Chaucer's *Wife of Bath's Prologue* and *Tale*

AN ANNOTATED BIBLIOGRAPHY 1900 TO 1995

Peter G. Beidler and Elizabeth M. Biebel

One of Chaucer's most popular and complex characters, the Wife of Bath has inspired a rich and diverse range of published scholarship. This work is the latest in the University of Toronto Press's Chaucer Bibliography series, a series that aims to provide annotated bibliographies for all of Chaucer's works. The volume summarizes twentieth-century commentary on Chaucer's *Wife of Bath's Prologue* and *Tale*. There are six sections in the bibliography, with items arranged chronologically in each section: editions and translations, sources and analogues, the marriage group, *gentillesse* or nobility, the *General Prologue*, the *Wife of Bath's Prologue*, and the *Tale*.

The editors have assembled a comprehensive bibliography covering not only standard English literature, medieval studies, and Chaucerian studies sources, but also lesser-known references and items published in languages other than English. Developments in Chaucer criticism are traced and grouped thematically, a particular benefit for those approaching Chaucerian studies for the first time.

PETER G. BEIDLER is Professor of English at LeHigh University in Bethlehem, Pennsylvania, where he has taught since 1968. He is also the author of *Geoffrey Chaucer's The Wife of Bath: Case Studies in Contemporary Criticism* (Bedford Books, 1996).

ELIZABETH M. BIEBEL is Adjunct Professor at LeHigh University.

(The Chaucer Bibliographies)

The Chaucer Bibliographies

Chaucer's
Wife of Bath's Prologue and *Tale*

AN ANNOTATED BIBLIOGRAPHY
1900 TO 1995

edited by Peter G. Beidler and Elizabeth M. Biebel

Published in association with the University of Rochester by
UNIVERSITY OF TORONTO PRESS
Toronto Buffalo London

© University of Toronto Press Incorporated 1998
Toronto Buffalo London
Printed in Canada
ISBN 0-8020-4366-6

Printed on acid-free paper

Canadian Cataloguing in Publication Data

Main entry under title:

Chaucer's Wife of Bath's prologue and tale : an annotated bibliography
1900–1995

(The Chaucer bibliographies ; [6])
Includes bibliographical references and index.
ISBN 0-8020-4366-6

1. Chaucer, Geoffrey, d. 1400. Wife of Bath's tale – Bibliography.
I. Beidler, Peter G.   II. Biebel, Elizabeth M.   III. Series.

Z8164.C43 1998   016.821'1   C98-931771-4

University of Toronto Press acknowledges the financial assistance to its publishing
program of the Canada Council for the Arts and the Ontario Arts Council.

For William and Marion Biebel
and Paul and Margaret Beidler
four wonderful parents

ᏇᏇ Contents

ℰ General Editor's Preface

The Chaucer Bibliographies will encompass, in a series of some eighteen volumes, a complete listing and assessment of scholarship and criticism on the writings of Geoffrey Chaucer (d. 1400), and on his life, times, and historical context. Five volumes — on Chaucer's short poems and *Anelida and Arcite*, on the translations, scientific works, and apocrypha, on the *General Prologue* to the *Canterbury Tales*, on the *Knight's Tale*, and on the *Tales* of the Miller, Reeve, and Cook — have already appeared. The present volume, on the *Wife of Bath's Prologue and Tale*, extends the coverage of the *Canterbury Tales* by taking up one of the best known and most studied of Chaucer's portraits. Additional volumes, on the *Pardoner's Prologue and Tale* and on several groupings of tales (the *Tales* of the Physician, Squire, and Franklin, the Friar, Summoner, Clerk, and Merchant, the Monk and Nun's Priest, and the Second Nun, Canon's Yeoman, Manciple, and Parson, with the Retractions) should appear during the course of the next year or so. Each volume in the series centers on a particular work, or a connected group of works; most contain material on backgrounds or related writings, and several will be wholly topical in their coverage (taking up music, the visual arts, rhetoric, the life of Chaucer, and other relevant subjects). Although the series perforce places unswerving emphasis on accuracy and comprehensiveness, the distinctive feature of the Chaucer Bibliographies is the fullness and particularity of the annotations provided for each entry. Annotations have averaged one-third to one-half page in the first six volumes; these thick descriptions of intellectual and critical activity (as opposed to simple itemizations or telegraphic summaries) have constituted more than four-fifths of each volume's content.

The individual volumes in the Chaucer Bibliographies series do not therefore constitute a reference work in the ordinary sense of that term. While they will enumerate virtually every publication on Chaucer worthy of notice and give complete coverage to materials from the twentieth century, they go far beyond the usual compilation, bibliographic manual, or guide to research. The bibliographies are not mechanical or machine-produced lists; each volume makes use of the intellectual engagement, learning, and insight of scholars actively at work on Chaucer. The series therefore serves not simply as the collection of all relevant titles on a subject, but as a companion and reliable guide to the reading and study of Chaucer's poetry. In this, the Chaucer Bibliographies represents an innovative and penetrating access to what Chaucer means, and has meant, to his readers. The project offers the full richness and detail of Chaucer's thought and world to a much wider audience than it has, even after one hundred years of energetic scholarship, ever before reached.

Before all else, then, the series provides a means of making practical headway in the study of earlier literature in English and in appreciating its broad cultural contexts. These volumes help make the writing of Chaucer — the earliest figure in the canon of great writers in the English language — more immediate, and more directly accessible to all readers. Although readers for six centuries have praised Chaucer as a moving, superb, complex writer, even teachers of his writing sometimes feel at a loss when faced with the linguistic, historical, and critical complexities packed into every line. Consequently, despite his canonical stature, Chaucer has often remained unread, or read only in translation or paraphrase. The goal of this project, at its first level, is to increase the numbers of those who read him with genuine understanding and pleasure by increasing the kinds of things that can be readily known about Chaucer. In offering such broad access to specialized knowledge, the Chaucer Bibliographies is effecting a major change in how Chaucer gets read, at what levels, and by whom.

The Chaucer Bibliographies seeks to intensify the comprehension and enjoyment of beginning readers in university, college, and high school classrooms, presenting themselves as tools to both students and teachers. The series will move undergraduates more quickly from the generalizations and observations of textbooks and instructors to a direct access to the richness and variety of Chaucer's writing, and to its connections with medieval realities and modern understandings. For graduate students, the books constitute a crucial resource for course work, exam preparation, and research. For non-specialist teachers of Chaucer in survey, masterpiece, and special topic courses, the series provides the means to a broader base of knowledge and to a more intense and shapely preparation than instructors, given the constraints of their work time, were previously able to manage. By clarifying and connecting both recent and long-available materials, and by making them readily accessible, the Chaucer Bibliographies refreshes the teaching and reading of Chaucer, and enables the development of alternative approaches to understanding his writing.

The series holds yet additional resources for specialist readers. The fullness and detail of the annotations in each volume will serve, in the first instance, as a check against duplication and redundancy in academic publication; individual scholars, and editors or readers at presses and journals, will be able to chart the place of a new or proposed work quickly. Likewise, Chaucerians engaged with a topic or set of issues will be able to advance or situate their work more readily by reference to the materials in the appropriate volumes within the series. In consolidating the massive work that has been done in the last century or so in medieval studies, and particularly on Chaucer, the bibliographies provide the ground on which new work in Chaucer can build. Their presence in the field will encourage more efficient research on restricted as well as expansive topics, and will likewise facilitate work on the ways in which institutions have fostered and used the reading and study of his writing.

In addition to Chaucerians, the series benefits other specialists in medieval literature in offering ready access to publications on Chaucer that touch on a variety of materials relevant to other fields. Whatever use the materials gathered in these volumes may have for particular queries or problems, they also address interests of a range of scholars whose expertise extends to Chaucer, but whose intellectual concerns have been stymied by the daunting mass of Chaucer scholarship. The Chaucer Bibliographies places interdisciplinary research before scholars in history, art history, and other related areas, and so makes multidisciplinary, collaborative work more possible and even more likely. In short, this massive effort to bring knowledge about Chaucer together strives to open up, rather than to close off, further innovative work on pre-modern culture.

Recent volumes in the series have analyzed, on average, nearly twelve hundred items each; the present volume, on the Wife of Bath, is not surprisingly the longest yet published. Their coverage takes in editions of Chaucer's writing, studies of language, manuscripts, and audiences, his sources and their contexts and intellectual connections, directly relevant background materials (eg, estates satire, medieval science, chivalry, the tradition of Boethius), and all publications (in whatever language) bearing directly on Chaucer's poetry. The early volumes have thoroughly fulfilled the promise of the series to sort out and make accessible materials that are confused or obscure, including early philological publications in German and Scandinavian languages, privately printed or scarce volumes, and recent work in Australia, Europe, Japan, and Korea. But even more strikingly, in bringing together all the materials on specific poems and subjects, these volumes have given new definition to the boundaries of Chaucer studies. Rather than working as a mopping-up operation, telling scholars what they already knew, these volumes attempt to contribute to a new flourishing of Chaucer research and criticism, enabling and even inspiring fresh and solidly grounded interrogations of the poetry. They stand not simply as the summation of a great tradition, but as an impetus for more intense and expanded understandings of Chaucer. The sweeping vision of late medieval writing offered in each volume represents a reconfiguration of knowledge that justifies and fosters informed work by an expanded community of scholars, of whom Chaucerians form merely the core.

In producing volumes that record all relevant titles and that specify — and thereby provide grounds for assessment of — the content and interconnections of Chaucerian criticism, the Chaucer Bibliographies defines a new space for itself as a reference tool in its own field, and potentially within affiliated fields as well. The volumes, published and projected, differ markedly in purpose and use from other introductory bibliographies and cumulative listings. Standard bibliographies — unmarked or minimally annotated compilations — furnish helpful listings of publications, but offer limited help to the specialist, and still less orientation or access to the uninitiated. Volumes in the Chaucer Bibliographies project take these publications as a base of information (and make reference to them), but the aim of each volume is to offer in-depth coverage of the works at hand. Contributors initially review annual and collected listings, but acquired learning, developed instincts, and the concentrated reading demanded for the preparation of each volume turn up leads and titles that complete the search. The series through its individual volumes seeks to stand as a definitive companion to the study of Chaucer, a starting point from which future work on the poet will proceed. It addresses itself to an audience beyond the community of professional Chaucerians, inviting non-Chaucerian scholars and non-specialist teachers and students to take part in the continuous process of understanding Chaucer.

The series achieves this inclusiveness through exhaustive itemization, full and strategic commentary, attention to backgrounds and corollary issues, and the demarcation of interrelationships and connected themes; annotations, cross-referencing, generous indices, and the report of significant reviews help insure this high level of comprehensiveness. Its design entails an examination of every relevant published item, in all foreign languages, though contributors rely on their own expertise and discretion in determining the choice and extent of annotations. Information on a 'ghost,' or an inaccessible but pointless item, may prove as valuable to users of these volumes as careful assessments of central books in the field; it is therefore crucial for contributors not to pass over inadvertently or deliberately omit any 'trivial' writings. The specification of items in these volumes should obviate the need for many vain entanglements in the trammels of scholarship as readers of Chaucer pursue their special interests.

The Chaucer Bibliographies is produced through the work of a diverse and distinguished array of experts. Its format — in which the individual efforts of autonomous scholars take their place within a single project's well articulated, coherent framework — accommodates in a peculiarly appropriate way its broad base and wide appeal. The authors of individual volumes include both distinguished and younger Chaucerians. The comprehensive work for each volume has been carried out over a period of years by an individual scholar or a team in close collaboration, conceiving each volume as a unified intellectual project. Having a collective of more than two dozen Chaucerians actively engaged in the same project has already led to a more thorough cross-checking, a richer array of suggestions and shared information, and a larger number of surprising finds — some obscure, some obvious — than any individual or more limited collaborative effort could have produced.

Since materials for the entire series have been electronically processed and stored, it will be possible for the University of Toronto Press to issue revised editions of volumes, and eventually to produce a general index to all volumes. Plans are underway to generate an updatable CD-ROM version of the Chaucer Bibliographies, which would combine data from multiple volumes and enable a variety of rapid searches through the materials. This electronic version will not replace the issue of individual volumes in hard copy, so that the series will continue to be accessible to a wide range of general users and scholars in a variety of formats.

The work of the Chaucer Bibliographies was sustained from 1989 to 1995 by a series of grants from the National Endowment for the Humanities (USA), through its Division of Research Programs; without NEH support, it would have been impossible for the collective efforts of the project to continue, or for the work of individual scholars to issue in published form. Library staff at the University of Rochester — in particular, Interlibrary Loan, and the Rossell Hope Robbins Library and its Curator, Dr. Alan Lupack — have provided invaluable and unstinting bibliographic and research aid. Patricia Neill, of the *Blake Quarterly* (University of Rochester), has furnished crucial editorial and technical expertise in the final stages of preparation. The final and pivotal phases of research and editing were resourcefully and meticulously carried out by Mara Amster, Jessica Forbes, Angela Gibson, and Jennifer Klein, at Rochester.

߆ Preface

In selecting, annotating, and indexing the wealth of scholarship that has been written on Chaucer's Wife of Bath, on the 32-line description of her in the General Prologue to the *Canterbury Tales*, on the 862-line *Wife of Bath's Prologue* to her tale, and on the 408-line *Wife of Bath's Tale*, we have been guided primarily by the needs of students and scholars. Those needs, we have assumed, are for accuracy, completeness, brevity, and handiness.

Although we are sure that some errors have crept in, we have made every reasonable effort to make sure that the bibliographical information for each of the many entries is accurate. We have searched in the standard bibliographies and in the footnotes to the books and articles we found there, for every reference we could find to the Wife of Bath and her tale. We have tried to keep our annotations brief and to the point, while at the same time giving readers enough information to guide them in selecting those items that they would need, for their own purposes, to read at full length. As for handiness, we have within each section listed items chronologically, so that those reading a section from front to back can gain a comprehensive sweep of the history of the criticism and growing complexity of the debate on the Wife of Bath and what is sometimes called her 'performance.' For readers who want to see what a certain critic may have said about the Wife of Bath, or what scholars may have written about some specific topic like the 'pillow lecture' in the *Wife of Bath's Tale*, we have provided a comprehensive alphabetical index of scholars and terms.

We have provided six large sections to the bibliography. In each section the items are arranged chronologically. The section on Sources and Analogues includes items that have to do primarily with the antecedents to the Wife of Bath materials — that rich array of biblical, philosophical, antifeminist, expository, and narrative materials that helped Chaucer develop his conception of the Wife of Bath and her performance. The section on the Marriage Group includes items connecting the Wife of Bath, her prologue, and her tale with certain other Canterbury tellers and tales that deal with marriage. The section on *gentillesse* deals with those items that have to do in a substantial way with the concept of gentility or noble behavior, particularly as they are revealed in the pillow lecture of the old new bride at the end of the *Wife of Bath's Tale.*

The other three sections concern the three narrative units of the Wife of Bath materials. The first — and shortest — is the description of the Wife of Bath in the General Prologue to the *Canterbury Tales.* The second — and longest — lists the many, many items that deal with the long personal narrative, variously called a confession, an autobiography, a diatribe, a sermon, and a tour de force, in which the Wife of Bath presents her views on virginity and multiple marriage, followed by an account of her marriages to her five husbands, three of them old and rich, two of them them younger. The third section collects together items that deal in a central way with the *Wife of Bath's Tale,* the Arthurian romance about a young rapist who is sent in quest of the answer to the question of what women most desire.

Because much of the scholarship on the Wife of Bath deals with materials that are appropriate to more than one of these sections, we have provided extensive cross references — indicated in bold-face numbers in the annotation section of a given entry — to material in those sections.

Although the Toronto Chaucer Bibliographies officially begin with works published in 1900, we have occasionally gone back before that date to note items we think will be of interest to users of this volume. Because we had to release the document halfway through 1996, our coverage of materials published in that year is at best incomplete.

We have tried to be consistent in our own spelling of certain key words. We use the spelling 'Alisoun,' for example, to refer to the Wife of Bath, even though some scholars spell it differently. We use the spelling 'Alison' to refer to the carpenter's wife in the *Miller's Tale.* We have used the spelling *gentillesse* consistently in our own usage of this word, though we have honored the spelling of other scholars if we quote something in which they spell the word differently.

No one can undertake a project of this magnitude without relying to a great extent on the help of others. We must first, of course, thank the General Editor Thomas Hahn, of the University of Rochester, for encouraging us in a project that grew every time we touched it. We are grateful, as well, to Mara Amster, Jessica Forbes, Penny Perrotto, Angela Gibson, James Knapp, and Jennifer Klein at the University of Rochester, for the grace and intelligence with which they saw the initial manuscript through the publication process. Kristen Pederson of the University of Toronto Press has assisted in bringing the volume to publication. Although we have never met Monica E. McAlpine, we are grateful to the example that her amazing annotated bibliography on Chaucer's *Knight's Tale*, also in this Toronto Series, provided us. We are indebted to Professor Mark E. Allen of the University of Texas, San Antonio, for sharing with us a working list of the bibliography he is compiling for the edition of the Wife of Bath materials that he and John Hurt Fisher are preparing for the *Variorum Chaucer*; to William J. Snell of Keio University for help in locating and annotating publications in Japanese journals; to Reinhard Hillefeld for help in annotating a Spanish-language article; to Charles French for help in translating the articles in German; to Jian 'Stan' Shi of Sichuan University in China for helping us to locate the many books and journals we have had to consult in Lehigh's own collection; and to Bill Fincke, Pat Ward, Jody Schmell, Barbara Parenti, Peggy Dilliard, and Evie Rivas of Lehigh University's InterLibrary Loan office. Without the gracious help of these last, who never once even *looked* annoyed when we trundled in — yet once more — with a timid request, 'Can you get us just this *one* more book? Surely this will be the last!'

Peter G. Beidler
Elizabeth M. Biebel

ℰ Abbreviations

LITERARY WORKS CITED

BD	*Book of the Duchess*
Bo	*Boece* (Boethius)
Buk	*Envoy to Bukton*
CA	*Confessio Amantis*
ClT	*Clerk's Tale*
Consol	*The Consolation of Philosophy* (John Gower)
Conv	*Convivio*
CT	*Canterbury Tales*
Dec	*Decameron* (Giovanni Boccaccio)
Div Com	*Divine Comedy* (Dante)
Flor	*Tale of Florent* (John Gower)
FranT	*Franklin's Tale*
FrT	*Friar's Tale*
GP	*General Prologue of CT*
Hen	*King Henry*
HF	*House of Fame*
Jov	*Adversus Jovinianum* (Jerome)
KnT	*Knight's Tale*
LGW	*Legend of Good Women*
LGWP	*Legend of Good Women Prologue*
ManT	*Manciple's Tale*
Mar	*Marriage of Sir Gawaine*
Mel	*Tale of Melibee*
MerP	*Merchant's Prologue*
MerT	*Merchant's Tale*
Met	*Metamorphosis* (Ovid)

MilP	*Miller's Prologue*
MilT	*Miller's Tale*
Mir	*Miroir de Mariage* (Eustache Deschamps)
MLT	*Man of Law's Tale*
MkT	*Monk's Tale*
NPT	*Nun's Priest's Tale*
Nug	*De nugis curialium*
PardP	*Pardoner's Prologue*
PardT	*Pardoner's Tale*
ParsT	*Parson's Tale*
PF	*Parliament of Fowls*
PhyT	*Physician's Tale*
Piers	*Piers Plowman*
PrT	*Prioress's Tale*
Rom	*The Romaunt of the Rose* (Chaucer)
RR	*Le Roman de la Rose* (Guillaume de Lorris and Jean de Meun)
RvT	*Reeve's Tale*
Scog	*Envoy to Scogan*
SGGK	*Sir Gawain and the Green Knight*
ShT	*Shipman's Tale*
SNP	*Second Nun's Prologue*
SNT	*Second Nun's Tale*
SqT	*Squire's Tale*
SumT	*Summoner's Tale*
TC	*Troilus and Criseyde*
Thop	*Tale of Sir Thopas*
Val	*Dissuasio Valerii ad ruffinum ne uxorem ducat* (Walter Map)
WBP	*Wife of Bath's Prologue*
WBT	*Wife of Bath's Tale*
Wed	*Weddynge of Sir Gawen and Dame Ragnell*

JOURNALS AND REFERENCE WORKS CITED

ABR	*American Benedictine Review*
Ang	*Anglia: Zeitschrift für Englische Philologie*

AnM	*Annuale Mediaevale*
AN&Q	*American Notes and Queries*
Archiv	*Archiv für das Studium der neueren Sprachen und Literaturen*
AUMLA	*Journal of the Association of Australasian Universities Language and Literature Association*
BlakeS	*Blake Studies*
BForum	*Book Forum: An International Transdisciplinary Quarterly*
BJRL	*Bulletin of the John Rylands Library*
CE	*College English*
CEA	*CEA Critic: An Official Journal of the College English Association*
ChauR	*Chaucer Review*
CLQ	*Colby Library Quarterly*
CL	*Comparative Literature*
CQ	*Cambridge Quarterly*
CR	*Critical Review*
CrSurv	*Critical Survey*
DA	*Dissertation Abstracts*
DAI	*Dissertation Abstracts International*
E&S	*Essays and Studies*
EAS	*Essays in Arts and Sciences*
EIC	*Essays in Criticism*
EJ	*The English Journal*
ELH	*ELH: A Journal of English Literary History*
ELN	*English Language Notes*
EM	*English Miscellany*
EngR	*English Record*
ES	*English Studies*
ESC	*English Studies in Canada*
Expl	*Explicator*
FCS	*Fifteenth-Century Studies*
GRM	*Germanisch-romanische Monatsschrift*
HUSL	*Hebrew University Studies in Literature and the Arts*
InG	*In Geardagum*

JASAT	*Journal of the American Studies Association of Texas*
JEGP	*Journal of English and Germanic Philology*
JRMMRA	*Journal of the Rocky Mountain Medieval and Renaissance Association*
KN	*Kwartalnik Neofilologiczny*
LauR	*Laurel Review*
LeedsSE	*Leeds Studies in English*
M&H	*Medievalia and Humanistica*
MA	*Le Moyen Âge*
MÆ	*Medium Ævum*
MedPers	*Medieval Perspectives*
MinnR	*Minnesota Review*
MLN	*Modern Language Notes*
MLQ	*Modern Language Quarterly*
MLR	*Modern Language Review*
MLS	*Modern Language Studies*
MP	*Modern Philology*
MS	*Mediaeval Studies*
MSE	*Massachusetts Studies in English*
N&Q	*Notes and Queries*
NCFJ	*North Carolina Folklore Journal*
NDEJ	*Notre Dame English Journal*
Neophil	*Neophilologus*
NM	*Neuphilologische Mitteilungen*
NMS	*Nottingham Medieval Studies*
PAPA	*Publications of the Arkansas Philological Association*
PBA	*Proceedings of the British Academy*
PCP	*Pacific Coast Philology*
PLL	*Papers on Language and Literature*
POMPA	*Publications of the Mississippi Philological Association*
PMLA	*Publications of the Modern Language Association*
PPMRC	*Proceedings of the PMR Conference: Annual Publication of the International Patristic, Mediaeval, and Renaissance Conference*

PQ	*Philological Quarterly*
R&L	*Religion and Literature*
RCEI	*Revista Canaria de Estudios Ingleses*
REL	*Review of English Literature*
RES	*Review of English Studies*
RLV	*Revue des langues vivantes*
RomR	*Romanic Review*
RPh	*Romance Philology*
SAB	*South Atlantic Bulletin*
SAC	*Studies in the Age of Chaucer*
SAQ	*South Atlantic Quarterly*
SFQ	*Southern Folklore Quarterly*
SMC	*Studies in Medieval Culture*
SMELL	*Studies in Medieval English Language and Literature*
SN	*Studia Neophilologica*
SoRA	*Southern Review: Literary and Interdisciplinary Essays* (University of Adelaide, Australia)
SP	*Studies in Philology*
Spec	*Speculum*
SSF	*Studies in Short Fiction*
TLS	*London Times Literary Supplement*
TSL	*Tennessee Studies in Literature*
TSLL	*Texas Studies in Literature and Language*
TSWL	*Tulsa Studies in Women's Literature*
UMS	*Unisa Medieval Studies* (University of South Africa, Pretoria)
UR	*University Review*
UTQ	*University of Toronto Quarterly*
W&L	*Women and Literature*
WHR	*Western Humanities Review*
YES	*Yearbook of English Studies*
YFS	*Yale French Studies*

‰ Introduction

Why has the Wife of Bath been the subject of more scholarly debate than any other pilgrim in the *Canterbury Tales*? The reasons are not hard to find. First, she is a woman, one of the first female characters of any depth or seriousness in British literature. Second, Chaucer has given scholars more to consider in her portrait and her performance than he has in those of any other pilgrim. We know about her clothes, her occupation, her husbands, her travels, her beliefs, her learning, her combativeness, her irreverence, her peculiar brand of feminism. Third, the close connections between her personality and her tale of rape, quest, and redemption have provided scholars with no end of material for analysis and debate.

The Wife of Bath gives scholars infinitely various fields to plow. Some have sought sources for her, for her learning, and for her tale. Others have seen her as the originator of a group of tales about marriage and as an early proponent of the concept of *gentillesse* — the notion that virtue resides in character rather than wealth, beauty, or class. Others still have seen her as an iconographic figure of Eve — the archetypal destroyer of the paradise that men have imagined they had before women existed. In the most recent decades, in particular, Alisoun of Bath has provided modern feminists with much material for debate. Is Alisoun an early feminist insisting on the rights and privileges of women, or is she merely a male-composed stereotype of the browbeating wife? In letting her speak her mind so boldly, has Chaucer given early voice to a complex woman, or has he merely appropriated her voice to give expression to his own male prejudices about women? Is her body a gross piece of flesh, variously attractive or repulsive to men, or is it a text in which scholars have inscribed their own fears and desires? In short, has she constructed herself, has Chaucer constructed her, or do we construct her for our own scholarly purposes and prejudices? So rich are Alisoun's portrait and performance that scholars have found many veins to mine, many coins to mint.

Indeed, it is possible to see the *Wife of Bath's Prologue* and *Tale* as a battleground for the various modern schools of scholarship. Early polite skirmishes were over the sources for and originality of the Wife of Bath's performace and its relationship to the performances of other Canterbury pilgrims, particularly those who speak of marriage. Later skirmishes were over the extent to which we are to read Alisoun as a 'real person' with a psychological profile, as an iconographic figure of carnality, as a caricatured representative of her 'estate,' as a middl-class woman, wife, and weaver, or merely as a literary artifact with nothing recoverable behind the words that describe her broad surfaces. The most recent battle lines have been drawn between more traditional scholars and feminists. Even in the feminist camp hostile divisions have developed as scholarship has moved more toward gender studies and the view that Alisoun and her performance, for all their lively humor and surface and concern for the rights and conditions of women, are finally little more than patriarchal constructs.

No attempt to capture in summary form the scope, richness, and diversity of the published scholarship on the Wife of Bath, her prologue, and her tale can avoid both surprisingly broad generalizations and annoyingly choppy specificity. This scholarship has been so diverse for so many years that it resists being captured in *any* summary. We hope, however, that the following pages will serve readers as both a general guide to important scholarship and a specific guide to the work of key scholars. We follow generally the broad divisions of this bibliography, with bold-face numbers referring to specific entries.

Sources, Analogues, and Alisoun

Chaucerian source and analogue study has been of early and enduring interest for scholars. Maynadier (**91**) provided early insights to the Wife of Bath and her performance, and Whiting, in Bryan and Dempster's *Sources and Analogues of Chaucer's Canterbury Tales* (**118**), provides texts of many possible sources for the *Wife of Bath's Prologue* and *Wife of Bath's Tale*. Morris's (**188**) cross-referenced book of sources and analogues and studies such as Calabrese's *Chaucer's Ovidian Arts of Love* (**203**) indicate the long-standing value placed on source study. The primary sources believed to have influenced the *Wife of Bath's Prologue* include Jean de Meun's portion of the *Roman de la Rose* and St. Jerome's *Adversus Jovinianum*.

As Koeppel (**86**) noted late in the nineteenth century, Alisoun's character reflects both La Vieille and Dame Nature in Jean de Meun's work. French (**124**) and Wetherbee (**180**), among others, also note the similarities and differences between Alisoun's character and that of La Vieille. Garbáty (**157**) suggests that Chaucer may have been familiar with the old woman of *Pamphilus de Amore* while developing Alisoun's character, and Muscatine (**158**) compares Alisoun to Gautier's La Veuve. Certain scholars also feel that the Good Woman of the Book of Proverbs served as a foil for Chaucer's creation of Alisoun. Historicists such as Manly (**287**) searched for an historical character whom Chaucer may have known and who served as an inspiration for the Wife. While Puhvel (**775**) and Gillam (**881**) were drawn to the historical personages of Alice Kytele and Alice Perrers, respectively, as inspirations for Chaucer's Alisoun, the frequency of the names *Alice* and *Alisoun* during Chaucer's day (**604**), and the common practice of women's remarrying, undermine the search for a non-fictional antetype for Alisoun.

St. Jerome's letter proves to be the source of much of the antifeminist and antimatrimonialist sentiments that Alisoun absorbed while hearing Jankyn read from his Book of Wikked Wyves. Some of the critics who have devoted their time to analyzing the correlation between St. Jerome's work and the *Wife of Bath's Prologue* are Woolcomb (**83**), Koeppel (**84**), and Barr (**192**). In the 1960's Silvia (**151, 164**) and Brennan (**160, 164**) both searched for a manuscript collection of antimatrimonial tracts, resembling Jankyn's book, with which Chaucer could have been familiar. Pratt (**142**) discusses the prevalence of antifeminist works among university clerics. Other source studies concerned with the contents of Jankyn's book include Wise's (**99**) suggestion that the story of Eriphile and Amphiaraus in Statius's *Thebaid* aided Chaucer in his incorporation of this tale into Jankyn's book, Pratt's (**127**) equation of some of Jankyn's *wikked wyves* with accounts found in the writing of John of Salisbury, and Schmitt's (**167**) more general account of the probable sources for Jankyn's book. Harbert (**169**) examines the various sources for Jankyn's book that Chaucer may have had access to, and notes the difficulty of making exact statements concerning Chaucer's sources. In reference to Jankyn himself, Green (**129**) feels that Chaucer used Richard de Bury's *Philobiblon* to familiarize himself with clerks. Steadman (**140**) provides accounts of several analogues to the burning of Jankyn's book, and Tatlock (**101**) believes Alisoun's final blow to Jankyn during their fight is similar to an incident in Map's *De Nugis Curialium*. Scholars have also debated the likelihood that Chaucer was aware of and used works by Isidore of Seville (**139**), Walter Map, Valerius Maximus, John of Salisbury (**83**), Matheolus (**122**), and by Theophrastus as reported in Jerome (**83, 139**). While Lowes (**97**), Wimsatt (**170**), and Mann (**197**) believe Deschamps' *Miroir de Mariage* was a source for Chaucer, Thundy (**177**) disagrees. Miller (**174**) provides a seemingly endless list of writers who could have been among Chaucer's sources for the *Wife of Bath's Prologue* and *Tale*. Chaucer's exact source for Alisoun's quotations from Ptolemy in the *Wife of Bath's Prologue* has been a particular subject of debate (**89, 107, 116, 173**). The influence of Ovid upon both the *Wife of Bath's Prologue* and *Tale* provides another area of study for critics. Portions of Alisoun's life may have been developed from the *Ars amatoria* (**108, 153**), and Alisoun also refers to this work (**110**). The Wife's references to Argus have been traced to Ovid's *Metamorphoses* (**108, 147**) and the *Amores* (**147**), and her reference to Pasiphäe might stem from the *Ovide moralisé* (**165**). Studies of Scripture, including the pertinence of a reference to Kings in Alisoun's performance (**175**) and to several passages from Proverbs (**84**), have been conducted throughout the twentieth century.

While Maynadier's early study of the analogues of the *Wife of Bath's Tale* focuses primarily on the English analogues that most closely reflect Alisoun's romance (the *Weddynge of Sir Gawen and Dame Ragnell, Marriage of Sir Gawaine, The Knight and the Shepherd's Daughter, King Henry*, and Gower's *Tale of Florent*), he also notes the parallel tales found in early Irish, German, and Norse literature. Root (**92**) looks at both sources and analogues for the *Wife of Bath's Tale*. Critics who have conducted comparative studies of the *Wife of Bath's Tale* and the *Tale of Florent* include Canby (**95**), who feels that while Gower's work may lack Chaucer's artistry, it has the more credible plot, and Fisher (**145**), who finds a legal connection in *Florent* that is absent in the *Wife of Bath's Tale*. Peck (**176**) and Beidler (**195**) show that *Florent* is not inferior to Alisoun's tale, while Pearsall (**154**) believes it is superior. Waterhouse and Stephens (**185**) as well as Fischer (**187**) note that each tale has been appropriately altered to reflect both its teller's personality and its author's point. Noting the similarities between the two tales, Sumner (**109**) suggests that Chaucer and Gower had access to a version of the loathly lady tale that is lost to us today. Among the studies that discuss the *Wife of Bath's Tale* in relation to the other English analogues, Kane (**130**) asserts the superiority of the *Weddynge of Sir Gawen and Dame Ragnell* over Chaucer's work, and Fichte (**202**) debates the probability that Chaucer had access to any of the other Arthurian loathly lady tales. Ackerman (**138**) and Shenk (**178**) also conduct comparative studies of these tales, while Dempster (**112**) and Huppé (**146**) examine Chaucerian additions and alterations to the folktale.

Many articles address Alisoun's loathly lady tale in light of its folk origins. Beach (**93**) and Albertini (**144**) examine the *Wife of Bath's Tale* for its connection to a variety of folktale traditions including, for example, the Cupid and Psyche tales. Albrecht (**133**) extends his study to include *Thomas of Erceldoune*. While Reinhard (**113**) links Chaucer's loathly lady to Norse and French traditions, Loomis (**117**) to the Breton lays of the Auchinleck manuscript, and Coomaraswamy (**121**) to Oriental analogues, the majority of studies that deal with the pervasiveness of the loathly lady tales connect the *Wife of Bath's Tale* to the Celtic tradition of tales in which a hag, representative of the sovereignty of the land, bestows her favor upon the future king of Ireland. Although Brown (**119**), Smith (**126**), Cary (**162**), Bollard (**189**), and Aguirre (**201**) have all conducted significant studies that treat the Celtic influence on the *Wife of Bath's Tale*, it is most likely that Eisner's *A Tale of Wonder* (**136**) will remain the foundational study of the dissemination of the loathly lady tale.

Another segment of the *Wife of Bath's Tale* that has been the focus of copious study is the pillow lecture the loathly lady delivers to the knight. Toynbee (**96**), Lowes (**102, 104, 105**), Sells (**134**), Bennett (**182**), and Boitani (**184**) explore Chaucer's indebtedness to Dante for his sentiments on *gentillesse*. Boethius (**105**), Seneca (**106**), and Boccaccio (**134**) are also credited for their important effects on Chaucer. Owen (**179**) has analyzed the glossings of the Hengwrt and Ellesmere manuscripts' scribes in reference to the pillow lecture. He lists the sources for this commentary as Jerome, Juvenal, Seneca, and Secundus. Other studies of the sources of certain motifs in the *Wife of Bath's Tale* include tracing the dancing ladies to an event in *De Nugis Curialium* (**115**), outlining the transformation motif in medieval exempla (**150**), highlighting patristic influence from John of Wales's *Communiloqium* (**172**), noting the Germanic origins of the time allotment of a-year-and-a-day (**183**), and observing a parallel to the marital dilemma in French farce (**191**).

Marriage Group

Hammond (**208**) is credited with coining the phrase "the Marriage Group." One of the criteria by which she defines this grouping of tales is the use of Jerome's *Adversus Jovinianum* as a source for the *Wife of Bath's Prologue*, the *Merchant's Tale*, and the *Franklin's Tale*. Believing that Chaucer formulated the idea for a Marriage Group late in the composition of the *Canterbury Tales*, Hammond also argues that Chaucer changed Alisoun's story from the *Shipman's Tale* to an Arthurian romance involving marital issues as a sign of his intent to develop an interlacing marriage theme in the *Canterbury Tales*. Kittredge, with his emphasis on the dramatic interplay among the tales (**210**), became the first major critical voice to promote the concept of a Marriage Group. He stresses the intertwining of themes among the tales of the Wife, Clerk, Merchant, and Franklin, and he includes the *Friar's Tale* and *Summoner's Tale* in the group. While these two tales do not focus on marriage, Szittya (**239**) points out that the tales do embrace the themes of authority and sovereignty. Olson (**237**) values these tales for their comic relief within the Marriage Group. The traditional view of the Marriage Group, then, is that Alisoun initiates a discussion to which the Franklin with his tale of a saved marriage of allegedly equal partners ultimately provides a happy ending. The Kittredge outline is reinforced by Baugh (**227**), Grose (**228**), and Murtaugh (**233**). Kaske (**236**) views the dramatic interchange in the Marriage Group as an ongoing debate. Over the years critics have discussed themes in addition to marriage that further connect these stories. Fisher (**225**), Schaefer (**229**), and Silvia (**230**) highlight the theme of *gentillesse* in the tales; Ginsberg (**246**) analyzes wish-fulfillment; and James (**253**) outlines a search for truth in the Marriage Group.

While the traditional view of the Marriage Group has been continually supported, several analyses take issue with the Kittredge model. Hinckley (**213**) is the first to challenge Kittredge's theory, arguing against the dramatic interchange among the pilgrims. Lyons (**215**) is also dissatisfied by the debate theory. Noting that over half of the Canterbury stories deal with concepts of marriage and sex, Leyerle (**240**) discredits the Marriage Group theory. Other critics choose to support the essence of Kittredge's theory, yet add their own variations to it, basing their opinions on both thematic unity and the issue of tale order.

Favoring an ordering of the *Canterbury Tales* that places Fragment VII before Fragment III, Lawrence (**211**) turns to tales preceding Alisoun's, specifically *Melibee*, to note the development of a marriage theme. Hemingway (**212**), as well, finds the issues of marriage introduced by the *Tale of Melibee*. In 1950, Lawrence (**218**) asserts that Chaucer placed the *Nun's Priest's Tale* before the *Wife of Bath's Prologue* and *Tale* so that it might belong to the Marriage Group. Glasser (**242**) and Johnston (**245**) cite Cecile and Valerian's relationship in the *Second Nun's Tale* for its continuation of Chaucerian commentary in marriage. Zong-qi (**254**) notes that marital issues are explored also in Fragments I and II of the *Canterbury Tales*.

Gentillesse

The most common thread in the scholarly criticism on the loathly lady's sermon on *gentillesse* is the praise given to Chaucer for his noble thoughts, to the old woman for her most eloquent delivery of the pillow lecture, and even to Alisoun for her ability to assess accurately the prevailing attitudes of her time and the faults that lay in her society's obsession with class. A trace of doubt in the motivation behind Chaucer's creation of the highly democratic sermon stems from Thomas (**273**), who notes Chaucer's own aristocratic status. Early criticism focuses on Chaucer's echoing of ideas found in Boethius' *Consolation of Philosophy* and Dante's *Convivio*. The loathly lady stresses the concept that true gentility originates as a God-given virtue that is neither hereditary nor class-based. Ward (**257**) credits Guillaume de Lorris for having like sentiments, Schofield (**258**) cites Seneca as another Chaucerian source, and Vogt (**261**) mentions numerous other writers who shared such egalitarian ideals. Vogt is unique among the critics in his belief that Chaucer was characteristically democratic for his time and was reiterating sentiments that were actually relatively common.

In addition to the sourcework concerning the *gentillesse* theme, critics examine other instances of *gentillesse* appearing in Chaucer's work, particularly in Chaucer's ballad *Gentillesse* and in the *Parson's Tale*. Albrecht (**264**) observes the intertextuality of the *gentillesse* theme — and the lack of it — within the Marriage Group. For example, the virtue of *gentillesse* is conspicuously absent in the marriage of January and May in the *Merchant's Tale*. Baker (**267**) reads the *Clerk's Tale* as containing a nobler treatment of *gentillesse* than that of the *Wife of Bath's Tale* because the Clerk possesses a heightened sense of the Divine. Fichte (**274**), however, does not see the *Clerk's Tale* as a superior rendering of this theme, finding that the loathly lady reveals more sympathy for humanity than does Griselda.

Kenyon (**262**) and Dempster (**263**) have analyzed the pronouns within the pillow lecture, and Williams (**269**) provides an historical hypothesis that the sermon on *gentillesse* comments on the relations between John of Gaunt and Katherine Swynford.

Alisoun in the *General Prologue*

Critical commentary on Alisoun's portrait in the *General Prologue* addresses such issues as whether the Wife's character was developed through Chaucer's consultation of medieval scientific tracts (**454**), his observation of an historical personage (**287**), and his familiarity with the estates structure of society (**340**). Alisoun has been interpreted as an individual in her own right (**381**), as a type character (**353**, **380**), and as an iconographic figure (**540**). Gottfried (**383**) observes that Alisoun is defined by her title of *Wife*. Many studies have been devoted to discovering the symbolic meanings of the manifold details Chaucer incorporated into Alisoun's portrait. Bowden (**296**) provides a thorough analysis of the picture Chaucer provided for us. And Sklute (**382**) reminds us that Chaucer leaves it to the reader to determine just how *worthy* a woman Alisoun is.

Alisoun's Appearance

Through her personal style of dress, Alisoun has combined an enormous hat and spurs with scarlet stockings. Whether Chaucer intended Alisoun to represent a fashionable woman or 'a carnival figure' (**389** p 179) is a contested issue. While Tupper (**289**), along with Hodges (**414**), notes an association between Alisoun's headgear and pride, Whitaker (**401**) mentions medieval connotations of sexual frustration and widowhood with hats. Wretlind (**297**) offers an historical parallel in his observation that Anne of Bohemia in 1382 began a fashion trend of voluminous headwear for women. Rowland (**324**) finds Alisoun's hat to be a manifestation of her femininity and her spurs to indicate her maintaining sovereignty in marriage, whereas Mertens-Fonck (**396**) feels that both the hat and the spurs symbolize knightly attire. Alisoun's fondness for the color scarlet has been interpreted to be a sign of vanity and to be reminiscent of court (**359**); evidence of her false motivation for pilgrimage (**360**); Alisoun's rejecting traditional widow's weeds (**413**); and even as a folk remedy for repelling venereal disease (**397**). Hodges outlines the differences between Alisoun's more practical, Mars-influenced pilgrim's outfit and her Venus-inspired Sunday dress (**414** pp 367–8). Some motivation for her attire is provided by Malone (**299**), who observes that Alisoun wishes to attract attention on the road, and by Lumiansky (**306**), who reminds us that getting attention is part of Alisoun's plan in her search for husband number six.

Artistic Renditions

Alisoun's colorful portrait as presented in the Ellesmere manuscript has served as a basis for additional commentary. Piper (**285**) remarks on the exquisite detail of the manuscript illumination. Jusserand (**286**) notes the historical accuracy of Alisoun's riding astride her horse. The gold net under Alisoun's hat caught the eye of Loomis (**320**), who felt that the net diverged from the traditional wimple, although Hussey (**326**) comments that Alisoun *is* wearing a wimple and this fashion would have been rather out-of-date. He also sees the Wife's whip as suggesting domination. Alisoun's blatant sexuality led to her being associated symbolically with the Whore of Babylon in William Blake's depiction of the Canterbury pilgrimage. Blake's artwork inspired the critical analysis of Kiralis (**332**), Stevenson (**360**), Allen (**361**), and Bowden (**367**).

The Grouping of the Pilgrims

Despite the fact that Alisoun is the sole secular female on the road to Canterbury and that she travels alone, critics have long sought to include her among the various subgroups of pilgrims they believe Chaucer created in order to present a microcosm of medieval society. These groupings may also aid us in perceiving any underlying strategy that Chaucer might have had in his specific ordering of the individual portraits. Emerson's 'provincial group,' consisting of the Shipman, Physician, Wife of Bath, Parson, and Plowman, seems to have set the standard of recognition for Chaucer's incorporation of the rising importance of the middle class in society. The Shipman, Physician, and Alisoun are further aligned because of their financial successes (**304**). Brooks (**315**) notes that while these three characters are proficient in their occupations, their morality is questionable. Mertens-Fonck (**395**) extends this concept of a lack of virtue by indicating that none of the three has found happiness in life. Lumiansky (**309**) discusses the deliberate juxtaposition of the Wife's portrait with that of the Parson, a placement that Howard (**336**) believes is a result of Chaucer's creating three subgroups of seven among his pilgrims. Since each group is introduced by an ideal character, the presentation of the Parson denotes the beginning of a new segment of society. Leicester (**402**) feels that the Parson follows Alisoun because he represents precisely what Alisoun is determined to rebel against: male authority. Evans (**356**) notes the contrast between Alisoun and the Prioress, as do Pittock (**341**), Valtz Mannuci (**351**), and Watanabe (**379**). Higdon (**338**) offers an interesting perspective that groups the pilgrims by means of music, thus placing added emphasis on Alisoun's knowledge of the *olde daunce.*

The Significant Details of Alisoun's Portrait

Not surprisingly, Alisoun's personality and its many idiosyncracies provide much fodder for literary scholars, and the variety of responses she has evoked from critics range from her being 'fundamentally cruel' (**292** p 117) to her being 'admirable for her adherence to the truth and to her nature' (**291** pp 40–1). Coghill (**298**) notes that the Wife's portrait

is filled with contradictions. Other scholars note Chaucer's artful
phrasing, specifically the puns that he uses to impute multiple levels of
meaning to Alisoun's portrait. The phrase *wandrynge by the weye*
(I.467) has been examined for its ambiguity (**311**), its insinuations that
Alisoun has an awareness of traveling both the road to heaven and the
road to hell (**313**), and its indication of Alisoun's morality (**394**). Tatlock
(**284**), Baum (**307**), and Taylor (**400**) observe the difficulty of
interpreting the meaning behind the word *withouten* (I.461) and the
subsequent ambiguity as to whether or not Alisoun had lovers in her
youth. Alisoun's desire to be the first to make offering in church has
been viewed as an indication of her greed (**317**), her insecurity (**334**),
and her middle-class coveting of privileges (**349**). Makarewicz (**300**)
believes that Alisoun's monetary donations to the church are not enough
to absolve her of all of her sins. In another observation of Alisoun's
love of wealth, Reisner (**347**) notes her acute awareness of the potential
for financial gain from marriage dowers. Her occupation of weaver
has encouraged scholars to align Alisoun with the archetypal old bawd
(**328**), with the Good Woman of Proverbs (**343**), and with Eve (**393**).
Hira (**329**) does not believe that Alisoun's weaving skills exceed those
of Flanders. That Alisoun bears the print of St. Venus' seal, Tupper
(**282**) feels, makes her a likely pilgrim, while Barnouw (**283**) suggests
that the cryptic Venus' seal is actually the gap between Alisoun's teeth.
Weissman (**371**) looks to Alisoun's originating from Bath as a symbol
of her sexuality, for the iconographic tradition associates the bath with
Venus and carnality. Critics have also made iconographic interpretations
of Alisoun's deafness. Hoffman (**344**) feels she cannot hear the call of
Christ, Sklute (**370**) believes her deafness comments upon her morality,
and Storm (**377**) stresses Alisoun's inability to perceive the truth.

Alisoun's Performance

What follows is a chronological review, by grouped decades, of the
enormous body of twentieth-century scholarship on the *Wife of Bath's
Prologue* and *Tale*. Our goal has been to note critical trends, the
application of different modes of critical theory, the responses of different
critics to one another on certain issues, and the most frequently discussed
incidents, details, and themes in the *Wife of Bath's Prologue* and *Tale*.
After developing this chronological perspective, we add a few sections

that treat important elements of Alisoun's performance that have received some critical attention throughout this century but did not fit easily into one specific set of decades.

Wife of Bath's Prologue: 1900–1930

Source study and tale order are the dominant critical foci of the early scholarship on the *Wife of Bath's Prologue*. Whether we term it a confessional work (**421**) or a dramatic monologue (**427**), the prologue is praised by the critics for being a 'revolutionary document' (**420** p 523), and a revelation both of Chaucer's perceptive awareness of the human condition and the depth of his scholarly knowledge (**432**). Critical opinion is not united, however, on whether Chaucer created the *Wife of Bath's Prologue* out of his own antifeminist sentiments (**425**) or from pure delight in human nature (**461**). Alisoun is also given a variety of critical evaluations. Is she the positive 'highly cultured woman' of Mackail (**433** p 19) or the 'eloquent' one of Iijima (**457** p 107)? Or is her prologue simply the 'careless chatter of an indomitable tongue,' as Ward ungenerously puts it (**425** p 120)? Comparisons of Alisoun's character are made with *Roman de la Rose* characters La Vieille (**420, 434, 442**) and Ami (**442**) and also with Boccaccio's Vedova in the *Corbaccio* (**445**). Other source studies include Hamilton's attempt to identify the Trotula found in Jankyn's book (**426**), a search for Chaucer's Ptolemaic source (**451**), and Chaucer's access to the Vulgate (**455**). In 1858, Boys (**418**), Carrington (**419**), and a critic known only as A.A. (**417**) each sought to discover the significance of the gap between Alisoun's teeth. Both A.A. (**417**) and Boys (**418**) connect Alisoun's dental composition with Venus, whereas Carrington (**419**) links *gat-tothed* directly to the teeth of a goat, recalling the lecherous nature of this animal.

While Shipley (**422**) and Skeat (**428**) concern themselves with tale order, Tatlock (**429**) and Lowes (**434**) add the challenge of dating Chaucer's composition of various tales to their studies, linking the *Wife of Bath's Prologue* and the *Merchant's Tale* together. Brusendorff (**456**) addresses the issue of the contested passages in the *Wife of Bath's Prologue*, passages that were marginally notated in certain manuscripts and whose authorship is thus uncertain. In *Five Hundred Years of Chaucer Criticism and Allusion* (**459**), Spurgeon gives particular emphasis to Pope's translation of Alisoun's performance.

Wife of Bath's Prologue: 1931–1960

Numerous articles in these decades devote themselves to word study. Important analyses of Chaucer's use of the word *worthy* to denote Alisoun's first three husbands (**465**) and of the rhyme content and original word usage of Chaucer in the *Wife of Bath's Prologue* (**478**) are conducted in the 1930's. In the 1940's, Kökeritz (**492**) searches for the meaning behind Alisoun's *secte*, Seaton (**489**) connects the expression *godde lief* to a Flemish saint, and Whiting (**494**) examines the significance of Alisoun's *colt's tooth*. Three studies of Chaucerian puns in the *Wife of Bath's Prologue* come out in the 1950's: two by Baum (**516, 524**) and one by Kökeritz (**510**). Rockwell (**521**) analyzes the *spiced conscience* of Alisoun's first three husbands. A handful of articles concern themselves with historical accounts of the Dunmow Flitch trials, the contest in which a gammon of bacon was awarded to a peacefully married couple (**475, 497, 503, 506**). Scholars often connect this event to Alisoun's disdain for bacon. Whiting (**472**), Pyle (**477**), and Bennett (**490**) conduct studies of the various proverbs found in the *Wife of Bath's Prologue*. Consideration is also given to issues of tale order. Some scholars support Alisoun's performance following the *Man of Law's Tale* (**466, 471, 527**), the Pardoner's performance following Alisoun's (**501**), and both *Melibee* and the *Nun's Priest's Tale* as appropriate preludes to the *Wife of Bath's Prologue* (**464**). Wyatt (**476**) notes how appropriate the *Shipman's Tale* would have been for a narrator with Alisoun's personality.

The so-called flaws in Alisoun's character are exposed by Bradley (**517**) and Mroczkowski (**526**). Shelley (**482**), however, highlights Alisoun's realistic approach to life, and Salter (**511**) calls attention to Chaucer's sympathy for a woman who has led a tragic life. In an earlier study, Patch (**479**) observes Chaucer's delight in this character of his creation, regardless of her erring ways. Lowes (**469**) praises Chaucer for his development of Alisoun, and, in appreciation of Chaucer's innovation, Moore (**484**) notes Chaucer's unique application of preaching techniques to a female character. Shaver (**475**), as well, analyzes the ecclesiastical basis of Alisoun's rhetoric. While many of these studies praise the originality of Chaucer's Alisoun, others link

Alisoun's character to personalities developed by different writers. Rutter (**463**) traces a long line of female characters that have been produced in the antifeminist tradition. Outlining these characters from classical antiquity to Chaucer's contemporaries, Rutter aligns Alisoun with the old woman of *Pamphilus de Amore*, La Vieille, and Ghismonda, among others. While Donaldson (**525**) also recognizes Alisoun as the product of antifeminism, he asserts that she challenges her audience to compare a real woman with the stereotypical, fictional product of misogynistic literature. Comparisons of Alisoun with some of Jean de Meun's creations include analyses that parallel Chaucer's Wife with La Vieille (**505**, **520**) and with Genius (**507**). Preston (**507**) observes similarities between the *Wife of Bath's Prologue* and works by Villon and Dunbar. Both Sedgewick (**481**) and Malone (**500**) relate Alisoun to Chaucer's Pardoner. Other topics that have received attention during this block of thirty years include the issue of virginity (**509**, **518**) and the marital woes of Alisoun's husbands (**499**, **513**).

Wife of Bath's Prologue: 1961–1970

Pratt (**533**) provides a detailed article concerning the development of Alisoun and her performance. He charts Chaucer's initial plan for the interrelation of various tales and their tellers and the eventual Chaucerian additions and alterations within the *Canterbury Tales* that ultimately led to the formation of the Marriage Group and Alisoun's subsequently being assigned a new story to narrate. Other studies of tale order include two discussions about the Bradshaw Shift (**536**, **617**), both of which remark upon the geographical inconsistency of the Rochester and Sittingbourne references. While Zimbardo (**583**) notes the dialectical unity between the *Wife of Bath's Prologue* and *Tale*, other critics have chosen to examine the *Wife of Bath's Prologue* in light of other portions of the *Canterbury Tales*. Viewing the *Wife of Bath's Prologue* as a rejoinder to the *Man of Law's Tale*, Whittock (**608**) does not view Alisoun's prologue as the initiating tale of the Marriage Group. Cox (**585**) believes that Alisoun's performance in its entirety is a reaction against the story of Constance. Noting that the Wife of Bath and Alison of the *Miller's Tale* share a name and a penchant for Oxford clerks, Hanning (**600**) supposes a direct connection between these two women. While not extending the comparison of these women as far as Hanning does, Mustanoja (**620**) does consider the appropriateness of the proper names of Alisoun and Alison, remarking that their name connotes flirting and love. In analyzing whom the *Shipman's Tale* was intended for, Sullivan (**535**) compares Alisoun with the wife of St. Denis and finds Alisoun to be the more independent of the two women. Both Verbillion (**582**) and Revard (**593**) discuss possible connections between Alisoun and the Pardoner. Moving out of the immediate realm of the *Canterbury Tales*, Overbeck (**592**) compares and contrasts Alisoun to the good women in Chaucer's *Legend of Good Women*. Returning to the concept of the interlacing of themes within the *Canterbury Tales*, Mogan (**619**) traces the presence of theological doctrine in the *Miller's Tale*, *Merchant's Tale*, *Parson's Tale*, and the *Wife of Bath's Prologue*. In this last, according to Mogan, Alisoun outlines her version of the *bona matrimonii*.

Marriage is a common theme in several critical articles in the 1960's. Margulies (**538**) analyzes the historical accurateness of the details of the medieval Church's marital laws and practices in the *Wife of Bath's Prologue*. Clemen (**543**), Mahoney (**555**), and Howard (**575**) also outline the elements of patristic doctrine, canon law, and Alisoun's adherence to orthodox concepts in her discussion of marriage. Noting that Chaucer centers the tensions between real and ideal marriages on his female characters, Cavalcanti (**542**) deems Alisoun a victim of love. Hoffman (**544**) and Mulvey (**564**) turn their attention to the marital woes that Alisoun recounts. Finding irony in the *Wife of Bath's Prologue*, Mulvey feels Alisoun's woe is of her own making. Cotter (**612**) examines the marital debt Alisoun wishes to exact from her husbands.

The strong emphasis that Alisoun places on sex in her marriages has prompted critics to pursue several themes. In tracing sexual imagery throughout the *Wife of Bath's Prologue*, Rowland (**565, 615**) produces two articles that outline the sexual connotations behind Alisoun's reference to grinding grain at a mill. Combining hagiographic detail with Alisoun's preoccupation with sex, Haskell (**573**) finds that the pilgrim's staff of St. Joce, a saint whom Alisoun is swift to swear by, has phallic symbolism. Silvia (**624**) examines the sexual imagery found in the contested passage of lines 44a-f, and Braddy (**571**) illustrates the erotic theme that runs through Alisoun's performance. Wagenknecht (**607**) feels that Alisoun is uneasy about her advancing age, while Brookhouse

(**599**) adds Alisoun's unease at never having had children. Another study of Alisoun's personality that specifically relates to sex is Nist's (**578**), which describes Alisoun as a self-proclaimed nymphomaniac. While many of these studies stress the woe in Alisoun's life, Howard (**553**) finds no tones of regret in the *Wife of Bath's Prologue*. Moving from issues of Alisoun's personality to the methodology she uses in presenting a convincing argument, Corsa (**549**) praises Alisoun's ability to rationalize. Unsure whether Alisoun's unusual applications of proverbs are deliberate or unconscious, MacDonald (**576**) wonders if Alisoun is being 'cleverly deceptive' or 'foolish' (p 457) in her performance. Curtis (**586**) also observes the tension between truth and falsehood in the *Wife of Bath's Prologue*. Her observation on the difficulty of determining what is believable in Alisoun's performance recalls Huppé's comment that Alisoun may be rewriting her personal history (**554** p 110). Rogers (**580**), however, finds Alisoun's argument so convincing that the *Wife of Bath's Prologue* becomes a manifesto that challenges Chaucer's society's conceptions of marriage. Rogers' opinions are in direct conflict with those of Jordan (**590**), who reads the *Wife of Bath's Prologue* as an argument that ultimately supports the antifeminist tradition. That not all critics would agree with Jordan's theory is illustrated by Payne (**546**), who highlights Alisoun's determined rejection of literary authority, and Pratt (**547**), who finds a symbolic representation of female triumph in the destruction of Jankyn's book.

One of the most influential and controversial readings of the 1960's is D.W. Robertson's *A Preface to Chaucer* (**540**). Robertson sees the Wife of Bath as an iconographic figure of carnality whose deafness indicates less a physical impairment caused by her husband than an inability to hear the truth of the very scriptures she quotes, someone who lives by the Old Testament rather than by the New: 'She is dominated by the senses or the flesh rather than by the understanding or the spirit, by oldness rather than newness. In short, the wife of Bath is a literary personification of rampant "femininity" or carnality' (p. 321). Gillie (**557**), Scholes and Kellogg (**581**), and Beichner (**584**) further this critical trend of reducing Alisoun to an allegorical figure, yet Parker (**621**), who stresses the Wife's individuality and her inconsistencies, rejects the practice of interpreting Alisoun through the iconographic tradition.

Wife of Bath's Prologue: 1971–1980

The topic of marriage, which includes, of course, Alisoun's husbands, seems to be the order of the day in this decade. While Nichols (**630**) believes Chaucer valued the sacredness of the sacrament of marriage and would therefore frown upon Alisoun's behavior, Spisak (**732**) is convinced that the Wife of Bath represents Chaucer's realistic appreciation of marriage. Klene (**759**) sees Alisoun's insistence upon role reversals in her marriages as indicating a world turned upsidedown. Fleissner (**655**) focuses on the numerical significance of Alisoun's having had five husbands, noting the Pythagorean equation of the number five with earthly love and marriage. The men Alisoun has married have been criticized as inadequate husbands (**668**), and Alisoun's capitalizing on male weakness for carnality is praised (**698**). Observing Alisoun's treatment of her spouses, Ruggiers (**700**) finds the marriages to be a source of comedy in the *Wife of Bath's Prologue*, and David (**689**) agrees. Tristram (**701**) highlights the imbalance of youth and age in comparing Alisoun's youthful wedding of older men and her espousing the young Jankyn later on in life. Chaucer's application of animal imagery, specifically mice and sheep, to Alisoun's first three husbands (**631**) aids his audience in their evaluation of Alisoun's early marriages. That these men were elderly and rich allows the reader to maintain sympathy with Alisoun as she victimizes them (**652**), and that they have no names (**691**) further distances the reader from them. Berggren (**706**) asserts that Alisoun is victimized in her early marriages and that her humiliation prompts the Wife to victimize these husbands in return. Plotting Alisoun's development through her successive marriages, Burlin (**707**) suggests that her early marriages instructed her in how to provide for herself, and, after the failure of her fourth marriage, Alisoun learns how to defend herself by using textual authority in her alliance with Jankyn. Burton (**724**) also maintains that in spite of her claim to the contrary, Alisoun's fourth marriage was indeed a defeating one, and he feels that her marriage to Jankyn indicates Alisoun's desire to be submissive.

Some intriguing relations between Alisoun and some of her fellow pilgrims have been proposed in this decade. Alisoun, after all, is a professional wife according to Lawler (**760**). It has been suggested that Alisoun and the Clerk have a 'courting relationship' (**662**), that Alisoun has her eye on the Clerk for a sixth husband (**673**), and that the

Clerk and Jankyn are one and the same person, the Clerk's *Envoy* being a secret declaration of love the meaning of which only Alisoun will discern (**717**). Other, more traditional studies concerning Chaucer's Clerk discuss the tension between Alisoun's performance and the *Clerk's Tale* and highlight the opposing carnal and aesthetic natures of these characters (**676, 756**). Noting the similarities between Alisoun of Bath and Alison of the *Miller's Tale*, Long (**696**) concocts an argument that fuses John of the *Miller's Tale* with Chaucer's Reeve and adds that this Reeve is also Alisoun's very-much-alive fourth husband. While Eliason (**653**) and de Weever (**754**) also observe parallels between the Wife of Bath and Alison of the *Miller's Tale*, they come to different conclusions. Palmer (**728**) finds no marital bliss in Alisoun's life, despite her reliance upon both authority and experience.

The tangible representation of authority in the *Wife of Bath's Prologue*, Jankyn's Book of Wikked Wyves has been considered primarily in light of its contents during the 1970's. Because Heloise is one of the women detailed in Jankyn's book, Hamilton (**638**) believes Chaucer envisioned Abelard's *Historia calamitatum* as one component of the book. The reference to Trotula is examined as a testament to the fame of the female doctor (**651, 702**), and while Rowland (**745**) stresses that Trotula is present in Jankyn's book because of sexual connotations of the word *trot*, Tuttle (**702**) would argue against such an interpretation. Bennett (**663**) notes that the contents of Jankyn's book may be located in the Merton College Library catalogue. While Knight (**657**) views the burning of Jankyn's book as Alisoun's rejection of authority, Diamond (**708**) sees Chaucer's creation of Alisoun as an affirmation of the misogynistic contents of Jankyn's book.

Studies that focus more on the relation of the *Wife of Bath's Prologue* to other sections of Chaucer's work include Alisoun's rejection of the absence of the world of experience in the *Man of Law's Tale* (**713, 720**) and the Parson's discussion of lechery as a response to the *Wife of Bath's Prologue* (**695**). Alisoun is compared to the wife of St. Denis (**719**), the Guildsmen's wives (**715**), the Pardoner (**670**), and Criseyde (**740**). Comparisons of Alisoun with women outside of Chaucer include her ties to La Vieille (**642**), to Dunbar's women (**660**), to the *mulier fortis* (**677**), to Eve (**687**), to the old-woman tradition in literature (**671**), to a character type from Roman comedy (**711**), and to the motif of the saved harlot, which includes Mary Magdalene (**726**).

Inconographic criticism is furthered by Ames (**705**) and Robertson (**762**).

As an autobiographical narrator, Alisoun has been accused of deception (**658, 699**), of inconsistent quotation of authority (**693**), and of admitting to being guilty of all the stereotypical female vices (**678**). While her dialogue may be 'rambling' (**667** p 109) according to some points of view, Alisoun earns critical praise both for being a skilled preacher (**682, 703**) and for being an artful rhetorician (**694, 727**). Scholars note that she is aware both of her difficult audience (**721**) and of her chance to make use of male stereotypes (**684**). Her non-penitential practices during Lent are called into question (**627**), as is her equation of her *quoniam* with the divine (**634**). Alisoun is labeled a nymphomaniac (**648**), an unrepentant sinner (**662**), a sociopath (**731**), and a tyrant (**735**). While critics believe she is indiscreet (**637**) and tends to rationalize her actions (**683**), Alisoun is also viewed to her credit as a representation of triumphant womanhood (**722**) and is recognized for drawing the line when it comes to committing adultery (**632**).

While some scholars feel that Alisoun's use of sex as a commodity has caused her guilt (**639**), Delany notes the historical relevance of the value placed on a woman's sexuality (**681**). Woolf (**749**) thinks that Alisoun's unbelievability causes readers not to censure her for using sex as an economic tool. Aers (**750**) observes that while Alisoun ostensibly marries Jankyn out of love, the practice of sexual economics still influences her.

In a landmark feminist article (**736**), Carruthers, while she also touches on the topic of sexual economics, focuses on Alisoun's complaint about the misogynistic stories of women in Jankyn's book of wicked wives. Alisoun draws a comparison with the fact that the stories in which men do combat with lions are always told by men. If the lions got to tell the tales, the lions would be the heroes who defeated the vicious men. Alisoun insists that if wives got to tell the tales about marriage, the stories would emphasize the wickedness of husbands. Try as he will, Carruthers insists, Chaucer cannot avoid having the Wife of Bath portray herself as the medieval patriarchy would have seen her. The immediate responses of two male scholars who criticized Carruthers for applying an historical context to Chaucer's work (**738**) and for focusing on feminist hermeneutics (**737**), suggest the broad resistance to early feminist readings of Chaucer.

Wife of Bath's Prologue: 1981–1990

While rather traditional analyses of Alisoun's personality and character are conducted during the 1980's — Singer's (**779**) evaluation of Alisoun as a fusion of a realistic individual and a more abstract, type-character provides an example of such work — Alisoun's sexuality becomes a pressing issue in this decade. Studies concerning Chaucer's use of puns focus on the words *quoniam* (**806**) and *queynte* (**811, 905**). Rowland (**777**) diagnoses the Wife as a nymphomaniac, and Collins (**834**) notes that Alisoun's frank depiction of her arousal by Jankyn's legs at her fourth husband's funeral is not the standard response of medieval women to the men in their world. Luecke (**786**) observes that Alisoun's sexual activity diminishes the potential influence of her narrative because Alisoun is no longer in the ideal feminine state of virginity. In another study that relates sexuality with language, Patterson (**801**) comments that while Alisoun has been aligned with a carnal nature through the tradition of antifeminist literature, Alisoun stresses the carnality of language itself in her prologue. According to Davenant (**769**), because of Alisoun's passionate nature Jankyn must beat her. Chaucer uses the Wife's fifth husband to illustrate the need to subdue the aggressive female in order to maintain patriarchal society. A few years later, Brewer (**831**) echoes this interpretation.

Not all critics readily accept the portrait of a dominated, subdued Alisoun. Noting numerous interpretational possibilities for the *Wife of Bath's Prologue*, Knapp (**863**) proposes that Alisoun *may* be presenting a defense of the emerging entrepreneurial woman. Knight (**864**) credits Alisoun with eluding the repressive traps of the patriarchy through, among other things, her ability to maintain her own business. The light in which an audience should view Alisoun's economic prowess is another facet of critical debate. While Knapp and Knight see the positive side of Alisoun's trade, Robertson (**776**) labels the Wife as an 'exploitative capitalist' and later writes (**871**) that she represents, for Chaucer, the absence of a steadfast society. Aers (**855**) also notes the decrease of humanism in light of the increase in capitalism during the fourteenth century, and he cites Alisoun's acceptance of sexual economics as an indicator of this devaluation of human worth.

Whether Alisoun triumphs over or is undone by the patriarchal society in which she lives, the fact that she struggles with the structural hierarchy is not contested. Her struggle has proven to be the basis for a web of critical themes. When we consider Alisoun's opening argument that ranks experience above authority, *experience* seems to serve as a heading for the categories of woman's voice, woman's wisdom, and the oral tradition, not to mention the issue of Alisoun's lion-painting complaint. *Authority*, then, encompasses topics such as Jankyn's book, the exegetical texts it contains, and, most specifically, the antifeminist attitudes with which such texts are saturated.

As Orme (**773**), Owen (**774**) and Sleeth (**914**) have observed, while Alisoun rails against patriarchal authority in her prologue, she does credit female authority, specifically the lore she inherited from her mother, the oral passage of experiential learning from one generation of women to the next. Sturges (**804**) notes that Alisoun, as well as the other female Canterbury tale-tellers, develops a tradition of female authority. Alisoun's vision of female authority differs from those of the religious female pilgrims in that she wishes to replace male domination with female governance rather than an alternative for a system that involves a hierarchical power structure. Alisoun's valuing of women's oral tradition is a prominent point in Schibanoff's (**872**) study, and Bishop feels that the *Wife of Bath's Prologue* reveals that a woman's main weapon is her gift of speech (**875**). Knapp (**945**), as well, outlines Alisoun's stress upon the value of female dialogue. Such consideration of woman's voice recalls Carruthers's discussion of Alisoun's lion-painting complaint (**736**), published in the late nineteen seventies. Carruthers's work seems to have spurred a number of articles that deal with the concepts of Alisoun as narrator and female encounters with patriarchal language. The lion-painting complaint itself has been regarded as a unifying message within the *Wife of Bath's Prologue* that tells the truth about the condition of women (**799**), a sentiment against misogyny shared by Christine de Pizan (**854**), an example of the subjective nature of writing (**876**), and a rhetorically self-negating speech (**898**). As for the premise behind Alisoun's complaint, that women have no true voice in the textual world of men, Kirkpatrick (**796**) views the *Wife of Bath's Prologue* as a challenge to the concept of ordered narrative, and Knapp (**932**) believes Alisoun attempts to rework the genres of antifeminist literature and romance in order to supply a definition of woman that is not dictated by masculine desire. Hanning (**819**) and Gottfried (**838**) both recognize the tension created by bringing the privatized form of feminine speech into the world of public, patriarchal discourse. Reminding us that Alisoun's female voice is ultimately the creation of a male author, Hansen (**944**) adds a significant factor for critical consideration when attempting to apply the criteria of feminine discourse to Alisoun's performance. Delany (**939**) notes that emphasis should also be placed on the silence found in the *Wife of Bath's Prologue*.

In *Chaucer's Sexual Poetics* (**922**) Dinshaw is one of the first, and certainly one of the most influential, feminist critics to suggest that we can profitably think of the Wife of Bath's body as a 'text' to be 'glossed' in various ways by men, particularly misogynist clerks. It can be sexual glossing, as when a man makes love to her: 'Glossing here is unmistakeably carnal, a masculine act performed on the feminine body, and it leads to pleasure for both husband and wife, both clerk and text' (p 125). But it can also be more harmful, since the 'text' is variously commented on by men, made fun of, beaten, raped, cast aside. In her own commentary Alisoun becomes a glossator, an assertive woman who successively mimics masculine discourse. Dinshaw's analysis may be united with Wetherbee's (**937**) work, which promotes the *Wife of Bath's Prologue* as a history of Alisoun's body. It has been suggested, however, that Alisoun manipulates others with her own ability to gloss (**839**). Body, text, and glossing become further related in discussions concerning Jankyn's Book of Wikked Wyves. Martin unites the concepts of bodies and language when she establishes the physical altercation between Alisoun and Jankyn as a manifestation of the detrimental effects of patriarchal language (**951**) for in the course of this fight the enraged Alisoun destroys a few leaves of her husband's book, and Jankyn, in retaliation, deafens his wife in one of her ears. While Barney (**783**) credits Jankyn's book as another source for Alisoun's learning, Neuss (**772**) believes the book inspired jealousy in Alisoun for it is against this work that she must compete for her husband's attentions. Leicester (**822**) envisions the book as being symbolic of Alisoun's and Jankyn's mutual delight in arguing with one another. Other critical studies that discuss Jankyn's book involve the women it brands as *wikked wyves* (**810, 862**), and Griffiths and Pearsall (**927**) provide a cost-estimate of Jankyn's possession, suggesting that the book would have been priced at several pounds.

In direct relation to the contents of Jankyn's book, the antifeminist tracts and Alisoun's ability to gloss exegetical material provide another focal point of critical scrutiny. Several scholars of the 1980's tend to view Alisoun's misquoting of Scripture as a comic device of Chaucer (**815, 829, 841**). While Reiss (**825**) perceives Alisoun's literal applications of biblical text as an indication of her inability to divine the spirit of the Word, Martin (**952**) highlights the significant meaning that emanates from Alisoun's interpretation of text, regardless of her method of approaching this work. Whereas Besserman believes Alisoun's exegesis does not compare favorably to other fourteenth-century commentaries, Stone (**890**) feels the alterations of the authoritative sources are fitting for a fourteenth-century woman's world.

Considering the specific biblical exegetes whom Alisoun challenges, Wurtele (**807**) compares Alisoun's logic with that of Jerome, and Wilson (**853**) examines the cultural connotations behind Jerome's selection of the grain barley in order to create an analogy for the state of marriage. Peck (**824**) produces a comparative study of Alisoun and St. Paul, and Knapp (**885**) notes the Augustinian influence on Alisoun's performance. Fleming's (**817**) discussion of Alisoun's more unorthodox conceptions of the Church's view of perfection calls to mind the association of Alisoun with the heretical Lollards. Although Hudson (**906**) finds some of Alisoun's language to reflect that of John Wyclif, Blamires (**918**) argues that Alisoun adheres to many of the practices the Lollards abhorred.

In addition to both Alisoun's and Jankyn's abilities to gloss, critics have analyzed the commentative glosses of the scribes who compiled the various manuscripts of the *Canterbury Tales*. Owen (**787**) provides a comparison of the Hengwrt and Ellesmere glossators, Fichte (**901**) studies the margins of these manuscripts, and Schibanoff (**913**) examines the Egerton manuscript glosses as well as those of the Ellesmere. Other textual studies include two by Blake, in which he outlines the development of Alisoun's performance (**784**) and comments upon Chaucer's shifting the *Squire's Tale* and the *Wife of Bath's Prologue* and *Tale* (**830**). Ruggiers (**828**) studies the various tale orderings preferred by noteworthy Chaucerian editors, and Koff (**908**) rejects the belief that the reference to Alisoun in the *Merchant's Tale* functions as an indicator of tale order. The study of thematic links among the tales of Fragment III also has received attention. Wasserman (**790**) perceives a philosophical debate between the notions of the concrete and the abstract in the stories, while Wallace (**960**) feels that anger provides a common motivation for these pilgrims to tell their tales. Both

Alford (**809**) and Hanning (**882**) focus on the issue of exegetical glossing as a common strand found within this fragment.

Along with thematic unity comes the concept of interrelation among the Canterbury pilgrims. A number of articles evaluate Alisoun's character in light of the Pardoner. Rhodes (**789**) highlights the commonality between Alisoun and the Pardoner, viewing them as sympathetic to one another because each must deal with his or her marginalized status. Leicester (**886**) notes that neither of these pilgrims' performances is well received by their immediate audience. Taylor (**892**) feels that Alisoun's performance serves as an intertextual forerunner of the *Pardoner's Prologue* and *Tale*, and Olson (**868**) believes that the Wife and the Pardoner, along with several other pilgrims, belong to an Epicurean sect governed by the flesh and corrupt reason. Articles that contrast these two characters note that Alisoun's morality, while by no means perfect, is of a higher caliber than that of the Pardoner (**802, 889**). Shoaf (**803**) observes that while Alisoun is jealous of the Pardoner's oratorical skills, he envies her sexual encounters.

As an increasing variety of schools of critical theory are applied to the process of analyzing Alisoun's performance, it is not surprising that a variety of scholars begin, in turn, to investigate these multiple methodologies. In response to Robertson's (**776**) previously discussed article that expresses disappointment in Alisoun's carnal and capitalistic nature, Gardner (**771**) points out that Chaucer does not detail any exploitative actions on Alisoun's part. He then notes that feminism was indeed an issue of Chaucer's era. Rejecting exegetical interpretation, Pearsall (**845**) believes Alisoun's relation to her audience, her middle-class status, and her coming from Bath distance her from the iconographic tradition. Fradenburg (**941**) also criticizes Robertsonian thought, observing that his accusation of Alisoun's self-serving textual interpretation is something of which he himself is guilty. His depicting Alisoun as a stereotypical female reinforces the patriarchal practice of creating binary opposition; he continues the tradition of viewing Alisoun as Other. Alkalay-Gut (**791**) debates the merits of applying contemporary feminist thoughts to the fourteenth century. Stressing the predominant power of the medieval patriarchy, Hansen (**904**) also advocates caution when discussing Alisoun's feminism. Nyquist (**954**) subsequently supports Hansen's awareness of the dissimilarities between medieval and modern gender relations. According to Straus (**915**), while Alisoun is entrenched in a masculine world, she does her best to subvert the dictates of masculine discourse. While Williams (**852**) devotes his article to examining the prevalent theories of critics who do not advocate deconstructive practices, O'Brien (**955**) actually labels Alisoun herself a deconstructionist. Adams (**808**) promotes an historical perspective, reminding us not to forget the cultural beliefs of the fourteenth century when analyzing Alisoun, and Howard (**884**) resurrects biographical criticism, comparing the wistfulness and sadness in Alisoun's voice with Chaucer's emotions in coping with Phillipa's death.

A number of articles concern works that influenced Chaucer and works that were influenced by Chaucer. Storm (**891**), Erzgräber (**879**), and Johnson (**907**) all highlight the effect medieval drama had upon Chaucer. The characters of Noah and his wife figure prominently in relating Alisoun to the antifeminist tradition in the first two of these articles. Influential across several centuries, Chaucer's Alisoun is credited with providing inspiration for Hoccleve (**950**), Dunbar (**770**, **826**, **848**), the author of *The Cobler of Cauterburie* (**877**), and the composer of the ballad *The Wanton Wife of Bath* (**895**). Numerous studies were devoted to Chaucer and Shakespeare in the 1980's. While parallels are drawn between Alisoun and Kate in *The Taming of the Shrew* (**794**, **931**) and the Wife of Bath and the Wives of Windsor (**797**), Alisoun is most frequently linked with Falstaff (**793**, **798**, **835**, **856**). Berry (**765**) discusses the powerful influence of Chaucer's *Wife of Bath's Prologue* on the Scriblerus Club, whose members included Gay, Pope, and Swift. As for twentieth-century art, Lammers (**909**) notes the common archetypal characterization of Alisoun and Joyce's Molly Bloom, and Prescott (**933**) reports on her collaborative efforts in creating choral works inspired by Chaucer's writing, one of which recounts the adventures of Alisoun.

Wife of Bath's Prologue: 1991–1996

A central concern of Chaucerian scholarship in the 1990's involves examining Chaucer's creation of Alisoun as an indication of his feelings toward the condition of women. Hagen (**971**) reflects that the medieval conception of women hindered Chaucer in his attempt to represent the female experience. She also notes that while Alisoun is often criticized for her preoccupation with sex, the Wife of Bath is the creation of a male author. While Astell (**963**) finds an ambivalent attitude in Chaucer, Mann (**975**) asserts that Chaucer dealt with gender stereotypes in order to reveal their effect on society. In another piece of her scholarly work, Mann (**976**) states that Chaucer exposes antifeminism in order to criticize the victimization of women. Carruthers (**992**) holds a belief similar to that of Mann, yet Delany (**994**) feels that however sympathetic towards women Chaucer might have been, he was the product of a culture that maintained a firmly-entrenched ambivalence towards women. Also recognizing Alisoun's male authorship, Lindley (**1004**) believes Alisoun vanishes from her performance just as surely as the dancing ladies in her tale disappear before the knight. While admitting that Alisoun does not dispel the antifeminist tradition, Dillon (**1023**) notes Alisoun's ability to expose truths about humanity, and Van (**1046**) argues that Alisoun creates a successful parody of antifeminist practices.

Any assault Alisoun makes against the patriarchy is typically seen in the form of verbal attack. While some scholars view Alisoun's speech acts as a means to gain mastery (**1024**), as a form of feminine power over authoritarian figures (**1045**), and as an exposé of the way speech can align itself more closely to fiction than to truth (**974**), other critics see Alisoun as reinforcing the antifeminist tradition because she is indeed so vocal (**975**). Both Hahn (**1000**) and Daileader (**1035**) examine the connection between woman's body and text.

Multiple critical methodologies are applied to the *Wife of Bath's Prologue* in these years. Osberg (**980**) and Storm (**983**) discuss the iconographic implications of Alisoun's adherence to the Old Law. Incorporating theories of Bakhtin, Breuer (**988**) and Wimsatt (**1016**) provide analyses that include the concept of dialogical discourse, and Wilson (**1015**) observes the carnivalesque qualities in the description of Alisoun's body. O'Brien (**1008**) studies the archetypal association of water with feminine power; Root (**1043**) applies Foucault to the *Wife of Bath's Prologue*. Crane (**993**) offers an historical parallel between Alisoun's burning of Jankyn's book and the Peasant's Revolt of 1381. In a Case Studies in Contemporary Criticism Series edition of the *Wife of Bath's Prologue* and *Tale*, Finke (**1059**) provides a Marxist reading of Alisoun's performance, Fradenburg (**1060**) supplies a psychoanalytic perspective, Hansen (**1061**) illustrates a feminist viewpoint, Leicester (**1062**) deconstructs Alisoun's performance, and Patterson (**1065**) treats new historicism, while Beidler (**1058**) outlines the variety of critical applications that have been used in studying the *Wife of Bath's Prologue* and *Tale*.

A few critical issues relating to Alisoun's performance have cut across the decades. Instead of discussing them as they appear within the chronological order of this introduction, we felt that separate sections would provide a more effective means of summarizing them.

...I am al Venerien / In feelynge, and myn herte is Marcien

In his *Chaucer and the Medieval Sciences* (**454**), Curry examines the accuracy of the Wife of Bath's horoscope and finds that Chaucer was well-versed in his understanding of planetary influence. Highlighting what grace and beauty Alisoun could have possessed had Venus been allowed to reign alone in Alisoun's stellar chart, Curry goes on to show how the effect of Mars in Taurus contributed to Alisoun's nature. Alisoun's horoscope has remained a common topic for critics throughout the century. The tension created between the Venusian and the Martian influences — expressed in terms of being loving and domineering (**646**) or being passionate and aggressive (**844**) — is the usual focus of discussion. Slaughter (**470**), Grose (**587**), and Elliott (**923**) point out how swift Alisoun is to use the concept of stellar influence as an excuse for her behavior, and Wood (**626**) adds that no one is required to follow the dictates of the stars. In his study of astrology and the *Canterbury Tales*, Hendricks (**883**) observes that the pilgrims who bring astrology into their tales reveal their materialism as well as their irresponsibility. Leicester (**948**) believes that since the study of the stars originates within the patriarchy, a horoscope is another manifestation of male power trying to keep women subjugated. Hamlin (**669**) and North (**910**) attempt to determine Alisoun's year of birth according to stellar position, and both scholars fix her date of birth as early in 1342. While Hira (**601**) debates whether or not Chaucer believed in horoscopes, Rutledge (**659**) conducts a study that aligns the *Canterbury Tales* with the various signs of the zodiac. It should come as no surprise that Alisoun's performance is associated with Scorpio, the eighth house of the zodiac, which governs the genitalia.

Murder will out?

In 1948, a tongue-in-cheek article was published in the *Baker Street Journal*. Using a discussion between Sherlock Holmes and Dr. Watson as his medium, Hall (**493**) has Holmes deduce that Alisoun persuaded Jankyn to help her murder her fourth husband. While critics remained silent upon the issue for several decades, Rowland (**649**), Palomo (**686**), Frank (**925**), and Wurtele (**916, 985**) each add supportive evidence for this alleged crime. The scholars generally feel that fear of his exposure provides a rationale for Jankyn's yielding sovereignty to Alisoun. Alisoun's guilt would also serve as an explanation for her rage when Jankyn details accounts of wives murdering their husbands in his book. Hamel (**741**) and Crane (**897**) defend Alisoun against this accusation.

Whether or not Alisoun is a widow on the Canterbury pilgrimage is another issue that has been contested throughout the twentieth century. In the mid-1960's, Huppé (**554**) supposes that Jankyn may be dead. Shortly thereafter, Silvia (**596**) asserts that Jankyn is alive and that Alisoun is keeping an eye out for a sixth husband because she has tired of her Oxford clerk. Schmidt (**1176**) challenges Silvia's hypothesis, suggesting that the moral of the *Wife of Bath's Tale* establishes Jankyn's death. Biggins (**665**) provides a list of critics and their opinions as to whether or not Jankyn is dead, and then, stressing Alisoun's title of *Wife* and her lack of mourning attire, comes out in favor of a living Jankyn. Combining the theory that Alisoun and Jankyn murdered Alisoun's fourth husband with the status of Jankyn, Palomo (**686**) theorizes that Jankyn was put to death for his crime and that Alisoun must seek atonement through her pilgrimage. Wurtele (**916**) also advances the murder theory, suggesting that Jankyn abandoned Alisoun because of their crime.

Alisoun and the Friar

Two topics that bear relation to one another frequently crop up in twentieth-century scholarly criticism on the Wife of Bath. They are Alisoun's insulting of the Friar and her equation of friars with incubi. Bennett (**1107**) finds the anti-mendicant portion of the *Wife of Bath's Tale* to be more critical of friars than Langland's work, yet Kiessling (**1209**) interprets Alisoun's remarks in a softer light, labeling them as a form of teasing. Mroczkowski (**1141**) has located a fourteenth-century exemplum that can be viewed as containing a critical comparison of friars and incubi, and Havely (**1310**) finds Chaucer's conception of friars reflected in Boccaccio's work. Braswell (**171**) finds in the work of Jacobus de Voragine an association similar to Alisoun's linking of friars with dust. Traversi (**1316**) argues that Alisoun's claim that the friars had replaced the incubi recalls the substitution of Christian morality for more liberal sexual practices.

This discussion of Alisoun's insulting of friars, which happens at an early point in her tale, provides us with the perfect transition to our survey of twentieth-century criticism of the *Wife of Bath's Tale*.

Wife of Bath's Tale: 1900–1930

Critical studies of the *Wife of Bath's Tale* at the beginning of the twentieth century focused predominantly on source and analogue study. Other pertinent early issues include the relation of the *Wife of Bath's Tale* to the *Wife of Bath's Prologue*, the connections between Alisoun's tale and the other Canterbury stories, and the influence that the *Wife of Bath's Tale* has had upon other writers. Snell (**1090**) notes a common theme of female sovereignty in marriage in the Wife's prologue and tale, and Cowling (**1091**) agrees that Alisoun's marital ideology is reflected in her Arthurian story. Curry (**1085**) points out that the Venusian aspect of Alisoun's horoscope enables her to relate a romance to her fellow pilgrims. In his studies on Chaucer's use of the Seven Deadly Sins as a motif in the *Canterbury Tales*, Tupper (**1078**) cites the *Wife of Bath's Tale* as evidence of Alisoun's sin of pride. Addressing Tupper's article, Lowes (**1079**), in his own study of the deadly sins in Chaucer, highlights the knight's condition of sloth and feels that Alisoun herself is a compilation of all of the seven sins. In the following year, Tupper (**1081**) echoes Lowes in his observation that the sins of pride and sloth are opposed by the virtue of *gentillesse*.

Spurgeon's (**1088**) study of early Chaucerian influence reveals the popularity of the *Wife of Bath's Tale*. She notes that Alisoun's performance was translated into both French and German, was retold by Dryden and Johnson, and influenced the work of Hoccleve and several other authors. While Canby (**1073**) discusses the tale's effect upon Dunbar's writing, Mackail (**1074**) finds the opening lines of the

Wife of Bath's Tale reflected in those of Keats' *Lamia*. Legouis (**1076**) comments upon Alisoun's reappearance in Chaucer's work, specifically in the *Envoy to Bukton*, and Vogt (**1086**) establishes the indebtedness of Fletcher and Favart to Chaucer's *Wife of Bath's Tale*.

Wife of Bath's Tale: 1931–1960

The ordering of the *Canterbury Tales* and Chaucer's replacement of Alisoun's initial fabliau by a romance are two of four issues frequently addressed in this span of thirty years. Pratt's (**1112**) examination of the *Canterbury Tales* leads him to his conclusion that since Alisoun is referred to in Fragments IV and V, these portions of Chaucer's work should be placed not far behind Fragment III. In defense of the Ellesmere order of the tales, Greenfield (**1118**) addresses the geographical problem created by the fact that the reference to Rochester follows the reference to Sittingbourne. Greenfield believes that the Summoner merely refers to Sittingbourne and that this character's remark should not be mistaken for an indication that the pilgrims have actually arrived in this town.

In the 1950's, Pratt (**1112**) explains that Chaucer initially intended to have Alisoun interrupt the Man of Law during the *Endlink* to the *Man of Law's Tale* and that she would then have told what is now the *Shipman's Tale*. Because the wife of St. Denis is duped by Daun John in the *Shipman's Tale*, Malone (**1111**) feels that Chaucer eventually decided to give Alisoun a tale in which the female characters have more control. Having cited the feminine pronouns found rather early on in the *Shipman's Tale* as the basis of his argument, Lowes (**1095**) comes to a similar conclusion. Chapman (**1130**) argues, however, that the feminine pronouns are not a piece of unfinished business that Chaucer neglected to correct after changing the gender of the tale's teller, but are a deliberate incorporation, the offering of a feminine perspective on marriage that complements the male view of marriage contained in the preceding lines. Lawrence (**1136**) believes that Alisoun was the original teller of the *Shipman's Tale* and supports this claim by highlighting the tale's theme and tone and by noting Chaucer's alterations of his source for this fabliau. It would seem that Kane (**1110**) would have preferred that Chaucer had Alisoun tell this ribald tale instead of giving her a romance to relate. All the beauty of the *Wife of Bath's Tale*, he feels, is undercut by its teller.

A significant number of articles from these three decades explore the knight's character, and the issue of his crime of rape — a rare topic in the first thirty years of twentieth-century criticism — also becomes a focal point for many critics. Roppolo (**1113**) believes that just as the loathly lady transforms outwardly, the knight undergoes an inner, or moral, transformation. Makarewicz (**1119**) notes that the *Wife of Bath's Tale* deals with the enlightenment of a sinner. In 1954, Salter (**1124**) writes that Chaucer incorporated the crime of rape into the *Wife of Bath's Tale* in order to stress the dramatic alteration of the knight's personality, and Townsend (**1125**) emphasized the serious nature of the knight as a character, that he is Alisoun's 'vision of masculine perfection' (p 3). Rather chivalrously, Donaldson (**1135**) views the knight's transformation as a tribute to the ability of women to influence goodness. Not all commentary, though, finds the knight to be an exemplary character. Slaughter (**1133**) expresses his doubts about the knight's accepting the higher truths of the pillow lecture and notes that the knight's feelings toward his bride change only after she reveals herself as a beautiful woman.

As for the rape itself, Coffman (**1105**) finds an analogue for the crime in hagiographical writings that detail the birth of St. Cuthbert. Recalling Andreas Capellanus' sanctioning of knights raping peasant women in *The Art of Courtly Love*, Huppé (**1108**) estimates the female victim was of the lower classes. Huppé does not condone the act but rather stresses the knight's violation of Christian and courtly codes of conduct. Gerould (**1115**) disagrees with Huppé's assertion that the rape victim came from a lower social order. Considering the rape in light of the teller, Gerould also assumes that the Wife of Bath details the crime of rape because she possesses a sex-obsessed nature and claims that an Arthurian knight would not be guilty of such conduct. Patch (**1099a**) believes that Alisoun does not feel that rape is a serious issue.

Wife of Bath's Tale: 1961–1970

Reflecting both the growth of scholarly publishing in almost all areas of literary study and a particular interest in the performance of the Wife of Bath, the amount of critical material on the *Wife of Bath's Tale* in the decade of the 1960's roughly equals the amount in the previous six decades. In the preceding discussion of the rape in the *Wife of Bath's*

Tale, we mentioned the critical tendency to link this sexual violation with Alisoun's own sexual nature. Severs (**1182**) comments upon the penchant that critics have for intertwining their analyses of the *Wife of Bath's Tale* with Alisoun's personality, noting that the Wife herself and not her romance is the attraction for many scholars. Indeed, Slade's (**1188**) article, published in the following year, stresses that the *Wife of Bath's Tale* should be approached by taking Alisoun's character into full consideration. While critics continually draw parallels between the *Wife of Bath's Prologue* and *Tale* — Mulvey's (**1161**) aligning Alisoun and Jankyn with the hag and the knight is a prime example of this methodology — several scholars, such as Malone (**1145**), explore contradictions that they find between the two sections of Alisoun's performance. Levy (**1158**) observes that while Alisoun is a proponent of female mastery in marriage, her romance ends with a woman's yielding to her husband. A later article of Levy's (**1192**) also explores the conflict between Alisoun's professed delight in a lusty husband and the decreased virility of husbands that is the result of their being dominated by their wives in both the *Wife of Bath's Prologue* and *Tale*. Whittock (**1184**) finds Alisoun to be ignorant of the true moral of her story: while she claims female sovereignty to be the desired goal in life, her romance stresses the goodness of yielding to the wills of others.

Holland (**1172, 1180**) applies various schools of criticism to the *Wife of Bath's Tale* in his two articles. He presents a Freudian, an allegorical, and an archetypal reading in the former and extends these readings, in addition to furthering a psychoanalytical approach, in the latter. The issue of class is raised by Brewer (**1177**), who emphasizes Chaucer's appreciation of the fact that the way an individual acts, not his or her birth, should determine status. Brookhouse (**1178**) calls attention to Alisoun's social-climbing instincts, believing that her aristocratic ambitions are revealed in her storytelling. Brookhouse also contends that the *Wife of Bath's Tale* reflects Alisoun's desire to regain her youth and beauty. This tendency to see the tale as a manifestation of wish-fulfillment is not universally accepted. Recalling Eleanor of Aquitaine's recommended pairing of young men with older women, Silverstein (**1142**) believes that Alisoun is not searching for her lost youth. While admitting that there are escapist tendencies in the *Wife of Bath's Tale*, Malone (**1145**) notes that Alisoun is accepting of her age in the *Wife of Bath's Prologue*.

Familiar facets of critical interest, for example the concepts of courtly love and chivalry, are dealt with in the 1960's. Broadbent (**1149**) unites the concept of courtly love with issues of class through his illustration of Alisoun's middle-class marriage to Jankyn. He also addresses the woman's desire to be both wife and mistress to her mate, a concept that Wagenknecht (**1183**) shows is contradictory to the courtly love tradition. While Bowden (**1163**) outlines the chivalric elements in the *Wife of Bath's Tale*, Hatton (**1165**) notes that Alisoun's tale reveals how this social code can be manipulated to serve the purposes of the individual. Continuing the debate surrounding the concept of the knight's conversion, Moorman (**1160**) defines the transformation as a movement towards an ideal nature, while Levy (**1192**) feels that the knight once again succumbs to his desire for a carnal existence when presented with his lovely bride.

Textual analysis is offered by Gardner (**1171**), who argues against the Bradshaw Shift, and by Ruggiers (**1174**) who feels that the *Wife of Bath's Tale* complements Alisoun's personality more than the *Shipman's Tale* would have. An historical approach is found in Wilks' (**1146**) article discussing the concepts of kingship and sovereignty and speculating that Chaucer applied his version of the loathly lady tale to the reign of Richard II.

The digressions in the *Wife of Bath's Tale*, according to Steinberg (**1155**), remind the reader of Alisoun's presence as she tells her tale. Schaar (**1175**) admires the depth of emotion Alisoun details in the Midas digression, and Allen and Gallacher (**1190**) continue the tradition of using the *Wife of Bath's Tale* to gauge Alisoun's character by reading her mistelling of the Midas story as an indicator of her inability to judge.

Wife of Bath's Tale: 1971–1980

One of the more popular topics for critical discussion in the 1970's is Chaucer's selection of a folk theme, that of the loathly lady tale, and his fusion of the folk element with the genre of the romance. Thomas (**1203**) feels that Chaucer held neither fairy-tale nor Arthurian elements in high regard, and Muscatine (**1210**) notes that Chaucer downplays the Celtic elements of fairy in the *Wife of Bath's Tale*. Other folk-oriented studies observe Chaucer's incorporation of a rape into the loathly lady tale (**1214**) and the absence of a father-figure in the Wife's tale as well as its analogues (**1282**). Articles that evaluate the *Wife of Bath's Tale* as a romance praise the coherence of the plot in comparison to the romances of the *Squire's Tale* and the *Tale of Sir Thopas* (**1232**), note the reversal of gender roles in the tale (**1255**), outline conventional romantic elements (**1262**), contemplate the inclusion of the magical in the genre (**1290**), and, more negatively, highlight the failure of Alisoun's tale as a romance (**1284**). Carpenter (**1221**) finds the loathly lady appearing in Texas folklore.

Articles that treat the issue of the relation of tale to teller offer a variety of opinions on the connections between Alisoun and her romance. Eliason (**1204**) examines Chaucer's inclusion of certain lines that clearly reflect Alisoun's character, and Pittock (**1217**) also addresses the Chaucerian tailoring of this romance in order that it might suit Alisoun. On the other hand, Knight (**1216**) feels that the rapid movement of the narrative's main plot allows the audience to forget Alisoun. Citing the *gentillesse* sermon as containing sentiments that seem contrary to Alisoun's nature, Brewer (**1220a**) underscores a conflict between tale and teller. Yet Evans (**1253**) feels that Alisoun's depiction of the unique relationship between the loathly lady and the knight reflects events in Alisoun's personal life. In keeping with this line of thought, Fyler (**1274**) observes that the Wife has placed herself into her narrative, specifically in the form of the old woman. Sato (**1277**) directly equates this woman with Alisoun and ascribes her transformation to wish-fulfillment. In agreement with Sato are Murtaugh (**1199**), Kean (**1208**), Rowland (**1211**), and Howard (**1244**). Engelhardt (**1224**) connects Alisoun with the loathly lady, but he also outlines parallels between Alisoun and the raped maiden. Carruthers (**1272**), however, asserts that Alisoun should *not* be identified with the loathly lady.

The closing elements of the *Wife of Bath's Tale* — the pillow lecture, the transformation of the loathly lady, and the knight's subsequent reformation (an ever-contested event) — receive their fair share of critical attention. Fisher (**1205**) remarks that the pillow lecture and choice the knight has between having either a beautiful or a faithful wife make the *Wife of Bath's Tale* highly appropriate for the Marriage Group. Focusing on the loathly lady's rhetorical means of persuasion, Spearing (**1212**) notes the repetitive wording of the pillow lecture, and Bloomfield (**1213**) discusses the scholastic elements of the speech. Sanders (**1227**) feels that the loathly lady employs feminine psychology, and Oberembt (**1245**) praises the old woman's wisdom and her reason, both of which further Alisoun's undermining of antifeminist thought. Wenzel (**1249**) notes the pulpit-like preaching of the sermon, and Mendelson (**1269**) finds that the loathly lady makes use of the questioning motif. Feeling that the loathly lady is unable to enlighten the knight with her words, Weissman (**1239**) finds no ultimate liberation for the old woman at the end. David (**1243**), however, believes that the old woman acquires 'sovereignty over herself' (p 156). While Nichols (**1200**) hypothesizes that the hag-turned-beauty will become a submissive spouse once she has achieved the enlightenment of her husband, Elbow (**1231**) believes that a mutual yielding, motivated by love, occurs at the end of the romance. Diamond (**1251**), however, views the tale skeptically, decrying it as a product of male fantasy that rewards a rapist with a lovely bride.

When considering the interrelation of the tales in Fragment III, Szittya (**1238**) feels that the *Friar's Tale* is a parody of the *Wife of Bath's Tale*, complete with a shape-shifting, fantastical character. Finding a debate to be the interconnecting theme, East (**1252**) notes that each of the three tales in Fragment III deals with authority versus experience. Owen (**1258**), however, believes that drama and the aggressive personalities of the Wife, Friar, and Summoner are the common threads in this fragment. Archetypal readings of the *Wife of Bath's Tale* were a popular method of critical evaluation in the 1970's. In his two articles, Brown associates the seasonal fertility myth with the loathly lady's transformation (**1242**) and outlines the evolution of the human consciousness (**1266**). While Atkinson (**1279**) believes the knight's transformation involves his reconciliation with his feminine side, Fritz (**1285**) outlines Alisoun's struggle to become whole, as she attempts to fuse her feminine and masculine sides. Elements of Bahktinian interpretation stem from Kern (**1288**), who highlights the carnival elements manifested in Alisoun's desire to undercut the patriarchy. Issues of class are raised in studies concerning Alisoun's social aspirations, the pillow lecture, and Chaucer's specific use of the terms *churl* and *gentil* (**1218, 1215, 1260**).

Wife of Bath's Tale: 1981–1990

While some of the *Wife of Bath's Tale* studies are interconnected, aside from a significant number of articles dedicated to the Midas digression, no overwhelming themes or patterns emerge in the 1980's. In dealing with the *Wife of Bath's Tale* as a romance, Quinn (**1327**) advocates studying the *Wife of Bath's Tale* in light of other Arthurian romances, believing that Chaucer's initial conception of this story included neither Alisoun as the narrator nor the loathly lady tale elements found within it. Finding little of Alisoun in the *Wife of Bath's Tale*, Fleming (**1349**) advocates comparing the romance to other Canterbury stories that are representative of the genre. Having produced such a study, Burrow (**1345**) finds that the five romances of the *Canterbury Tales* are non-traditional romances. Knight (**1353**) comments that, despite its deviance from traditional romance motifs, the *Wife of Bath's Tale* ends with a marriage in which the husband is sovereign. While Crane (**1361**) notes as well the resistance of the romance genre to transmitting any thematic intimations of the liberation of women, Dinshaw (**1382**) feels that Alisoun undermines this genre in her narration of the *Wife of Bath's Tale*. Folks (**1394**) finds the *Wife of Bath's Tale* to be an ironic rendition of the romance. Articles that explore Alisoun's design behind the telling of her romance find the *Wife of Bath's Tale* to be an illustration of feminine power (**1315**), a vindication of female counsel (**1301**), and a subversive replacement of the patriarchy (**1377**). Not all critics, though, feel that Alisoun accomplishes such goals. Patterson (**1313**) notes the dependence Alisoun has on both masculine language and desire, which limits the power of her own voice, and Delany (**1363**) argues that any attempt to determine what women most desire emphasizes the marginalized role of women.

While some studies that examine the loathly lady may praise the rhetorical techniques she employs in the pillow lecture (**1299, 1392**), others are less complimentary. Bishop (**1305, 1358**) feels that the loathly lady wearies the knight with the length of her talk to the point where he yields to her. Blanch (**1332**) feels that the old bride provides the knight with no choice through her employment of the law. The old woman's transformation is viewed as a gift of mercy (**1320**) and as a movement representative of the shift from the letter to the spirit of the law (**1326**). Pearsall (**1338**) feels that the true transformation in the *Wife of Bath's Tale* is the knight's reformation, just as Orme (**1298**) believes that the edification of the knight to be the primary theme in this romance. While Grennen (**1352**), Fisher (**1374**), and Martin (**1399**) find correlations between the old woman's pillow lecture and Alisoun's views, Benson

(**1344**) finds no reflection of Alisoun in either the loathly lady or her noble speech. While Mehl (**1355**) and Simmons-O'Neill (**1389**) find that the *Wife of Bath's Tale* indicates Alisoun's own life-experiences, Alisoun's romance is sometimes seen as an expression of the Wife's desire to conquer death (**1293**), her desire for her lost youth (**1350**), and a 'fantastical representation of Alisoun's life' (**1368** p 68). Leicester (**1323**) feels that Alisoun comes to realize through her tale-telling that her energy and spirits are still vitally alive despite her advancing age.

The Midas digression is seen in various lights: as an example of moral orders (**1300**); as an iconographic condemnation of the senses conquering reason (**1328**); as a negative reflection upon Alisoun (**1334**, **1359**); as a reminder of Alisoun's presence as narrator (**1340**); as an exposure of the condition of women (**1390**); and as an indication of the unrealistic qualities of language (**1372**).

Scholars have identified various themes in the *Wife of Bath's Tale*. Among these are the importance of pleasure (**1303**), the healing power of love (**1324**), and the need for a code of conduct for husbands (**1318**). The marriage of the loathly lady and knight has been examined in light of the relationship between the public and private worlds (**1307**) and in connection with Chaucer's alterations of the fidelity clause (**1321**) and the focus on power in the marital dilemma as opposed to the analogous versions of the loathly lady tale (**1325**). Other analogue studies include those of Roney (**1314**), Frese (**1335**), and Green (**1385**). In one of the few source studies conducted during the 1980's, Kirkpatrick (**1311**) relates the pillow lecture to the contents of Dante's *Convivio*.

Blake (**1295**) examines scribal concern over the feminine pronouns in the *Shipman's Tale*, Cooper (**1306**) finds parallel structuring between the compositions of Fragment I and Fragment III, while Mann (**1398**) outlines a balancing of anger and patience that occurs between many of the tales in Fragment III and Fragment V. Sklute (**1330**), however, finds no unity between the *Wife of Bath's Tale* and the *Friar's Tale*. Iconographic studies continue: the dancing ladies of the *Wife of Bath's Tale* are equated with cupidity (**1296**); a Synagogue figure is transformed into an Ecclesia figure (**1347**); and Alisoun's rendering of an old wives' tale associates her with the Old Testament (**1348**). A few articles examine Chaucerian influence: Harris (**1309**) compares Jane Austen's Anne Elliot with the loathly lady; Bowden (**1360**) recounts Alisoun's effect on eighteenth-century literati; Cooper (**1391**) conducts a study that focuses on Alisoun's influence on writers during the period of 1395-1670; and Windeatt (**1403**) thinks that the translator of *Partonope of Blois* had the *Wife of Bath's Tale* in mind when depicting certain scenes.

Wife of Bath's Tale: 1991–1995 and beyond

The exploration of desire and power seems to be the dominant feature among the critical articles of the first half of the 1990's. Eberle (**1407**), Mann (**1413**), Taylor (**1416**), Tigges (**1426**), and Wood (**1427**) stress the poetic justice that occurs when the knight is stripped of the power vested in him by patriarchal society and is forced to assume the role of a potential rape victim when he finds that he must marry the loathly lady. Both Neuse (**1421**) and Petty (**1436**) depict the *Wife of Bath's Tale* as an assertion of a woman's ability to achieve power through language. Slover (**1458**) demonstrates that while both Alisoun and the loathly lady relinquish their recently acquired mastery to their husbands, these women possess both authority and the ability to regain this mastery. Keeping in mind the issue of what women most desire, Hallissy (**1432**) denies any suggestions that what Alisoun longs for is her former good looks. Tigges (**1426**) notes that the *Wife of Bath's Tale* reveals that one thing women do *not* want is to be raped. Bowman (**1405**) advocates that Alisoun's romance should be read with a focus on the interplay between male and female desire in the text. Recalling Chaucer's becoming a widower, Zauner (**1428**) asserts that it was Philippa's memory that spurred Chaucer to explore the question of what it is that women most desire.

As a testimony to the enduring nature of source and analogue study, Ireland (**1411**) and McKinley (**1420**) conduct word study and analysis of interiority that recall the loathly lady tales, while Wilson (**1439**) exposes the influence of Seneca on the pillow lecture in the *Wife of Bath's Tale*. Recent scholarship on *Wife of Bath's Tale* shows such vigor that there is every indication that it will continue unabated.

Chaucer's *Wife of Bath's Prologue* and *Tale*

ଊ Editions and Translations

The *Wife of Bath's Prologue* and the *Wife of Bath's Tale* are among the most frequently edited and anthologized works of Chaucer — along with the tales of the Knight, the Nun's Priest, and the Pardoner. There are several reasons for the popularity of the Wife of Bath narratives. The most important is the sparkling vividness of Alisoun herself, but it is also significant that her tale is seen as a charming representative of the medieval romance. Because both prologue and tale treat sexual matters with comparative decorum, they have been seen as appropriate for students.

The standard scholarly edition for thirty years was the 1957 second edition of F.N. Robinson (**38**), but it has been replaced by the 1987 third edition of Robinson's text, now called the *Riverside Chaucer*, edited by Larry D. Benson (**72**). A separate edition of the Wife of Bath materials is being prepared by Mark Allen and John H. Fisher for the *Variorum Chaucer* project (**82**). For important discussions of the textual and editing traditions of Chaucer's work, see *Editing Chaucer: The Great Tradition*, ed. Paul G. Ruggiers (Norman, OK: Pilgrim Books, 1984).

Listed below in chronological order are the most important editions and translations. We have made no attempt to list every edition in every student textbook or British literature survey anthology. Nor have we included here works like Vera Chapman's *The Wife of Bath* (New York: Avon, 1978), an imaginative novel which begins with Harry Bailly's pinching the Wife of Bath's bottom as he helps her down from her horse and ends with her marriage to the Franklin in Canterbury Cathedral. Unless otherwise indicated, page numbers at the end of each bibliography entry below refer to the inclusive pages of the *WBP* and *WBT* together.

There were several early printed editions, such as Thomas Wright's three-volume set of 1847–51 (*The Poetical Works of Geoffrey Chaucer: A New Text* [New York: Crowell]), but significant editorial work on the *Canterbury Tales* may be said to begin with Furnivall's Six-Text edition, published by the Chaucer Society in eight parts between 1869–77, the earliest edition in the list below. Wright's edition, for example, is based on the Harley 7334 manuscript and was not improved by reference to other manuscripts. Still, the earlier editions are sometimes worth consulting for various reasons. Wright expresses a strong antipathy toward modern English translations: 'We may well be allowed to wonder that any Englishman of taste should refuse the comparatively trifling labor of making himself acquainted with his own language of little more than four centuries ago, for the satisfaction of reading and understanding the poetry of his glorious countryman Geoffrey Chaucer. Changing and mutilating is not, in my opinion, the right way to make anything popular' (volume 1, p 17). To give some indication of the style and accuracy of the various translations into Modern English, we reproduce in the summary annotation of the various translations the lines devoted to the rape scene at the start of the *WBT* (lines 882–8). The items are presented in chronological order.

1 *A Six-Text Print of Chaucer's Canterbury Tales*. Ed. Frederick J. Furnivall. Chaucer Society Publications, First Series, Part 4. London: N. Trübner, 1869–77. Pp 334–70.
The text is printed in parallel columns as it appears in six mss. This publication can be said to mark the beginning of modern textual analysis of the *CT* by making accessible in parallel format six of the oldest mss: Ellesmere, Hengwrt, Cambridge Gg.4.27, Corpus Christi, Petworth, and Lansdowne 851. There is usually not a great difference in the six mss. For the first lines of the *WBT*, for example, the six mss have these six readings — all close, but each distinctive in some small way:
Ellesmere, 'In tholde dayes / of Kyng Arthour';
Hengwrt, 'In tholde dayes / of the kyng Arthour';
Cambridge, 'In olde dayis of kyng Arthour';
Corpus, 'In olde dayes of the king arthour';
Petworth, 'In the olde dayes of the king arthour'; and

Lansdowne, 'In the olde daies of the kinge Arthoure.'
[Note: this six-text, parallel-column edition is not to be confused with Furnivall's separate edition in 1868 of the Cambridge University Library Gg.4.27 ms of the *CT*, also published by the Chaucer Society (London: Trübner, 1868), with the Wife of Bath materials on pp 167–203.]

2 *The Canterbury Tales: by Geoffrey Chaucer, from the Text and with the Notes and Glossary of Thomas Tyrwhitt, Condensed and Arranged under the Text: A New Edition.* New York: D. Appleton, 1880. Pp 157–88.

There is no introduction or glossary to this edition, but it is clearly meant to be an inexpensive version based on Tyrwhitt's earlier and more scholarly edition of 1775–8 and his five-volume 1830 edition. The notes at the bottom of the page are minimal and mostly give the meanings of difficult or obsolete words but occasionally refer to Tyrwhitt's notes or opinions. No line numbers are given.

3 *The Canterbury Tales.* Ed. Alfred W. Pollard. 2 volumes. London: Macmillan, 1894. Volume 2: 1–50.

Contains brief notes at the bottom of the pages and, at the end of volume 2, a brief 'Glossary of Common Words' (pp. 461–75). This edition was almost immediately superseded by the great Skeat edition (**4**).

4 *The Complete Works of Geoffrey Chaucer.* Ed. W.W. Skeat. London: Oxford University Press, 1894. The Oxford Chaucer, in six volumes with a supplementary volume VII, 1897; rpt 1899, and many times thereafter through 1963. Volume IV: 320–56.

This edition is based on the Ellesmere but is collated with the other mss in Furnivall's *Six-Text* edition (**1**). The volumes were issued between 1894 and 1897 (volumes IV and V, the ones of central concern for Wife of Bath studies, were published in 1894). The extensive notes in Volume V are the basis for a description of the Wife of Bath, pp 291–313 for *WBP*, and pp 313–22 for *WBT*. The extensive glossary in volume VI: 1–309 is still useful. This was in every sense a landmark edition, and is still the beginning point for many scholars, though the Ellesmere-base is now often seen to be problematic.

5 *The Student's Chaucer, Being a Complete Edition of His Works, Edited from Numerous Manuscripts.* Ed. Walter W. Skeat. New York and London: Macmillan; Oxford: Clarendon, 1895. Pp 565–81.

This edition was reprinted many times through 1967 as the Chaucer volume in the Oxford Standard Authors series. It is the 1894 text (**4**), without the textual or explanatory notes, but with a useful 'glossarial index' at the end. This text was published in 3 volumes for the World's Classics Series (London: Oxford University Press, 1903–6). This Skeat text was the one from which several generations of readers learned their Chaucer. The introductory material offers little more than a brief account of the life of Chaucer and some hints about how to read his language. There are no on-page glosses or explanatory notes.

6 *The Works of Geoffrey Chaucer, now newly imprinted* [The Kelmscott Chaucer]. Ed. F.S. Ellis. Hammersmith, Middlesex: William Morris at the Kelmscott Press, 1896. Pp 104–17.

Based on Skeat's 1894 edition (**4**), this edition contains three woodcut illustrations of the *WBT*: on p 112, the knight, on horseback, coming up to the old woman; on p 114, the knight and his ugly bride in their marital chamber; and on p 115, the knight and his young bride in the same room, she standing naked. For a useful discussion of the history of this lavish book, see John T. Winterich's introduction to the facsimile edition (**41**).

7 *The Works of Geoffrey Chaucer* [The Globe Edition]. Ed. Alfred W. Pollard, H. Frank Heath, Mark H. Liddell, and W.S. McCormick. London and New York: Macmillan, 1898/rev 1928; rpt often, including Freeport, NY: Books for Libraries Press, 1972. Pp 154–71.

Text is based on the Ellesmere ms, conservatively emended by collation with the other mss in Furnivall's 1869–77 *Six-Text* edition (**1**) and Harley 7334. This edition was used as the basis of the important *Concordance to the Works of Geoffrey Chaucer*, ed. J.S.P. Tatlock and A.G. Kennedy (Washington: Carnegie Institute of Washington, 1927). In the 1928 revision Pollard included some corrected readings based on the *Concordance*. At the foot of the page are explanatory and textual notes. This important Globe edition should not be confused with Pollard's earlier separate edition (**3**) of the *CT*.

8 *The Cambridge Ms. Dd.4.24, of Chaucer's Canterbury Tales. Completed by the Egerton MS. 2726 (The Haistwell Ms.).* Part 1. Ed. Frederick J. Furnivall. Chaucer Society Publications, First Series, Numbers 95 and 96. London: Kegan Paul, Trench, Trübner & Co., 1901. Pp 167–203.

This is an unpunctuated transcript of the Cambridge ms Dd.4.24, showing the location of the virgules or slash marks. The edition includes some brief marginal comments by a scribe or early reader. In a special section at the end following page 688 are a number of fine woodcuts by W.H. Hooper based on the Ellesmere miniatures and on six of the illustrations of Cambridge Gg.4.27, 'being those that were not cut out of the Ms. by some scoundrel.' The pages of these last sections of Hooper illustrations are not numbered, but the two woodcuts of the Wife of Bath are easily located.

9   *The Select Chaucer.* Ed J. Logie Robertson. Edinburgh and London: William Blackwood, 1902. Pp 159–63.

This edition is an effort to make available to students portions of a large number of Chaucerian poems. Few of the tales selected are complete, but some of the parts omitted are summarized in prose. The *WBP*, for example, is summarized by the Wife's having 'unburdened her mind of her own long and varied experiences of the married state' (p 159), and the rape scene is summarized thus: 'a knight or bachelor of the Court, for an act of villainy, was condemned to death' (p 159). Fewer than a hundred lines from the *WBT* are quoted, most of those from the old woman's sermon on *gentillesse*. The lines presented are 'based on the readings of the Ellesmere and Harleian MSS, slightly modified by collation of these with such other authorities as are given in Dr Furnivall's Six-Text Print, and in the editions of Dr Morris and Dr Skeat' (p iii). An introduction with information about Chaucer's life, times, grammar, diction, versification, and pronunciation runs to nearly 50 pages. A few notes to the Wife of Bath materials appear on pp 163–4, and a brief glossary closes the volume, pp 95–109.

10 *Tales of the Canterbury Pilgrims: Retold from Chaucer and Others.* By F.J. Harvey Darton. Introduction by F.J. Furnivall. Illustrations by Hugh Thompson. London, New York: Wells Gardner, Darton and Co., 1904. Pp 147–59.

This version is more a loose rendition in modern English than a translation. The *WBT*, for example, is called 'The Old Woman and the Knight' and the rape scene in the tale runs thus: 'It happened that there was at King Arthur's Court a young knight, in the full vigour and pride of his strength, who one day, as he was riding out, came upon a maiden walking all alone. She was very beautiful, and the sight of her made him forget his knighthood. He went up to her, and tried to carry her off with him by force. But before he could succeed help came, and he was seized and taken before the King' (p 153). On page 149 there is a line drawing of Alisoun knocking Jankyn into the fire and on page 155 a drawing of the knight coming upon the old woman.

11 *The Works of Geoffrey Chaucer and Others, Being a Reproduction in Facsimile of the First Collected Edition 1532, from the Copy in the British Museum, with an Introduction by Walter W. Skeat.* [Ed. William Thynne.] London: Alexander Moring (De La Mare Press) and Henry Frowde (Oxford University Press), nd [1905]. Pp 98–112.

This is a facsimile of the first collected edition, made in 1532, of the works of Chaucer and other writers. Published by William Thynne, this edition is something of a 'first folio' of Chaucer's works, dated exactly a century before the First Folio of Shakespeare. It was for several centuries the world's primary source of knowledge about what Chaucer wrote. Though it contained many errors of text and ascription, it is still valuable for those who want to know what generations of students of Chaucer were led to believe he wrote. Skeat's introduction to this limited edition of 1000 copies is still useful for anyone interested in the early printed history of Chaucer's works. Skeat discusses, for example, the five earlier printed editions of *CT*: Caxton's first (1477–8), Caxton's second (1483), Pynson's first (1493), Wynkyn de Worde's (1498), and Pynson's second (1526). It is unfortunate that Thynne based his edition on Caxton's inferior first edition, because Thynne's became the 'standard Chaucer' for the next several centuries.

12 *Chaucer's Canterbury Tales for the Modern Reader.* Ed. Arthur Burrell. Everyman's Library. London: J.M. Dent; New York: Dutton, 1908; rpt often through 1948. Pp 252–82.

Prints the *CT* with modernized spelling, punctuation, and vocabulary: 'The spelling has been slightly modernized, modernized just enough to leave its quaintness and take away some of its difficulty' (p viii). Seven of the tales (not including the Wife of Bath's) are left unmodernized: 'They are so broad, so plain-spoken, that no amount of editing or alteration will make them suitable for the twentieth century' (pp vii–viii). The base text is not indicated, but the introduction admits that 'there is no pretence that this version is the Chaucer of the scholar, or the Chaucer of any recognized text' (p viii). The lines are not numbered.

13 *The Ellesmere Chaucer, Reproduced in Facsimile.* Preface by Alix Egerton. 2 volumes. Manchester: Manchester University Press, 1911.

The Ellesmere is one of the most important mss of Chaucer. Written apparently by the same scribe who had earlier done the Hengwrt ms, the Ellesmere is lavishly illustrated with many fine portraits of Chaucer and the other Canterbury pilgrims, including the Wife of Bath, at the opening of each tale. The Ellesmere was scribally 'improved' in ways not always pleasing to modern scholars and has been the basis of most editions of Chaucer. The then-owner, the third Earl of Ellesmere, made the copy available for reproduction. This facsimile is now rare, and is of limited use in any case, since the quality of the reproduction is poor and since neither foliation nor paging are provided. The Huntington Library in San Marino, CA, now owns the Ellesmere (EL 26 C 9), which was made available in 1995 in a fine color facsimile (**79**). The new facsimile renders this 1911 facsimile quite obsolete.

14 *The Complete Poetical Works of Geoffrey Chaucer*. Trans. John S.P. Tatlock and Percy MacKaye. (The Modern Reader's Chaucer). Illustrations by Warwick Goble. New York: Macmillan, 1912/rev 1938. Pp 157–78.

This prose translation of the 'complete poetical works' is actually not complete at all, since the translators not only clean up the text to eliminate the 'excessive coarseness' of the original, but also excise entirely some episodes that are 'incurably gross or voluptuous' (p vii). The translators, for example, silently delete lines 115–34 in *WBP* about the function of 'members of generation.' The rape scene is rendered thus: 'And so befell that this King Arthur had a lusty young knight in his court, who on a day came riding from the river; and it happed that he saw a maid walking ahead alone as she was born, and her he ravished' (p 171). There is no cross-referencing in this translation to the line numbers in any edition. This edition was reissued without the introduction or illustrations in paperback by the Free Press (Toronto: Collier-Macmillan, 1966).

15 *The Canterbury Tales of Geoffrey Chaucer. Illustrated after Drawings by W. Russell Flint*. 3 volumes. A Riccardi Press book published for the Medici Society. London: Philip Lee Werner, 1913; reissued in one volume in 1928. Volume 2: 77–114 in the 3-volume edition; pp 313–50 in the one-volume edition.

Published in a limited edition of 500 copies, this edition uses Skeat's 1895 text (**5**). Several colored illustrations appear in the three-volume edition: opposite volume 2, p 88, the Wife of Bath walking out by night; opposite p 92, Jankyn and Alisoun; and opposite p 112, the knight pulling back the curtain to see, standing outside his bed-enclosure, a lovely young light-haired bride, dressed in white. Only the last of these is reproduced in the one-volume edition, opposite p 350. No line numbers are given.

16 *The College Chaucer.* Ed. Henry Noble MacCracken. New Haven: Yale University Press, 1913; rpt 1915, 1918, 1920. Pp 237–72.

Text is based on Ellesmere, with some variants printed at the foot of the page. There are a few scattered on-page explanatory notes, but an extensive glossary appears on pp 605–713. 'The editorial apparatus has been compressed within the smallest possible compass, while a glossary of greater than average fullness supplies the place of the usual notes'(p v).

17 *Geoffrey Chaucer's Canterbury Tales, nach dem Ellesmere Manuscript mit Lesarten, Anmerkungen und einum Glossar.* Ed. John Koch. Heidelberg: Carl Winter's Universitätsbuchhandlung, 1915. Pp 112–35.

Text is based on Ellesmere, with notes on variants at the foot of the page. There is introductory discussion — now dated — of mss, editions, and sources of the CT, and an extensive glossary, all in German. The textual and explanatory notes at the bottom of the page are brief.

18 *Selections from Chaucer.* Ed. William Allan Neilson and Howard Rollin Patch. New York: Harcourt, Brace, and Co., 1921. Pp 378–85.

This edition was apparently meant for students who could not handle Chaucer's sexual or scatalogical passages. It includes portions of the *WBP* (lines 1–8, 45–86, 453–8, 469–502, 525–32, 543–606, 627–46, 669–96, 747–66, 771–828), run together without ellipses to warn readers that lines have been omitted. The *WBT* is not included. The text is based on Skeat (**4**), but the spelling has been somewhat modernized and there are a few changes introduced from other texts. There are no explanatory notes. The brief list of variant readings at the end gives only one variant in the Wife of Bath materials. A reasonably extensive glossary appears on pp 425–505. The introduction contains some useful background material, but it is sometimes quirky: 'Although the feudal system prevented any realization of the principle of equal opportunity, it served to check inordinate ambitions on the part of the serf to leap into the nobility in a day, and it put the responsibility for government and social power in the hands of people trained for generations to its necessity' (p xii).

19 *Canterbury Tales.* Ed. John M. Manly. New York: Holt; London: Harrap, 1928. Pp 279–308.

'In no sense an attempt at a critical text' (p vi), this incomplete and sanitized edition is designed for 'use in senior high school and elementary college work' (p v) — that is, for young people who presumably cannot handle sexually explicit or scatological material. The text skips a number of lines in the *WBP* without ellipses: 37–43, 51–52, 87–90, 115–53, 201–02, 331–36, 465–68, 508–12, 533–42, 607–08, 728–36, and 767–68. The text is based on the Ellesmere and uses the Ellesmere order but is corrected from other mss. Still somewhat useful are the notes and the extensive introductory materials relating to Chaucer's life, the history of the period, and key concepts of astronomy and astrology. Opposite p 278 is the manuscript illustration of the Wife of Bath (on horseback, and wielding a whip) from Cambridge ms Gg.4.27. Notes appear on pp 574–86, a glossary pp 659–707.

20   *The Canterbury Tales by Geoffrey Chaucer.* Ed. Walter W. Skeat. New York: The Modern Library, 1929. Pp 284–316.

This edition is from Skeat (**4**), but it includes no notes and only a minimal section on language and meter (pp 579–82) and a brief glossary (pp 583–602). A brief introduction by Louis Untermeyer identifies Chaucer as 'the father of English poetry, and perhaps the prince of it' (p vi).

21   Item cancelled.

22   *The Works of Geoffrey Chaucer.* 8 volumes. Shakespeare Head Press. Oxford: Blackwell, 1929. Volume 2: 138–79.

This limited edition (375 copies, plus 11 on velum) prints the 1898 Pollard et al. edition (**7**). There are no notes, annotations, or glossary. A small color miniature of the Wife 'freely rendered' by Hugh Chesterman from the Ellesmere miniature appears at the bottom of p 164.

23   *The Canterbury Tales of Geoffrey Chaucer, together with a version in modern English verse by William Van Wyck, illustrated by Rockwell Kent.* 2 volumes. New York: Covici- Friede, 1930. Volume 2: 262–89.

This limited edition of 999 copies has the Van Wyck iambic pentameter translation printed in parallel columns with the Middle English text, the source of which is not indicated. Here is the rape: 'And so it happened, this King Arthur too, / Had in his court a glad young knight and gay / Who rode in from the river one fine day, / And saw a naked maiden wondrous fair, / As she was laving in the river there. / And there and then in spite of all she said, / By very force he took her maidenhead' (p 281). Rockwell Kent's portraits are impressions rather than attempts to extrapolate from the *GP* descriptions or any manuscript illuminations.

24 *Tales from Chaucer: The Canterbury Tales*. Re-told by Eleanor Farjeon. Illustrations by Marjorie Walters. London: Medici Society, 1930; rpt Newton, MA: Charles T. Branford, 1959. Pp 86–93.

This book is less a translation of the *CT* than a prose 'rendering' or 'retelling' or 'abbreviation' of it for young readers. The reteller writes in her brief introduction about the difficult decisions she had to make: 'I have had to decide between the complete omission of certain tales in which particular incidents would prevent their being given to young people, and the suppression or alteration of the incidents' (p v). She opted for the latter. She gives us the *MilT*, for example, with Absolon kissing not Alison's buttocks but Nicholas's bearded face, and there is no mention of a fart. Here is the rape in the *WBT*: 'Well, it so happened that this King Arthur had among his knights a jolly young fellow, who, as he came riding one day from hawking, insulted a maiden he found walking alone' (p 89). There are no notes, but the reteller acknowledges her debt to those of Pollard (**7**). Walters' black-and-white illustration of the Wife of Bath at the top of p 86 appears to be based in a general way on the Ellesmere miniature.

25 *The Complete Works of Geoffrey Chaucer: Student's Cambridge Edition*. Ed. F.N. Robinson. Boston: Houghton Mifflin; London: Oxford University Press, 1933. Pp 91–106.

Supplanted Skeat's one-volume edition and remained the important edition until it was replaced by Robinson's second edition in 1957 (**38**). This edition is strong where Skeat was weak: it has useful introductory materials on the life of Chaucer, the canon and chronology of his works, and his language, as well as introductions to each of the various works and extensive explanatory and textual notes. For explanatory notes on the Wife of Bath materials, see pp 801–08, for textual notes, pp 1007–08. There is a glossary at the end of the volume. The text is based on the Ellesmere, 'in accordance with the opinion and practice of all recent editors' (p 1004). Robinson admits, in so many words, that he has been rather free in altering the text for his edition: 'In textual method the present editor does not belong to the severest critical school. When the readings of the "critical text" or of a superior archetype appeared unsatisfactory or manifestly inferior, he has accepted help from other authorities more often than the strict constructionists might approve' (p xxxiii).

26 *Canterbury Tales*. Rendered into Modern English by J.U. Nicolson. With Illustrations by Rockwell Kent. Garden City, NY: Garden City Publishing Company, Inc., 1934. Pp 311–44.

This verse translation in Modern English iambic pentameter couplets is of questionable faithfulness to the original. The description of the rape in *WBT*, for example, reads thus: 'And so befell it that this King Arthur / Had at his court a lusty bachelor / Who, on a day, came riding from river; / And happened that, alone as she was born, / He saw a maiden walking through the corn, / From whom, in spite of all she did and said, / Straightway by force he took her maidenhead' (p 334). An illustration of the Wife of Bath sitting under a tree appears after p 334. Gordon Hall Gerould's introduction is brief and of little consequence. The lines are not numbered.

27 *The Canterbury Tales*. Translated into Modern English Verse by Frank Ernest Hill. London: Longmans, 1935. Pp 286–317.

A preface tells us that some of the tales in this verse translation into iambic pentameter couplets were drafted as early as 1913. The rape scene in the tales reads: 'Now at King Arthur's court / There dwelt a knight, a lusty one and gay; / And from the river as he rode one day / He saw a maid, and felt great longing for her. / She was alone as when her mother bore her; / And soon this maid, despite her very head, / By force he ravished of her maidenhead' (p 308). The lines are not numbered.

28 *The Canterbury Tales of Geoffrey Chaucer*. Ed. Edwin Johnston Howard and Gordon Donley Wilson. New York: Prentice Hall, 1937/ rev and corrected Oxford, OH: Anchor Press, 1942 [cited]/rev 1947. Pp 70-97.

The textual authority for this incomplete set of the *CT* is not indicated. The 30-page introduction includes historical, biographical, and linguistic background information. Notes to the *WBP* and *WBT* appear on 156–61. A useful glossary is on pp 167–99.

29 *The Text of the Canterbury Tales, studied on the basis of all known manuscripts*. Ed. John M. Manly and Edith Rickert, with the aid of Mabel Dean, Helen McIntosh and Others, With a Chapter on Illuminations by Margaret Rickert. 8 volumes. Chicago: The University of Chicago Press; London: Cambridge University Press, 1940. For information on the Wife of Bath materials, readers will have to look in several places: for the classification of mss, volume 2: 191–217; for the text, volume 3: 233–83; for variants, volume 6:1–288.

This monumental work, based on photostatic copies of all of the known mss, was done at the University of Chicago. It demonstrated the complexity of relations among the 80-odd mss of the *CT* (only 50-odd have more-or-less complete sets of the tales). The text, which is close to the Hengwrt, is printed without punctuation. This work is still fundamental for anyone wanting to examine the complex relations among the various mss and the many variants to individual readings. The editors state their opinion that the five variant or contested passages (totalling 32 lines) were probably added by Chaucer at the request of a friend.

30 *Canterbury Tales*. Selected and Edited by Robert D. French. New York: Appleton-Century-Crofts, 1948. Pp 25–57.

Based on the Ellesmere ms, this small edition includes only the *GP* and the tales of the Wife of Bath, the Friar, the Pardoner, the Prioress, the Nun's Priest, and Chaucer's Tale of Sir Thopas. There are a minimal introduction, same-page glosses, and a closing glossary. This edition was reprinted unrevised, but with an updated bibliography after 1960 (but with the same 1948 copyright date) by Appleton-Century-Crofts as a Crofts Classic.

31 *The Canterbury Tales by Geoffrey Chaucer; Done into Modern English Verse by Frank Ernest Hill and Newly Revised for This Edition*. New York: Limited Editions Club, 1948. Pp 269–301.

This slightly revised version of Hill's translation of the *CT* has, in the translator's words, 'a considerable number of minor improvements upon the original rendering' (p xx) — the reference being to Hill's earlier translation (**27**). No change in the wording of the rape incident, however, appears. A colorful drawing of the Wife of Bath appears opposite p 297.

32 *Chaucer's Canterbury Tales (Selected): An Interlinear Translation*. Ed. Vincent F. Hooper. Great Neck, NY: Barron's Educational Series, 1948; rpt often through 1962. Pp 304–83.

This edition includes the *GP* and the tales of the Knight, Prioress, Nun's Priest, Pardoner, Wife of Bath, and Franklin. In alternating lines, the original Chaucerian lines are followed by italicized modern English translations: 'The running translation is intended to make the process of familiarization as painless as possible, and also to give needed assistance over the more difficult passages; thus restoring Chaucer's original intention of being completely intelligible and providing his reader with unalloyed pleasure' (p viii). The source of the Middle English text is not indicated. Although the translation is line-by-line, it is really a prose translation. The rape scene runs thus: 'And it so happened that this King Arthur / Had in his house a lively young knight, / Who one day came riding from the river. / And it chanced that, alone as she was born, / He saw a maid walking ahead of him, / From which maid at once, in spite of her protests, / By sheer force he stole her maidenhood' (p 360). There is a brief, mostly biographical, introduction, but there are no notes or glossary.

33 *The Portable Chaucer*. Ed. and trans. Theodore Morrison. New York: Viking, 1949/rev 1975; rpt many times. Pp 218–53.

This edition contains verse translations (sometimes condensations) of the *GP* and a dozen tales and is based on the 1933 Robinson edition (**25**). The rape scene runs: 'It chanced that Arthur had a knight who came / Lustily riding home one day from hawking, / And in his path he saw a maiden walking / Before him, stark alone, right in his course. / This young knight took her maidenhead by force' (p 244). No line numbers are given, but note that this translation reduces Chaucer's seven lines to five. This edition was reprinted by Penguin after 1977. In the revised version the Wife of Bath materials can be found on pp 207–40.

34 *The Canterbury Tales*. Translated into Modern English by Nevill Coghill. Harmondsworth: Penguin, 1951/rev 1958, 1960, 1975 [cited]. Pp 276-310. Rev 1977; rpt many times. Pp 215-51.

By far the most popular verse translation of the *CT*, this edition has the *GP* and all the tales except *Mel* and *ParsT*. Coghill claims to have used both Skeat 1894 (**4**) and Robinson 1933 (**25**) as the basis for his translation. The Wife of Bath materials are in iambic pentameter couplets. The rape scene runs thus: 'Now it so happened, I began to say, / Long, long ago in good King Arthur's day, / There was a knight who was a lusty liver. / One day as he came riding from the river / He saw a maiden walking all forlorn / Ahead of him, alone as she was born. / And of that maiden, spite of all she said, / By very force he took her maidenhead' (p 300). No line numbers are given, but note that Chaucer's seven lines are expanded here to eight. A later edition is illustrated (Penguin, 1977, and frequently reprinted), but the illustrations have no direct connection with the Wife of Bath or her tale.

35 *A Chaucer Reader: Selections from the Canterbury Tales*. Ed.

Charles W. Dunn. New York: Harcourt, Brace, and Company, 1952. Pp 85–120.

This edition, based on the Manly and Rickert 1940 text (**29**) includes the *GP*, Sir Thopas, and the tales of the Prioress, the Nun's Priest, the Franklin, and the Pardoner, as well as the Wife of Bath materials and translations of the tales of the Reeve, the Clerk, and the Canon's Yeoman. There are line-by-line, same-page glosses and a few explanatory notes but no glossary.

36 *The Canterbury Tales — Selections — Together with Selections from the Shorter Poems*. Ed. Robert Archibald Jelliffe. The Modern Student's Library. New York: Scribner, 1952. Pp 193–227.

This edition is based on the Ellesmere ms, but 'for reasons which appear good and sufficient to the editor, a few lines here and there have been dropped' (p iii). Lines omitted from the *WBP* include 115–54, 331–32, 443–50, and 729–36. The introductory materials include a brief biography of Chaucer, but it is a fanciful reconstruction of Chaucer's starting out on a trip to Canterbury: 'One April morning, almost six hundred years ago, Geoffrey Chaucer set out from London as one of a company of pilgrims' (p 1). This section ends, 'Geoffrey Chaucer must have been a most enjoyable and stimulating person to know' (p 14). It also has sections on Chaucer as poet, on Chaucer's times, and on his language. Although the introduction says that 'notes ... have been added to the text' (p iii), in fact there are no textual notes whatever. A glossary (pp 315–77), however, is of some help.

37 *The Canterbury Tales*. Trans. into Modern English Prose by R.M. Lumiansky. New York: Holt, Rinehart and Winston, 1954. Pp 201–24.

This is an expansion of a 1948 partial prose translation, but in that edition the translator had included only summaries of some of the tales (*PrT*, *MkT*, *Mel*, and *ParsT*). This 1954 edition has full translations of all of the tales. It is based on Robinson's 1933 edition (**25**). The rape scene is translated thus: 'It happened that King Arthur had in his court a lusty squire who one day rode along the river where he saw a girl walking ahead of him, alone as she was born, and, despite her resistance, he ravished her' (p 217). A brief introduction justifies translating Chaucer on the basis that 'the reader can concern himself immediately with literary analysis of the *Tales* rather than with the rather arduous task of line-by-line translating' (p xviii). The complete *GP* is given in Middle English on pp 459–82, but with no line numbers, notes, or glossary. In

1960 Washington Square Press republished the original 1948 edition (with the tales of Melibeus, the Prioress, the Parson, and the Monk presented only in summary, though the *GP* and *NPT* are given in full at the end in Middle English). The translation of the Wife of Bath materials appears on pp 153–76 of the 1960 edition.

38 *The Works of Geoffrey Chaucer*, 2nd ed. Ed. F.N. Robinson. Boston: Houghton Mifflin, 1957; rpt in paperback, London: Oxford University Press, 1974. Text pp 76–88, explanatory notes pp 697–704, textual notes pp 891–92.

This fine second edition supplanted Robinson's 1933 edition (**25**) as the standard edition for graduate courses and for virtually all scholarship. The text is based on the Ellesmere but is sometimes altered by reference to other editions, particularly the Hengwrt, Cambridge Dd.4.24, Cambridge Gg.4.27, Corpus, Petworth, Lansdowne, and Harley 7334, as well as to Thynne's edition and to the unpublished Cardigan and Morgan mss. Robinson sometimes accepted readings from mss or editions that have little authority. The textual notes list some of the important variants, but are silent on the many decisions and emendations that make the Robinson text more regular than it probably was in Chaucer's own exemplar. Robinson's tale order is that of the Ellesmere, in ten fragments. In this second edition Robinson incorporates some changes based on the comprehensive eight-volume Manly-Rickert edition of 1940 (**29**), but he repeats his disclaimer from the first edition that he does not belong to 'the severest critical school' and that he has 'accepted help from other authorities more often than the strict constructionists might approve' (p xxxvii). Because the second Robinson edition is the basis of the now-standard 'third edition' known as the *Riverside Chaucer*, edited by Larry D. Benson in 1987 (**72**), Robinson's editing continues to influence many readers of Chaucer.

39 *Canterbury Tales*. Ed. A.C. Cawley. Everyman's Library. London: Dent; New York: Dutton, 1958/rev 1975, 1990 and 1992. Pp 158–91.

Because of its low cost and handy size, this has been a popular student text of Robinson's second edition (**38**), which it reproduces. Glosses of difficult words appear at the right, but glosses of phrases and lines are found at the bottom of the page. There are brief notes at the end on pronunciation, grammar, and versification.

40 *Chaucer's Poetry: An Anthology for the Modern Reader*. Ed. E. Talbot Donaldson. New York: Ronald Press Co., 1958/rev 1975. Pp

191–230.

Based on Hengwrt, with brief glosses and notes at the bottom of the page. A long closing commentary has discussions of Chaucer's language, his life, and the individual tales. Donaldson, a proponent of the New Criticism, purposefully gives almost no historical background material. Notes appear at the bottom of the page, with commentary on the Wife of Bath materials appearing on pp 1075–8. Donaldson uses a somewhat modernized spelling to make the reading easier for twentieth-century readers. He was highly influential as a Chaucer scholar, and his edition, with its full commentaries, has influenced many students, particularly in U.S. colleges.

41   *The Works of Geoffrey Chaucer. A Facsimile of the William Morris Kelmscott Chaucer, with the Original 87 Illustrations by Edward Burne-Jones and a Glossary for the Modern Reader.* Ed. F. S. Ellis. Introduction by John T. Winterich. Cleveland and New York: World Publishing Company, 1958. Pp 104–17.

This is a facsimile reissue of the Kelmscott Chaucer, originally published in 1896 (**6**). Winterich's extended introduction gives information about William Morris, his Kelmscott Press (named after Morris's country home in Gloucestershire), and the lavish care that went into the production and illustration of the original. We learn, for example, that Burne-Jones averaged a week on each of the 87 illustrations. Curiously, the introduction makes no mention of the contribution of F.S. Ellis, who is listed in a colophon as the editor, though it does say that the text is based on the Ellesmere and on Skeat's 1894 edition (**4**). A glossary (p xiii-xx), also based on Skeat, is printed before the facsimile proper as the only effort to help modern readers understand what the Kelmscott Chaucer actually says.

42   *The Age of Chaucer.* Ed. William Frost. Englewood Cliffs, NJ: Prentice-Hall, 1951; rpt often. 2nd ed 1961. Pp 152–87 in 2nd ed.

This teaching edition contains, in additions to many of the works in the *CT* (Knight, Miller, Wife of Bath, Friar, Clerk, Franklin, Pardoner, Prioress, Nun's Priest), a translation of *Sir Gawain and the Green Knight* and several Middle English lyrics. For the text of the Chaucer materials the editor consulted the Manly and Rickert 1940 edition (**29**), as well as the Donaldson 1958 (**40**) and the Robinson 1957 (**38**). This edition has a generous but general introduction and same-page glosses but no terminal glossary.

43 *The Canterbury Tales of Geoffrey Chaucer*. Ed. Daniel Cook. Garden City, NY: Doubleday (Anchor), 1961. Pp 114–201.

This edition contains the tales of the Miller, the Pardoner, the Prioress, and the Nun's Priest, as well as the *WBP* and *WBT*. The text is based on Furnivall's six-text edition (**1**) but especially on the Hengwrt and Ellesmere mss. There is a sketchy introduction but no glossary. The meanings of unfamiliar words and some explanatory materials are given on pages facing the text.

44 *Chaucer*. Ed. Louis O. Coxe. The Laurel Poetry Series, 1188. New York: Dell Pub. Co., 1963. Pp 126–46.

This edition, based on Skeat 1895 (**5**) and Robinson 1957 (**38**), contains the *WBP* but not the *WBT*. There is a brief closing glossary but no on-page glosses or notes: 'I have deliberately refrained from explaining topical, historical, astrological, etc., references because there is for all practical purposes no end to the process once started' (p 24).

45 *Chaucer's Major Poetry*. Ed. Albert C. Baugh. New York: Appleton-Century-Crofts; London: Routledge and Kegan Paul, 1963; Englewood Cliffs, NJ: Prentice-Hall, 1963. Pp 382–402.

Includes all of Chaucer's poetry but none of his prose except the Retraction. Extensive glosses and notes appear at the bottom of the page, supplemented by a full glossary at the end of the volume. Introductory material includes sections on Chaucer's life, language, and versification. The text is based on Ellesmere, but adopts the Bradshaw Shift, which moves the Wife of Bath materials away from the MLT and places it later, after *NPT* in Fragment VII (B^2). Along with Robinson (**38**), Donaldson (**40**) and Fisher (**63**), this edition has been widely influential in U.S. colleges.

46 *Chaucer: Canterbury Tales/Tales of Canterbury*. Ed. A. Kent Hieatt and Constance Hieatt. New York: Bantam Books, 1964. Pp 182–239.

The *GP* and the tales of the Knight, Miller, Wife of Bath, Merchant, Franklin, Pardoner, Prioress, and Nun's Priest are included in this dual-language edition. Based on Skeat's 1895 text (**5**), this edition has line-by-line translations on facing-pages but almost no editorial or explanatory aids. The rape scene runs: 'It so happened that this King Arthur / had in his house a lusty bachelor, / who one day came riding from the river; / and it happened that he saw a maiden / walking before him, alone as she was born. / And from this maiden then, against her will, / and by pure force, he took her maidenhood' (p 223).

47 *Geoffrey Chaucer: The Canterbury Tales*. A Prose Version in Modern English by David Wright. New York: Random House (Vintage), 1964. Pp 174–97.

All of the *CT* except *Mel* and *ParsT* are included in this prose translation based on Robinson 1957 (**38**). The rape scene runs: 'Well, it so happened that in King Arthur's court there was a gay young knight; and one day he was riding home from hawking by the river when he chanced to see a maiden walking all by herself; and in spite of all she could do he took her maidenhood from her by main force' (p 190).

48 *The Wife of Bath's Prologue and Tale from the Canterbury Tales by Geoffrey Chaucer*. Ed. James Winny. Cambridge: Cambridge University Press, 1965. Pp 35–75.

This stand-alone edition of the *WBP* and *WBT* is designed for classroom rather than scholarly use. The text is based on Robinson (**38**), but 'the punctuation has been revised, with special reference to the exclamation marks. Spelling has been partly rationalized, by substituting *i* for *y* wherever the change aids the modern reader and does not affect the semantic value of the word' (p 33). The long introduction is still useful, but now somewhat dated, for example, by declarations that the Wife of Bath was probably not a weaver because 'the estates of five husbands should have left her financially independent, and when had she time to acquire such expertise?' (p 6). There are no same-page glosses, but a short glossary appears at the end. The editor provides generous notes in a separate section (pp 76–119). Two brief appendices give Chaucer's ballad on *Gentillesse* and a short excerpt on Theophrastus from Jerome's *Jov*.

49 *Geoffrey Chaucer: A Selection of His Works*. Ed. Kenneth Kee. Toronto: Macmillan of Canada, 1966. Pp 58–99.

Based on the Ellesmere and Hengwrt mss, this volume contains several of Chaucer's short poems, the *GP*, and the tales of the Wife of Bath, the Merchant, the Franklin, the Nun's Priest, and the Pardoner. There is a helpful introduction and same-page glosses and brief notes but no glossary.

50 *Selections from The Tales of Canterbury and Short Poems*. Ed. Robert A. Pratt. Boston: Houghton Mifflin, 1966. Pp 190–221.

Includes the *GP* and 18 tales (all but *Mel*, *MkT*, *SNT*, *CYT*, and *ParsT*). Based on the Robinson text (**38**) but with many alterations from Manly and Rickert (**29**). The 46-page introductory matter is still useful. Simple glosses appear in the right margins, with longer notes at the bottom of the page. The simple glossary at the end of the book is almost useless. This book was later to be expanded by the editor into the *The Tales of Canterbury, Complete* (**61**).

51 *The Canterbury Tales of Geoffrey Chaucer*. Selected and Adapted by A. Kent Hieatt and Constance Hieatt. Illustrations by Gustaf Tenggren. New York: Golden Press, 1968. Pp 44–52.

Clearly designed for children, this prose 'adaptation' of the tales of the Knight, Wife of Bath, Friar, Clerk, Nun's Priest, Pardoner, Canon's Yeoman, Manciple, and Man of Law will be of limited interest to scholars. The *WBP* is only three short pages, and the sanitized rape scene runs: 'It happened, then, that there was a young knight at the court of King Arthur, and one day he carried off a young maiden against her will' (p 47).

52 *Geoffrey Chaucer. The Works, 1532. With Supplementary Material from the Editions of 1542, 1561, 1598, and 1602*. Ed. D.S. Brewer. Menston, Yorkshire: Scholar Press, 1969 and 1974; rpt by Scholar Press, 1974 and 1976.

The 'pages' of this early and important printed edition are not numbered, but the *WBP* and *WBT* appear on folios 39v–46r. Based on Thynne's 1532 edition, with material from later editions added, this edition is useful for those who want to see Chaucer as it would have been available to Shakespeare, Spencer, Milton, Dryden, and Pope — and most of the rest of the world, as well. See also **11**.

53 *Geoffrey Chaucer: The Canterbury Tales, A Selection*. Ed. Donald R. Howard, with the assistance of James Dean. The Signet Classic Poetry Series. New York: New American Library, 1969. Pp 261–98.

Besides the *WBP* and *WBT*, this edition includes the *GP* and the tales of the Knight, Miller, Reeve, Shipman, Prioress, Thopas, Nun's Priest, Merchant, Franklin, and Pardoner. The text is 'eclectic' but especially indebted to the Manly and Rickert 1940 edition (**29**). The text is considerably standardized in spelling so as to suggest more clearly the modern meanings of words. There is a brief introduction, and brief notes and glosses appear at the bottom of the page. The glossary contains two pages of 'basic words.'

54 *Selections from Geoffrey Chaucer's The Canterbury Tales*. Ed. Francis King and Bruce Steele. Melbourne: F. W. Cheshire, 1969. Pp 206–70.

Among other selections, the editors include the *GP* and the tales of the Miller, Pardoner, Prioress, Nun's Priest, Wife of Bath, and Manciple. The text is based on the Hengwrt and on Manly and Rickert 1940 (**29**). The text appears on right-hand pages with rather full notes on the facing left-hand page.

55   *The Literature of Medieval England.* Ed. D.W. Robertson, Jr. New York: McGraw Hill, 1970. Pp 538–52.

The text is from Skeat 1895 (**5**). The notes and glosses are gathered together at the end of the tale on pp 552–8. A brief introductory note describes the Wife of Bath as a variant of the Old Whore and her fifth husband as an echo of Adam 'and of all those after him who have struggled unsuccessfully, as most of us do, to keep a firm rein on effeminacy' (p 538).

56   *Geoffrey Chaucer: Canterbury-Erzählungen.* Trans. Detlef Droese. Illustrations by Otto Karl. Zürich: Manesse Verlag, 1971. Pp 267–305.

The German translation of the Wife of Bath's tale is entitled 'Die Erzälung der Frau von Bath.' The illustrations are from Caxton woodcuts.

57   *The Canterbury Tales.* Ed. John Halverson. New York: Bobbs-Merrill, 1971. Pp 149–88.

Includes the *GP* and the tales of the Knight, Miller, Reeve, Wife of Bath, Friar, Summoner, Clerk, Merchant, Franklin, Pardoner, Prioress, and Nun's Priest. The text is based on the Ellesmere, as reflected in Robinson (**38**) and Manly and Rickert (**29**). Brief notes appear at the foot of the page and a glossary appears at the end.

58   *The Canterbury Tales.* Ed. J.A.W. Bennett. A Facsimile Edition of Caxton's Second Edition. Cambridge: Cornmarket Reprints, 1972.

This is not really a new 'edition' at all, but a facsimile reproduction of Samuel Pepys' copy of the second (1484) William Caxton edition of the *CT*, a copy he apparently acquired around 1696. The editor wrote the brief headnote and arranged for facsimiles of certain leaves missing from Pepys' copy to be supplied from another of the only 13 extant copies of the book. The pages are not numbered or foliated, but the *WBP* and *WBT* appear at the end of the first half of the volume, after *FkT* and before *ClT*. The Caxton woodcut of the Wife of Bath sitting side-saddle appears just opposite the start of the *WBP*. There are no notes or glosses of any kind, and Caxton's black-letter print is a strain to read, in part because Caxton provided no punctuation.

59 *A Choice of Chaucer's Verse*. Selected with an introduction by Nevill Coghill. London: Faber, 1972.

Selections and excerpts of original texts based on Skeat 1895 (**5**) with facing Modern English verse paraphrases. Several selections from the Wife of Bath appear with Coghill's translation on facing pages: from the *WBP*, pp 220–7, and the *gentillesse* sermon in *WBT*, pp 70–3.

60 *The Wyf of Bathe, by G. Chaucer*. Illustrated by Gregory Irons. San Francisco: Bellerophon Books, 1973.

This edition of the *WBP* and *WBT* uses without alteration the 1957 Robinson text (**38**). On every page are line drawings appropriate to a coloring book. Neither the pages nor the lines are numbered, but the booklet contains a total of 48 pages.

61 *The Tales of Canterbury, Complete*. Ed. Robert A. Pratt. Boston: Houghton Mifflin Co., 1974. Pp 252–84.

The 1974 edition is similar to Pratt's 1966 *Selections* (**50**), but here with the complete *CT* and without the short poems. This edition is based on Robinson but with upwards of 70 alterations from the Manly and Rickert text (**29**). On p 270 is an illustration of 'The Children of Venus,' following line 697. This edition accepts the Bradshaw Shift by moving the Wife of Bath materials to after *NPT* rather than after *MLT*. There are introductory discussions of tale order, language, 'suggestions for reading Chaucer,' and a brief glossary at the end of the volume.

62 *The Wife of Bath's Prologue and Tale and the Clerk's Prologue and Tale from The Canterbury Tales*. Ed. Gloria Cigman. New York: Holmes and Meier, 1976. Pp 31–84.

Nothing is said about the base mss used for this edition. There is a long general introduction. The extensive foot-of-page notes are augmented by explanatory notes, pp 140–76.

63 *The Complete Poetry and Prose of Geoffrey Chaucer*. Ed. John H. Fisher. New York: Holt, Rinehart, and Winston, 1977/rev 1989. Pp 107–26.

Text is based on the Ellesmere ms and follows the Ellesmere order with the Wife of Bath materials following after the *MLT*. Important variants in Hengwrt and other mss are given in textual notes at the bottom of the page. Also at the bottom of the page are glosses and explanatory notes. At the end of the volume are essays on 'the place of Chaucer,' Chaucer in his time, and Chaucer's language and versification. This text rivals the Robinson (**38**) and *Riverside Chaucer* (**72**) in importance and general usefulness, especially for advanced students.

64 *Geoffrey Chaucer: I racconti di Canterbury*. Trans. Cino Chiarini and Cesare Foligno. Firenze: Biblioteca Universale Rizzoli, 1978. Pp 161–88.

This Italian translation of the *CT* includes 'Il racconto della donna di Bath.'

65 *The Canterbury Tales. A Facsimile and Transcription of the Hengwrt Manuscript, with Variants from the Ellesmere Manuscript*. Ed. Paul G. Ruggiers. Introductions by Donald C. Baker and by A.I. Doyle and M.B. Parkes. Volume I of *A Variorum Edition of the Works of Geoffrey Chaucer*. General Editor, Paul G. Ruggiers. Norman: University of Oklahoma Press; Folkstone, Kent: William Dawson and Sons, 1979. Pp 226–89.

This useful edition gives a photographic facsimile of the Hengwrt ms and, on facing pages, a transcription of the hand-written script in printed form, reproducing the virgules or slash marks (/) that constitute virtually the only punctuation in the ms. The facing pages also show the variants in the Ellesmere ms, made a little later and by the same scribe, but this time with apparently greater editorial supervision and direction.

66 *Chaucer's Canterbury Tales Complete, in Present-Day English*. Trans. James J. Donohue. Dubuque, Iowa: Loras College Press, 1979. Pp 306–39.

This prose translation, based on the Robinson 1933 edition (**25**), is in iambic pentameter couplets. The rape scene runs: 'It happened that King Arthur entertained / At court a knight unfledged and out of hand, / Who one day cantered from the hawking land / And saw before him where along the road, / Alone as she was born, a maiden strode. / And from that maid, despite her very blood, / By simple force he reft her maidenhood' (pp 329–30).

67 *Poetical Works. A Facsimile of Cambridge University Ms Gg.4.27*. Introductions by M.B. Parkes and Richard Beadle. 3 volumes. Norman, OK: Pilgrim Books in Association with Cambridge: D.S. Brewer, 1979.

This ms is important in that it represents the only surviving fifteenth-century effort to collect in one volume most of Chaucer's poetry. The pages of the facsimile are not numbered, but what remains of the *WBP* and *WBT* appears on folios 201r–216v, at the end of volume 1 and the start of volume 2. A color reproduction of a miniature of the Wife of Bath from folio 211r appears near the end of volume 3, just before the extended commentary on pp 1–69.

68 *The Canterbury Tales*. Ed. N.F. Blake. York Medieval Texts, second series. London: Edward Arnold, 1980. Pp 177–215.

This edition is distinctive in that it is based almost entirely on the Hengwrt ms, including what most scholars see as an inappropriate ordering of the tales, with the Wife of Bath materials appearing immediately after the unfinished *CkT*. The editor does not include the five passages that are usually printed in the *WBP* — lines 44a–f, 575–84, 609–12, 619–26, and 717–20 — though he does include them from Ellesmere and other mss in an appendix. He uses the traditional line numbering, with gaps in the numbering between, for example, 574 and 585, alternating with his consecutive numbering of the Hengwrt without the additional lines. Glosses and explanatory notes appear at the bottom of the page. Blake's edition has generally been considered too conservative, too devoted to the Hengwrt alone, to have gained wide acceptance or academic adoption.

69 *The Canterbury Tales*. Trans. Martin Lehnert. Illustrations by Edward Burne-Jones. Leipzig: Insel-Verlag, 1981. Pp 211–49.

This modern German verse translation has useful notes. The illustrations are reproductions of the William Morris Kelmscott Chaucer woodcuts, reproduced in the 1958 facsimile (**6** and **41**).

70 *The Canterbury Tales/Die Canterbury-Erzählungen: Mittelenglisch/Deutsch*. Trans. and annotated by Heinz Bergner, Waltraud Böttcher, Günter Hagel, and Hilmar Sperber. Ed. Heinz Bergner. Stuttgart: Philipp Reclam Jun., 1982. Pp 228–99.

The Middle English text of the *CT* is based on Robinson (**38**), with the modern German translation of 'Der Prolog der Frau von Bath' and 'Die Erzählung der Frau von Bath' on facing pages. Useful commentary, notes, and bibliography appear on pp 496–517.

71 *The Canterbury Tales*. Trans. David Wright. Oxford: Oxford University Press, 1985; rpt in Oxford: World Classics Series, 1986. Pp 219–50.

This verse translation, apparently based on Robinson (**38**), does not pretend to reproduce all of the poetic qualities of the Chaucerian originals: 'I have preferred to sacrifice, for the sake of the immediacy, directness, and plain speech that make up the real poetry of the original, any strict adherence to Chaucer's rhyme schemes' (p xx). The rape scene runs: 'Now it so happened that this King Arthur / Had in his court a bold knight-bachelor / Who one day was hawking by the river, / And it so chanced, as he was riding home, / He met a maiden walking all alone, / And thereupon, though she fought long and hard, / The knight took by main force her maidenhood' (p 241). This verse translation is not to be confused with the same translator's 1964 prose translation (**47**).

72 *The Riverside Chaucer.* 3rd ed. Ed. Larry D. Benson. Boston: Houghton Mifflin, 1987. Pp 105–22.

This now-standard edition of all of the works of Chaucer is based on Robinson's second edition (**38**) and so harks back ultimately to the Ellesmere and follows the Ellesmere order. Brief glosses appear at the bottom of the page, with longer and more complicated ones, by Christine Ryan Hilary, appearing in a special section of explanatory notes on pp 864–74. Textual notes appear on pp 1126–7. This edition supplants most previous ones as the one favored for graduate courses and scholarly citation, though some scholars distrust the Ellesmere scribe's possible 'improving' on Chaucer and the editors' judgment in matters of punctuation and the insertion of the letter *e* to regularize the meter.

73 *Canterbury Tales.* Selected, translated, and adapted by Barbara Cohen. Illustrations by Trina Schart Hyman. New York: Lothrop, Lee and Shepard Books, 1988. Pp 46–63.

This prose translation is apparently for young people. The rape scene runs thus: 'It so happened that King Arthur had in his court a young man who one day was riding by a river. He saw a maiden walking all alone. In spite of all she could do, he forced himself upon her' (p 55). Colorful illustrations appear on p 54 (the Wife of Bath) and p 59 (queen's court with the knight giving his answer).

74 *The Canterbury Tales: A Selection.* Retold by Selina Hastings. Illustrations by Reg Cartwright. New York: Henry Holt, 1988. Pp 60–7.

This children's version is a prose retelling of the original. The tale begins, 'Long ago, back in King Arthur's time, there lived a Knight known for his love of pleasure. Riding by the river one day, he met a pretty girl walking by herself and, ignoring all her pleas, he threw her to the ground and attacked her' (p 62). The illustrations include the Wife of Bath (p 61), Arthur's castle (p 62), three dancing ladies (p 63), the knight coming upon the old woman (p 64), and an empty bed (p 66).

75 *The Canterbury Tales: Nine Tales and the General Prologue.* Ed. V.A. Kolve and Glending Olson. New York: W.W. Norton and Company, 1989. Pp 105–35.

The copy text for this edition was Skeat 1894 (**4**). In addition to the Wife of Bath material, the nine tales include the tales of the Knight, the Miller, the Reeve, the Clerk, the Franklin, the Pardoner, the Prioress, and the Nun's Priest. Notes appear at the bottom of the page. In the second part of the volume are excerpts from source and background materials. For the Wife of Bath the editors provide translations of selected writing of Jean de Meun, Gautier le Leu, Theophrastus, Saint Jerome, Walter Map, various biblical verses, and Gower's *Flor*.

76 *The Canterbury Tales: The General Prologue and Twelve Major Tales in Modern Spelling.* Ed. Michael Murphy. Lanham, MD: University Press of America, 1991. Pp 148–83.

The base text for this modern-spelling edition is the Hengwrt edition as presented in the Furnivall 1869–77 six-text edition (**1**). The editor has altered the spelling to make the task of reading Chaucer easier for modern readers: 'This edition is not a translation. Spelling is the only major difference from the texts in standard editions used by scholars. The grammar, the syntax, and the vocabulary of this modspell edition remain essentially unchanged from the language of the original' (p xv). The rape scene in 'modspell' reads: 'And so befell it, that this king Arthur / Had in his house a lusty bachelor, / That on a day came riding from the river / And happened that, alone as she was born, / He saw a maiden walking him beforn, / Of which maid anon, maugre her head, / By very force he raft her maidenhead' (p 173). Notes appear at the bottom of the page.

77 *The Tales of the Clerk and the Wife of Bath.* Ed. Marion Wynne-Davies. Routledge English Texts. London: Routledge, 1992. Pp 27–70.

This edition is based on the Hengwrt ms, but the editor 'sometimes followed Ellesmere, especially for indentation in long and complicated passages' (p 22), and for the contested passages — either authorial or scribal revisions — not in the Hengwrt ms. These last are included in brackets. Brief glosses appear at the bottom of the page with longer explanatory notes gathered at the end, pp 149–73. A glossary appears on pp 183–202. The introduction gives brief summaries of Chaucer's life, the social and cultural backgrounds of his time, and his language. What is most distinctive about this edition is the feminist tone of its introduction (with a section on 'Women in the Medieval Period') and its extended 'Critical Commentary,' pp 119–47. The editor invites us to see the Wife of Bath and Griselda of the *ClT* not merely as contrasting types but as similar, or at least complementary, in their basic situations and experiences. Speaking of the rape in the *WBT*, she says that it 'demonstrates the absolute power of one person over another and, as such, it may act as a metaphor for men's control over women — this time focusing upon sexuality rather than language. What the Wife's tale allows us to see is the continuing thematic display of gender and control, the "sovereyntee" in marriage, but it simultaneously foregrounds the horrors of such domination when taken to extremes' (p 123).

78 *The Canterbury Tales.* Trans. Ronald L. Ecker and Eugene J. Crook. Palatka, FL: Hodge & Braddock, 1993. Pp 154–86.

The editors base their translations on the Robinson edition (**38**) but have also consulted other editions. This is one of the few translations that provides line numbers for easy reference. The rape scene reads: 'It happened that King Arthur had with him / A bachelor in his house; this lusty liver, / While riding from his hawking by the river, / Once chanced upon, alone as she was born, / A maiden who was walking — soon forlorn, / For he, despite all that she did or said, / By force deprived her of her maidenhead' (p 177). At the end of the volume is a brief glossary of proper and special terms.

79 *The Canterbury Tales: The New Ellesmere Chaucer Facsimile (of Huntington Library MS EL 26 C 9).* Ed. Daniel Woodward and Martin Stevens. Tokyo and San Marino, CA: Yushodo and Huntington Library Press, 1995.

This full-color facsimile runs to 240 leaves (480 pages) in the size of the original ms. The ms contains 23 portraits of the Canterbury pilgrims at the start of each of their tales. The Ellesmere is also adorned with ornate capital letters and border designs, some of them in gold. This new facsimile supersedes the Manchester University Press facsimile of 1911 (see **13**).

80 *The Canterbury Tales Project: The Wife of Bath's Prologue.* Ed. Peter Robinson, with Contributions from Norman Blake, Dan Mosser, Stephen Partridge, and Elizabeth Solopova. Cambridge: Cambridge University Press, 1996.

This new kind of edition of the *WBP* is available on CD-ROM. When the project is complete and includes other works besides the *WBP*, it will supersede, for most scholarly purposes, both the Furnivall six-text edition of 1869–77 (**1**) and the Manly and Rickert eight-volume text of 1940 (**29**). The project makes it possible to compare on-line reproductions and transcriptions of 58 versions of the *WBP* and make detailed collations. Scholars can, for example, compare almost instantaneously variant spellings of words in the *WBP*.

81   *The Wife of Bath's Prologue and Tale*. Ed. Peter G. Beidler. Case Studies in Contemporary Criticism Series. Boston: Bedford Books of St. Martin's Press, 1996. Pp 44–85.

This newly edited text (based on Hengwrt but modernized somewhat) is followed by five case studies in contemporary criticism. The text contains a biographical and historical sketch and a critical history of the Wife of Bath materials. This is followed by five introductory explanations by series editor Ross C. Murfin of five critical approaches, each followed by a critical essay written for this volume: a new historicist approach by Lee Patterson (**1065**), a Marxist approach by Laurie Finke (**1059**), a psychoanalytic approach by Louise O. Fradenburg (**1060**), a deconstructionist approach by H. Marshall Leicester (**1062**), and a feminist approach by Elaine Tuttle Hansen (**1061**). Extensive glosses appear at the right of the text, with longer explanatory notes at the bottom of the page.

82   *The Variorum Wife of Bath's Prologue and Tale*. Ed. John H. Fisher and Mark Allen, with assistance of Joseph B. Traherne. In *The Variorum Edition of the Works of Chaucer*. Norman: University of Oklahoma Press, forthcoming.

Although this edition is not yet completed, it will be of fundamental importance to anyone interested in the Wife of Bath and her performance. The text will be based on the Hengwrt. The introduction will include a textual commentary and a critical commentary with discussions of dating, sources and analogues, relations with other tales, and a review of criticism through 1990.

ဢ Sources and Analogues

83 Woolcomb, W.W. 'The Sources of the *Wife of Bath's Prologue*: Chaucer not a Borrower from John of Salisbury.' In *Essays on Chaucer, His Words and Works*. Chaucer Society Publications III.7. London: Trübner, 1876; rpt 1900. Pp 293–306.

There are parallels between the *WBP* and John of Salisbury's *Policraticus* in the passages that incorporate Theophrastus (p 297). Chaucer's source for this material was Jerome, however, not John. Chaucer also derived passages attributed to Tertullian, Abelard, and Heloise from Jerome.

84 Koeppel, Emil. 'Chauceriana.' *Anglia* 13(1891), 174–86. [In German.] Woolcomb incorrectly cites sources for III.362–4 and III.366–9. Chaucer uses Proverbs 30:21, 23 and not Proverbs 30:15 for his source in these passages (p 176). Jerome indirectly cites Proverbs 30:21, 23 in *Jov*. Other portions of *Jov* in the *WBP* are well known.

85 Toynbee, Paget. 'The Author of Chaucer's Book *Cleped Valerie*.' *Academy* 40(1891), 588–9.

While Francisque Michel believed the author of *Valerie* was Valerius Maximus, Walter Map actually wrote the work. Neither Chaucer nor Jean de Meun knew the identity of the author of this source.

86 Koeppel, Emil. 'Chauceriana.' *Anglia* 14(1892), 227–67. [In German.] Alisoun's life history is closely compared to that of La Vieille. Passages from the *WBP* closely parallel segments of *RR* (pp 250–5). Portions of the *gentillesse* sermon also reflect passages from this work of Jean de Meun (p 256). Alisoun resembles Dame Nature.

87 Stokes, Whitley. 'The Marriage of Sir Gawain.' *Academy* 41 (1892), 399.

Both Gower's *Flor* and Chaucer's *WBT* were probably based on a Celtic source.

88 Toynbee, Paget. 'The *Liber de Nuptiis* of Theophrastus in Medieval Literature.' *Academy* 41(1892), 616–7.

While Chaucer used Theophrastus' *Liber Aureolus de Nuptiis* for III.282ff, it is difficult to discern if he was aware of Theophastus' connection with Jerome's *Jov*. The names of both men are listed in Alisoun's description of Jankyn's book.

89 Boll, Franz. 'Chaucer und Ptolemaeus.' *Anglia* 21(1899), 222–30. [In German.]

Alisoun's quotations of Ptolemy are not to be found in the *Almagest*. Contrary to Skeat's opinion, Chaucer did not derive his Ptolemy from *RR*. Abulwafe Mubaschschir's *Albuguafe*, which details Ptolemy's life and works, would have been available as a source in Chaucer's time (p 229). Alisoun should be viewed as neither highly frivolous nor as overtly scholarly, but as a medieval storyteller who knows her apocrypha (p 230).

90 Görbing, F. 'Die Ballade The Marriage of Sir Gawain in ihren beziehungen zu Chaucers Wife of Bath's Tale und Gowers Erzählung Von Florent.' *Anglia* 23(1901), 405–23. [In German.]

While the phrasing of the riddle in *Flor*, *WBT*, and *Mar* differs, what the riddle asks and the answer to it are the same in all these works (p 410). In his phrasing, Gower loses much of the humor that is found within the loathly-lady tales because he concentrates too much on his source. Chaucer manages to maintain the humor and wit found in the ballad.

91 Maynadier, G.H. *The Wife of Bath's Tale: Its Sources and Analogues.* London: David Nutt, 1901.

The *WBT* and its English analogues, *Flor*, *Wed*, *Mar*, and *Hen*, have parallels to medieval Irish, Germanic, and Norse tales. French Grail romances contain descriptions of ugly hags that parallel the British tales. Neither the French nor the Icelandic tales served as sources for the British works. The importance of the theme of sovereignty in the Celtic and British tales suggests that the Irish tales influenced the British (p 80). It is difficult to determine if this influence was direct or if it was mediated though the Scandinavians or the Welsh. Chaucer's *WBT* differs from its English counterparts in its rape scene. A similar incident occurs, however, in *The Knight and the Shepherd's Daughter* (p 111). Chaucer also has a unique version of the marital dilemma.

92 Root, Robert Kilburn. *The Poetry of Chaucer: A Guide to Its Study and Appreciation.* Boston: Houghton-Mifflin, 1906/rev 1922; rpt 1934; rpt Gloucester, MA: Peter Smith, 1950, 1957.

The summary of *WBT* makes clear its place in the Marriage Group. Sources for the *WBT* include Gower's *CA*, the ballads *Wed, Mar,* and *Hen.* The themes of the hag's pillow lecture can also be found in Dante, Petrarch, Boccaccio, and the *Rom.* While some may feel that the content of the lecture is more in keeping with Chaucer himself than with the Wife, Chaucer's decision to have the Wife deliver this tale is aesthetically appropriate. See **427**.

93 Beach, Joseph Warren. 'The Loathly Lady: A Study in the Popular Elements of the *Wife of Bath's Tale*, with a View to Determining Its Story-Type.' Dissertation: Harvard University, 1907.

The *WBT* has strong folktale connections. It is related to the Night-Beast tales, Cupid and Psyche tales, and Lost Animal Spouse tales. The loathly lady tales include motifs such as the disenchantment through marriage and the fairy mistress. Tales such as *Beauty and the Beast* and *The Frog Prince* contain similar disenchantment concepts. Chaucer's version of the loathly lady tale contains Alisoun's humor and includes many original characteristics in comparison with Gower's *Flor.* The *WBT*'s rape incident bears a parallel to *The Knight and the Shepherd's Daughter.* Chaucer's tale is related to the Irish loathly lady tales.

94 Derocquigny, J. 'A Possible Source of Chaucer, *Canterbury Tales*, A 4134 and D 415.' *MLR* 3(1908), 72.

Derocquigny suggests that two similar lines, *With empty hand men may na haukes tulle* from the *RvT* and *With empty hand men may none haukes lure* from the *WBP,* share lines 7820–5 of *RR* as their source.

95 Canby, Henry Seidel. *The Short Story in English.* New York: Henry Holt, 1909; rpt New Haven: Yale University Press, 1913.

While it lacks the satire, digression, and artistry of *WBT,* Gower's *Flor* has a more plausible plot than its analogue (p 63). *WBT* is most likely a Breton lay. Alisoun's voice reappears in Dunbar's *Tua Mariit Wemen and the Wedo* (p 98).

96 Toynbee, Paget. *Dante in English Literature from Chaucer to Cary*, Volume I. London: Methuen & Co., 1909.

Lines 253–82, 290–309, and 312–4 of the *WBT* are transcribed to show Chaucer's indebtedness to Dante for the hag's pillow lecture (pp 13–4).

97 Lowes, John Livingston. 'Chaucer and the *Miroir de Mariage.*' *MP* 8(1910–11), 165–86, 305–34.

See **434**.

98 ———. 'Illustrations of Chaucer. Drawn Chiefly from Deschamps.' *RomR* 2(1911), 113–28.

The Wife of Bath's passion for going on pilgrimages is paralleled in chapters 11, 37 and 42 of Deschamps' *Mir* (pp 120–1). The Wife's lines III.551–3 correspond directly to the heading of the *Mir*'s chapter 43, 'Comment femmes procurent aler aux pardons, non pas pour devocion qu'elles aient, *mais pour veoir et estre veues.*' Lines 1407–18 in the *Mir* describe in detail a woman's shoes which recall those of the Wife of Bath.

99 Wise, Boyd Ashby. *The Influence of Statius upon Chaucer.* New York: Phaeton Press, 1911; rpt 1967.

Statius's account of Eriphile's betrayal of Amphiaraus in the *Thebaid* would have provided Chaucer with the detail he used for the story in Jankyn's book.

100 Tatlock, John S.P. 'Boccaccio and the Plan of Chaucer's *Canterbury Tales.*' *Anglia* 37(1913), 69–117.

The motivation for confession in the *CT*, primarily exemplified by the Pardoner, Alisoun, and the Canon's Yeoman, is similar to that of the *Ameto*. The themes of the Marriage Group reflect the contents of the *Ameto* as well (95–6). The nymph Agape's marriage to a senile man parallels Alisoun's first three marriages as well as the marriage of January and May in the *MerT*.

101 ———. 'Notes on Chaucer: The *Canterbury Tales.*' *MLN* 29(1914), 140–44.

The Wife of Bath's 'final revenge' (p 143) of hitting Jankyn when he stoops to kiss her bears a resemblance to a story of two thieves in Walter Map's *Nug*. A wounded thief slays his partner for not capturing his murderer by stabbing him as he bends down to kiss the dying man.

102 Lowes, John Livingston. 'Chaucer and Dante's *Convivio.*' *MP* 13(1915), 19–33.

Chaucer's familiarity with Dante's *Conv* and its fourth *Tractate*'s treatment of the nature of *gentillesse* allows him to combine 'the fine democracy of Jean de Meun's conception of true nobility ... with Dante's loftier idealism' (p 20). The phrase *antica ricchezza* appears six times in Dante's *Tractate* and the words 'old richesse' occur twice in *WBT* and once in *Gentilesse*. Chaucer shares Dante's belief that 'God is the sole source of *Gentilezza*' (p 20) as well as the concept that *gentillesse* is a hereditary trait (p 24). Chaucer's III.1152–8 resemble 34–3 in Dante's canzone and the hag's commentary on poverty reflects 'Dante's exposition of riches as *cagione di male*' (p 26).

103 Jefferson, Bernard L. *Chaucer and the Consolation of Philosophy of Boethius*. New York: Gordian Press, 1917; rpt 1968; rpt NY: Haskell House, 1965.
See **259**.

104 Lowes, John Livingston. 'Chaucer and Dante.' *MP* 15(1917), 705–35.
In Canto VIII of the *Paradiso*, *'the active virtue of the spheres'* (p 734) governs heredity. Chaucer seems to have remembered this portion of Dante when Alisoun refers to astrology's influence in forming her personality, III.604-20.

105 ———. 'The Second Nun's Prologue, Alanus, and Macrobius.' *MP* 15(1917), 193–202.
While Chaucer relies heavily on Dante's *Conv* for the sermon on the origins of *gentillesse* in the *WBT*, he also had Book III, prose iv, of *Consol* in mind. The passage in Boethius' work led him to Servius' commentary on the *Aeneid* which deals with the subject of 'contagioun of the body' (p 198). This 'partial source' (p 201) of *WBT* is a source for the *SNP* as well, but whether Chaucer drew upon the works of Albericus, Macrobius, or Servius for his writing is unknown.

106 Ayers, Harry M. 'Chaucer and Seneca.' *RomR* 10(1919), 1–15.
Seneca's influence on Chaucer is found in *Mel, ParsT, MLT,* and *WBT*. Chaucer's familiarity with Seneca's 44th and 2nd epistles is seen in the hag's discourse on *gentillesse* and poverty (pp 8-9). She refers directly to Seneca in III.1168–76 and 1183–90.

107 Steele, Richard. 'Chaucer and the "Almagest."' *Library* 10(1919), 243–7.
See **451**.

108 Koch, John. 'Chaucers Belesenheit in den römischen Klassikern.' *Englische Studien* 57(1923), 8–84. [In German.]
Chaucer drew his reference to Argus in the *WBP* from *Met* (p 12). Alisoun's acquisition of five husbands reflects her knowledge of the

Ars amatoria (p 40). An anecdote of Socrates appears in the *WBP* (p 76). Seneca's finding honesty in poverty is reflected in the *WBT* (pp 60–1). There are two references to Juvenal in the *WBT*.

109 Sumner, Laura. 'The Weddynge of Sir Gawen and Dame Ragnell.' *Smith College Studies in Modern Languages* 5(1924), vii–xxix.

Of the English loathly lady tales, the *WBT* and *Flor* are highly similar in plot. Of the differences between Chaucer's and Gower's versions, the most significant is that Chaucer's knight is a rapist (p xx). It is probable that Chaucer and Gower knew a version of the loathly lady tale that we do not have today. This version was most likely derived from the Irish tradition of loathly lady tales in which a choice is given and the hero's function is not divided as it is in the Gawain loathly lady tales (pp xxiii–xxv).

110 Shannon, Edgar Finley. *Chaucer and the Roman Poets.* Cambridge: Harvard University Press, 1929.

Alisoun refers to Ovid's *Ars Amatoria* (III.680) and to Ovid directly when she recounts her version of the Midas story (p 318).

111 Rutter, George. 'The Wife of Bath.' *Western Reserve University Bulletin* 34(1931), 60–4.

See **463**.

112 Dempster, Germaine. *Dramatic Irony in Chaucer.* Stanford: Stanford University Press, 1932; rpt New York: Humanities Press, 1959.

Chaucer employs dramatic irony in portions of the *WBT* that differ from its analogues. Because the folktale genre neither contains complex dramatic irony nor tends to focus on 'secondary episodes,' Chaucer presumably 'added the rape episode for sake of its humorous effect' (p 304). Chaucer's ironic juxtaposition of the knight's manly stance with his humbling speech in III.1034–6 stems either from his own creative originality or from his familiarity with the 'boon motif ... [which] Chaucer may very well have found ... already combined with the question story of Gower' (p 304). Departing from tradition, Chaucer describes the knight's feelings for his wife in a concise manner, thereby increasing the dramatic suspense.

113 Reinhard, John Revell. *The Survival of Geis in Mediaeval Romance.* Halle: Niemeyer, 1933.

In *Kath Sarit S gara*, Chrétien's *Perceval*, the Didot-*Perceval*, and the *WBT*, the lady can assume a hag-like appearance by her own volition (p 345). The hag is linked with sovereignty in the *WBT* and several

Celtic loathly lady tales (p 356).

114 Lowes, John Livingston. *Geoffrey Chaucer and the Development of His Genius*. Boston: Houghton Mifflin, 1934; rpt (with different pagination) Bloomington: Indiana University Press, 1958; rpt through 1962.

See **469** and **1095**.

115 Train, Lilla. 'Chaucer's *Ladyes Foure and Twenty*.' *MLN* 50(1935), 85–7.

The passage concerning the dancing ladies in *WBT* creates 'the feeling of the supernatural' (p 86). A similar event occurs in *Nug*. Both passages serve as transitions, taking the reader from a realistic world to a magical one.

116 Young, Karl. 'Chaucer's Aphorisms from Ptolemy.' *SP* 34(1937), 1–7.

Flügel discovered that the aphorisms of Ptolemy in III.180–3 and 324–7 are located in Gerard of Cremona's translation of the *Almagestum*. Chaucer's immediate source may have been Walter Burley's *Vita Omnium Philosophorum et Poetarum*.

117 Loomis, Laura Hibbard. 'Chaucer and the Breton Lays of the Auchinleck MS.' *SP* 38(1941), 14–33. Rpt in *Adventures in the Middle Ages: A Memorial Collection of Essays and Studies*. New York: Burt Franklin, 1962. Pp 111–30.

Chaucer may have been familiar with three Breton lays, *Sir Degaré*, *Le Freine*, and *Sir Orfeo*, found in the Auchinleck ms, a work compiled 'in the second quarter of the fourteenth century' (p 14). In both the *WBT* and *Sir Orfeo*, 'a woeful knight wandering in a forest comes upon ... [a] fairy dance' (p 26). A rape occurs in *Sir Degaré*, 'He binam hire here maidenhod' (I.111), that parallels the similar incident in the *WBT*, 'By verray force, he rafte hir maydenhed' (III.888). 'When we reflect that no other known version of the Loathly Lady story has the rape incident for its introduction ... the probability that [Chaucer] borrowed it from something already associated in his mind with *Britoun* fairy tale is heightened' (pp 30–1).

118 Whiting, Bartlett J. 'The *Wife of Bath's Prologue*' and 'The *Wife of Bath's Tale*.' In *Sources and Analogues of Chaucer's Canterbury Tales*. Ed. W.F. Bryan and Germaine Dempster. Chicago: University of Chicago Press, 1941; rpt New York: Humanities Press, 1958. Pp 207–22 and 223–68.

Most of the quotations taken from Jerome fall in the first 150 lines of the *WBP*. The portion based on Theophrastus has been incorporated in about 100 lines after III.198. The *Mir* portions lie in the 200 lines after III.198. The *RR*'s influence runs throughout the *WBP* and the final part of Chaucer's work contains *Val*'s influence (p 208). Excerpts from *Jov* (pp 208–12), *Val* (pp 212–3), *RR* (pp 213–5), and *Mir* (pp 215–22) are provided. The *ShT* was replaced by the *WBT* as a more fitting story for its teller. The *WBT* acts as an *exemplum* for the *WBP*. The separate motifs of the loathly lady tale and the life-saving answer to a question are combined in the *WBT* as well as in its analogues. Gower's *Flor* (pp 224–35), *Mar* (pp 235–41), and *Wed* (pp 242–64) are provided, as well as Ovid's account of Midas in the *Met* (p 265), Dante's *Conv*, which tells of the virtue of gentility, (pp 265–6), and similar sentiments from *RR* (pp 267–8).

119 Brown, Arthur C.L. *The Origin of the Grail Legend.* Cambridge: Harvard University Press, 1943.

Celtic tales contain an ugly fée, much like the hag in *Wed* and *Mar* (p 210). The fée is representative of the Sovereignty of Ireland and the hero who wins her obtains kingship of the land. See **1102**.

120 Moore, Arthur K. 'Alysoun's Other Tonne.' *MLN* 59(1944), 481–3. See **484**.

121 Coomaraswamy, Ananda K. 'On the Loathly Bride.' *Spec* 20(1945), 391–404.

The English loathly lady tales have Oriental parallels in which the loathly lady is analogous to the dragon or snake that is disenchanted. The Oriental loathly lady is representative of the Undine or the psyche, who is disenchanted by her marriage to a hero (p 393).

122 Moore, Arthur K. 'Chaucer and Matheolus.' *N&Q* 190(1946), 245–8. While there is no proof that Chaucer was familiar with Matheolus' *Lamentations*, 'three-fourths of the polemical matter of the *Wife of Bath's Prologue*' (pp 245–6) closely resembles the work. Parallel themes include marital debt, a wife's strategic self-defense by attacking her husband, the mourning practice for deceased husbands, and the fate of a widow's wealth in her new husband's hands. Chaucer could have encountered a French translation of Matheolus written in 1371–2 by Jehan le Fèvre.

123 Pratt, Robert A. 'Karl Young's Work in the Learning of Chaucer.' In *A Memoir of Karl Young.* New Haven: Privately printed, 1946.

In an address given at Columbia University, Karl Young discussed his book-in-progress concerning two volumes 'each represented in a number of manuscripts which Chaucer must have known' (p 52): the *Liber Catonianus* and a volume 'similar in content to the prized possession of Jankyn ... a compilation of Latin anti-matrimonial pamphlets, including Valerius, Theophrastus, and Jerome' (p 53). Chaucer did not have to ferret out antifeminist literature but simply incorporate the work he had at hand. Young died before completing his book on Chaucer.

124 French, Robert Dudley. *A Chaucer Handbook*, 2nd ed. New York: Appleton-Century-Crofts, 1947.

Chaucer borrows much from La Vieille's character to create the Wife, specifically 'the wiles which she believes that all women employ in their dealings with men' (p 272). Chaucer has, however, tempered the more 'harsh and disillusioned' (p 272) aspects of La Vieille in his rendering of Alisoun. Other portions of the *RR*, such as Ami's relating the condition of the jealous husband, have been borrowed. Jerome, Theophrastus, Map, and Deschamps are Chaucer's other sources. Outlines of the ballads *Wed*, *Mar*, and *Hen* reveal their parallels to *WBT*. 'It is probable that the original of the *WBT* was some version of the story of the Loathly Lady which had been developed beyond the more primitive stage represented by the old ballads' (p 284). Gower probably consulted this same source for *Flor*.

125 Whiting, B.J. 'A Colt's Tooth.' In *Mediaeval Studies in Honor of Jeremiah Denis Matthias Ford*. Ed. Urban T. Holmes, Jr. and Alex J. Denomy. Cambridge: Harvard University Press, 1948. Pp 321–31.
See **494**.

126 Smith, Roland M. 'The Six Gifts.' *Journal of Celtic Studies* 1(1949), 98–104.

Chaucer may have had indirect access to an Irish source for the list of qualities women want in their husbands found in the *WBT, NPT,* and *ShT*. The romance *Tochmarc Emire* contains a list of the *na sé buada, 'the six triumphs,'* for which women love Cuchulain, as does *Tain Bo Cualnge* and *Bricriu's Feast*. The gifts are listed in triads. 'The use of the double triad, or hexad, leans heavily in favor of an Irish (or at least Celtic) origin for Chaucer's lines enumerating the *thynges sixe*' (pp 102–3). 'It is worth noting that among Chaucer's secular tales only triads trip from the tongue of the Wife of Bath with her marked Celtic affinities' (p 103).

127 Pratt, Robert A.. 'A Note on Chaucer and the *Policraticus* of John of Salisbury.' *MLN* 65(1950), 243–6.

There is 'a series of parallels between portions of Book VIII of John's treatise and a passage near the close of the *Wife of Bath's Prologue*' (p 244). In III.765–71, Alisoun relates Jankyn's stories of women who violently slay their husbands. These stories of the Widow of Ephesus, Jael and Sisera, and Judith and Holofernes are recorded in the *Policraticus* in precisely the same order as the Wife lists them.

128 Slaughter, Eugene. 'Clerk Jankyn's Motive.' *MLN* 65(1950), 530–4. See **499**.

129 Green, A. Wigfall. 'Chaucer's Clerks and the Mediaeval Scholarly Tradition as Represented by Richard de Bury's *Philobiblon*.' *ELH* 18(1951), 1–6.

Richard de Bury's *Philobiblon* served Chaucer as a source of information about medieval scholars and aided him in developing his clerks. The clerkly love of books described in this work is reflected in Jankyn's fury when Alisoun damages his book (p 4).

130 Kane, George. *Middle English Literature: A Critical Study of the Romances, the Religious Lyrics, Piers Plowman*. London: Methuen, 1951; rpt New York: Barnes and Noble, 1970.

Wed is superior to the *WBT* because it relates its story 'more honestly than does the Wife of Bath' (p 27). See **1110**.

131 Roppolo, Joseph P. 'The Converted Knight in Chaucer's *Wife of Bath's Tale*.' *CE* 12(1951), 263–9. See **1113**.

132 Preston, Raymond. *Chaucer*. New York: Sheed and Ward, 1952; rpt New York: Greenwood Press, 1969. See **507** and **1116**.

133 Albrecht, William P. *The Loathly Lady in 'Thomas of Erceldoune': With a Text of the Poem Printed in 1652*. Albuquerque: University of New Mexico Press, 1954.

Much like Melusina and the hags of the *WBT* and Irish sovereignty tales, Thomas of Erceldoune's mistress undergoes a transformation in which she regains her beauty (p 7). While in *Flor*, *Mar*, and *Wed*, the crime is forgotten in light of the quest, the *WBT* fuses its crime with the riddle (p 58). While Chaucer's technique is, in part, responsible for this linking, this union also suggests a double-transformation Cupid and Psyche source tale for the *WBT*.

134 Sells, A. Lytton. *The Italian Influence in English Poetry: From Chaucer to Southwell.* Bloomington: Indiana University Press, 1955. Chaucer was influenced by Dante's *Conv*, and, perhaps, by Boccaccio's *Corbaccio* and *Ameto* for the *WBT* (p 52).

135 Schlauch, Margaret. *English Medieval Literature and Its Social Foundations.* Warsaw: Panstowowe Wydawnictwo Naukowe, 1956, 1967; rpt New York: Cooper Square Publishers, 1971.
See **519** and **1132**.

136 Eisner, Sigmund. *A Tale of Wonder: A Source Study of the Wife of Bath's Tale.* Wexford, Ireland: John English and Company, 1957.
The loathly lady tales appear to have originated in Irish mythology and the hag's role in them was that of an earth goddess. She later developed into a symbolic representation of Ireland. In Wales, her story was aligned with Arthurian tales. The Bretons brought the tales to France and, ultimately, the story arrived in England. Of five variations of the loathly lady tale (Irish myths, English Arthurian versions, the hag-visiting group, the *fier baiser* cycle, and Perceval legends), the absence of linkage between all but the Irish tales suggests independent development. Eight motifs of the Irish tales are traced in the variants. The transformation motif is found virtually untouched in the English, hag-visiting, and Perceval tales. The concept of sovereignty of the land became transformed into sovereignty over a husband in the English analogues. The motifs of the heroine as dispenser of food or drink, the heroine's association with a succession of Irish kings, and the Irish hunt are absent from the English Arthurian tales. The concept of enchantment is present in the English tales, usually with the enchanter being a stepmother. The presence of Irish sun god Lugh, who serves as hero or heroic prototype in the myths, was reworked to focus on the king's sister's son and eventually developed into the royal-nephew-as-hero motif. Gawain is an example of this role in *Wed* and *Mar*. The concept of choice, which in the Irish involves accepting or rejecting the hag, was transformed into the beautiful-by-day-or-night dilemma and the marital dilemma of the *WBT*. Three motifs found exclusively in the English Arthurian tales are the rape in the *WBT*, the quest to learn what women most desire, and the anger of the instigator of the quest.

137 Schulze, Konrad. 'Zu Chaucers *Weib von Bath* und Shakespeare's *Kaufmaun von Vendig.*' GRM 8(1958), 103–5. [In German.]
The *gentillesse* sermon has parallels with *RR*. Juvenal is a probable

source of Chaucer for this portion of the *WBT.*

138 Ackerman, Robert W. 'The English Rimed and Prose Romances.' In *Arthurian Literature in the Middle Ages: A Collaborative History.* Ed. Roger Sherman Loomis. Oxford: Clarendon Press, 1959; rpt 1961. Pp 480–519.

The Irish analogues of the loathly-lady tale were brought into the Gawain cycle (p 503). Of the multiple versions of the story, only three involve Arthurian elements: *Wed, Mar,* and *WBT. Wed* and *WBT* have similar plots, but in *Wed,* Arthur's life is in danger and Gawain saves him, while in *WBT* the knight must save himself. The knight is repelled by the hag and therefore his wedding is privately carried out, whereas Gawain is determined to do his duty and marries his bride publicly. The knight has the condition of either fidelity or unfaithfulness added to the marital dilemma of *Wed.* The fidelity choice is in keeping with the antifeminist elements in the *WBP* (p 503). While the hag is under no one's spell, Ragnell has been transformed by her stepmother. The ballad *The Knight and the Shepherd's Daughter* could have provided Chaucer with the idea of having the knight commit rape. In both the *WBT* and this ballad, a queen pronounces judgment (p 502). Chaucer's incorporation of the rape scene and the queen as judge may have stemmed from the courtly love tradition. The Wife's digressions are Chaucer's innovations.

139 Pratt, Robert A. 'Chaucer and Isidore on Why Men Marry.' *MLN* 74(1959), 293–4.

While some portions of the Wife's diatribe against her first three husbands have been taken from Theophrastus, the passage III.257–62 does not truly reflect *Liber Aureolus de Nuptiis.* These lines are reminiscent of a passage found in Isidore of Seville's *Etymologiarum Libri XX,* a work well known in Chaucer's time. Isidore's reasoning on why men marry could be found in Hrabanus Maurus' *De Rerum Naturis,* Hugutio Pisanus' *Magnae Derivationes,* and Johannes Balbus de Janua's *Catholicon.*

140 Steadman, John M. 'The Book-Burning Episode in the *Wife of Bath's Prologue*: Some Additional Analogues.' *PMLA* 74(1959), 521–5.

The Book of Sinbad contains a story similar to the *WBP*'s book-burning incident. *Studien über Weibertücke* ('The Man Who Understood Female Wiles') recounts the story of a young man who has collected tales of female trickery yet who falls prey to such wiles. Feeling his text is worthless, the youth burns the compilation and eventually marries.

Versions of this story include the Greek *Syntipas*, the Castilian *Enxemplo del Mancebo que non queria casar fasta que sopiese las maldades de las mugeres* and the Persian poet Nachschebi's *Tuti-nameh*. A reference to the destroying of a text on woman's wiles is also found in the twelfth- or thirteenth-century Italian poem *Castigabricon*. The primary parallels between the *WBP* and these works are the following: a 'youth shows an inordinate regard for a "book of wikked wyves"' (p 524); he is bested by an older woman and is prompted to destroy his text; the youth is usually a scholar; and the issues of '*maistrie* and matrimonial felicity' (p 524) are involved. The *WBP* differs from these tales in respect to 'the composition of the "book of wikked wyves," the motives for burning it, and the relationship between the two principal characters' (p 524). Chaucer may have been familiar with the Castilian and Italian works; however, it is doubtful he had direct access to the other tales.

141 Mroczkowski, Przemyslaw. 'Incubi and Friars.' *KN* 8(1961), 191–2. See **1141**.

142 Pratt, Robert A. 'Jankyn's Book of Wikked Wyves: Medieval Antimatrimonial Propaganda in the Universities.' *AnM* 3(1962), 5–27. That an Oxford cleric like Jankyn would have had a Book of Wicked Wives adds credence to the theory that antifeminist works abounded at universities for the purpose of encouraging celibacy. Peter Abelard and John of Salisbury were influenced by Jerome and Theophrastus, as was Walter Map. Only one ms of 60 credits Map with *Val*; others credit such authors as St. Cyprian, Jerome, and Valerius Maximus. Due to its high stylization, *Val* commentators provided copious annotations for the work. It is plausible that John Waleys is the author of approximately 200 pages of commentary on 15 pages of *Val*, now housed in the Lambeth Palace Library. If this is so, Map's *Val* may be connected with Paris as well as with Oxford, where it was commented on by Trevet and Ridewall (p 20).

143 ———. 'Saint Jerome in Jankyn's Book of Wikked Wyves.' *Criticism* 5(1963), 316–22. See **547**.

144 Albertini, Vergil R. 'Chaucer's Artistic Accomplishment in Molding the *Wife of Bath's Tale*.' *Northwest Missouri State College Studies* 28(1964), 3–16. The elements of eager love, fairies, and transformation unite the *WBT*

to the Cupid and Psyche folk tales, more specifically to the subgroup of the Melusina tales, whose female character is of the otherworld (pp 3–4). The plots and parallel phrases of the *WBT* and *Flor* are compared and contrasted (pp 6–9). While Chaucer's source for the rape is unknown, it may come from the Cupid and Psyche tales, which considered marriage to be a rape of virginity, a transformation of the female (p 12). The *WBT* may be considered a story of double transformation. The pillow lecture and Midas digression are in keeping with Alisoun's life experiences.

145 Fisher, John H. *John Gower: Moral Philosopher and Friend of Chaucer*. New York: New York University Press, 1964.

Gower's *Flor* contains a legal connection that is absent from the *WBT* (p 195). His *Vox clamantis* contains a description of an evil woman that is a pale anticipation of Alisoun. See **225**.

146 Huppé, Bernard F. *A Reading of the Canterbury Tales*. Albany: State University Press of New York, 1964/rev 1967.

There are five major points of difference between the *WBT* and its analogues: the introduction contains Alisoun's insulting of the Friar; the riddle quest is assigned because of a rape; the hag is given one line of description and keeps her marriage desire a secret; the pillow lecture is a Chaucerian innovation; and the dilemma has fidelity added to the beauty choice. Through these alterations, Chaucer molds the tale to Alisoun's personality (p 132). It exemplifies the *WBP* and caters to Alisoun's wish-fulfillment. See **554**.

147 Hoffman, Richard L. 'Ovid's Argus and Chaucer.' *N&Q* 210(1965), 213–6.

Alisoun's reference to Argus has its foundations in both Ovid's *Amores* and the *Met* (p 214).

148 ———. 'Ovid and the "Marital Dilemma" in the *Wife of Bath's Tale*.' *AN&Q* 3(1965), 101–2.

Ovid discusses the inverse relationship between the beauty of women and marital fidelity in his *Amores*.

149 Levy, Bernard S. 'Chaucer's Wife of Bath, the Loathly Lady, and Dante's Siren.' *Symposium* 19(1965), 359–73.

See **1158**.

150 Miller, Robert P. 'The *Wife of Bath's Tale* and Mediaeval Exempla.' *ELH* 32(1965), 442–56.

The transformation motif of the *WBT* is related to medieval *exempla* on the powers of the virtue of obedience against lechery (pp 442–3). These *exempla* include writings by Odo of Cheriton and Jaques de Vitry, the *Vitae Patrum*, and the *Speculum morale*. The similarities between such *exempla* and the *WBT* include the three stages of the knight's purgation and the two stages of his reformation (p 452).

151 Silvia, Daniel S., Jr. 'Glosses to the *Canterbury Tales* from St. Jerome's *Epistola Adversus Jovinianum*.' *SP* 62(1965), 28–39.
    The *MLT*, *WBP*, and *ClT* contain the most glosses of Jerome. In the *WBP*, the majority of glosses are Latin source citations that come from either the Vulgate or *Jov* (p 29). Two books served as sources for the *WBP*: *Jov* and an anthology similar to Jankyn's book (p 31). The uneven distribution of glosses may be accounted for by Pratt's (**533**) suggestion that Chaucer enlarged his original *WBP*. Chaucer would have used the marginal notations as guidelines for his writing.

152 Hoffman, Richard L. 'Ovid and the Wife of Bath's Tale of Midas.' *N&Q* 211(1966), 48–50.
    Alisoun manipulates Ovid's account of the Midas legend in *Met* (p 48). Alisoun distorts the story because of her habit of misrepresenting text. The Wife's deafness to the underlying meaning of Scripture may be associated with Midas' own inability to prefer the lofty music of Apollo over the music of Pan.

153 ———. *Ovid and the Canterbury Tales*. Philadelphia: University of Pennsylvania Press, 1966.
    Ovid's *Remedia Amoris* and *Ars Amatoria* are reflected in Alisoun's knowledge of both remedies of love and the old dance. Ovid's *Ars Amatoria* influenced Alisoun's defense of adultery, her description of her drunkenness, her attending public functions, her finding a new husband at her old husband's funeral, and her reference to Pasiphäe. The *Met* contributed to Alisoun's references to the mad crow and to Argus. The story of Midas is found in the *Met*. Alisoun's version is compared to the original tale (pp 145–9). See **322** and **574**.

154 Pearsall, Derek. 'Gower's Narrative Art.' *PMLA* 81(1966), 475–84.
    By traditional narrative standards, *Flor* is superior to *WBT*. It contains a detailed description of the hag's ugliness and portrays Florent in a noble light. Chaucer's reworking the tale to conform to his teller indicates that he is writing at a different artistic level than Gower.

155 Pratt, Robert A. 'Chaucer and the Hand that Fed Him.' *Spec* 41(1966), 619–42.

Chaucer was familiar with some form of John Waleys' *Communiloquium* and used it as a source for portions of the *CT*. In the Ellesmere ms version of the *WBP*, glossings of and quotations from Valerius Maximus, Proverbs, and Jerome resemble John Waleys' work more closely than they do the original sources (pp 620–4). Portions of the pillow lecture also resemble the *Communiloquium*.

156 Scholes, Robert, and Robert Kellogg. *The Nature of Narrative*. New York: Oxford University Press, 1966.

See **581**.

157 Garbáty, Thomas Jay. '*Pamphilus, de Amore*: An Introduction and Translation.' *ChauR* 2(1967), 108–34.

The dramatic poem *Pamphilus, de Amore* had much influence on medieval writers. Chaucer may well have known the work itself, but he was also familiar with its influence on *RR* (p 109). The poem's old woman, Anus, is a prototype for La Vieille. An English translation of the play is provided (pp 111–34).

158 Muscatine, Charles. 'The Wife of Bath and Gautier's *La Veuve*.' In *Romance Studies in Memory of Edward Billings Ham*. Ed. Urban T. Holmes. Hayward: California State College Press, 1967. Pp 109–14.

It is possible that Gautier's *La Veuve* was among Chaucer's sources for his *WBP*. The works have similar dramatic monologues and imagery. The character La Veuve shares Alisoun's sexual drive, is a widow, is skilled in weaving, and has had both old-and-wealthy and young-and-poor husbands. Both works end with a fight that brings about peace.

159 Schaar, Claes. *The Golden Mirror: Studies in Chaucer's Descriptive Technique and Its Literary Background*. Lund: C.W.K. Gleerup, 1967.

See **1175** and **594**.

160 Brennan, John Patrick, Jr. 'The Chaucerian Text of Jerome *Adversus Jovinianum*: An Edition Based on Pembroke College, Cambridge MS 234.' *DAI* 28(1968), 4622–3A.

The passages Chaucer incorporated from Jerome's work into the *CT*, including those in the *WBP*, resemble those found in MS Pembroke College 234.

161 Hoffman, Richard L. 'The Influence of the Classics on Chaucer.' In *Companion to Chaucer Studies*. Ed. Beryl Rowland. New York: Oxford University Press, 1968/rev 1979 [cited]. Pp 162–75/62–73.

Juvenal's *Tenth Satire* influenced *WBT* III.1192–4 (p 63). Elements of John Waleys' *Communiloquium* are found in both *WBP* and *WBT*.

162 Cary, Meredith. 'Sovereignty and Old Wife.' *PLL* 5(1969), 375–88.
The English loathly lady tales are similar only in general outline to the Irish analogues (p 375). While the English analogues all begin with an issue of honor, only the *WBT* includes a female definition of this concept by making the knight's prey a woman (pp 376–7). Chaucer's other alterations redefine sovereignty in feminine terms, grant authority to the women at court, and elevate the dignity of women by not belaboring the hag's description. The *gentillesse* sermon serves to educate the knight (p 384). In both the *WBT* and the Irish analogues, the hag doesn't keep sovereignty but yields it to her love.

163 Duncan, Edgar H. 'Chaucer's *Wife of Bath's Prologue*, Lines 193–828, and Geoffrey of Vinsauf's *Documentum*.' *MP* 66(1969), 199–211.
See **613**.

164 Silvia, D.S., and John P. Brennan, Jr. 'Medieval Manuscripts of *Jerome against Jovinian*.' *Manuscripta* 13(1969), 161–6.
A list of the 87 mss containing complete copies of *Jov* is given (pp 162–6).

165 Witlieb, Bernard L. 'Chaucer and the *Ovide Moralisé*.' *N&Q* 215(1970), 202–7.
Alisoun's reference to Pasiphäe may have been derived from the *Ovide moralisé* (p 206).

166 Gardner, Averil. 'Chaucer and Boethius: Some Illustrations of Indebtedness.' *University of Cape Town Studies in English* 2(1971), 31–8.
See **1196**.

167 Schmitt, Charles B. 'Theophrastus in the Middle Ages.' *Viator* 2(1971), 251–70.
Chaucerian critics have analyzed extensively Chaucer's incorporation of Theophrastus's, Jerome's, and Map's antimatrimonial writings into Jankyn's book (pp 263–4).

168 Hamilton, Alice. 'Helowys and the Burning of Jankyn's Book.' *MS* 34(1972), 196–207.
See **638**.

169 Harbert, Bruce. 'Chaucer and the Latin Classics.' In *Geoffrey Chaucer: The Writer and His Background*. Ed. Derek Brewer. London: G. Bell and Sons, 1974; rpt Athens, OH: Ohio University Press, 1975; rpt Cambridge: D.S. Brewer, 1990. Pp 137–53.

Chaucer's access to mss much like Jankyn's book, which combines medieval and classical works, makes it difficult to pinpoint his sources (pp 140–1).

170 Wimsatt, James I. 'Chaucer and French Poetry.' In *Geoffrey Chaucer: The Writer and His Background*. Ed. Derek Brewer. London: G. Bell and Sons, 1974; rpt Athens, OH: Ohio University Press, 1975; rpt Cambridge: D.S. Brewer, 1990. Pp 109–36.

Chaucer's familiarity with French romances and lays probably influenced his *WBT*, *FranT*, and *SqT* (p 112). Deschamps' *Mir* also influenced Alisoun's performance (p 134).

171 Braswell, Laurel. 'Chaucer and the Legendaries: New Sources for Anti-Mendicant Satire.' *ESC* 2(1976), 373–80.

Alisoun's and the Summoner's insults against the Friar reflect parallels in the legends of St. Michael the Archangel and St. Francis of Assisi (p 374). The Summoner's equation of friars with flies echoes the *Speculum perfectionis* and Jacobus de Voragine's *Legenda aurea*. Alisoun's comparison of friars to dust is also an image found in Jacobus' work. Her comment about friars and women reflects an account in *The South English Legendary* concerning incubi (p 377).

172 Murphy, Francis X. 'Chaucer's Patristic Knowledge.' *PPMRC* 1(1976), 53–7.

John Waleys' *Communiloquium sive summa collationum* provided Chaucer with many patristic excerpts for the *WBT*. Some of the writers included in the handbook are Seneca, Jerome, John of Salisbury, and Cicero (p 54).

173 Metlitzki, Dorothee. *The Matter of Araby in Medieval England*. New Haven: Yale University Press, 1977.

Alisoun's preference for experience over authority echoes the beliefs of Peter Alfonsi (p 19) and Adelard of Bath (p 48), who were influenced by the doctrines of Arab masters. While Alisoun credits Ptolemy with valuing the authority of experience, the proverbs she quotes actually come from Arabian philosophy found in the *Disciplina Clericalis* and the *Secret of Secrets* (p 111). Ptolemy places these proverbs in the preface of his *Almagest*.

174 Miller, Robert P., ed. *Chaucer: Sources and Backgrounds*. New York: Oxford University Press, 1977.

Details that comprise Alisoun's portrait, *WBP*, and *WBT* have been found in Jacobus de Voragine's *The Golden Legend*, Ovid's *Remedia*

Amoris, Amores, and *Ars amatoria*, the *Sarum Missal*, Theophrastus's *Liber Aureolus de Nuptiis*, Jerome's *Jov*, Map's *Val*, and Jean de Meun's *RR*. Additional works related to and contrasted with the *WBP* include Augustine's *De civitate Dei*, Deschamps' *Mir*, Gower's *Vox clamantis*, Capellanus' *De amore*, Anglicus' *De proprietatibus rerum*, Solomon's proverbs, and Abelard's *Historia Calamitatum*. A work involved with the relationship of Alisoun and the Friar is William of Saint-Amour's *De periculis*.

175 Cook, Robert. 'Another Biblical Echo in the *Wife of Bath's Prologue*?' *ES* 59(1978), 390–4.

Alisoun's reference to her husband's secret act of pissing on a wall (III.534) reflects a similar phrase that appears six times in the books of Kings. In the sixth, I Kings 25:22 is part of the story of Abigail, whose life parallels Alisoun's in that a new husband is found quickly after the convenient death of an unfaithful husband. Unlike Alisoun, the humble Abigail is known for her prudent speech (p 393).

176 Peck, Russell A. *Kingship and Common Profit in Gower's 'Confessio Amantis.'* Carbondale: Southern Illinois University Press, 1978.

While Gower's *Flor* differs markedly from the *WBT*, it is not necessarily the inferior work (p 46). The variations between these analogues suit the intent behind the individual works.

177 Thundy, Zacharias P. 'Matheolus, Chaucer, and the Wife of Bath.' In *Chaucerian Problems and Perspectives: Essays Presented to Paul E. Beichner, C.S.C.* Ed. Edward Vasta and Zacharias P. Thundy. Notre Dame: University of Notre Dame Press, 1979. Pp 24–58.

The *Lamentations* of Matheolus, translated into French in the early 1370's by Jehan le Fèvre, has often been disregarded by Chaucer critics, but the work is actually a great source for the *WBP*, *MerT*, and *NPT*. In the *WBP* and *WBT*, there are 122 parallels to this work, 88 of them being verbal parallels (p 26). Detailed tables note the verbal parallels by corresponding line numbers (pp 28–33). It is probable that Deschamps was not one of Chaucer's sources for the *WBP*.

178 Shenk, Robert. 'The Liberation of the "Loathly Lady" of Medieval Romance.' *JRMMRA* 2(1981), 69–77.

Near the end of *Wed*, the poet prays to Christ that both genders escape the trials of life (p 69). As exemplified in *Wed* and *WBT*, such liberation can only occur when a person grants his will to another. Arthur learns both humility when he must ask Gawain to marry Ragnell and the lesson that a king should not be imprudent. When Gawain humbles himself to the hag, he is rewarded with a beautiful, obedient wife. In promising obedience, the hag submits to another's will, and both characters obtain freedom.

179   Owen, Charles A., Jr. 'The Alternative Reading of *The Canterbury Tales*: Chaucer's Text and the Early Manuscripts.' *PMLA* 97(1982), 237–50.

The glossators of the Hengwrt and Ellesmere mss commented frequently on the pillow lecture (p 24). Sources for the glossing include Jerome, Juvenal, Seneca, and 'Secundus.' See **787**.

180   Wetherbee, Winthrop. 'Some Implications of Nature's Femininity in Medieval Poetry.' In *Approaches to Nature in the Middle Ages: Papers of the Tenth Annual Conference of the Center for Medieval and Early Renaissance Studies*. Ed. Lawrence D. Roberts. Binghamton: Medieval and Renaissance Texts and Studies, 1982. Pp 47–62.

Alisoun possesses not only traits of Jean de Meun's La Vieille but characteristics of his Dame Nature as well (p 60). As Chaucer's representative of females, Alisoun embodies some of the challenges of Nature.

181   Ando, Shinsuki. 'A Note on Line 1196 of the *Wife of Bath's Tale*.' *Poetica* 15/16(1983), 154–9.

The source for III.1196 is Vincent of Beauvais' *Speculum historiale*, and Chaucer's *bisyness* is his translation of *remotio curarum*. A modern interpretation of this would be 'a very great remover of worries' (p 157).

182   Bennett, J.A.W. 'Chaucer, Dante and Boccaccio.' In *Chaucer and the Italian Trecento*. Ed. Piero Boitani. Cambridge: Cambridge University Press, 1983. Pp 89–113.

Alisoun credits Dante for her tale's treatment of *gentillesse* and III.1127–30 is a parallel of the *Purgatorio* VII, 121–3 (p 106).

183   Blanch, Robert J. 'The Legal Framework of "A Twelvemonth and a Day" in *Sir Gawain and the Green Knight*.' *NM* 84(1983), 347–52.

The year-and-a-day time allotment is a tradition in the Germanic judicial system that was incorporated into the English legal system.

184   Boitani, Piero. 'What Dante Meant to Chaucer.' In *Chaucer and the Italian Trecento*. Ed. Piero Boitani. Cambridge: Cambridge University Press, 1983. Pp 115–39.

The *gentillesse* sermon was inspired by Dante's *Conv* (p 131). Alisoun considers Dante to be a font of moral wisdom in III.1125-6 (pp 132–3).

185 Waterhouse, Ruth, and John Stephens. 'The Backward Look: Retrospectivity in Medieval Literature.' *SoRA* 16(1983), 356–73.

In Gower's *Flor* the hag explains that she was put under a spell. Once readers receive this information, they may more clearly perceive retrospectively the inner struggle Florent undergoes in his tale and understand that their perception of the hag has come from Florent's point of view (p 363). It is through Florent's accepting his penance that he may perceive the hag in her original state. Her transformation motivates him to renounce the self completely (p 364). In the *WBT*, Chaucer's decision to omit any reference to the hag's being enchanted can suggest that the beautiful maiden in the knight's bed is an illusion. The knight's perception of the hag, not the hag herself, is transformed.

186 Wurtele, Douglas. 'The Predicament of Chaucer's Wife of Bath: St. Jerome on Virginity.' *Florilegium* 5(1983), 208–36.

See **807**.

187 Fischer, Olga C.M. 'Gower's *Tale of Florent* and Chaucer's *Wife of Bath's Tale*: A Stylistic Comparison.' *ES* 66(1985), 205–25.

Gower and Chaucer both suit their tales to their tellers. While the Confessor tells *Flor* as an exemplum from which he is removed, Alisoun is enmeshed in her tale and its theme of sovereignty. Alisoun incorporates fairy elements and works to build suspense in the *WBT*, whereas the Confessor narrates in a matter-of-fact style. Alisoun's digressions, complex sentence structure, and her active, direct, and stylized speech reveal her personal and artistic involvement with her tale. While Gower's work lacks the intricacy of Chaucer's, its bland style is appropriate for the tale's function in *CA*.

188 Morris, Lynn King. *Chaucer Source and Analogue Criticism: A Cross-Referenced Guide*. New York: Garland, 1985.

Chaucer's sources and analogues are indexed according to his works, the sources' and analogues' authors, the sources' genre, and the sources' or analogues' titles. The sources and analogues of the *WBP* may be found on pp 194–6 and those for the *WBT* on pp 196–9.

189 Bollard, J.K. 'Sovereignty and the Loathly Lady in English, Welsh, and Irish.' *LeedsSE* 17(1986), 41–59.

The insignificance of transformation in French tales containing a loathly lady discounts the theory that such tales came to England through France (p 45). The English tales do not specifically unite the concept of sovereignty with transformation. Here sovereignty is a separate issue, a choice that the hag gives the hero. This association differs from the Irish *flaithius*, the association of sovereignty with land and kingship. While Irish analogues culminate in transformation, the English analogues weave transformation into a four-step plot: the riddle, the promise to wed the hag, the transformation, and the yielding to the hag in marriage (pp 48–9). The differences between the *WBT* and its analogues reveal the variations an author can achieve in a particular tale.

190 Mertens-Fonck, Paule. 'Tradition and Feminism in Middle English Literature: Source-Hunting in the Wife of Bath's Portrait and in *The Owl and the Nightingale.*' In *Multiple Worlds, Multiple Words: Essays in Honor of Irene Simon.* Ed. Hena Maes-Jelinek, Pierre Michel, and Paulette Michel-Michot. Liège: Université de Liège, 1987. Pp 175–92.
See **396**.

191 Axton, Richard. 'Gower — Chaucer's Heir?' In *Chaucer Traditions: Studies in Honour of Derek Brewer.* Ed. Ruth Morse and Barry Windeatt. Cambridge: Cambridge University Press, 1990. Pp 21–38.
Chaucer's decision to make Alisoun the narrator of a tale similar to *Flor* 'may be viewed as part of his creative response to Gower' (p 33).

192 Barr, Jane. 'The Vulgate Genesis and St. Jerome's Attitude to Women.' In *Equally in God's Image: Women in the Middle Ages.* Ed. Julia Bolton Holloway, Joan Bechtold, and Constance S. Wright. New York: Peter Lang, 1990. Pp 122–8.
Jerome's translation of Genesis is usually highly accurate, except where passages refer to women. His solid knowledge of Hebrew suggests that the errors in these passages stem from bias. While some of Jerome's translations indicate a harshness toward women, others reveal tenderness towards them.

193 Nolan, Edward Peter. *Now Through a Glass Darkly: Specular Images of Being and Knowing from Virgil to Chaucer.* Ann Arbor: University of Michigan Press, 1990.
In the *Purgatorio*, Dante's Statius uses female images to convey his concepts of bodily generation. Conversely, Chaucer's Wife of Bath uses the language of clerks to discuss her notions of the generative process (pp 204–9).

194 Wicher, Andrzej. 'A Discussion of the Archetype of the Supernatural

Husband and the Supernatural Wife as It Appears in Some of Geoffrey Chaucer's *Canterbury Tales.*' *REAL: Yearbook of Research in English and American Literature.* Ed. Herbert Grabes, Hans-Jürgen Diller, and Hartwig Isernhagen. 7(1990), 19–60.

See **256**.

195 Beidler, Peter G. 'Transformations in Gower's *Tale of Florent* and Chaucer's *Wife of Bath's Tale.*' In *Chaucer and Gower: Difference, Mutuality, Exchange.* Ed. R.F. Yeager. Victoria, B.C.: University of Victoria, 1991. Pp 100–14.

Gower's *Flor* is not inferior to the *WBT*. It merely has 'different purposes' (p 100) than Chaucer's work. *Flor* stresses a noble knight's ability to transform an enchanted hag. Key differences between the two include the characterization of the knight and hag, the nature of the crime committed, the quest-setter, the quest, the surety, the return, the riddle's answer, the marriage, the marital dilemma, and the disenchantment.

196 Green, Richard Firth. 'An Analogue to the "Marital Dilemma" in the *Wife of Bath's Tale.*' *ELN* 28(1991), 9–12.

The French farce, *Les deux maris et leurs deux femmes*, contains a rough parallel to the marital dilemma of the *WBT* and suggests that the origins of the dilemma may not lie in classical literature.

197 Mann, Jill. *Geoffrey Chaucer.* Feminist Readings. Atlantic Highlands: Humanities Press International, 1991.

Chaucer's sources for the *WBP* have much 'dialogic potential' (p 74) for ironic exposition. Deschamps' *Mir* contains both male and female voices. The *RR* contains a more intricate working of speeches-within-speeches, and Chaucer's use of the same device exceeds Jean de Meun's elaborateness. See **976** and **1413**.

198 Minnis, A.J. 'De Vulgari Auctoritate: Chaucer, Gower and Men of Great Authority.' In *Chaucer and Gower: Difference, Mutuality, Exchange.* Ed. R.F. Yeager. Victoria, B.C.: University of Victoria, 1991. Pp 36–74.

Chaucer may have been exposed to the 'virtuous Dido' (p 42) of *Jov*, because we know he used this work as a source for the *WBP* and *FrT*. Alisoun reveals her respect for Dante (III.1125–6).

199 Wimsatt, James I. *Chaucer and His French Contemporaries: Natural Music in the Fourteenth Century.* Toronto: University of Toronto Press, 1991.

While many remarks concerning marriage made by the *Mir*'s Repertoire de Science are present in the *WBP*, Lowes (**434**) assumed the *Mir* had more influence upon Chaucer than it actually did. Thundy's scholarship (**177**) proves that both the *Lamentations* of Matheolus and Jehan le Févre's translation of it were more influential than the work of Deschamps.

200 Galloway, Andrew. 'Marriage Sermons, Polemical Sermons, and the *Wife of Bath's Prologue*: A Generic Excursus.' *SAC* 14 (1992), 3–30. Alisoun's initial scriptural reference to the Wedding at Cana recalls a 'tradition of sermons' (p 5) concerning the topic of marriage. The number and content of these sermons on marriage indicate the medieval concern with this sacrament. Alisoun's discussion of 'the functions of genitalia' (p 7) aligns itself with sermons that discuss the carnal aspect of marriage. Medieval marriage sermons frequently employ misogynistic themes yet also promote women. The *WBP* relates thematically to Jacobus de Voragine's thirteenth-century three-sermon series on Cana. These sermons contain a striking passage that encourages wives to 'never be silent or passive when confronted by their husbands' sins' (p 11), and recall Alisoun's chiding of her husbands. Other parallels include antifeminist material, the type of woman one should marry, the qualities men desire in their wives, and the proper form of correcting a wife. Alisoun's 'professionalizing of a sermon tradition' (p 28) provides a unifying question for Fragment III, that of who 'owns' discourse, 'a theme of profound cultural power in the fourteenth century' (p 28).

201 Aguirre, Manuel. 'The Riddle of Sovereignty.' *MLR* 88(1993), 273–82. A 'fundamental continuity' (p 276) exists between the English and Irish analogues to the *WBT* that may be found by examining both the similarities and differences between the tales. The English stories may be divided into three sections, each of which contains a riddle-motif that is absent in *Echtra mac n-Echach*. In the *WBT*, for example, the sections are the rape and the knight's quest, the hag's information and its accompanying price of marriage, and events of the wedding night. Each riddle is presented to the knight by a woman and its answer involves female sovereignty, a subject which seems unreasonable to the knight. In the British analogues, this unreasonable nature of the answers magnifies the challenge of the male questor and gives 'a verbal shape to the test ... central to which stands the loathly hag' (p 276). That the English analogues contain two polarized women, innocent victim and evil spell-caster, ties in with the most significant discrepancy between the English and Irish stories: the issue of sovereignty. The concept of female sovereignty is present in all of the English analogues in the form of a female insistent upon obtaining power within her marriage. In the Irish tale, the Sovereignty of Ireland is given by a woman to a future king (pp 275–6). All versions of this story 'contain a statement about woman and her symbolic nature' (p 278). In the Irish tradition, woman is associated with the non-rational otherworld; she represents the fertile earth goddess. Only in *Wed* does the woman have a connection with land. The absence of a land issue in the other English versions marks woman's movement away from an association with Sovereignty of the land and toward the more unreasonable, irrational Sovereignty of love (p 279). In the *WBT*, the motif of courtship is represented by the rape, whereas in the other analogues it is symbolized by the hunt. The absence of the evil stepmother highlights the deliberate nature of the hag. This emphasis is in keeping with Alisoun's role as narrator of this story; it reflects her 'high-minded feminism' (p 280) and her unreasonable nature. Woman's movement away from the land in literature corresponds to her marginalization in patriarchal society. She increasingly became associated with the realm of the emotions and its unreasonableness.

202 Fichte, Joerg O. 'Images of Arthurian Literature Reflected in Chaucer's Poetry.' *Archiv* 230(1993), 52–61.

There is no direct intertextual relationship between the *WBT* and its analogues. Because the ms containing *Wed* and *Mar* is of the fifteenth century, it is uncertain if Chaucer had access to a loathly lady tale with an Arthurian setting (p 58). While *Wed* may be seen as a parody of the classical romance, the *WBT*, which does not contain the classical elements of chivalry, an otherworld adversary, and an explanation for the hag's enchantment, cannot be viewed as a 'further reduction of the classical model' (p 59).

203 Calabrese, Michael A. *Chaucer's Ovidian Arts of Love*. Gainesville: University Press of Florida, 1994.

Alisoun's performance relates intertextually to Ovid's work. In her battle against antifeminism, Alisoun 'becomes a new Ovid and composes a new art of love' (p 83). The literary, textual, and social problems in Alisoun's performance are expressed in Ovidian terminology, yet Chaucer adds to them an individual's struggle for identity and for love (p 110).

204 Evans, Dansby. 'Chaucer and Eliot: The Poetics of Pilgrimage.' *MedPers* 9(1994), 41–7.

In *The Waste Land*, Eliot shares Chaucer's penchant for twisting sources, such as Chaucer's having Alisoun tell her own version of Ovid's Midas story in *Met* (p 43). Both writers expected their audiences to recognize their alterations.

205 Olson, Glending. 'The Marital Dilemma in the *Wife of Bath's Tale*: An Unnoticed Analogue and Its Chaucerian Court Context.' *ELN* 33(1995), 1–7.

A ballad of Eustache Deschamps contains a *demande d'amour* that addresses the dilemma of a young knight having either a young and beautiful wife or a middle-aged one. The courtly nature of Deschamps' work suggests that the marital dilemma in the *WBT* stems more from an aristocratic genre than from either the antifeminist tradition or popular topoi (p 5). The marital dilemma is Alisoun's critique of the limiting stereotypes of women.

206 Vasta, Edward. 'Chaucer, Gower, and the Unknown Minstrel: The Literary Liberation of the Loathly Lady.' *Exemplaria* 7(1995), 395–418.

English writers who made use of the loathly lady tradition employed the loathly lady's powers of renewal for the betterment of an individual character. They began, however, to push away 'from their own official culture in order to call for its renewal' (p 398) by using the carnivalesque traits of the grotesque and humor in their work. Gower's *Flor* lacks humor and is steeped in the conventions of the official culture. His lengthy and grotesque description of the loathly lady contains no laughter. The renewal in this tale is merely on the personal level. In his *WBT*, Chaucer uses 'fewer formal legalities' (p 404) and 'places the culture's ideology at his tale's heart' (p 405). While the pillow lecture negatively addresses the shallow values of wealth, beauty, youth, and nobility and promotes spiritual virtues, it supports the official ideology of Chaucer's world. Chaucer's addition of the issue of female sovereignty in the marital dilemma goes against his culture's conception of women. Chaucer also supports women by having a female narrator tell this. That the loathly lady in the *WBT* lacks the full description Gower gave her makes her abstract and a representation of 'violated females who seek to correct ... male violators' (p 407), who are represented by the knight. Chaucer's alterations, however, do not transform the official culture. This transformation is accomplished by the author of *Wed*.

∞ The Marriage Group

207 Root, Robert Kilburn. *The Poetry of Chaucer: A Guide to Its Study and Appreciation*. Boston: Houghton Mifflin, 1906/rev 1922; rpt 1934; rpt Gloucester, MA: Peter Smith, 1950, 1957.
See **92** and **427**.

208 Hammond, Eleanor Prescott. *Chaucer: A Bibliographical Manual*. New York: Macmillan, 1908; rpt New York: Peter Smith, 1933.
'Yet a third class of narratives in the *CT* is what I may term the Marriage Group' (p 256). The *WBP, MerT,* and *FranT* rely upon Jerome's *Jov* as a source. The conception of the Marriage Group occurred later in Chaucer's life and caused Chaucer to transfer Alisoun as teller of the *ShT* to the teller of the *WBT*.

209 Moore, Samuel. 'The Date of Chaucer's Marriage Group.' *MLN* 26(1911), 172–4.
Chaucer's *Buk*, composed in late 1396, contains a reference to the Wife of Bath; therefore, it serves as a terminal date for the *WBP*'s completion. The presence of both Jerome's influence and that of *Mir* in *WBP, MerT, FranT,* and the A prologue of *LGW* suggests these works were written at about the same time. If the *LGW*'s A prologue may be dated around June 1394, the Marriage Group may be dated in the period from 1393–6. Moore cites Chaucer's complaint in his *Scog* that his muse is asleep as evidence that he had not begun working on the Marriage Group. The *Scog* was composed in 1393.

210 Kittredge, George L. 'Chaucer's Discussion of Marriage.' *MP* 9(1912), 435–67. Rev *Chaucer and His Poetry*. Cambridge: Harvard University Press, 1915; rpt many times; with an Introduction by B.J. Whiting in 1970.
The tales reveal the interrelations of the pilgrims in Chaucer's 'human

comedy' (p 435). The *WBP* stands as 'a scornful, though good-humored, repudiation of what the Church teaches' (p 439) regarding chastity and advocates a wife's maintaining sovereignty over her spouse. Because the *WBP* is not connected to any previous tale and Alisoun directly addresses this speech to her fellow travelers, Chaucer must have intended that the Wife promote a new topic of discussion among the pilgrims (pp 439–40). The Wife's discourse regarding the church's view of virginity and her diatribe against clerks would have offended the celibate, sober Clerk who, like Jankyn, was a graduate of Oxford. While the main point of the *ClT* is to parallel Griselda's submissive relationship with Walter and humanity's ideal response to the will of God, the Clerk cannot resist directing his moral to the Wife and *all her sect*. The Clerk's specific use of the word *soverayntee* (IV.114) shows he is providing a rejoinder to the Wife's story: 'The Clerk is answering the Wife of Bath; he is telling of a woman whose principles in marriage were the antithesis of hers' (p 446). The Clerk's *Envoy* pays an 'ironic tribute' (p 450) to the Wife and paves the way for the *MerT* which is also connected to the *WBP*. January protests against marrying an older woman. Justinus uses some of the Wife's language; IV.1670–3 parallels III.489–90. In IV.1685 the Wife is called by name. Proserpine's attitude towards doctrine reflects that of the Wife, and her argument with Pluto resembles one of the Wife's confrontations with a husband. The *FranT* also refers back to the *WBT* in its emphasis on the concept of *gentillesse*, the focal point of the hag's pillow lecture to her knight (pp 461–4).

211　Lawrence, William W. 'The Marriage Group in the *Canterbury Tales*.' *MP* 11(1913), 247–58.

While there is a Marriage Group, the *WBP* doesn't function as the initial introduction of the discussion. The *WBP* is connected to preceding tales, specifically *Mel*, which is a 'prose counterpart' (p 252) to the *WBT*. In both tales a wife obtains mastery over her husband, as does Alisoun over Jankyn in the *WBP*. The knight's lines to the hag (III.1230–1, 1235–8) could easily have been spoken by Melibeus to Prudence. The list of tragedies in the *MkT* that involve a woman proving to be a man's undoing may be a forerunner of Jankyn's book (p 254 n 2). The *NPT* undercuts the value of a woman's counsel that was found in *Mel*. *PhyT* and *PardT* should be moved further ahead in the collection so that the Wife may continue the marriage debate with her words.

212　Hemingway, Samuel B. 'Chaucer's Monk and Nun's Priest.' *MLN*

31(1916), 479–83.

The Marriage Group does not begin with *WBP*. The Wife 'has been attacked, and she heatedly replies with an attack upon the clerical ideal of celibacy' (p 482). The celibacy issue is first introduced in *MkP* by Harry Bailly and continued by him in the epilogue to the *NPT*. The subject of marriage is initiated with *Mel*. Ideally, there should have been a link between the *NPT* epilogue and the *WBP*, but if it were ever written, it has been lost.

213 Hinckley, Henry B. 'The Debate on Marriage in the *Canterbury Tales*.' *PMLA* 32(1917), 292–305.

While the *WBP* and *MerT* alone focus on marriage, they do not 'take issue' (p 301) with each other nor form part of the Marriage Group. The reference to the Wife in the *MerT* (IV.1685–7) is 'the most striking lapse of dramatic propriety' (p 301) in the *CT*. The theme that unifies the *WBP* with *WBT* is Alisoun's search for a sixth husband. The *ClT* 'was not intended to answer the Wife of Bath' (p 295). If it were, the Clerk's acknowledgement that women possess more humility and loyalty than do men (IV.932–8) should contain an ironic reference to the Wife. The only 'co-ordination' (p 299) between these tales is IV.1170–2. These lines and the *Envoy* are 'later additions' (p 299) to the *ClT*, intended to satirize the *ClT*, not the Wife. The *FranT* was not designed to end the marriage debate, because it precedes the *SNT* which recounts 'the unconsummated marriage of St. Cecelia' (p 303). Fragment V should be placed before III, because Dorigen's condition would motivate the Wife to speak, and both the Franklin and the Wife share similar views of *gentillesse* (p 294).

214 Brown, Carleton. 'The Evolution of the Canterbury "Marriage Group."' *PMLA* 48(1933), 1041–59.

Chaucer revised the ending of the *ClT* in order to connect this tale more closely to both the *WBT* and the *MerT*. The *MerP* was composed later than the *MerT*. The *MerT*, which closely parallels portions of *Mir*, originally preceded *WBT* (p 1045). That the portions of the *WBP* that parallel *Mir* fall after III.198 suggests Chaucer expanded *WBP* after he decided to develop a tale other than what is now the *ShT* for Alisoun.

215 Lyons, Clifford P. 'The Marriage Debate in the *Canterbury Tales*.' *ELH* 2(1935), 252–62.

'It is possible to admit that certain tales present a schematized pattern of ideas without interpreting them as long speeches in a battle of ideas and personalities' (p 254). While the links between the tales usually provide the reader with an understanding of the relationship between tale, teller, and fellow pilgrims, the *WBP* is not connected to a previous tale. 'In the link between the Prologue and Tale there is no mention whatsoever of marriage or of the Wife's ideas' (p 256), and a debate doesn't occur in the subsequent links. The Clerk's mentioning the Wife in his tale is a 'realistic reference' (p 259), not an indication of debate. The negative viewpoints on marriage and women found in the *MerT*'s *Endlink* are 'sufficiently common sentiments' (p 260) and are not a direct attack on the Wife.

216 Mariella, Sister. 'The *Parson's Tale* and the Marriage Group.' *MLN* 53(1938), 251–6.

A portion of the *ParsT* summarizes the Marriage Group debate. Because the attitude of this passage concerning the creation of Eve was typical of medieval religious literature, it is uncertain whether the passage is Chaucerian or a translation from a source.

217 Dempster, Germaine. 'A Chapter on the Manuscript History of the *Canterbury Tales*: The Ancestor of Group *d*; the Origin of Its Texts, Tale-order, and Spurious Links.' *PMLA* 63(1948), 456–84.

Two-thirds of the prototype d ms came from the broken prototype c ms and the remaining third consisted of new copies of a text that resembled the prototype c ms. The Hengwrt ms or one of its derivatives contributed the Squire/Franklin and Merchant/Squire links. The editor of the prototype d ms constructed a sequence of the tales in which the *WBP* followed the *MerT* and the *FranT* followed the *ClT* (p 475).

218 Lawrence, William Witherle. *Chaucer and the Canterbury Tales*. New York: Columbia University Press, 1950; rpt 1964.

Despite Kittredge's opinions (**210**), Alisoun's performance should follow the *NPT* (p 125), a tale that Chaucer has adjusted so that it might fit into the Marriage Group (p 136). Alisoun is not attacking the Clerk in the *WBP* but is trying to insult the Nun's Priest (p 138).

219 Albrecht, W.P. 'The Sermon on Gentilesse.' *CE* 12(1951), 459.

See **264**.

220 Dempster, Germaine. 'A Period in the Development of the *Canterbury Tales* Marriage Group and of Blocks B² and C.' *PMLA* 68(1953), 1142–59.

Once Chaucer developed the Marriage Group, he decided to make ordering and linking arrangements with previously written tales so that the Marriage Group would be properly introduced and supported. *Mel* and the *NPT* would now function as precursors of the Marriage Group and the *ClT* was placed into the debate itself.

221 Makarewicz, Sister Mary Raynelda. *The Patristic Influence on Chaucer*. Washington, D.C.: Catholic University of America Press, 1953.

See **300, 509,** and **1119**.

222 Savage, James E. 'The Marriage Problems in the *Canterbury Tales*.' *MLQ* 9(1955), 27–9.

The hag desires to be both lover and wife to the knight, entities that are never fused in the courtly love tradition. A masculine version of this desire is found in Averagus who wants to be both husband and lover to Dorigen.

223 Owen, Charles A., Jr. 'The Development of the *Canterbury Tales*.' *JEGP* 57(1958), 449–76.

See **527**.

224 Howard, Donald R. 'The Conclusion of the Marriage Group: Chaucer and the Human Condition.' *MP* 57(1960), 223–32.

The real issue of Chaucer's Marriage Group is begun in the *WBP* when Alisoun challenges the higher value the Church places on virginity, the medieval state of perfection, than on marriage (p 224). While the Clerk examines attaining Christian perfection in marriage and while the Merchant has a slight incorporation of this issue in his tale, the concept of perfection loses its place of importance as a topic to that of sovereignty. The Franklin does not conclude the debate. Whether the *SNT* or the *PhyT* was meant to follow the *FranT*, the *FranT* was to have been followed by a story dealing with virginity. In the *SNT*, there is chastity in marriage. Cecile and Valerian present a union which incorporates the Christian perfection that is absent in the marriage of Dorigen and Arveragus.

225 Fisher, John H. *John Gower: Moral Philosopher and Friend of Chaucer*. New York: New York University Press, 1964.

Within the Marriage Group, mastery is the negative power and *gentillesse* is the positive thread. Gower was first to combine the theme of *gentillesse* in marriage in *Flor* and *Mirour de l'omme*. See **145**.

226 Hodge, James L. 'The Marriage Group: Precarious Equilibrium.' *ES* 46(1965), 289–300.

The *WBT* and the *ClT* present an unbelievably chivalric husband and an unrealistically submissive wife. The conflicting views of the *WBT* and *ClT* call for a more realistic and less self-serving perspective of marriage (p 290). The Merchant's experiences have him tell a tale devoid of happiness in marriage and debasing of courtly love. While his courtesy will not allow him to rebuke the Merchant, the Squire tells an idealistic tale that exalts the chivalric code (p 292). The *ShT* does attack the Merchant through the merchant of St. Denis. While it is meant to resolve the marriage debate, the *FranT*, placed between the *MerT* and the Host's unfavorable comments, leaves both courtly love and marriage in an uncomfortable position (pp 298–9).

227 Baugh, Albert Croll, ed. *A Literary History of England*. New York: Appleton-Century-Crofts, 1967. Book 1 of 4. Pp 3–312.

While the Wife of Bath begins the discussion on marriage, counter attack of her opinions is stalled by the argument between the Friar and the Summoner. The *ClT* reverses the Wife's vision of female sovereignty. The *MerT* examines marriage between youth and age. Neither the *SqT* nor the *FranT* has marriage as a main theme, yet the *FranT* does depict a happy marriage. The *FranT* is thus seen as the end of the debate, and it is assumed that the Franklin's view of marriage is also Chaucer's.

228 Grose, M.W. *Chaucer: Literature in Perspective*. London: Evans Bros.; New York: Arco, 1967.

Before the Clerk can respond to Alisoun's introduction of the marriage debate, the Friar and the Summoner have a realistic conflict. The Clerk's concluding lines, concerning the way women like Alisoun make their husbands miserable, prompt the Merchant to discuss his own tribulations (p 137). The Franklin provides a final example of domestic bliss. See **587**.

229 Schaefer, Willene. 'The Evolution of a Concept: *Gentilesse* in Chaucer's Poetry.' *DA* 27(1967), 3850.

The Marriage Group should be renamed the *Gentillesse* Group, because *gentillesse* is established by the *WBT*, *SqT*, and *FranT*. The *ClT* elaborates upon Alisoun's definition of the concept and the *MerT* attempts to negate it. See **270**.

230 Silvia, D.S. 'Geoffrey Chaucer on the Subject of Men, Women, Marriage, and *Gentilesse*.' *RLV* 33(1967), 227–36.

The Marriage Group is not a debate on which gender should have mastery but an analysis of human relationships and *gentillesse*. The

FranT is the only Marriage Group tale that establishes a happy marriage without either partner yielding to the other (p 230). This is because *gentillesse* replaces the need for mastery.

231 Hornstein, Lillian Herlands. 'The Wyf of Bathe and the Merchant: From Sex to "Secte."' *ChauR* 3(1968), 65–7.

The Clerk's reference to the Wife of Bath's *secte* (V.1171) may be interpreted in a legal sense. In medieval law, a plaintiff needed the support of *secta*, people who would verify the plaintiff's charge (p 66). The Clerk supports Alisoun's testimony of marital woe. Alisoun and the Merchant are of the same *secte*, in that both relate the trials of marriage.

232 Lawlor, John. *Chaucer.* London: Hutchinson University Library, 1968.

The debate of the Marriage Group is a 'holiday affair' (p 142) that revolves around the dichotomy of authority and experience. See **330**.

233 Murtaugh, Daniel M. 'Women and Geoffrey Chaucer.' *ELH* 38(1971), 473–92.

Chaucer connects the antifeminist tradition with courtly love in the Marriage Group (pp 473–4). He was perhaps influenced by Jean de Meun's association of the politics of authority, the economics of property, and the concept of mastery in love in *RR*. The tales of the Marriage Group work to dispel the fantastical views of women and create an ideal of marriage between peers. See **1199**.

234 Cherniss, Michael D. 'The *Clerk's Tale* and *Envoy*, the Wife of Bath's Purgatory, and the *Merchant's Tale*.' *ChauR* 6(1972), 235–54.

The Clerk's reference to the Wife of Bath in his *Envoy* revives the theme of marriage which gets lost in the spiritual moral of the *ClT* (p 242). The subtle irony of the *Envoy* suggests that women who dislike Griselda can model themselves after Walter and be instruments of God's will. Such wives, like Alisoun, put their husbands through purgatory. In the *MerT*, January anticipates the paradise of marital bliss, which for May is a hell (p 250). While Justinus warns that marriage is purgatory, it is not until the garden scene that January sees what a false paradise his marriage is.

235 Martin, William Eugene. 'Concepts of Sovereignty in the *Canterbury Tales*.' *DAI* 32(1972), 5236.

The Marriage Group debates several conceptions of sovereignty and reveals how these ideals pertain to individual relationships and society.

236 Kaske, R.E. 'Chaucer's Marriage Group.' In *Chaucer the Love Poet*.

Ed. Jerome Mitchell and William Provost. Athens: University of Georgia Press, 1973. Pp 45–65.

The parallels and contrasts between the tales of the Marriage Group suggest that the pilgrims are consciously taking part in a debate (p 46). The Marriage Group focuses on the issues of sovereignty and sex in marriage. These issues are related, for Christianity advocates the husband's sovereignty provided he does not over-value sex. When this is the case, the wife gains sovereignty through sexuality. Alisoun advocates the elevation of sex, and subsequently female sovereignty, as a marriage value (p 51). The *ClT* supports the Christian view (p 54). Because January is consumed with lust, he is subject to May (p 56). The *FranT* tries to fuse the best qualities of Christian marriage and courtly love in an imperfect world (pp 59–65).

237 Olson, Clair C. 'The Interludes of the Marriage Group in the *Canterbury Tales*.' In *Chaucer and Middle English Studies in Honour of Rossell Hope Robbins*. Ed. Beryl Rowland. London: Allen & Unwin, 1974. Pp 164–72.

The two interludes of the Marriage Group, the *FrT/SumT* and the *MerT/SqT*, are purposefully placed. The *FrT* and *SumT* provide comic relief and reflect Alisoun's coarse humor. The *SumT* is the emotional climax of this interlude (p 167). In the second interlude the cynicism of the *MerT* is countered by the fantastical *SqT*. The *SqT* eases what would have been a sharp contrast between the *MerT* and the idealistic *FranT*.

238 Hieatt, A. Kent *Chaucer, Spenser, Milton: Mythopoeic Continuities and Transformations*. Montreal: McGill-Queen's University Press, 1975.

Certain Thynne editions of the *CT* place the *FranT* before the *WBT*, *FrT*, *SumT*, and *ClT*, thereby eliminating the culmination of the Marriage Group (pp 24–5). The *FranT* and *WBT* are romances with 'supernatural overtones' (p 60). Both the *WBP* and *MerT* ironically explore stereotypical relationships and move from male to female sovereignty. The harmony of the *FranT* criticizes both the *WBP* and *WBT* and underscores the Boethian concept of love found in the *KnT* (p 70).

239 Szittya, Penn R. 'The Green Yeoman as Loathly Lady: The Friar's Parody of the *Wife of Bath's Tale*.' *PMLA* 90(1975), 386–94.

The *FrT* and the *SumT* are part of the Marriage Group because both deal with authority and sovereignty, albeit in a different context than the marriage-oriented tales. See **1238**.

240 Leyerle, John. 'Thematic Interlace in the *Canterbury Tales.' E&S* 29(1976), 107–21.

Bailly's plan that the pilgrims' tales should be separate units does not 'account for the complicated interconnectedness of the Marriage Group' (p 108). Marriage and sexuality thematically link over one half of all the tales. See **695**.

241 Berggren, Ruth. 'Who *Really* Is the Advocate of Equality in the Marriage Group?' *MSE* 6(1977), 25–36.

The Clerk's mistaking Alisoun's desire for equality for an advocacy of female dominance leads him to tell a story of male dominance which counters her theme of *gentillesse* (pp 29–30). The Merchant attacks Alisoun by denouncing her theme of courtly love (p 31). The *FranT* serves to show how destructive a woman can be if she is allowed independence in marriage. See **706** and **1250**.

242 Glasser, Marc D. 'Marriage and the *Second Nun's Tale.' TSL* 23(1978), 1–14.

The marriage in the *SNT* provides an opposite view of Alisoun's and the Merchant's opinions on marriage (p 7). It moves away from the St. Venus-dominated marriages of the Marriage Group (p 11).

243 Richmond, Velma Bourgeois. 'Pacience in Adversitee: Chaucer's Presentation of Marriage.' *Viator* 10(1979), 323–54.

Critical commentary that views the Marriage Group 'as a debate about sexual dominance' emanates from early twentieth-century attitudes concerning Alisoun's impropriety (p 324). When one considers Chaucer's own marriage, a union that was predominantly a happy one despite the questionable paternity of Thomas Chaucer and the Cecily Champain incident, a theme of *pacience in adversitee* seems applicable to the Marriage Group. These tales portray the difficulties of marriage and reveal that tolerance is a key to attaining domestic bliss (p 353).

244 Fichte, Joerg O. *Chaucer's 'Art Poetical': A Study in Chaucerian Poetics.* Tübingen: Gunter Narr Verlag, 1980.

Several of the *CT* offer different views of love in marriage. The *WBP* and *WBT* incorporate female sovereignty into this view, while the *ClT* focuses on submission. *Mel* adds prudence; the *NPT* adds imprudence. The *FranT* blends truth with love.

245 Johnston, Mark E. 'The Resonance of the *Second Nun's Tale.'* Mid-Hudson Language Studies 3(1980), 26–38.

Chaucer uses the *SNT* to explore further the issues raised by the

Marriage Group. It serves to 'temper' (p 31) the *WBT* and Alisoun's issues of sovereignty.

246 Ginsberg, Warren. 'The Lineaments of Desire: Wish-Fulfillment in Chaucer's Marriage Group.' *Criticism* 25(1983), 197–210.

Alisoun's dreams of her youth have her living 'within the margins of romance literature' (p 200). Reflective of her trade, Alisoun both weaves and interprets her dreams. Alisoun shares traits with the Parson, the Knight, and Lady Fortune. The Franklin is Alisoun's 'male counterpart' (p 204), for he too desires youth. The *FranT* reflects its teller's belief that 'more is better' (p 206). The Clerk also tells a tale of wish-fulfillment.

247 Hagen, Susan K. 'The Wife of Bath, the Lion, and the Critics.' In *The Worlds of Medieval Women: Creativity, Influence, Imagination*. Ed. Constance H. Berman, Charles W. Connell, and Judith Rice-Rothschild. Morgantown: West Virginia University Press, 1985. Pp 130–8.

Alisoun's lion-painting complaint applies to Kittredge and his Marriage Group theory. Alisoun's performance concerns 'female prerogative' (p 132), not marriage. She is asserting her experience and her right to judge between marriage and virginity in the *WBP*, not focusing on marital woe. The *WBT* also deals with a woman's right to make choices outside of man's governance (p 135). The Clerk's reference to Alisoun is critical of what she says about clerks, and the *ClT* is about humanity's relationship to God (p 131).

248 Payne, Robert O. *Geoffrey Chaucer*, 2nd ed. Boston: Twayne, 1986.

The Marriage Group is the most famous and most debated of Chaucer's 'groupings' in the *CT* (pp 117–8). Fragment ordering and theme pose difficulties in defining this group. Alisoun does not seem to be reacting to any other pilgrim or tale in her performance. The Wife's age softens her argument and makes it more acceptable than it would be had it come from a character like Alison of the *MilT*.

249 Peck, Russell A. 'Social Conscience and the Poets.' In *Social Unrest in the Late Middle Ages: Papers of the Fifteenth Annual Conference of the Center for Medieval and Early Renaissance Studies*. Ed. Francis X. Newman. Binghamton: Center for Medieval and Early Renaissance Studies, 1986. Pp 113–48.

Chaucer's Marriage Group could 'have been viewed ... as a churchmen group' (p 139) because Alisoun is surrounded by the ecclesiastical Pardoner, Friar, Summoner, and Clerk. Alisoun resembles Lady Meed.

250 Rogers, William E. *Upon the Ways: The Structure of the Canterbury*

Tales. English Literary Studies Monograph Series, vol. 36. Victoria, B.C.: University of Victoria, 1986.

Fragments III–V of *CT* are not a Marriage Group. They are thematically linked by 'the value and significance of earthly experience' (p 52). The *WBT* is a response to the *MLT*. The hag's discourse on poverty rebukes the Man of Law's views of wealth. Alisoun calls upon temporal authority to deal with rape, while the Man of Law turns to divine intervention.

251 Haahr, Joan G. 'Chaucer's "Marriage Group" Revisited: The Wife of Bath and Merchant in Debate.' *Acta* 14(1987), 105–20.

Alisoun and the Merchant have social status, class and marital woe in common. They both value sex, and their focusing on sexuality in marriage reveals their contempt for clerical authority. While Alisoun derives her knowledge from experience, the Merchant relies on theory (p 112). Both Alisoun and the Merchant recount harsh retribution in their performances.

252 Stone, Brian. *Chaucer.* Penguin Critical Studies. London: Penguin Books, 1987.

While Kittredge's Marriage Group includes *FrT* and *SumT*, tales that do not focus on marriage, the concept of the Marriage Group underscores the importance of marriage as a theme to Chaucer. See **890** and **1366**.

253 James, Max H. 'Chaucer's "Contemporary" Search for *Steadfastnesse* and *Trouthe.' Christian Scholar's Review* 18(1988), 118–35.

Chaucer's search for truth unifies the Marriage Group. In the *WBP* and *WBT*, Alisoun advocates freedom of choice for a good marriage (pp 122–5). The marriage in the *ClT* represents the union of humankind with Christ, and Griselda embodies the true qualities of Christians and the Church (pp 125–9). While the *MerT* is fraught with deceit, it serves to illustrate how humans become blind to the truth (pp 129–31). The *FranT* exemplifies the importance of faithfulness to marriage and to one's own integrity (pp 131–5).

254 Zong-qi, Cai. 'Fragments I–II and III–V in the Canterbury Tales: A Re-Examination of the Idea of the "Marriage Group."' *Comitatus* 19(1988), 80–98.

Chaucer initiates a discussion of marital woe in Fragments I–II of the *CT*. He explores marriages involved with abstract ideals, *KnT* and *MLT*, and marriages concerned with sex and money, *MilT* and *RvT*. The juxtaposition of spiritual and physical union is continued in Fragments

III–V. The *WBT* is in contrast with the *ClT*. The *MerT* parodies both issues, while the *FranT* provides a resolution to the debate in its presentation of a marriage having both lofty ideals and physical love.

255 Stephens, John, and Marcella Ryan. 'Metafictional Strategies and the Theme of Sexual Power in the *Wife of Bath's* and *Franklin's Tales*.' *NMS* 33(1989), 56–75.

Chaucer presents a 'bleak view' (p 73) of gender relationships in his Marriage Group. 'Woman is continually re-created in these tales through the perceptions of her expressed through fictional narrators' (p 61). *WBT* contains a thematic interchange between speech acts and sexual acts and also between sexual power and verbal power.

256 Wicher, Andrzej. 'A Discussion of the Archetype of the Supernatural Husband and the Supernatural Wife as It Appears in Some of Geoffrey Chaucer's *Canterbury Tales*.' *REAL: Yearbook of Research in English and American Literature*. Ed. Herbert Grabes, Hans-Jürgen Diller, and Hartwig Isernhagen. 7(1990), 19–60.

The unity of the Marriage Group is based on the foundation that each of the tales has in traditional stories of supernatural partners (p 22). The *MLT* is related to *The Maiden Without Hands* folktales that are in turn linked to *The Man on a Quest for His Lost Wife* stories, which deal with a missing supernatural wife (p 23). The *ClT* may be connected with *The Search for the Lost Husband* tale type (p 30). The *WBT* is also related to *The Man on a Quest for His Lost Wife* stories, which are known as the *Swan Maiden* tales (p 37). The *FranT* 'appears to be the result of a curious truncation of a Cupid and Psyche tale' (p 45). All the Marriage Group tales bear a relation to the Cupid and Psyche tradition.

৪ *Gentillesse*

257 Ward, Adolphus W. *Geoffrey Chaucer*. English Men of Letters. Ed.
John Morley. New York: Harper and Brothers, 1901.
After finding similar sentiments in Boethius, Guillaume de Lorris, and
Dante, Chaucer constructed his finest discourse on the true essence of
gentillesse in the *WBT*. See **425**.

258 Schofield, William Henry. *Chivalry in English Literature: Chaucer,
Malory, Spenser and Shakespeare*. Cambridge: Harvard University
Press, 1912; rpt Port Washington, New York: Kennikat Press, 1964.
Chaucer sets forth his views on *gentillesse* through the voice of the
hag in *WBT*. Boethius, Dante, and Seneca are the intellectual authorities
behind her discourse (pp 68–70). The *ParsT* and the ballad *Gentillesse*
also express Chaucer's feelings on this subject.

259 Jefferson, Bernard L. *Chaucer and the Consolation of Philosophy
of Boethius*. New York: Gordian Press, 1917; rpt 1968; rpt New York:
Haskell House, 1965.
The origin of enlightened beliefs concerning *gentillesse* is the *Consol*.
In the *WBT*, Chaucer both quotes Boethius and names him as an authority
on the subject (p 94). The hag echoes Boethius' main points regarding
gentillesse: that it is a virtue, that it is not inherited, and that its origin is
divine. Since Dante's *Conv* also contains these premises, it is moot to
argue whose influence was stronger on Chaucer (p 100).

260 Iijima, Ikuzo. *Langland and Chaucer: A Study of the Two Types of
Genius in English Poetry*. Boston: Four Seas, 1925.
The sermon on *gentillesse* is a praiseworthy, democratic piece. See
457.

261 Vogt, G.M. 'Gleanings for the History of a Sentiment: Generositas Virtus,
Non Sanguis.' *JEGP* 24(1925), 102–24.

Root and Wells are wrong in thinking that Chaucer's view of the origins of *gentillesse* in *WBT* is uncharacteristically democratic for his time. Copious citations treat this theme, such as Seneca, Juvenal, Boethius, Wace, Andreas Capellanus, Guiliemus Peraldus, Gaydon, Jean de Meun, and Frère Lorens, among others. The medieval mindset, however, accepted distinct differences between the classes. While it was argued that all descended from Adam, the *Cursor Mundi* noted that three distinct classes were formed through Noah's sons: the free from Shem, knights from Japhet, and thralls from Ham (p 110). Many other sources comment upon the inequality of Adam and Eve's children.

262   Kenyon, John S. '*Wife of Bath's Tale* 1159–62.' *MLN* 54(1939), 133–7

The text of the *WBT* should be emended to solve what appears to be a contradiction in Chaucer's usage of the term *gentillesse*. When speaking of *Thy gentillesse* (III.1162), the hag is referring to the false gentillesse of the knight, yet the line reads, *Thy gentillesse cometh fro God allone*. This statement is not in keeping with the hag's speech on the nature of true gentillesse. If III.1159's *For gentillesse* and 1162's *Thy gentillesse* are switched, the contradiction is eradicated. The two phrases may have initially been interchanged as a result of scribal error; however, there is no ms evidence on which to base this theory.

263   Dempster, Germaine. "'Thy Gentillesse" in *Wife of Bath's Tale* D 1159–62.' *MLN* 57(1942), 173–6.

The usage of second-person pronouns in III.1159–62 is in conflict with the general nature of lines III.1146–58. If *thou* is translated as *any one*, as in parallel interpretations of Boethius' *Consol*, the hag's lines are not a direct attack upon the knight but an address to all.

264   Albrecht, W.P. 'The Sermon on Gentilesse.' *CE* 12(1951), 459.

'The desirability of gentilesse in love and marriage is a theme linking' (p 459) the Marriage Group. The hag's assertion that *gentillesse cometh fro God allone* (III.1162) is validated by Griselda, Canacee, Dorigen, and Arveragus. It is the absence of this virtue that 'perverts the marriage of January and May' (p 459). The pillow lecture also makes the Wife a 'victim of dramatic irony,' because the hag's 'partial relinquishment of mastery' (p 459) undermines Alisoun's concept of marriage.

265   Coghill, Nevill. *Geoffrey Chaucer*. London: Longmans, Green, and Company, 1956 [cited]. Rpt in *British Writers and Their Works*. Vol 1.

Ed. Bonamy Dobreé and J.W. Robinson. Lincoln: University of Nebraska Press, 1963. Pp 7–68.

In the hag's discourse on *gentillesse* Chaucer focuses on the concept of this virtue initiating with Christ (pp 25–6). See **518**.

266 Gaylord, Alan Theodore. 'Seed of Felicity: A Study of the Concepts of Nobility and *Gentilesse* in the Middle Ages and in the Works of Chaucer.' *DA* 20(1959), 3741.

Chaucer's extensive writing on the concept of *gentillesse* outside of the *WBT* and his ballad is an expression of his concern over society's distancing itself from the true spirit of this term.

267 Baker, Donald C. 'Chaucer's Clerk and the Wife of Bath on the Subject of *Gentilesse*.' *SP* 59(1962), 631–40.

Alisoun views the two themes of her tale, woman's sovereignty and the divine origin of *gentilesse*, as one because the knight chooses to accept the tenets of her pillow lecture and yields authority to her. The theme of *gentillesse* is also found in the *ClT*. Walter disagrees with his advisors and prefers his bride to possess natural, not hereditary, *gentillesse* (p 634). Griselda's character serves to prove the theory that nobility is God-given and will manifest itself. While Alisoun views *gentillesse* 'as license to rule,' the Clerk sees it in a broader light, finding it to be 'the mark of the true servant, the servant of God' (p 638). The *ClT* serves as a commentary on the *WBT*. 'It is an amused tale of wifely patience in answer to her strident demands for womanly equality and ... subtle instruction as to the nature of true *gentilesse*' (pp 638–9).

268 Fisher, John H. *John Gower: Moral Philosopher and Friend of Chaucer*. New York: New York University Press, 1964.

See **145** and **225**.

269 Williams, George. *A New View of Chaucer*. Durham: Duke University Press, 1965.

The sermon on *gentillesse* manifests Chaucer's concern for women abandoned by their men. III.1154 is an admonition to John of Gaunt against his leaving Katharine Swynford (pp 158–9).

270 Schaefer, Willene. 'The Evolution of a Concept: *Gentilesse* in Chaucer's Poetry.' *DA* 27(1967), 3850.

While Chaucer's sources for his *gentillesse* sermon have been determined, there is no widely accepted theory of how this word operates in his work. He seems to be establishing a private standard for the secular world in his humanistic rendering of this concept. See **229**.

271 Silvia, D.S. 'Geoffrey Chaucer on the Subject of Men, Women, Marriage, and *Gentilesse.*' *RLV* 33(1967), 227–36.
See **230**.

272 Coghill, Nevill. *Chaucer's Idea of What Is Noble.* Oxford: Oxford University Press, 1971.
Chaucer uses the pillow lecture to go beyond his predecessors' discourse on *gentillesse* (p 15). His ultimate vision is that of Christ, the source of this virtue.

273 Thomas, Mary Edith. *Medieval Skepticism and Chaucer.* New York: Cooper Square, 1971.
Chaucer's preoccupation with the true nature of *gentillesse* seems surprising when one considers his aristocratic affiliations. The *WBT* contains evidence of Chaucer's familiarity with similar views on *gentillesse* in Dante, Seneca, Jean de Meun, and Boethius (p 90). Chaucer's incorporating this theme into his ballad *Gentillesse* and his translating Boethius' *Consol* also indicate the depth of his interest in this area. See **633** and **1203**.

274 Fichte, Joerg O. '*The Clerk's Tale*: An Obituary to *Gentilesse.*' In *New Views on Chaucer: Essays in Generative Criticism.* Ed. William C. Johnson and Loren C. Grubner. Denver: Society for New Language Study, 1973. Pp 9–16.
In the *ClT*, Chaucer attempts to reveal 'that the concept of absolute *gentillesse* is inoperable in a capricious and volatile society, represented in this tale by Walter and his people' (p 9). Chaucer's conception of *gentillesse* may be realized by examining his translation of Boethius' *Consol*, the *WBT*, and *Gentillesse*. In Boethius' work, true *gentillesse* is associated with behavior, not birth. This concept is echoed in the hag's pillow-lecture in *WBT* which establishes God as the origin of *gentillesse*. Chaucer's ballad notes the specific virtues of this God of *gentillesse*. Chaucer's usage of the word *gentillesse*, however, is not restricted to the moral concepts mentioned previously. His 91 mentionings of the word connote courtesy, good conduct, noble birth, polite reference, and religious qualities. At times the word refers to ignoble characters like May (p 11). The term *gentil* is also linked to such base characters as the Pardoner and Summoner. Since such a variety of definitions applies to this word, 'there are three levels on which Chaucer conducts his test to find an operable definition of actual *gentilesse*' (p 12). While popular consensus classifies the term with noble birth, the more

enlightened will recognize the Boethian philosophy. On the third level, Griselda's character is a close personification of this quality. The only virtue she lacks is pity; she shows no emotion for her children when Walter removes them. By making Griselda a more sympathetic character through his commentary and dramatization of her condition, Chaucer takes away from the exemplary style of the tale. Chaucer's comments in IV.621–3 indict not only Walter's behavior but also Griselda's excessive, unreasonable submission (p 14). Since Griselda is not a true example of *gentillesse*, the *ClT* is not a 'positive answer to the *WBT*' (p 14). The hag embodies *gentillesse* more perfectly than Griselda, for she pities the knight errant.

275 Schaefer, Ursula. *Hofisch-ritterliche Dictung und sozial-historische Realität: Literatursoziologische Studien zum Verhältnis von Adelsstruktur, Ritterideal und Dichtung bei Geoffrey Chaucer.* Neue Studien zur Anglistik und Amerikanistik 10. Frankfurt: Peter Lang, 1977. [In German.]

Alisoun's social position adds to the intensity of the *gentillesse* sermon and its commentary on birth and nobility (p 312). The pillow lecture stems from Alisoun's observations of her world.

276 Gray, Douglas. 'Chaucer and Gentilesse.' In *One Hundred Years of English Studies in Dutch Universities: Seventeen Papers Read at the Centenary Conference, Groningen, 15–16 Jan. 1986.* Ed. G.H.V. Bunt, E.S. Kooper, J.L. Mackenzie, and D.R.M. Wilkinson. Amsterdam: Rodopi, 1987. Pp 1–27.

The pillow lecture is the 'moral climax' (p 18) of *WBT*. The *gentillesse* sermon is an elaborate and intelligent persuasion delivered with rational conviction.

277 Allen, Valerie. 'The "Firste Stok" in Chaucer's *Gentilesse*: Barking up the Right Tree.' *RES* (n.s.) 40(1989), 531–7.

Chaucer's ballad *Gentillesse*, Scogan's *Moral Balade*, and the *WBT* all cite God as the source of *gentillesse* (pp 532–3).

278 Saul, Nigel. 'Chaucer and Gentility.' In *Chaucer's England: Literature in Historical Context.* Ed. Barbara Hanawalt. Minneapolis: University of Minnesota Press, 1992. Pp 41–5.

The Chaucerian ballad *Gentillesse* provides a strong 'subtheme' (p 43) for many of the Canterbury stories, especially the *WBT*. Chaucer's reworking of the loathly lady tale establishes the pillow lecture as his own view of gentility. Alisoun's view of gentility diverges from that of the Franklin.

279 Hudson, Harriet E. 'Construction of Class, Family, and Gender in Some Middle English Popular Romances.' In *Class and Gender in Early English Literature: Intersections*. Ed. Britton J. Harwood and Gillian Overing. Bloomington: Indiana University Press, 1994. Pp 76–94.

The medieval nobility's separation from gentility 'set the stage for the *gentilesse* debate' (p 81) of the *WBT*.

ℰℴ The Wife of Bath in the General Prologue

280 Koch, John. 'Chauceriana.' *Anglia* 6(1883), 104–6. [In German.]
In his edition of the *CT*, William Morris is unaware that the work *Jobi Ludolfi alias Leutholf dicti ad suam Historiam Aethiopicam Commentarius* can provide further illumination of I.459–60.

281 Hinckley, Henry Barrett. *Notes on Chaucer: A Commentary on the Prolog and Six Canterbury Tales.* Northhampton: Nonotuck Press, 1907; rpt New York: Haskell House, 1964, 1970.
Provides commentary on I.448, 453, 454, 457, 462, 463, 463–6, 467, 468, 472–3, 475, and 476 (pp 37–9). See **1072**.

282 Tupper, Frederick. 'Saint Venus and the Canterbury Pilgrims.' *Nation* 97(1913), 354–6.
In Bartholomew the Englishman's thirteenth-century *De Proprietatibus Rerum*, Venus is the star of pilgrimages. That Alisoun is marked by the print of Venus and is Venusian in character makes her a likely pilgrim.

283 Barnouw, A.J. 'The Prente of Seinte Venus Seel.' *Nation* 103(1916), 540.
Primitive superstition and ritualistic practices support the concept of the gap between teeth allowing magic into or the soul out of the body. Women like Alisoun, who have gap-teeth, were believed to be experts in the field of love. Hence Alisoun's being *gap-tothed* is the print of St. Venus.

284 Tatlock, John S.P. 'Puns in Chaucer.' In *Flügel Memorial Volume*. Leland Stanford Junior University Publications, University Series.

Stanford: Stanford University Press, 1916. Pp 228–32.

Chaucer employs puns to suggest a double meaning. For example, I.460–1 is an open-ended statement on whether or not Alisoun had lovers in her youth (p 229).

285 Piper, Edwin Ford. 'The Miniatures of the Ellesmere Chaucer.' *PQ* 3(1924), 241–56.

The portraits of the pilgrims in the Ellesmere ms capture the realistic images of Chaucer's *GP*. The text, however, takes predominance over the figures. The Wife of Bath is depicted as an expert horseperson. She is a bold, gilt-bedecked figure. Minute details include metal tips on her whip, a jointed bit in her horse's mouth, a double-rigged saddle, and five-pointed spurs (p 245).

286 Jusserand, J.J. *English Wayfaring Life in the Middle Ages.* Trans. Lucy Toulmin Smith. New York: Putman, 1925; rpt London: Ernest Brown, 1950.

In the fourteenth century the majority of female travelers rode astride, much like the depiction of Alisoun in the Ellesmere illumination (p 103).

287 Manly, John Matthews. *Some New Light on Chaucer: Lectures Delivered at the Lowell Institute.* New York: Holt, 1926; rpt 1951; rpt Gloucester, MA: Peter Smith, 1959.

While Curry (**454, 1085**) believes Alisoun's character was constructed through concepts of medieval science, it is more likely that she was developed from a real person. Many women were occupied as weavers in Chaucer's time. Chaucer would most likely have visited the Bath area as a result of his position as deputy forester (p 232). The Bath Records Society indicates not only that *Alice* and *Alisoun* were extremely popular names but also that several of these women had multiple marriages in their lifetimes.

288 Quiller-Couch, Sir Arthur T. *The Age of Chaucer.* London: J.M. Dent and Sons, Ltd., 1926; rpt New York: AMS Press, 1972.

A modern English rendition of the *GP* account of the Wife is accompanied by the illustration of her from the Ellesmere ms.

289 Tupper, Frederick. *Types of Society in Medieval Literature.* New York: Holt, 1926; rpt New York: Biblo and Tannen, 1968.

The book's third section, 'The Eternal Womanly' (pp 107–59), deals with the relationships between the sexes. The medieval patriarchy viewed a wife's disobedience, a sin closely connected to that of pride, as a violation of a sacrament. The Wife's enormous head-covering is symbolically associated with the sin of pride. The chapter lists many examples and excerpts from antifeminist literature, many of which appear in both Jankyn's book and in romance literature of the courtly love tradition. The Wife, 'the vulgarian, tells a courtly tale and gives the largest expression to views of gentleness' (p 158). While Chaunticleer functions as the 'true precursor' (p 157) of the Wife, the characters Virginia and Cecilia serve as counterpoints to Alisoun's opinions.

290 Hammond, Eleanor Prescott, ed. *English Verse between Chaucer and Surrey.* Durham: Duke University Press; London: Cambridge University Press, 1927; rpt New York: Octagon, 1965, 1969.

Hoccleve refers to the Wife of Bath in his *Dialogue with a Friend* (p 72).

291 Erskine, John. *The Delight of Great Books.* Indianapolis: Bobbs-Merrill, 1928. Pp 33–49.

Alisoun's uninhibited character may not be virtuous, but she is admirable for her adherence to the truth and to her nature (pp 40–1).

292 Cazamian, Louis. *The Development of English Humor.* New York: Macmillan, 1930; rpt Durham: Duke University Press, 1951, 1952.

Chaucer's humorous treatment of women is less vicious than that of Jean de Meun. The Wife is fundamentally cruel; she is a character of 'magnificent impudence,' 'high color,' and 'loud prattling' (p 117).

293 Camden, Carroll, Jr. 'Chauceriana.' *MLN* 47(1932), 360–2.

Both Manly (**19**) and Liddell (**7**) have glossed *worthy* as a positive reference to an individual; however, a more suitable definition of the word would be that of a comment on someone's proficiency at a certain, not necessarily positive, thing. Chaucer's noting the Wife as being worthy might signify her ability to be a stereotypical woman. See **465**.

294 Piper, Edwin Ford. *Canterbury Pilgrims.* Whirling World Series. Iowa City: Clio Press, 1935.

Two poems about Alisoun, one based on her *GP* portrait and the other on the *WBP*, reveal her influence on literature (pp 38–9).

295 Ford, Ford Madox. *The March of Literature: From Confucius' Day to Our Own.* New York: Dial Press, 1938.

Chaucer exhibits his democratic tendencies by allowing lower class pilgrims like Alisoun to mingle with aristocratic ones (p 405).

296 Bowden, Muriel. *A Commentary on the General Prologue to the Canterbury Tales.* New York: Macmillan, 1948/2nd ed, 1967.

'[I]f we meet the Wife in the *GP* with fourteenth-century understanding, we shall know her well from that epitomized account' (p 214). The Wife's being *of biside Bathe* (I.445) corresponds to St. Michael-juxta-Bathon, a parish known for its weaving industry but not for the quality of its goods. The Wife exhibits pride in her insistence on being the first to make church offering. Her 'well set-up appearance ... is in keeping with the strong directness of her character' (p 217). Alisoun's multiple marriages would not have shocked a medieval audience (widows with property were attractive commodities), yet her freedom would have been seen as unusual. Bowden incorporates Owst's belief that the good woman of Proverbs 8:10–2, a frequent reference of fourteenth-century homilists, is another of Chaucer's sources for the Wife (**579**). The medieval custom of a vernacular banns ceremony outside the church before the Latin service began explains why Alisoun has had her husbands *at chirche dore* (I.460). The Wife's *gat-tothed* (I.468) appearance has been interpreted as a sign of 'much travel and of good fortune' (p 220), dishonesty, and being destined for love. Only one parallel can be found between the Wife and La Vieille of the *RR*: both claim to have had *oother compaignye in youthe* I.461. Alisoun would have witnessed many sights on her multiple pilgrimages (pp 221–5).

297 Wretlind, Dale E. 'The Wife of Bath's Hat.' *MLN* 63(1948), 381–2.
Although Manly (**19**) asserts that the Wife's headgear is of an outmoded fashion, Alisoun's enormous hat is in keeping with Queen Anne's introducing large head-dresses to English fashion in 1382.

298 Coghill, Nevill. *The Poet Chaucer*. London: Oxford University Press, 1949/2nd ed, 1967.
The Wife of Bath is the sole pilgrim whose portrait contains contradictions (p 105). Alisoun and the Prioress signify the medieval period's polarized conception of women. See **495** and **1109**.

299 Malone, Kemp. *Chapters on Chaucer*. Baltimore: Johns Hopkins Press, 1951; rpt 1961.
The Wife of Bath travels alone and is not part of one of Chaucer's subgroups of pilgrims (p 150). Alisoun's description covers 32 lines of the *GP* (p 152). She intends her outlandish dressing to attract attention to her (p 203). See **500** and **1111**.

300 Makarewicz, Sister Mary Raynelda. *The Patristic Influence on Chaucer*. Washington, D.C.: Catholic University of America Press, 1953.
According to Augustine, Alisoun's generous offerings at church are

still not enough to atone for her extreme vices (p 195). Alison of the *MilT*, May, and the wife in the *ShT* are all dim reflections of Alisoun. Griselda is her antitype. See **509** and **1119**.

301 Duncan, Edgar Hill. 'Narrator's Points of View in the Portrait-Sketches, Prologue to the *Canterbury Tales*.' In *Essays in Honor of Walter Clyde Curry*. Nashville: Vanderbilt University Press, 1954. Pp 77–101.

Much of Alisoun's portrait looks toward further explanation in the *WBP* and stems from Chaucer's perspective as omniscient narrator. Other details, however, come from a restricted point of view (p 100).

302 Hoffman, Arthur W. 'Chaucer's Prologue to Pilgrimage: The Two Voices.' *ELH* 21(1954), 1–16. Rpt in *The Canterbury Tales: Analytic Notes and Review*. Ed. Mina Mulvey. New York: American R.D.M. Corp., 1965. Pp 127–42.

The Wife of Bath is on a secular pilgrimage, spurred by Venus to find her next husband and by Mars to conquer him. Alisoun straddles the line 'between the secular and the profane' (p 5). Several of the pilgrims have a reference to love in their *GP* portraits. The Wife's concerns her knowledge of the *olde daunce* (p 15).

303 Severs, J. Burke. 'Did Chaucer Rearrange the Clerk's *Envoy*?' *MLN* 69(1954), 472–8.

Once he decided to place the *MerT* after the *ClT*, Chaucer added his reference to Alisoun to the Clerk's *Envoy* in order to provide significant motivation for the *MerP* (p 473).

304 Swart, J. 'The Construction of Chaucer's *General Prologue*.' *Neophil* 38(1954), 127–36.

In the *GP*, the Wife is grouped with the Shipman and the Physician because all three are economically well-off. Alisoun's deafness is a detail that explains in part the incredible volume of her actions and dress; it also places an emphasis on 'the imperfections of her character' (p 133). Chaucer's depiction of the Wife is harsh; it is only later in the *CT* that the reader is presented with a more sympathetic rendering of Alisoun.

305 Baldwin, Ralph. *The Unity of the Canterbury Tales. Anglistica*, Vol 5. Copenhagen: Rosenkilde and Bagger, 1955. Excerpts rpt in *Chaucer Criticism: The Canterbury Tales*. Ed. Richard Schoeck and Jerome Taylor. Notre Dame: University of Notre Dame Press, 1960. Pp 14–51.

While Alisoun is one of the most complex characters of the *CT*, her central characteristic is being an archwife (p 49).

306 Lumiansky, R.M. *Of Sondry Folk: The Dramatic Principle in the Canterbury Tales*. Austin: University of Texas Press, 1955.

Alisoun's assertiveness and her sensuality are the keys to her 'militant feminism' (p 119). While some critics feel that the reference to Alisoun's unsurpassed skill in textiles is ironic, Alisoun's aggressive drive to succeed makes it likely that she became the best in her field. Alisoun's concern with her appearance is appropriate for a woman seeking a husband. See **513** and **1127**.

307 Baum, Paull F. 'Chaucer's Puns.' *PMLA* 71(1956), 225–46.

Alisoun's portrait contains puns on the words *charity* (I.452), and *without* (I.461). See **516** and **1128**.

308 Bradley, Sister Ritamary, C.H.M. 'The *Wife of Bath's Tale* and the Mirror Tradition.' *JEGP* 55(1956), 624–30.

See **517**.

309 Lumiansky, R.M. 'Benoit's Portraits and Chaucer's General Prologue.' *JEGP* 55(1956), 431–8.

Contrary to Lowes' opinion that the portraits in the *GP* were constructed without any influence from Benoit de Ste. Maure's depiction of the Trojan War personalities (**98**), there are significant parallels between the two works (p 435). Both authors combine an individual's appearance with his personality. Just as Benoit made two major groupings between the Greeks and Trojans that are subdivided by family relations, Chaucer created divisions in his catalogue of pilgrims. Chaucer groups his characters by family ties, profession, morality, and acquaintance. The Wife's and the Parson's portraits have been placed together to effect a striking contrast (p 436).

310 Slaughter, Eugene Edward. *Virtue According to Love, in Chaucer*. New York: Bookman Associates, 1957.

Alisoun represents a religio-philosophical system, deals with the virtue of charity, and embodies the vices of pride, wrath, incontinence, and idle talk (p 233). See **522** and **1133**.

311 Baum, Paull F. 'Chaucer's Puns: A Supplementary List.' *PMLA* 73(1958), 167–70.

The Wife's experience with *wandrynge by the weye* (I.467) 'is something between a pun and a poetical ambiguity' (p 170). See **524**.

312 Owen, Charles A., Jr. 'The Development of the *Canterbury Tales*.' *JEGP* 57(1958), 449–76.

See **527**.

313 Biggins, Dennis. 'Chaucer's *General Prologue*, A 467.' *N&Q* 205(1960), 129–30.

The phrase *wandrynge by the weye* (I.467) may have both a 'double figurative' (p 129) and a literal meaning. It ironically implies that Alisoun knows about traveling the roads to heaven and to hell.

314 Magoun, Francis P., Jr. *A Chaucer Gazetteer*. Chicago: University of Chicago Press, 1961.

Geographic definitions augment the place names in the *CT* as well as Chaucer's other works. Bath appears not only in its *GP* reference but is used in *WBP* as well. See also Boulogne, Cologne, Galicia, Ghent, Ypres, Jerusalem, Rome and Saint James. See **532**.

315 Brooks, Harold F. *Chaucer's Pilgrims: The Artistic Order of the Portraits in the Prologue*. New York: Barnes and Noble, 1962; rpt 1968.

The middle-class Alisoun, Shipman, and Physician excel in their trades yet have dubious moral natures. Alisoun's portrait shares travel experience with the Knight, and it may be contrasted with that of the Prioress (pp 31–2).

316 Reidy, John. 'Grouping of Pilgrims in the *General Prologue* to the *Canterbury Tales.*' *Papers of the Michigan Academy of Science, Arts, and Letters*. Ed. Hubert M. English, Jr. Ann Arbor: University of Michigan Press, 1962. 47(1962), 595–603.

The Shipman, Physician, Wife of Bath, Parson, and Plowman form a heterogenous group that Emerson has labeled 'provincial' (p 601).

317 Nevo, Ruth. 'Chaucer: Motive and Mask in the "General Prologue."' *MLR* 58(1963), 1–9.

Money provides a key to understanding the order of the pilgrims in the *GP*. Those belonging to the most wealthy segments of society and those who have the potential to gain financial strength come before those who are most likely to earn little in life. The Wife, who is involved in a trade, belongs to the lower middle class; therefore, her portrait falls after upper middle class members such as the Franklin and before the peasant class (p 5). Chaucer employs subtle irony in order to comment upon the worldliness of some of his pilgrims. Alisoun's coverchiefs and her desire to be the first to make an offering at church reveal the extent to which the power of money influences her. The Wife's stance on the morality of virginity and multiple marriages 'exemplifies the easy-going conscience of the majority of pilgrims' (p 8). Her elevation of herself over moral standards reveals her cupidity.

318 Bowden, Muriel. *A Reader's Guide to Geoffrey Chaucer*. New York: Farrar, Straus, and Company, 1964; rpt Farrar, Straus and Giroux 1966 and 1970.

Alisoun's garb is admired (pp 113–4). See **548a** and **1163**.

319 Hoffman, Richard L. 'The Wife of Bath as Student of Ovid.' *N&Q* 209(1964), 287–8.

Alisoun might well have been familiar with Ovid's *Remedia Amoris*. Jankyn's book contains the *Ars Amatoria* and could also have had other Ovidian works in it. While her knowledge of the *olde daunce* is not in keeping with the theme of the *Remedia*, Alisoun is notorious for her personalized interpretation of text.

320 Loomis, Roger S. *A Mirror of Chaucer's World*. Princeton: Princeton University Press, 1965.

The Ellesmere ms portrait of the Wife is an almost-accurate representation of Chaucer's description of her, except for the fact that there is a gold net, as opposed to a wimple, under her hat (Fig 94). A miniature from the Bodley 264 ms illustrates the custom of the church door marriage ceremony (Fig 114). The bridal party approaches the church where the groom waits with the priest and his server. See **563**.

321 Mulvey, Mina. *The Canterbury Tales: Analytic Notes and Review*. Woodbury, NY: Illustrated World Encyclopedia, 1965.

The *GP* description of Alisoun is recounted (p 20). See **564** and **1161**.

322 Hoffman, Richard L. *Ovid and the Canterbury Tales*. Philadelphia: University of Pennsylvania Press, 1966.

Ovid's *Remedia Amoris* and *Ars Amatoria* are reflected in Alisoun's knowledge of both remedies of love and the old dance. See **153** and **574**.

323 Muscatine, Charles. '*The Canterbury Tales*: Style of the Man and Style of the Work.' In *Chaucer and Chaucerians: Critical Studies in Middle English Literature*. Ed. D.S. Brewer. London: Nelson, 1966. Pp 88–113.

See **577**.

324 Rowland, Beryl. 'The Horse and Rider Figure in Chaucer's Works.' *UTQ* 35(1966), 246–59.

Alisoun's equestrian skills 'emphasize her unfortunate ambivalence' (p 254). Her spurs have sexual symbolism and comment upon her dominating her husbands. Her feminine hat indicates that she can be yielding.

325 Curtis, Penelope. 'Chaucer's Wife of Bath.' *CR* 10(1967), 33–45.
See **586**.

326 Hussey, Maurice. *Chaucer's World: A Pictorial Companion.* Cambridge: Cambridge University Press, 1967.
In the Ellesmere portrait of the Wife, Alisoun brandishes a whip, symbolic of domination, and wears a wimple, an out-of-date fashion for her time. She straddles her horse as a man would (Fig 75). See **589**.

327 Druker, Trudy. 'Some Medical Allusions in the *Canterbury Tales.*' *Medical Arts and Letters* 1(1968), 444–7.
The physical details of Alisoun's portrait suggest that she suffers from 'mild chronic hypertension' (p 445). She has suffered a perforation of the eardrum and her deafness adds to her propensity to talk in order that she might not have to listen. Her gap teeth are merely gap teeth.

328 Garbáty, Thomas Jay. 'Chaucer's Weaving Wife.' *JAF* 81(1968), 342–6.
Alisoun represents the archetypal literary character of the old bawd. Alisoun's occupation of weaving underscores this connection.

329 Hira, Toshinori. 'Two Phases of Chaucer, Moral and Mortal.' In *Maekawa Shun'ichi Ky ju Kanreki Kinen-ronbunsh : Essays and Studies in Commemoration of Professor Shunichi Maekawa's 61st Birthday.* Ed. Maekawa Shunichi. Tokyo: Eihosha, 1968. Pp 91–114.
Alisoun belongs to the group of human, as opposed to ideal, pilgrims. Her weaving abilities could not have exceeded those of Flanders. Alisoun's social rank contributes to her pride (p 97). See **601**.

330 Lawlor, John. *Chaucer.* London: Hutchinson University Library, 1968.
The 'fixed' characters of the Pardoner and the Wife of Bath offer dramatic continuity between their *GP* portraits and their autobiographical prologues (p 113). Alisoun represents ungoverned human nature. See **232**.

331 Smith, Walter. 'Geoffrey Chaucer, Dramatist.' *Interpretations* 1(1968), 1–9; rpt 1985.
The pilgrims are listed as *dramatis personae* with an annotation for each character. Alisoun may be compared to Falstaff, and the *WBP* is excellent.

332 Kiralis, Karl. 'William Blake as an Intellectual and Spiritual Guide to Chaucer's *Canterbury Pilgrims.*' *Blake Studies* 1(1969), 139–90.

Blake criticized Stothard's print of the pilgrims because he depicted a young and fair Wife of Bath (p 141). In his artwork, Blake placed Alisoun near both the Miller and the Merchant, suggesting that these men are attracted to her. The Prioress and Alisoun mark contrasting subdivisions within the painting. Both women are dressed in sensual clothing, but the Prioress's sexuality is subtly stated compared to Alisoun's revealing neckline (p 148). This difference in allure aligns the Wife with Rahab and the Prioress with Tizrah in Blakean mythology (p 153).

333 Alderson, William L., and Arnold C. Henderson. *Chaucer and Augustan Scholarship*. Berkeley: University of California Press, 1970. See **1189**.

334 Lenaghan, R.T. 'Chaucer's *General Prologue* as History and Literature.' *Comparative Studies in Society and History* 12(1970), 73–82.
The pilgrims who are tradespeople must all face the trials of economic competition. Such struggle leads to manifestations of insecurity; hence, Alisoun needs to be first to make her offering in church (p 77). Alisoun does, however, know how to relax.

335 Burgess, Anthony. 'Whan that Aprille.' *Horizon* 13.2 (1971), 45–59.
French artist Zevi Blum has produced illustrations for five of the tales. In her portrait, Alisoun holds a whip under her skirt (p 49).

336 Howard, Donald R. 'The *Canterbury Tales*: Memory and Form.' *ELH* 38(1971), 319–28.
In the *GP*, Chaucer has arranged his pilgrims into three groups of seven, 'each headed by an ideal portrait' (p 324). This arrangement accounts for the Parson's and Plowman's placement between Alisoun and the Miller.

337 Hussey, S.S. *Chaucer: An Introduction*. London: Methuen; New York: Barnes and Noble, 1971/rev 1981.
The exaggerated language of the Clerk's *Envoy* indicates that the Clerk finds female characters such as Griselda and Alisoun to be too extreme (p 171).

338 Higdon, David Leon. 'Diverse Melodies in Chaucer's *General Prologue*.' *Criticism* 14(1972), 97–108.
The pilgrims may be divided into three groups according to their relation to music. These groups are categorized by song, dance, and harmony; noise, loudness, and discord; and silence and hostility to music (p 101). The Wife might belong to the first group because her laughter produces

a melody (p 103). That the Wife can *laugh and carpe* (I.474) and participate in *the olde daunce* (I.476) is an example of how musical associations reveal a character's nature. In this first group of pilgrims, the flesh and the spirit are not in harmony with one another (p 104).

339 Knight, Stephen. *The Poetry of the Canterbury Tales.* Sydney: Angus and Robertson, 1973/rev 'The Poetry of the *Wife of Bath's Prologue* and *Tale.*' *Teaching of English* 25(1973), 3–17.

The vitality of Alisoun's character is reflected in the varied metrics of her *GP* portrait and from stresses in the lines. See **657** and **1216**.

340 Mann, Jill. *Chaucer and Medieval Estates Satire: The Literature of Social Classes and the General Prologue to the Canterbury Tales.* Cambridge: Cambridge University Press, 1973.

Medieval estates lists viewed women as a separate class that was usually subdivided by marital status (p 121). While Alisoun's character has been molded by Jean de Meun's La Vieille, Alisoun differs from the old woman in that she still possesses a lusty attractiveness (p 126). That Alisoun weaves, is guilty of pride, loves pilgrimages, and is preoccupied with fashion makes her a typical female in the estates tradition. While some of these traits are considered as weaknesses, they are Alisoun's strengths.

341 Pittock, Malcolm. *The Prioress's Tale [and] the Wife of Bath's Tale.* Notes on English Literature. Oxford: Blackwell, 1973.

Alisoun's lively coarseness in manner, speech, and dress stands in contrast with the delicate nature of the Prioress. See **658** and **1217**.

342 Rutledge, Sheryl P. 'Chaucer's Zodiac of Tales.' *Costerus* 9(1973), 117–43.

See **659**.

343 Engelhardt, George J. 'The Lay Pilgrims of the *Canterbury Tales*: A Study in Ethology.' *MS* 36(1974), 278–330.

Alisoun has only weaving in common with the Good Woman of Proverbs. Her passionate nature stems from stellar influence (p 321). See **668** and **1224**.

344 Hoffman, Richard L. 'The Wife of Bath's Uncharitable Offerings.' *ELN* 11(1974), 165–7.

Alisoun cannot hear Christ's call to be charitable and to achieve reconciliation with people before making offering. Her wounded pride often ironically places her outside of charitable feelings when she is performing a charitable service.

345 Kernan, Anne. 'The Archwife and the Eunuch.' *ELH* 41(1974), 1–25. See **670**.

346 Parr, Roger P. 'Chaucer's Art of Portraiture.' *SMC* 4(1974), 428–36. The interrelation between the brief, introductory portraits of the *GP* and the pilgrims' personalities that are found within their tales can be seen through 'the rhetorical repetition of vivid and pertinent characteristics' (p 431). *GP* lines 468, 463, 526, 460, 446 correspond with III.603, 495, 435, 636, respectively.

347 Reisner, Thomas A. 'The Wife of Bath's Dower: A Legal Interpretation.' *MP* 71(1974), 301–2. Chaucer emphasizes Alisoun's having married her husbands at church door in order to stress her shrewdness concerning her marriage dowers. Alisoun bargained for her rights before getting married.

348 Thorpe, James. *A Noble Heritage: The Ellesmere Manuscript of Chaucer's Canterbury Tales*. San Marino: The Huntingdon Library, 1974. The *GP* contains clear portraits of the pilgrims (p 4). This book contains a color centerfold piece of all the Ellesmere ms pictures of the pilgrims. See **1229**.

349 Green, Eugene. 'The Voice of the Pilgrims in the *General Prologue* to the *Canterbury Tales*.' *Style* 9(1975), 55–81. The voices of the various pilgrims intermix with that of Chaucer's narrating persona in the *GP*. The Gildsmen's wives and Alisoun voice their desire for privileged places in church (p 77).

350 Kelly, Henry Ansgar. *Love and Marriage in the Age of Chaucer*. Ithaca: Cornell University Press, 1975. Chaucer's appreciation of Ovidian comedy and irony is evinced by Alisoun's knowledge of the *olde daunce* (p 73). Alisoun's weddings recount the medieval contracts involved in marriage (p 179). She is aware of the potential for sin in marriage (pp 270–1).

351 Mannucci, Loretta Valtz. *Fourteenth-Century England and the Canterbury Tales*. Milan: Coopli, 1975. The Wife represents the condition of women in the *CT*. She is the Franklin's counterpart, a foil for the Prioress, and a gauge by which to read the male pilgrims' stance on the woman question (p 135). The physical description of Alisoun's person calls for sympathy from the reader (p 138). See **684** and **1234**.

352 Weissman, Hope Phyllis. 'Antifeminism and Chaucer's

Characterizations of Women.' In *Geoffrey Chaucer: A Collection of Original Articles.* Ed. George D. Economou. New York: McGraw-Hill, 1975. Pp 93–110. Rpt in *Critical Essays on Chaucer's Canterbury Tales.* Ed. Malcolm Andrew. Toronto: University of Toronto Press, 1991. Pp 106–25.

See **687** and **1239**.

353 Hawkins, Harriett. *Poetic Freedom and Poetic Truth: Chaucer, Shakespeare, Marlowe, Milton.* Oxford: Clarendon Press, 1976.
While Chaucer provides a unique portrait of Alisoun, the reader is not given an explicit description of her looks. Eye and hair color, for example, have been omitted. Through this selective detailing of her person, the Wife is seen in terms of a personality type rather than an individual (p 121). See **691**.

354 Ruggiers, Paul G. 'A Vocabulary for Chaucerian Comedy: A Preliminary Sketch.' In *Medieval Studies in Honor of Lillian Herlands Hornstein.* Ed. Jess B. Bessinger, Jr., and Robert R. Raymo. New York: New York University Press, 1976. Pp 193–225.
While Alisoun's portrait initially appears as an impostor or *alazon*, she is later exposed as a more sophomoric character (pp 213–4). See **700** and **1246**.

355 Zacher, Christian K. *Curiosity and Pilgrimage: The Literature of Discovery in Fourteenth-Century England.* Baltimore: Johns Hopkins University Press, 1976.
Chaucer may have been influenced by Jean de Meun's symbolic equation of a lover's sexual goal with elements of a pilgrim's progress. Alisoun's yearning for travel and her lust signify her unstable marriage (p 109).

356 Evans, Gillian Rosemary. *Chaucer.* Glasgow: Blackie, 1977.
The Wife's bold portrait provides an intriguing contrast to that of the courtly Prioress. Her being an old wife ensures her knowledge of folk medicines and legends (p 81). The Wife's awareness of planetary rule indicates how pervasive the influence of astrology was in the medieval period (p 52). Chaucer's audience would recognize the role of the stars in Alisoun's life as well (p 108). The book provides an illustration of Venus and her revelling 'children' (Fig 30) and a copy of Blake's depiction of the pilgrims (Fig 41). See **1253**.

357 Gardner, John. *The Poetry of Chaucer.* Carbondale: Southern Illinois University Press, 1977.
Alisoun is misguided by reason and is therefore proud. Her physiognomy,

her life history, and an allegorical reading of her portrait emphasize her sexuality (pp 238–9). See **713** and **1254**.

358 Miller, Robert P., ed. *Chaucer: Sources and Backgrounds*. New York: Oxford University Press, 1977.

See **174**.

359 Morgan, Gerald. 'The Universality of the Portraits in the *General Prologue* to the *Canterbury Tales*.' *ES* 58(1977), 481–93.

The Wife of Bath embodies, as Mann (**340**) has outlined, the medieval estate of woman drawn from antifeminist tradition (p 485). This tradition characterizes woman as the personification of pride and lechery. Alisoun's astrological chart ensures that she possesses these vices. Martian influence is also responsible for the Wife's military accessories (p 489). Chaucer finds pride to be a vice common among the *bourgeoisie*, for the Wife's worldliness is reflected in that of the Gildsmen's wives (p 486). Chaucer's position as wool customs controller from 1374 to 1386 familiarized him with many specifics of the textile industry. Alisoun comes from the Bath area but not from the town itself because it would be in the outlying districts that wool and a good water supply might be found. 'What Chaucer has in mind here is surely the nature of the cloth industry rather than the parish of St. Michael *juxta Bathon*' (p 488). The scarlet color of the Wife's stockings and gowns not only signifies her vanity but calls to mind life at court. The Wife's deafness may be considered in a figurative sense; she doesn't hear the things with which she doesn't agree.

360 Stevenson, Warren. 'Interpreting Blake's Canterbury Pilgrims.' *CLQ* 13(1977), 115–26.

According to Blakean mythology, in the artist's painting of the pilgrims, the Wife of Bath is in the state of Rahab (p 123). The chalice she holds calls to mind the Whore of Revelations' cup. The cross about her neck signifies institutionalized religion and the seven or ten spires of the church in the background may be linked with the beast in Revelations who has seven heads and ten horns. There are seven horns on the Wife's hat and she wears a ruff that has ten points. The morning star of Venus, also of Lucifer, is visible between Alisoun's legs and is also present in the sky above the church (p 124).

361 Allen, Orphia Jane. 'Blake's Archetypal Criticism: *The Canterbury Pilgrims*.' *Genre* 11(1978), 173–89.

The Miller, the Merchant, and the Wife of Bath either relate stories about sex 'or exhibit themselves as characters preoccupied with sex' (pp 80-1). In terms of Blakean mythology, both the Wife and the Prioress are viewed as Orc-Luvah characters because they are linked with frustrated desire (p 181). In Blake's portrait of the Wife, Alisoun bears a strong resemblance to the Whore of Babylon. Her large hat recalls the Pope's tiara and has 'an ironic suggestion of a halo' (p 181). Her gaudy dress reveals much of her upper torso, but her exposed flesh is hidden in part by a cross and a heart-shaped necklace that dangles between her breasts (p 181).

362 Brewer, Derek, ed. *Chaucer: The Critical Heritage*. Volume 1, 1385–1837. Volume 2, 1837–1933. London: Routledge and Kegan Paul, 1978. Volume 1 provides commentary on and references to the Wife of Bath by Lydgate, Scogan, Harrington, Braithwait, Dryden, Warton, Blake, Hazlitt, an unknown author (p 311), and Hippisley. Volume 2 includes similar works by Lowell, Mackail, Kittredge, and Manly.

363 Martin, Loy D. 'History and Form in the *General Prologue* to the *Canterbury Tales*.' *ELH* 45(1978), 1–17.
Alisoun is one of several pilgrims who are linked with a specific geographical location in order to emphasize 'that persons from all over England come together for pilgrimages' (p 5). The fact that the Wife is unmarried on this trip represents the 'disjunction between pilgrimage and ordinary life' (p 10).

364 Item cancelled.

365 Whitbread, L. 'Six Chaucer Notes.' *NM* 79(1978), 41–3.
Alisoun's ruddy complexion (I.458) is explained in the *WBP* by Mars' influence in her horoscope. The reference to Christ's encounter with the Samaritan woman, who has had five husbands, may be a reminder of a 'prohibition on more than five husbands' (p 42) for Alisoun.

366 Olsen, Alexandra Hennessey. 'Chaucer and the Eighteenth Century: The Wife of Bath and Moll Flanders.' *Chaucer Newsletter* 1(1979), 13–5.
Since Defoe mentions the *GP* in his writing, he was most likely familiar with the Wife of Bath's character and used her when creating Moll Flanders. Both Alisoun and Moll have had five husbands and various lovers. Only two of Moll's marriages are legitimate and Alisoun debates the validity of her marriages after her first widowing. The two women recognize the financial and social benefits of marriage. Both women are sly and enjoy fine clothing, and they rely on clothwork skills to

support themselves. Moll's midwife parallels Alisoun's gossip. They both discuss theology knowledgeably.

367 Bowden, Betsy. 'The Artistic and Interpretive Context of Blake's *Canterbury Pilgrims.' Blake* 13(1980), 164–90.

William Blake types the Wife of Bath as the Whore of Babylon in his painting of the pilgrims. There is symmetry between her and the Prioress, despite their being placed apart from one another in the picture (p 164). Alisoun is depicted with a goblet in her right hand, nearly-naked breasts, and spread legs. She stares at the oblivious Parson (Fig 1).

368 Holloway, Julia Bolton. 'Medieval Pilgrimage.' In *Approaches to Teaching Chaucer's Canterbury Tales.* Ed. Joseph Gibaldi. Consultant editor, Florence H. Ridley. New York: The Modern Language Association of America, 1980. Pp 143–8.

Alisoun, a practiced yet false pilgrim, wears scarlet and not the traditional white garb of a pilgrim (p 146). See **757**.

369 Lawler, Traugott. *The One and the Many in the Canterbury Tales.* Hamden, CT: Archon Books, 1980.

See **760**.

370 Sklute, Larry. 'Catalogue Form and Catalogue Style in the *General Prologue* of the *Canterbury Tales.' SN* 52(1980), 35–46.

Chaucer makes use of some traditional catalogue devices in his portraits in the *GP*. The Wife of Bath's association with the Samaritan Woman is derived from 'religious typology' (p 35). Chaucer does not merely adhere to the literary custom of allowing physical attributes to be interpreted symbolically; he recognizes the narrative potential in the details of his descriptions. While the Wife's deafness is a commentary on her moral status, this condition is later revealed to be the result of her battle with Jankyn (p 40). Chaucer also develops a psychological portrait of his pilgrims through their interaction in the links of the *CT*.

371 Weissman, Hope Phyllis. 'Why Chaucer's Wife Is from Bath.' *ChauR* 15(1980), 11–36.

The concept of the bath as a symbol of 'sexual indulgence' (p 12) emphasizes Alisoun's lustful nature. Medieval iconography provides evidence of the bath being perceived as a place of carnality, the bathhouse of Venus. Alisoun's living *biside Bath* reveals how misogynistic culture has banished her from being a 'woman in her human fullness ... the human in the fullness of its flesh' (p 25).

372 Diekstra, F. 'Chaucer's Way with His Sources: Accident into Substance

and Substance into Accident.' *ES* 62(1981), 215–36.

The highly realistic characterization of Alisoun, drawn from material in *RR*, *Jov*, *Mir*, and the fabliau tradition, affects a reader's allegorical interpretation of her. Alisoun should be viewed in neither a strictly iconographic nor an ultra-realistic light (pp 220–1).

373 Donaldson, E. Talbot. 'Adventures with the Adversative Conjunction in the *General Prologue* to the *Canterbury Tales*; or, What's Before the But?' In *So Meny People, Longages and Tonges: Philological Essays in Scots and Mediaeval English Presented to Angus McIntosh*. Ed. Michael Benskin and M.L. Samuels. Edinburgh: Authors, 1981. Pp 355–66.

In Alisoun's portrait, I.445–6 is a specific example of the use of the '*but* sympathetic' (p 363). It suggests that Alisoun's capabilities as a wife were hindered by her deafness. The *but* of I.462 is a coy remark that should interest the reader in Alisoun's story.

374 Plummer, John F. 'The Women's Song in Middle English and Its European Backgrounds.' In *Vox Feminae: Studies in Medieval Women's Song*. Ed. John F. Plummer. Kalamazoo: Medieval Institute Publications, 1981. Pp 135–54.

Several songs in both Middle English and French relate a willful woman's pleasure and pride in her sexuality. The women are, like the Wife of Bath, satirically portrayed (pp 147–8).

375 Reiss, Edmund. 'Chaucer's Thematic Particulars.' In *Signs and Symbols in Chaucer's Poetry*. Ed. John P. Hermann and John J. Burke, Jr. University, AL: University of Alabama Press, 1981. Pp 27–42.

Chaucer's use of *worthy* to describe characters like Alisoun is ironic (p 28). The references to Alisoun in the *ClT* and *MerT* as well as her similarity to Alison of the *MilT* requires the reader to reevaluate situations (p 30). The details of Alisoun's portrait offer thematic particulars. Alisoun's head-gear is a parody of Jerome's red cardinal's hat, and, through her wearing the hat, Alisoun appears as a parody of authority (p 31).

376 Robertson, D.W., Jr. 'Simple Signs from Everyday Life in Chaucer.' In *Signs and Symbols in Chaucer's Poetry*. Ed. John P. Hermann and John J. Burke, Jr. University, AL: University of Alabama Press, 1981. Pp 12–26.

See **776**.

377 Storm, Melvin. 'Alisoun's Ear.' *MLQ* 42(1981), 219–26.

Iconographic interpretation views the ear as the key to the perception of truth. Deafness is thus the sign of hindering the reception of truth, and Alisoun's deafness leads to her misrepresentation of authority (p 223). Abbot Godfrey associates the ringing of only one ear with humanity's relation to God before Christ became man. This belief associates Alisoun with the Old Law and the temporal world. The deafening blow she receives from Jankyn is a transformation that aligns her physical state with her spiritual condition.

378 Kollmann, Judith J. '"Ther is noon oother incubus but he": *The Canterbury Tales*, *Merry Wives of Windsor*, and Falstaff.' In *Chaucerian Shakespeare: Adaptation and Transformation*. Medieval and Renaissance Monograph Series, 2. Ed. E. Talbot Donaldson and Judith J. Kollmann. Ann Arbor: Michigan Consortium for Medieval and Early Modern Studies, 1983. Pp 43–68.
See **797**.

379 Watanabe, Ikuo. 'Two Women Pilgrims — the Prioress and the Wife of Bath.' *Tenri University Journal* 137(1983), 176–96. [In Japanese.] Alisoun and the Prioress represent vastly different female types, yet they share some similarities.

380 Bosse, Roberta Bux. 'Female Sexual Behavior in the Late Middle Ages: Ideal and Actual.' *FCS* 10(1984), 15–37.
While Alisoun and the Prioress provide examples of medieval femininity, they are fictional type-characters who were created for aesthetic purposes (p 15).

381 Murphy, Ann B. 'The Process of Personality in Chaucer's *Wife of Bath's Tale*.' *Centennial Review* 28(1984), 204–22.
While many details about Alisoun stem from antifeminism, others add to her individuality and render her a sympathetic character. Her portrait blurs the tension between authority and experience with its attention to 'class, materialism, money, and power' (p 207). See **823** and **1325**.

382 Sklute, Larry. *Virtue of Necessity: Inconclusiveness and Narrative Form in Chaucer's Poetry*. Columbus: Ohio State University Press, 1984.
The pilgrims represent a perspective of the world in their tales. Alisoun advocates experience over authority (p 96). Details of her portrait have implications concerning Alisoun's morality, yet they also contribute to her individuality. While Alisoun's having five husbands underscores her femininity, the reader must judge whether this trait is indeed *worthy* (pp

107–8). See **1330**.

383 Gottfried, Barbara. 'Conflict and Relationship, Sovereignty and Survival: Parables of Power in the *Wife of Bath's Prologue.*' *ChauR* 19(1985), 202–24.

Alisoun's title of wife is typical of woman's being defined by her marital status, a concept the *WBP* does not challenge. Alisoun's portrait details her knowledge gleaned from experience. See **838**.

384 Lindskoog, Verna de Jong. 'Chaucer's Wife of Bath: Critical Approaches in the Twentieth Century.' *DAI* 45(1985), 2520A.

Critical commentators on the Wife of Bath, *WBP*, and *WBT* provide many diverse opinions and use evidence from Alisoun's performance to substantiate their arguments. Two large divisions of criticism include realistic and non-realistic criticism. Since the nature of criticism is relevant to its particular time and atmosphere, an ordering of criticism is recommended before an analysis of the commentary occurs.

385 Miyoshi, Yoko. 'Why Is It the Tale of the Wife of Bath?' In *Symposium on the Wife of Bath.* Medieval English Studies Symposia 2. Ed. Hisashi Shigeo, Hisao Tsuru, Isamu Saito, and Tadahiro Ikegami. Tokyo: Gaku Shobo, 1985. Pp 30–47. [In Japanese.]

Medieval economic history reveals both why Chaucer located Alisoun in Bath and why marrying five times was not unusual for a woman at this time.

386 Sheehan, Michael M. 'The Wife of Bath and Her Four Sisters: Reflections on a Woman's Life in the Age of Chaucer.' *MH* 13(1985), 23–42. Rpt. in *Critical Essays on Chaucer's Canterbury Tales.* Ed. Malcolm Andrew. Toronto: University of Toronto Press, 1991 [cited]. Pp 187–204.

In the *CT*, women of the landed and free estate would be represented by the woman married to Chaucer's Knight. Rural peasant women are reflected in the widow of the *NPT,* and their urban counterparts can be found in the background women of the *CkT*. Religious women are exemplified by the Prioress, and Alisoun represents the women of the growing middle class. Potential circumstances from birth through death in the lives of these women are analyzed.

387 Shigeo, Hisashi. 'The Wife of Bath.' In *Symposium on the Wife of Bath.* Medieval English Studies Symposia 2. Ed. Hisashi Shigeo, Hisao Tsuru, Isamu Saito, and Tadahiro Ikegami. Tokyo: Gaku Shobo, 1985. Pp 101–22. [In Japanese.]

Difficulties in interpreting Alisoun exist in light of both her portrait and her performance.

388 Alford, John A. 'The Wife of Bath Versus the Clerk of Oxford: What Their Rivalry Means.' *ChauR* 21(1986), 108–32.

The tensions between Alisoun and the Clerk must be explored in order that their individual identities might be fully understood. As complete opposites in their *GP* portraits, the two are destined to clash. Their conflict is a historical one, reflecting the differences between the rhetorical discourse of Socrates and the philosophical language of Plato. The physiognomy of Alisoun and the Clerk correspond to the personified conceptions of rhetoric and philosophy (p 120). Alisoun's performance is also rhetorical while the *ClT* is related through logical discourse.

389 Cook, Jon. 'Carnival and the *Canterbury Tales*: "Only Equals May Laugh."' In *Medieval Literature: Criticism, Ideology, and History*. Ed. David Aers. New York: St. Martin's Press, 1986. Pp 169–91.

Alisoun exemplifies a carnival figure in her public speech and dress (p 179).

390 Cooper, Helen. 'Chaucer and Joyce.' *ChauR* 21(1986), 142–54.

Comparing the *CT* with *Ulysses* reveals a parallel between Alisoun and Molly Bloom. The two women are similar in ego, in their freedom from moral censorship, and in their sexual freedom (p 149).

391 Pearsall, Derek. 'Chaucer's Poetry and Its Modern Commentators: The Necessity of History.' In *Medieval Literature: Criticism, Ideology, and History*. Ed. David Aers. New York: St. Martin's Press, 1986. Pp 123–47.

While history cannot refute Robertson's (**762**) claim that Alisoun was a bondswoman, the basis of Robertson's assessment is iconographic. History becomes anti-historical in such cases (p 140).

392 Puhvel, Martin. 'The Wife of Bath's "Remedies of Love."' *ChauR* 20(1986), 307–12.

Alisoun's knowledge of *remedies of love* (I.475) may imply that she was familiar with erotic, perhaps magical, stimulants. She may have resorted to love potions in order to win back her fourth husband. The references in Jankyn's book to Lucilia's and Deianira's accidentally destructive uses of love potions suggest that Alisoun's attempts at regaining her husband's affections had fatal results.

393 Rowland, Beryl. 'Chaucer's Working Wyf: The Unraveling of a Yarn-Spinner.' In *Chaucer in the Eighties*. Ed. Julian N. Wasserman and

Robert J. Blanch. Syracuse: Syracuse University Press, 1986. Pp 137–49.

Chaucer makes Alisoun a weaver because of the archetypal associations of weaving with women (p 142). As an archwife, Alisoun is aligned with Eve and the sin of concupiscence.

394 Hanning, Robert W. 'Appropriate Enough: Telling "Classical" Allusions in Chaucer's *Canterbury Tales.*' In *Florilegium Columbianum: Essays in Honor of Paul Oskar Kristeller*. Ed. Karl-Ludwig Selig and Robert Somerville. New York: Italica Press, 1987. Pp 113-23.

Chaucer's phrase *wandrynge by the weye* (I. 467) is indicative of Alisoun's delinquent morality (p 117).

395 Mertens-Fonck, Paule. 'Art and Symmetry in the *General Prologue* to the *Canterbury Tales.*' In *Actes du Congrès d'Amiens, 1982*. Ed. Société des Anglicistes de l'Enseignement Supérieur. Paris: Didier, 1987. Pp 41–51.

The Shipman, the Physician, and the Wife of Bath may be grouped together in the *GP* by Chaucer's evaluation of them (p 48). None of the three relates well to humanity and none have attained bliss. Alisoun is figuratively deaf to the words of other people. The *GP* reveals Alisoun as she appears to others, yet the *WBP* shows both how she appears to herself and how she wants to be perceived. The ending of the *WBT* exposes Alisoun's unfulfilled desire for a marriage of true love.

396 ———. 'Tradition and Feminism in Middle English Literature: Source-Hunting in the Wife of Bath's Portrait and in *The Owl and the Nightingale.*' In *Multiple Worlds, Multiple Words: Essays in Honour of Irène Simon*. Ed. Hena Maes-Jelinek, Pierre Michel, and Paulette Michel-Michot. Liège: Université de Liège, 1987. Pp 175–92.

In his construction of Alisoun's portrait, Chaucer not only drew from the account of the *mulier fortis* of Proverbs 31 but also from the Adulterous Woman of Proverbs 7 (p 177). Alisoun's hat, hose, and spurs reflect traditional details of a knight's description (p 182). Alisoun's resemblance to a knight, connected with the clerkly Jankyn, is reflective of a series of medieval debates on love held between knights and clerks.

397 Renn, George A., III. 'Chaucer's *Prologue.*' *Explicator* 46(1988), 4–7.

That Alisoun wears red stockings may be a preventative folk remedy against contracting a venereal disease (p 5).

398 Roberts, Ruth Marshall. 'Chaucer, An Androgynous Personality.'

POMPA (1988), 137–42.

Chaucer possessed an 'androgynous ability' (p 137) that allowed him to create female characters such as Criseyde and Alisoun. He begins his depiction of Alisoun with an objective portrait and then allows her to reveal her struggles with guilt and advancing age.

399 Elliott, Ralph. 'Chaucer's Garrulous Heroine: Alice of Bath.' *SMELL* 4(1989), 1–29.

Chaucer's readers are provided with three portraits of the Wife of Bath, found in the *GP*, the *WBP*, and in Alison of the *MilT* (pp 3–4). Alison's life seems to resemble what the Wife's would have been like at eighteen. The *GP* portrait, containing many hints about Alisoun's character which will be revealed further on in the *CT*, presents a fully energetic woman. See **923** and **1383**.

400 Taylor, Karla. *Chaucer Reads 'The Divine Comedy.'* Stanford: Stanford University Press, 1989.

Chaucer creates deliberate ambiguity around Alisoun. That she was *withouten* other company (I.461) can imply that she did or did not have lovers in her youth (p 80–1).

401 Whitaker, Elaine E. 'Chaucer's Wife of Bath and Her Ten Pound Coverchief.' *PAPA* 15(1989), 26–36.

Alisoun's headgear 'both condemn[s] and exonerate[s] her' (p 27). Books such as Robert Mannyng's *Handlyng Synne* find women's coverchiefs to be 'accessories of the devil' (p 27). Fourteenth-century life viewed them as being reflective of sexual frustration and of widowhood.

402 Leicester, H. Marshall, Jr. 'Structure as Deconstruction: "Chaucer and Estates Satire" in the *General Prologue*, or Reading Chaucer as a Prologue to the History of Disenchantment.' *Exemplaria* 2(1990), 241–61.

Many of the details of Alisoun's portrait in the *GP* are indefinite and less informative than those belonging to pilgrims in higher estates. In his description of the third estate, the class that breaks down the medieval hierarchy, Chaucer struggled with the issue of incorporating stereotypical attitudes towards these people and his actual details (p 249). Alisoun's portrait anticipates her performance and does not focus on her character in respect to its estate. Because her aggressive appearance presents a threat to the patriarchy, Alisoun is followed in the *GP* by the Parson, a representative of male authority.

403 Luttrell, Anthony. 'Englishwomen as Pilgrims to Jerusalem: Isolda Parewastell, 1365.' In *Equally in God's Image: Women in the Middle Ages*. Ed. Julia Bolton Holloway and Constance S. Wright. New York: Peter Lang, 1990. Pp 184–97.

While it is rare to find a woman's own written account of her pilgrimages, men often provided commentary on the increasing number of female pilgrims such as Chaucer's Wife of Bath. At times commentary proved hostile (p 184).

404 Fineman, Joel. *The Subjectivity Effect in Western Literary Tradition: Essays Toward the Release of Shakespeare's Will*. Cambridge: MIT Press, 1991.

See **968**.

405 Frese, Dolores Warwick. *An Ars Legendi for Chaucer's Canterbury Tales: Re-Constructive Reading*. Gainesville: University of Florida Press, 1991.

The portraits of Alisoun and the Pardoner seem to have benefited from late Chaucerian revisions of the *GP* that unite details with later-revealed events, such as Alisoun's deafness being eventually explained by the blow she receives from Jankyn (pp 99–101). Chaucer makes use of the 'medieval trope of clothing-or-cloth as text' (p 196) combining Alisoun's occupation of weaver with her elaborate dress. Even the *curtyn* (III.1249) in the *WBT* adds to this motif. Alisoun's concern with her 'array' (p 197) may be tied in with Chaucer's allowing her to recite her performance before the Clerk and the Merchant provide their tales.

406 Mertens-Fonck, Paule. 'Life and Fiction in the *Canterbury Tales*: A New Perspective.' In *Poetics: Theory and Practice in Medieval English Literature*. Ed. Piero Boitani and Anna Torti. Suffolk: Brewer, 1991. Pp 105–15.

See **979**.

407 Frese, Dolores Warwick. 'The Names of Women in the *CT*: Chaucer's Hidden Art of Involucral Nomenclature.' In *A Wyf Ther Was: Essays in Honour of Paule Mertens-Fonck*. Ed. Juliette Dor. Liège: Université de Liège, 1992. Pp 155–66.

In her drive for domestic sovereignty, the Wife resembles Queen Medb, the personification of the Sovereignty of Ireland. While some have compared Alisoun to the Whore of Babylon, a more apt resemblance may be found in the Queen of Sheba, who sought to gain both the wisdom of Solomon and his pleasures (pp 163–4). The reader can glean this association from subtle Chaucerian clues. After noting where the Wife comes from, the expert reader 'would supply the invisible but uxoriously potent name that exegetes would most often find "biside Bath," *id est*, BATH SHEBA, mother of said Solomon' (p 164). The Wife's having traversed many streams on her pilgrimages draws a parallel with the iconographic depiction of the Queen of Sheba in which she has webbed feet. The Queen forded many streams of wisdom as she drew closer to Solomon.

408 Haas, Renate. 'Lionesses Painting Lionesses? Chaucer's Women as Seen by Early Women Scholars and Academic Critics.' In *A Wyf Ther Was: Essays in Honour of Paule Mertens-Fonck*. Ed. Juliette Dor. Liège: Université de Liège, 1992. Pp 178–92.

In his 1913 dissertation, Emil Meyer associates the worst characteristics of the Wife of Bath with contemporary women who were seeking to better themselves (p 183). In contrast, Maria Koellreutter's academic writing links the Wife's more lewd traits with equally bawdy habits of men (p 185).

409 Knapp, Peggy A. 'Varieties of Medieval Historicism.' *Chaucer Yearbook* 1(1992), 157–75.

Historicism is essential for the critical evaluation of texts. Gadamer, Hirsch, and Habermas have all explored language's ability to transfer its meaning from the past to the present. The influence of these scholars has affected the perspective of Alisoun that noteworthy critics such as Curry, Robertson, Aers, and Patterson reveal.

410 Martin, Priscilla. 'Chaucer and Feminism: A Magpie View.' In *A Wyf Ther Was: Essays in Honour of Paule Mertens-Fonck*. Ed. Juliette Dor. Liège: Université de Liège, 1992. Pp 235–46.

David Aers has coined the term *magpie* to refer to those critics who apply bits of various forms of post-structural criticism to medieval literature (p 235). Although Aers may not be in favor of such pluralistic criticism, there is a rationale behind this practice. When various disciplines are applied to a piece of literature they may enhance one another. The Wife of Bath may be viewed in many aspects (p 241). Her portrait in the *GP* can be interpreted 'with reference to theological models, contemporary society, intertextuality with other literary works and with the visual arts' (p 242). The Wife wears masculine accessories, assumes the male roles of 'the soldier and the preacher' (p 242) and uses her textile skills to earn money, not to enhance her domestic situation as the

Good Woman of Proverbs does. She is the voice of the marginalized medieval woman; in the *WBP* she outlines sex and marriage in capitalistic terms. The *WBP* also lends itself to the study of feminine discourse (pp 244–5). In revealing a new perspective on the origin of *gentillesse* in the *WBT*, Alisoun supports a 'reordering of society' (p 244). By analyzing genre, such as perceiving how the *WBT* differs from the *KnT* as a romance, the reader may note cultural changes and comments on gender perceptions (p 243).

411 Strohm, Paul. *Hochon's Arrow: The Social Imagination of Fourteenth-Century Texts*. Princeton: Princeton University Press, 1992.
See **1014**.

412 David, Alfred. 'Old, New, and Yong in Chaucer.' *SAC* 15(1993), 5–21.
Chaucer uses the word *new* ironically throughout the *GP*. Alisoun's new shoes (I.457) belie her being worn out from her numerous relationships (p 14). See **1430**.

413 Hallissy, Margaret. *Clean Maids, True Wives, and Steadfast Widows: Chaucer's Women and Medieval Codes of Conduct*. Westport, CT: Greenwood, 1993.
Alisoun's taste in clothing exhibits her wealth and her non-adherence to traditional widow's garb. See **1024** and **1432**.

414 Hodges, Laura F. 'The Wife of Bath's Costumes: Reading the Subtexts.' *ChauR* 27(1993), 359–76.
While the clothing of many of the pilgrims is not detailed, much attention is given to Alisoun's wardrobe. Alisoun's dress reveals her class, wealth, pride, and practicality (pp 360–2). Allegorically, her elaborate head-gear connotes pride. While her Martian-influenced traveling costume suggests that she has a wayward nature (p 367), the outfit is not as excessive as Alisoun's Venusian-inspired Sunday garb, which may be classified as 'harlot's attire' (p 368).

415 Boswell, Jackson Campbell and Sylvia Wallace Holton. 'References to the *Canterbury Tales*.' *ChauR* 29(1995), 311–36.
References to Alisoun are found in the works of Rolland, Holland, Hakewill, Boys, Crakanthorp, Barker, Donne, and Hobson (pp 333–6).

416 Slover, Judith. 'A good wive was ther of biside Bath.' In *Chaucer's Pilgrims: An Historical Guide to the Pilgrims in the Canterbury*

Tales. Ed. Laura C. Lambdin and Robert T. Lambdin. Westport, CT: Greenwood, 1996. Pp 243–55.

Alisoun's portrait reflects the pretensions of her social class. Marrying at the age of twelve was not uncommon for medieval women. Many of the issues Chaucer raises concerning marital fidelity, widowhood, fashion, and antifeminism have significance for a modern audience (pp 246–9). Alisoun proves herself *worthy* through her financial capabilities, her charity, her faithfulness to Jankyn, and her going on pilgrimages. 'While neither obedient nor meek, she was true to herself' (p 250). See **1458**.

ℰ The Wife of Bath's Prologue
1900-1930

417 A.A. 'Gat-toothed and Venus.' *N&Q* (2nd ser) 6(1858), 199.
In the *WBP* Alisoun is *gaptothed*; she has lost a tooth in her aging.
Venus' seal is described in Cornelius Agrippa's *De Occulta
Philosophia* as a cross that has among its features three ornamented
points and one blank one. This blankness is a gap, and a Venus seal
may thus be identified as 'something with a gap in it' (p 199).

418 Boys, Thomas. 'Gat-tothed.' *N&Q* (2nd ser) 5(1858), 392.
Gat-tothed is defined in Todd's edition of Johnson's *Dictionary* as
goat-toothed. That the goat is sacred to Venus adds meaning to III.603–
4. Alisoun feels that her teeth are an attractive feature.

419 Carrington, F.A. 'Gat-toothed.' *N&Q* (2nd ser) 5(1858), 465.
While Boys suggests *gat-tothed* means that Alisoun's mouth contains
the teeth of a goat, this expression should be interpreted figuratively,
specifically in the sense that elderly men who pursue young women are
labeled *old goats*.

420 Lounsbury, Thomas R. *Studies in Chaucer: His Life and Writings*.
Volume 3. New York: Harper and Brothers, 1892; rpt New York: Russell
and Russell, 1962.
For its time, the *WBP* is a 'revolutionary document' (p 523) that attacks
accepted norms. Chaucer heightens Alisoun's argument by having her
use Jerome's *Jov* as a basis for her attack. While Chaucer derived
hints of Alisoun's character from La Vieille, he added individualistic
details to Alisoun's portrait (p 526). It is in the *WBP* that Chaucer extends

himself most from societal tradition. Alisoun's appearances in literature outside of her performance indicate Chaucer's contentment with his creation. In Tyrwhitt's edition of the *CT*, as well as some sixteenth-century editions, III.143–4 reads *Let hem with bread of pure wheat be fed, / And let us wives eaten barley bread.* Rendering the lines as *Let hem be bread of pured wheate seed / And let us wives hoten barley bread;* is more in keeping with Jerome (pp 306–8). See **1067**.

421 Brink, Bernard ten. *History of English Literature.* Volume 2. Trans. William Clarke Robinson. New York: Henry Holt and Co., 1893; London: George Bell, 1901.

The *WBP* could have been entitled her 'confession.' Her character is in striking contrast with that of Griselda. She is the physical representation of the female depicted by the antifeminist tradition (p 126). A plot summary of the *WBP* may be found on pp 127–30. The *WBP* is a remarkable work because it contains an awareness of humanity along with its comedy. The *MerT* offers a variation on the themes of the *WBP*. Chaucerian revision groups the Wife with the Summoner and the Friar and creates a fragment filled with 'vivid characteristics and stirring action' that combines 'dramatic satire with a high art of presentation' (p 160). Picturing the figures of the Pardoner and the Wife juxtaposed against one another when he interrupts her speech adds to the comedy of the scene. See **1068**.

422 Shipley, George. 'Arrangement of the *Canterbury Tales.*' *MLN* 10(1895), 260–79.

The Merchant's and the Clerk's references to Alisoun establish that their tales follow Alisoun's performance (p 274). The Franklin's combining the Clerk's theme of patience with Alisoun's theme of mastery indicates his tale should follow theirs (p 276).

423 Braithwait, Richard B. *A Comment upon the Two Tales of Our Ancient, Renouuned, and Ever Living Poet Sir Jeffray Chaucer, Knight.* London: W. Godbid, 1665. Text quoted from *Richard Brathwait's Comments in 1665 upon Chaucer's Tales of the Miller and the Wife of Bath.* Ed. C.F.E. Spurgeon. Chaucer Society Publications, 2nd ser, 33. London: Kegan Paul, Trench, Trübner, 1901.

Alisoun borrows from Scripture for her arguments (p 34). For her, husbands are a necessity. Alisoun approves of virginity yet advocates carnality and sovereignty in marriage. She causes her first three husbands to repent their marriages. Alisoun's diatribe against them is put into seventeenth-century prose (pp 46–52) as are her propositioning of Jankyn (pp 59–60) and some of her proverbs. The plot of the *WBP* is explained in full. See **1069**.

424 Mead, William. 'Prologue of the Wife of Bath.' *PMLA* 10(1901), 388–404.

The *WBP* and *PardP* are similar in their confessional style and the *WBP* is Chaucer's most creative prologue. While it is lengthy, none of its material is extraneous. 'It is an early account of the taming of a shrew' (p 389). Alisoun is earthy, proud, and fresh, and she may be likened to Falstaff and to Mrs. Caudle. While Chaucer may have had a living model for Alisoun, he did draw material from *RR*'s La Vieille. Yet Chaucer makes Alisoun more energetic, optimistic, and witty than Jean de Meun's character. Alisoun's topic of woe in marriage was a popular theme in the Middle Ages. Chaucer also made use of *Jov* and some works of Theophrastus for the *WBP*.

425 Ward, Adolphus W. *Geoffrey Chaucer*. English Men of Letters. Ed. John Morley. New York: Harper and Brothers, 1901.

The *WBP* is a 'careless clatter of an indomitable tongue' (p 121). It is the height of Chaucer's satire against women (p 154). Along with the *MilT*, the *WBP* records the origins of miracle plays in English drama (p 186). See **257**.

426 Hamilton, George L. '"Trotula."' *MP* 4(1906), 377–80.

The Trotula mentioned as one of the authors in Jankyn's book may well have been the eleventh-century female medical student of Salerno who was widely known for her writings.

427 Root, Robert Kilburn. *The Poetry of Chaucer: A Guide to Its Study and Appreciation*. Boston: Houghton-Mifflin, 1906/rev 1922; rpt 1934; rpt Gloucester, MA: Peter Smith, 1950, 1957.

The *WBP* is a dramatic monologue that reveals the influence of the Italian Renaissance upon English literature. Chaucer exhibits his modernity in choosing as his focal character a middle-class woman who denounces chastity. Chaucer's elaboration upon *RR*'s La Vieille in order to create the Wife's character develops Alisoun into a realistic individual as opposed to an abstract character. Other sources used in constructing the tale are Theophrastus' *Liber Aureolus de Nuptiis*, Jerome's *Jov,* and Walter Map's *Val*. A summary of the main points of the Wife's argument against virginity and of her personal history indicates that Chaucer uses the Wife to express his own ideas concerning the

Church's stance on celibacy. While the Wife's appetites might have offended Chaucer's contemporaries, Chaucer maintains a moral stance by showing that beneath the Wife's bold appearance lies unhappiness. See **92**.

428 Skeat, Walter W. *The Evolution of the Canterbury Tales.* Chaucer Society Publications, 2nd ser, 38. London: Kegan Paul, Trench, Trübner, and Co., 1907 (for the issue of 1903); rpt New York: Haskell, 1968.

In Chaucerian mss, Fragment III is 'always a distinct group' (p 24). While Furnivall is correct in assuming the *ShT* was initially meant for Alisoun, he inappropriately believes that it was to have been her second tale and not her first (p 28).

429 Tatlock, John S.P. *The Development and Chronology of Chaucer's Works.* Chaucer Society Publications, 2nd ser, 37. London: Kegan, Paul, Trench, Trübner and Co., 1907; rpt Gloucester: Peter Smith, 1963.

Chaucer originally intended the *ShT* to be told by the Wife. Afterwards, he wrote the *WBP. ShT*'s 1194–1209 and 1363–7 are similar to *WBP*'s 337–56 and 257–62, which deal respectively with the manner in which wives dress and the benefits of a husband. There are also parallels between the wife in *ShT* and Alisoun. The earliest possible date for the *WBP* is 1388 and the latest, based upon a reference in *Buk* to the Wife, is the end of 1396. Chaucer's incorporation of Jerome in both the *WBP* and the G-prologue of *LGW* (p 212) moves this time frame back to 1394. The *MerT* follows chronologically as a 'masculine rejoinder' (p 208) to the *WBP*. There are ten parallel passages between *MerT* and *WBP* (pp 201–2). In both writings Chaucer incorporates Theophrastus, Walter Map's *Val*, and quotes from *ParsT*. Other relations between the writings are found in January's resemblance to an old husband of the Wife and May's similarity to Alisoun (see IV.2187–2206, 2368–2415 and III.443–50, 226–34). January also discusses the perils of marrying an old woman. *MerT*'s 1682–8 contain a direct reference to the Wife, a 'dramatic impropriety' (p 204) on Chaucer's part in having a tale character refer to a pilgrim. The lines belong not to Chaucer, but to Justinus.

430 Derocquigny, J. 'A Possible Source of Chaucer, *Canterbury Tales*, A 4134 and D 415.' *MLR* 3(1908), 72.

See **94**.

431 ———. '"Wayte what" = "Whatever."' *MLR* 3(1908), 72.

In line 51 of the *WBP*, the words *Wayte what* function as an idiom for *whatever*, a synonym for the phrase *look what*.

432 Saintsbury, George. 'Chaucer.' In *The Cambridge History of English Literature*, Volume 2. Cambridge: Cambridge University Press, 1908; rpt New York: Macmillan, 1920. Pp 179–224.

Chaucer's artistry is responsible for his readers' not being shocked by the *WBP* (p 206). The *WBP* allows Chaucer to display both his scholarly learning and his awareness of humanity (p 209).

433 Mackail, John William. *The Springs of Helicon*. London: Longmans Green, & Co., 1909 [cited]. Excerpted in *Chaucer: The Critical Heritage*. Volume 2. Ed. Derek Brewer. London: Routledge and Kegan Paul, 1978. Pp 285-99.

The value Chaucer placed on 'academic learning' can be derived by noting that 'he lavishes it most freely on that highly cultured woman, Alison of Bath' (p 19). See **1074**.

434 Lowes, John Livingston. 'Chaucer and the *Miroir de Mariage*.' *MP* 8(1910–11), 165–86, 305–34.

Not only was Deschamps' *Mir* accessible before its author died, but Chaucer had specific access to the work as well. Deschamps' misogynistic satire of marriage inspired portions of *MerT*, the Wife of Bath, *LGWP*, *MilP*, and *FranT*. While there are differences between the Wife of Bath and Jean de Meun's La Vieille in *RR*, the wife in *Mir* parallels Alisoun with a mutual love of pilgrimages, valuing of church offerings, and managing one's husband. Both writers incorporate Theophrastus and Jerome in their works. While Chaucer refers directly to Theophrastus, he sometimes consults Deschamps' use of the Greek writer (pp 314–5). Both works include maternal influence on controlling spouses (p 316), a scene containing a housemaid and a husband (p 317), and similar strategies for spousal control (p 318). The words the Wife puts into her husband's mouth parallel those spoken by Repertoire to Franc Vouloir (p 319). Chronologically, *WBP* must have preceded *MerT*, which refers to it, as well as *LGWP*. In comparing III.707–10 with *LGWP*'s A.261–63, Lowes finds that the Wife's lines are part of a well-developed argument, whereas the God of Love's lines seem to be tacked on (p 330). Drawing on the fixed date of 7 June 1394 for *LGWP*, *WBP* dates from 1393 or early 1394.

435 ———. 'Illustrations of Chaucer. Drawn Chiefly From Deschamps.' *RomR* 2(1911), 113–28.

See **98**.

436 Moore, Samuel. 'The Date of Chaucer's Marriage Group.' *MLN* 26(1911), 172–4.
See **209**.

437 Wise, Boyd Ashby. *The Influence of Statius upon Chaucer*. New York: Phaeton Press, 1911; rpt 1967.
See **99**.

438 Kittredge, George L. 'Chaucer's Discussion of Marriage.' *MP* 9(1912), 435–67. Rev *Chaucer and His Poetry*. Cambridge, MA: Harvard University Press, 1915; rpt many times; with an Introduction by B.J. Whiting in 1970.
See **210**.

439 Snell, F.J. *The Age of Chaucer*. London: G. Bell and Sons, Ltd., 1912. A summary of the plot of the *WBP*, noting its appeal 'as a study of human nature, of matrimonial adventure' (p 207).

440 Lawrence, William W. 'The Marriage Group in the *Canterbury Tales*.' *MP* 11(1913), 247–58.
See **211**.

441 Edmunds, E.W. *Chaucer and His Poetry*. London: Harrap, 1914; rpt New York: AMS, 1971.
Alisoun reveals her character much as the Pardoner exhibits himself (p 176). Her witty, unabashed recounting of her experiences does not reduce her to the Pardoner's contemptible status. A brief summary of the *WBP* and *WBT* convey a reader's delight in Alisoun (pp 176–81).

442 Fansler, Dean D. *Chaucer and the Roman de la Rose*. New York: Columbia University Press, 1914; rpt Gloucester, Mass: Peter Smith, 1965.
There are approximately thirty passages parallel to the *RR* in the *WBP* (p 166). Alisoun is a modification of La Vieille, and her character also resembles Ami. The specific parallel lines in the two works are noted and compared (pp 168–74).

443 Tatlock, John S.P. 'Notes on Chaucer: The *Canterbury Tales*.' *MLN* 29(1914), 140–4.
See **101**.

444 Lowes, John Livingston. 'Chaucer and the Seven Deadly Sins.' *PMLA* 30(1915), 237–71.
See **1079**.

445 Cummings, Hubertis M. *The Indebtedness of Chaucer's Works to the Italian Works of Boccaccio: A Review and Summary*. New York:

Phaeton Press, 1916; rpt 1967.

While Alisoun does share some traits with the Vedova in Boccaccio's *Corbaccio*, it is doubtful that this Italian work influenced Chaucer in his creation of the *WBP* (pp 43–4).

446 Hemingway, Samuel B. 'Chaucer's Monk and Nun's Priest.' *MLN* 31(1916), 479–83.

See **212**.

447 Tupper, Frederick. 'Chaucer's Sinners and Sins.' *JEGP* 15(1916), 56–106.

See **1081**.

448 Hinckley, Henry B. 'The Debate on Marriage in the *Canterbury Tales.*' *PMLA* 32(1917), 292–305.

See **213**.

449 Lowes, John Livingston. 'Chaucer and Dante.' *MP* 15(1917), 705–35.

See **104**.

450 Grimm, Florence. *Astronomical Lore in Chaucer.* Studies in Language, Literature, and Criticism, No. 2. Lincoln: University of Nebraska, 1919; rpt New York: AMS Press, 1970.

The Wife's 'amorousness and pugnaciousness' (p 63) are qualities she inherited from the influence of Venus and Mars in her horoscope. The tension between the Wife and the Clerk stems from the opposition of the personality traits she has obtained from the effect of the planet Venus in her star sign with the characteristics he has inherited from the planet Mercury (p 64).

451 Steele, Richard. 'Chaucer and the "Almagest."' *Library* 10(1919), 243–7.

Tyrwhitt was unable to locate the points of reference in Ptolemy's 'Almagest' to which the Wife refers in III.180–3 and 323–7. They can be found, however, in Gerard of Cremona's introduction to 'the only translation of Ptolemy in existence in the fourteenth century' (p 244).

452 Wedel, Theodore O. *The Mediaeval Attitude towards Astrology: Particularly in England.* Yale Studies in English, 60. New Haven: Yale University Press; London: Humphrey Milford and Oxford University Press, 1920; rpt New York: Archon, 1968.

The passage on astrology in the *WBP* reveals many of the stellar doctrines of Chaucer's day, some of which Chaucer may not have accepted as true (pp 151–2).

453 Tatlock, J.S.P. 'The Source of the Legend, and Other Chauceriana.'

SP 18(1921), 419–28.

Alisoun's reference to herself in the third person in III.311 is a common feature in medieval literature outside of Chaucer (p 425).

454 Curry, Walter Clyde. 'More about Chaucer's Wife of Bath.' *PMLA* 37(1922), 30–51 [cited]. Rev in *Chaucer and the Medieval Sciences*. Oxford: Oxford UP, 1926/rev New York: Barnes and Noble, 1960.

If we are fully to understand the Wife's characterization, 'constant reference must be made to what the mediaeval mind believed to be truths found in the "science" of celestial physiognomy and perhaps of geomancy' (p 30). The influences of Venus, Mars, and the star-sign Taurus relieve the Wife from taking responsibility for her personality. The Wife's being born in the house of Taurus results in her pleasure-loving personality and her stocky build (p 34). While the presence of Venus in Taurus should have endowed the Wife with beauty and an agreeable personality, the additional influence of Mars corrupts both the Wife's complexion and her nature, giving her an adulterous appetite (p 40). Since Chaucer did not specify 'which face of the sign was in the ascendant at the time of her birth' (p 41), the exact location of the mark of Taurus on the Wife's neck is unknown. The mark of Venus is more than likely located on her genitalia as is the mark of Mars which corresponds to the Martian mark on her face (pp 42–3). The Wife's character represents 'a conflict in astral influence' (pp 43–8). See **1085**.

455 Landrum, Grace W. 'Chaucer's Use of the Vulgate.' *PMLA* 39(1924), 75–100.

Chaucer most likely had access to a copy of the Vulgate. It may be inferred from *WBP* that Jankyn owned one (p 76). While using Jerome as a source for Alisoun's reference to the Samaritan woman, Chaucer adds the detail of the well from the Vulgate. Jerome does not comment about the well (p 95).

456 Brusendorff, Aage. *The Chaucer Tradition*. London: Oxford University Press, 1925; rpt Oxford: Clarendon Press, 1968.

Chaucer's placing III.575–84, 609–12, 619–26, 717–20 in the margins of his ms has caused the omission of these lines from the Oxford group of mss and all but one of the All England mss (p 86). Rearranging the Ellesmere ms so that III.613–8 would fall between 608–9 would make more sense.

457 Iijima, Ikuzo. *Langland and Chaucer: A Study of the Two Types of Genius in English Poetry*. Boston: Four Seas, 1925.

Chaucer is indebted to Jean de Meun for the *WBP*. The pleasure-loving Wife uses Scripture in a highly immoral manner. Despite her crudeness, she is extremely clever. See **260**.

458 Jones, Richard F. 'A Conjecture on the *Wife of Bath's Prologue*.' *JEGP* 24(1925), 512–47.

The first 193 lines of the *WBP* initially preceded the *ShT*.

459 Spurgeon, Caroline F.E. *Five Hundred Years of Chaucer Criticism and Allusion 1357–1900*. 3 volumes and a supplement. Cambridge: Cambridge University Press, 1925; rpt New York: Russell and Russell, 1960.

The *WBP* has been translated by Pope, has been referred to in the work of Skelton, has influenced Selden and Skot, and has been commented upon by Nashe. See **1088**.

460 Walker, Hugh. *English Satire and Satirists*. New York: J.M. Dent, 1925; rpt New York: Octagon Books, 1965.

While the *WBP* is antimatrimonialist in theme as well as a 'satire upon the lascivious woman' (p 23), it also contains dramatic elements.

461 Cowling, George. *Chaucer*. London: Methuen, 1927; rpt Freeport, NY: Books for Libraries Press, 1971.

In the *WBP* Chaucer derides neither women nor people who have chosen celibacy. He merely sees the humor of women's cunning and views marriage as a more natural choice for humans (p 168). See **1091**.

462 Rickert, Edith. '"Goode lief, my wyf."' *MP* 25(1927–8), 79–82.

That Goodelief is the name of Bailly's wife is doubtful when one considers that Alisoun uses the expression *goode lief* to address her fourth husband (III.431). The name Goodelief was common during the fourteenth century. Chaucer could have used the words for two distinct purposes.

&bsp; The Wife of Bath's Prologue 1931-1960

463 Rutter, George. 'The Wife of Bath.' *Western Reserve University Bulletin* 34(1931), 60–4.

Rutter outlines 'a definite literary tradition of the treatment of women' (p 64) to which the Wife belongs. His list includes, among others, Anus from the Latin play *Pamphilus, de amore*, La Vieille, the characters in William Dunbar's *Tua Mariit Wemen and the Wedo*, and Boccaccio's Ghismonda. 'The chief characteristics of the women mentioned seem to be carnality, deceit, a love of liberty in action, and a passion for dominance, all revealed by their talk' (p 64).

464 Baldwin, Charles Sears. *Three Medieval Centuries of Literature in England 1100-1400*. Boston: Little Brown, 1932; rpt New York: Phaeton, 1968.

Bailly's comparing Goodelief to Prudence and the *NPT* are cues for the *WBP*. See **1092**.

465 Camden, Carroll, Jr. 'Chauceriana.' *MLN* 47(1932), 360–2.

For a true appreciation of Chaucer's intentions behind his usage of *worthy*, one must appreciate what the medieval ideal of perception of a person was. His ironic obliqueness is revealed in his referring to the Wife's first three husbands as *worthy men in hir degree* (p 360). See **293**.

466 McCormick, Sir William. *The Manuscripts of Chaucer's Canterbury Tales: A Critical Description of their Contents*. With the assistance of Janet E. Heseltine. Oxford: Clarendon, 1933.

The Man of Law's *Epilogue* was originally absent from approximately 20 mss (p xvi). The *MLT* is followed by the *WBP* in 15 mss. See **1096**.

467 Parsons, Coleman O. 'A Scottish Sequel to the *Wife of Bath's Prologue.*' *Scottish Notes and Queries* 11(1933), 33–5.

The ballad *The Wanton Wife of Bath* appeared in print in 1670. It functions as a sequel to the *WBP* and deals with the Wife's adventures in heaven. A 1700 Scottish version of the English ballad, *The New Wife of Beath Much Better Reformed, Enlarged and Corrected than It Was Formerly in the Old Uncorrect Copy with the Addition of Many Other Things*, adds a moral dimension to the story.

468 Coffman, George R. 'Old Age from Horace to Chaucer. Some Literary Affinities and Adventures of an Idea.' *Spec* 9(1934), 249–77.

For the purpose of accurate characterization, Horace outlines the stages of man's life and the primary traits of an old man in his *Ars Poetica* (pp 249–50). Chaucer treats old age rather lightly. Alisoun does reflect upon the joys of youth and realistically accepts the coming of age in III.474–8.

469 Lowes, John Livingston. *Geoffrey Chaucer and the Development of His Genius*. Boston: Houghton Mifflin, 1934 [cited]; rpt (with different pagination) Bloomington: Indiana University Press, 1958; rpt through 1962.

While the *WBP* is 'marred by' its 'breach of decorum' (p 217), Chaucer's creation of Alisoun's self-revealing character shows his greatness as a writer. See **1095**.

470 Slaughter, Eugene E. '"Allas! Allas! That ever love was sinne!"' *MLN* 49(1934), 83–6.

While III.614 is usually interpreted as the Wife's regret that the church doesn't favor multiple marriages, the line has an added dimension. The Wife knows Jerome advocates chastity in marriage. Her enjoyment of sexual intercourse, however, is in conflict with this religious belief. 'In extenuation of both causes of uneasiness — incontinency and several marriages — she pleads her inclination due to astrological influences' (p 86).

471 Tupper, Frederick. 'The Bearings of the *Shipman's Prologue.*' *JEGP* 33(1934), 352–72.

The Ellesmere ms, along with twelve other mss, places the *WBP* after the Man of Law's *Endlink*. Alisoun was to have been the initial teller of the *ShT* (pp 356–8). The mss which place the Squire instead of the

Shipman in the *Endlink* are the victims of scribal error.

472 Whiting, Bartlett J. *Chaucer's Use of Proverbs*. Cambridge: Harvard University Press, 1934.

Alisoun values the realistic qualities of proverbs and uses them more than any other pilgrim. There are 'fourteen proverbs and twenty-five sententious remarks' in the *WBP* (pp 92–99). See **1097**.

473 Lyons, Clifford P. 'The Marriage Debate in the *Canterbury Tales*.' *ELH* 2(1935), 252–62.

See **215**.

474 Piper, Edwin Ford. *Canterbury Pilgrims*. Whirling World Series. Iowa City: Clio Press, 1935.

See **294**.

475 Shaver, C.L. 'A Mediaeval French Analogue to the Dunmow Flitch.' *MLN* 50(1935), 322–5.

In addition to the work of Tyrwhitt and du Fail which proves that 'the practice of awarding a gammon of bacon to that married couple who could truthfully swear that they had never rued their bargain' (pp 323–4) existed in Brittany, there is Jacques de Vitry's *Sermones Feriales et Communes*. This work, dated between 1229–40, gives evidence that the flitch contest was conducted 'long before Chaucer gave it literary immortality' (p 325).

476 Wyatt, A.J., ed. *The Links of the Canterbury Tales and the Wife of Bath's Prologue*. London: Sidgwick and Jackson, 1935.

The *WBP* not only reveals Alisoun's mind-set but is 'a marvelous example of homogeneity inspired upon the most heterogeneous materials' (p 7).

477 Pyle, Fitzroy. 'A Metrical Point in Chaucer.' *N&Q* 170(1936), 128.

The lines of Jankyn's proverb, III.655–8, differ in meter from the *WBP*. While Skeat (**4**) felt the meter was irregular, Pyle notes it is a standard four-beat verse. Variations of this proverb can be found in *Reliquiae Antiquae, i. 233* and Juliana Berners' *Treatise on Hunting*, ed. 1486.

478 Mersand, Joseph. *Chaucer's Romance Vocabulary*. Brooklyn: Comet Press, 1937/2nd ed, 1939.

The *WBP* contains a 43.85 percentage of rhyming romance words (p 87). It also contains 17 words first used by Chaucer. See **1099**.

479 Patch, Howard Rollin. *On Rereading Chaucer*. Cambridge: Harvard University Press, 1939.

The robust Alisoun embodies the creative impulse and female instinct, yet she does not exemplify an ideal character (p 161). Alisoun and

Jankyn love one another and also love to fight. Chaucer does not wholly agree with all Alisoun has to say, yet he delights in her (p 247). See **1099a**.

480 Bayon, H.P. 'Trotula and the Ladies of Salerno: A Contribution to the Knowledge of the Transition between Ancient and Medieval Physick.' *Proceedings of the Royal Society of Medicine* 33(1940), 471–4.
Alisoun's reference to Trotula in the *WBP* may reflect Chaucer's awareness of the copies of this physician's work in the Canterbury Library (p 474).

481 Sedgewick, G.G. 'The Progress of Chaucer's Pardoner, 1880–1940.' *MLQ* 1(1940), 431–58.
The dynamics of the Pardoner's interruption of the *WBP* support the placing of the *PardT* after and not before Alisoun's performance (p 446). His admiration of Alisoun's preaching inspires him to tell a confessional prologue (p 448).

482 Shelley, Percy Van Dyke. *The Living Chaucer*. Philadelphia: University of Pennsylvania Press, 1940.
While Alisoun does quote authorities in the *WBP*, she does so only in conjunction with the opinions she has formulated through her own experiences (p 216). Her frank and realistic approach to life is seen in her defense of marriage and advocacy of female sovereignty. See **1100**.

483 Whiting, Bartlett J. 'The *Wife of Bath's Prologue.*' In *Sources and Analogues of Chaucer's Canterbury Tales*. Ed. W.F. Bryan and Germaine Dempster. Chicago: University of Chicago Press, 1941; rpt New York: Humanities Press, 1958. Pp 207–22.
See **118**.

484 Moore, Arthur K. 'Alysoun's Other Tonne.' *MLN* 59(1944), 481–3.
The Wife's reply to the Pardoner's question whether or not he should marry is based on the *qui capit uxorem* motif. While Chaucer was familiar with the incorporation of this motif in *Mir*, he 'was probably the first to cast a woman in the role of the ecclesiastical raconteur who invariably renders this recitation' (p 482).

485 Utley, Francis Lee. *The Crooked Rib: An Analytical Index to the Argument about Women in England and Scots Literature to the End of the Year 1568*. Columbus: Ohio State University Press, 1944; rpt New York: Octagon Books, 1970.
Alisoun doesn't realize that clerks can be a source of praise for women (p 14). Most medieval laments of wives are satires like *WBP*, which is

a confession (pp 40–1). Chaucer's *LGW* and the Marriage Group inspired much antifeminist satire (p 55). The mss of the authorities that Alisoun quotes are catalogued (pp 125–7). Alisoun's character has influenced Hoccleve, Idley, Waleys, Dunbar, and Skot. Works containing similarities to Alisoun and her performance include those of Sempill, Skelton, Gosynhill, and works possibly authored by Turberville and Lydgate.

486 Whiting, B.J. 'Some Chaucer Allusions, 1923–1942.' *N&Q* 187(1944), 288–91.

Little work has been done in examining Chaucerian allusions in literature of the twentieth century. In Louis Paul's 1937 *Hallelujah, I'm a Bum*, the character Resin meditates on the Wife's character and puts III.27–38 into modern English. Another allusion to III.38 occurs in p 153 of the work (p 289). Bellamy Partridge's *Country Lawyer* of 1939 refers to the Wife's gossip. See **1104**.

487 Moore, Arthur K. 'Chaucer and Matheolus.' *N&Q* 190(1946), 245–8. See **122**.

488 Schlauch, Margaret. 'The Marital Dilemma in the *Wife of Bath's Tale*.' *PMLA* 61(1946), 416–30.

See **1106**.

489 Seaton, Ethel. 'Goode Lief My Wife.' *MLR* 41(1946), 196–202.

Alisoun's use of *goode lief* in connection with patience in marriage may be seen as being highly appropriate if one connects it to the Flemish saint Godeleva, the submissive virgin-wife, who was murdered by her husband.

490 Bennett, H.S. *Chaucer and the Fifteenth Century*. Volume 2, Part 1 of the Oxford History of English Literature. Oxford: Clarendon Press, 1947; rpt with corrections, 1965.

Many topics in the *WBP* have come from sermon material (p 20). Proverbs as well contribute to the *WBP*, adding to the depiction of characters (p 79). See **1107**.

491 French, Robert Dudley. *A Chaucer Handbook*, 2nd ed. New York: Appleton-Century-Crofts, 1947.

See **124**.

492 Kökeritz, Helge. 'The Wyf of Bathe and al hire secte.' *PQ* 26(1947), 147–51.

Kittredge (**210**) derived his opinion that Alisoun is 'a member of a mysterious, heretical sect with the sinister aim of putting her second heresy into universal practice' (p 148) from his interpretation of the

Clerk's addressing his tale to the Wife and *al hir secte* (IV.1171) as a reference to a heretical organization. Another of the *NED*'s definitions of sect, that of 'a class or kind (of persons)' (p 149), suggests that the Clerk is referring to all women.

493   Hall, Vernon, Jr. 'Sherlock Holmes and the Wife of Bath.' *Baker Street Journal* 3(1948), 84–93.

After reading *WBP*, Holmes concludes that Alisoun and Jankyn murdered her fourth husband. Alisoun used her dream to plant ideas of murder in Jankyn's head. Holmes bases his deductions on the facts that Jankyn is the only husband for whom Alisoun prays (p 86), that Alisoun verbally stumbles in *WBP* and almost reveals her secret (p 88), and that Alisoun calls Jankyn a thief during their fight (p 89). Fear that Alisoun might expose him as a murderer accounts for Jankyn's submission in marriage.

494   Whiting, B.J. 'A Colt's Tooth.' In *Mediaeval Studies in Honor of Jeremiah Denis Matthias Ford*. Ed. Urban T. Holmes, Jr., and Alex J. Denomy. Cambridge: Harvard University Press, 1948. Pp 321–31.

The expression 'a colt's tooth' 'is not recorded in English before Chaucer nor after him until 1588' (p 321). The Wife uses this phrase (III.602) to emphasize her youthful lust for Jankyn despite her advancing age. The Reeve also makes use of the expression in I.3888. Chaucer uses the adjective *coltish* (IV.1847) to describe January's sexuality. Because Deschamps uses the idiom in two of his ballads, Whiting feels that Chaucer may have adopted this phrase from him.

495   Coghill, Nevill. *The Poet Chaucer*. London: Oxford University Press, 1949/2nd ed, 1967.

The *WBP* 'is the first autobiography in English fiction' (p 106). While Alisoun is extremely self-aware, she does not know whether love or power is her ultimate goal. Her desire for both causes her unsettled nature. The comedy of *WBP* is rooted in the tragedy that Jankyn hits Alisoun (p 109). The Wife's womanly wiles and passion allow her to attain sovereignty over Jankyn. See **298** and **1109**.

496   Moore, Arthur K. 'The Pardoner's Interruption of the *Wife of Bath's Prologue*.' *MLQ* 10(1949), 49–57.

The Pardoner's interruption of the Wife serves as a catalyst for Alisoun to begin her diatribe against matrimony. 'The continuation is a modified antifeminist satire which the Wife converts to burlesque ... gaining complete victory over the advocates of the traditional Church view' (p 49). The Pardoner's recognition of the Wife as a *noble prechour*

(III.165) reveals his 'approval of the Wife's shrewd examination of the Scriptural authority for the Church's attitude toward marriage and celibacy' (p 50). While the Wife does intend to answer the Pardoner's question, the primary motive behind her response is an attack upon the clergy. In order to introduce misogynistic themes, Alisoun describes the trials of married men. This technique is found in *Mir* and *Val*. The Wife uses conventional examples from antiquity in her speech; 'Adam and Sampson are everywhere mentioned in antifeminist documents' (p 55), and she duly offends the Friar and Clerk with her sermon.

497   Hench, Atchison L. 'Dunmow Bacon, 1949.' *CE* 11(1950), 350.
The four gammons awarded to peaceful couples in England in 1949 provide a modern illustration for Alisoun's comment about the Dunmow flitch.

498   Pratt, Robert A. 'A Note on Chaucer and the *Policraticus* of John of Salisbury.' *MLN* 65(1950), 243–6.
See **127**.

499   Slaughter, Eugene. 'Clerk Jankyn's Motive.' *MLN* 65(1950), 530–4.
'Jankyn contracted an irregularity in marrying a widow which excluded him forever from clerical orders' (p 530). According to Thomas Aquinas, a priest may not violate the sacraments because he is the one who administers them. I Timothy 3:2 and 12 and the First and Fourth Toledo Councils declare the 'impediment to receiving orders' if one marries 'a woman who is not a virgin' (p 531). 'Chaucer, indeed, has motivated Jankyn's relation to the Wife of Bath — and the conflict between her and the Clerk of Oxford — not only by the general consequences woman brings upon man, but also by the specific effects a woman ... works upon a clerk who falls under her power' (p 534).

500   Malone, Kemp. *Chapters on Chaucer*. Baltimore: Johns Hopkins Press, 1951; rpt 1961.
Both the Wife and the Pardoner provide self-revelations in their prologues. See **299** and **1111**.

501   Owen, Charles A., Jr. 'The Plan of the Canterbury Pilgrimage.' *PMLA* 66(1951), 820–6.
The placement of Fragment VI within *CT* is partially influenced by the Pardoner's interruption of *WBP*, which would prove anticlimactic if it took place after *PardT* and the Host's insulting of him.

502   Speirs, John. *Chaucer the Maker*. London: Faber and Faber, 1951, 1954/2nd ed, 1960, 1962; rpt 1964, 1967, 1972.

WBP is 'self-revelatory and self-explanatory,' and Alisoun 'glories unashamedly in her way of life' (p 137). Because she has been criticized by the church patriarchy, Alisoun herself becomes a critic of this institution. Adopting clerkish techniques, she uses the Bible to support her opposing views on virginity. After recounting the sensual glories and the marriages of her youth, the Wife recognizes that she has aged. She intertwines the more sacred aspects of her story (her pilgrimages, Lent, her fourth husband's funeral) with the more profane (her lust for Jankyn, etc.). The Wife adheres to the 'natural law' of her horoscope, knowing that it 'is in conflict with moral law as interpreted by the Church' (p 144). In her fifth marital conflict, Alisoun 'is armed with shrewd knowledge ... of human nature' (p 145), a weapon that will aid her in gaining sovereignty over her husband. In his use of '*ensamples* to madden his wife the Clerk overreaches himself, becoming himself a fantastic-comic figure' (p 146). *WBP* ends 'in buffoonery of vivid melodrama' (p 146). See **1114**.

503 Steer, Francis W. *The History of the Dunmow Flitch Ceremony*. Essex Record Office Publications, 13. Chelmsford: Essex County Council, 1951.
WBP is one of several literary works that give historical evidence of the Flitch trials (p 7).

504 Gerould, Gordon Hall. 'Some Dominant Ideas of the Wife of Bath.' In *Chaucerian Essays*. Princeton: Princeton University Press, 1952. Pp 72–80.
Chaucer reveals his awareness of the flaws of courtly love and in human attitudes towards sex in *WBP*. There should be a distinction between the creator and the character he creates (p 73). Alisoun's integrated character revolves around her instinct and emotions (p 79). See **1115**.

505 Gunn, Alan M.F. *The Mirror of Love: A Reinterpretation of 'The Romance of the Rose'*. Lubbock: Texas Tech Press, 1952.
La Vieille's use of authority to support her arguments parallels Alisoun's learned references in *WBP*.

506 Hench, Atchison L. 'The Dunmow Flitch Trials of 1949.' *SFQ* 16(1952), 128–31.
A detailed account of a twentieth-century Dunmow Flitch Trial shows that it is a descendant of the one to which Alisoun refers in III.217–8.

507 Preston, Raymond. *Chaucer*. New York: Sheed and Ward, 1952; rpt New York: Greenwood Press, 1969.

A parallel may be drawn between Alisoun and *RR*'s Genius. *WBP* reflects Villon's *La Belle Heaulmière* and Dunbar's *Of Manis Mortalitie*. The Wife's command of ecclesiastical learning is to be attributed in part to 'the maligned Church of the fourteenth century' (p 245). A ballad concerning Alisoun's arrival at heaven's door 'and the replies of that lady to the Biblical persons who refused her admittance' was composed in the Elizabethan Age. Unfortunately, 'the copies were burnt' (p 245). See **1116**.

508 Schlauch, Margaret. 'Chaucer's Colloquial English: Its Structural Traits.' *PMLA* 67(1952), 1103–16.

WBP provides examples of the following: colloquial repetition occurring when interrupting clauses are not present (III.362), anticipatory pushing forward of noun phrases and clauses that are later 'recapitulated through a pronoun' (p 1106), omitting of formal antecedents (III.639f), illogical parataxis (III.853f), and shifting from first person plural pronouns to the singular third person (III.257–9). See **1117**.

509 Makarewicz, Sister Mary Raynelda. *The Patristic Influence on Chaucer*. Washington, D.C.: Catholic University of America Press, 1953.

In the Marriage Group Chaucer addresses not only the issue of sovereignty but also that of marriage-vs-virginity. The core of this debate is found in *WBP* (p 12). Alisoun counters and manipulates Jerome's opinion of virginity. Church support of virginity as the ideal state stemmed from the writings of Augustine and his doctrine of *caritas*. Patristic opinion on marriage is discussed (pp 64–8). Jerome incorporated Scripture and classical scholarship, such as that of Theophrastus, into his *Jov* (p 35). The passages of *WBP* for which Chaucer has used Jerome are compared to their source throughout this work. Alisoun's pride is revealed in her desire to obtain sovereignty over her husbands (pp 191–2). Because the Seven Deadly Sins are related, Alisoun's pride leads to lechery. See **300** and **1119**.

510 Kökeritz, Helge. 'Rhetorical Word-Play in Chaucer.' *PMLA* 69(1954), 937–52.

Punning occurs among the words *preamble*, *preambulation*, and *amble* in III.830–8. See **1122**.

511 Salter, F.M. 'The Tragic Figure of the Wyf of Bath.' *Proceedings and Transactions of the Royal Society of Canada* 48(1954), 1–13.

The Wife of Bath is the creation of an overtly moral writer whose 'sympathy and pity were more and more enlisted' as he 'worked on the portrait of the Wyf' (p 13). There is no comedy in Alisoun's three marriages to 'old, worn-out lechers and drunken sots' (p 11). Alisoun's definition of these men as being *goode* (III.196) should not be interpreted as 'virtuous' (p 11) but as well-made matches. There is tragedy in Alisoun's being married at twelve, in her fourth husband's infidelity, and in the brevity of her happy fifth marriage. 'It was not "bacon" she desired, but children' (p 13) and her ill-matched marriages prevented her from having them. See **1124**.

512 Schaar, Claes. *Some Types of Narrative in Chaucer's Poetry*. Lund Studies in English, 25. Lund: C.W.K. Gleerup; Copenhagen: Ejnar Munksgaard, 1954.

Chaucer makes use of close chronological narrative in *WBP*. Alisoun's fight with Jankyn is recounted in specific detail. The incident is fully developed and equal attention is given to both characters. The precision of the passage matches that of the fight in *RvT*.

513 Lumiansky, R.M. *Of Sondry Folk: The Dramatic Principle in the Canterbury Tales*. Austin: University of Texas Press, 1955.

The *WBP* is a piece of well-wrought dialectic. It should not be seen as divisible into two parts. Alisoun's speech before the Pardoner's interruption is a necessary prelude to her argument (p 121). The woe of marriage is that of husbands who didn't yield sovereignty to their wives, not Alisoun's personal tribulations. Alisoun begins her argument by overturning the concepts of a single marriage in one's life and of the importance of virginity. The antifeminist contents of Jankyn's book assert that wives give their husbands woe (p 124). Alisoun's performance is a response to the *NPT* (p 126). In her fourth and fifth relationships, Alisoun assumes the role of her first three husbands. See **306** and **1127**.

514 Owen, Charles A., Jr. 'Morality as a Comic Motif in the *Canterbury Tales*.' *CE* 16(1955), 226–32.

The bawdy *ShT*, originally intended for Alisoun, reflects her antagonism towards morality. While Alisoun is suitable for the telling of a story of 'perfidity and prostitution' (p 287), the wife of St. Denis's 'exposure would have exposed herself' (p 227). Alisoun's attack upon antifeminism transforms a sober subject into comedy (p 231).

515 Shain, Charles E. 'Pulpit Rhetoric in Three Canterbury Tales.' *MLN* 70(1955), 235–45.

Because she is arguing against theological doctrine, Alisoun employs figurative language and biblical authorities in her performance (p 241).

516   Baum, Paull F. 'Chaucer's Puns.' *PMLA* 71(1956), 225–46.

In the *WBP*, there are puns made with the words *age* (III.113), *array* (235), *borel* (355f), *cross* (484), *dalliance* (565), *dangerous* (513f), *definition* (25), *dight* (398), *lecherous* (466), *lees* (302), *pre-amble* (837f), *proof* (247), *quaint* (332, 444), and *tail/tale* (466). See **307** and **1128**.

517   Bradley, Sister Ritamary, C.H.M. 'The *Wife of Bath's Tale* and the Mirror Tradition.' *JEGP* 55(1956), 624–30.

Alisoun's self-revelation relies heavily 'on the tradition of mirror literature and allusion' (p 624), in which wit and folly function as thesis and antithesis. The tradition of the medieval mirror centers on the presentation of a perfect example juxtaposed against reality. The *WBP* explores the contrast between holy wisdom and life experiences. In Alisoun's world, female wisdom consists of deception and wiles. 'The conflict between wisdom and self-indulgence becomes cosmic in the discussion of Mercury as opposed to Venus' (p 625). The animal imagery applied to the Wife exposes her self-indulgent nature. Certain references, such as those concerning gold, extend the 'ironic contrast between wisdom and worldly "purveyaunce"' (p 626). This contrast may be applied thematically to the *CT*. The portraits in the *GP* expose 'what the characters are and what they ought to be' (p 627).

518   Coghill, Nevill. *Geoffrey Chaucer*. London: Longmans, Green, and Company, 1956 [cited]. Rpt in *British Writers and Their Works*. Volume 1. Ed. Bonamy Dobrée and J.W. Robinson. Lincoln: University of Nebraska Press, 1963. Pp 7–68.

Chaucer asserts the 'pre-eminence of virginity' (p 40) in several of the pilgrims' tales, including the *WBP*. Alisoun's theme of sovereignty runs through several of the other tales (p 45). See **265**.

519   Schlauch, Margaret. *English Medieval Literature and Its Social Foundations*. Warsaw: Panstowowe Wydawnictwo Naukowe, 1956, 1967; rpt New York: Cooper Square Publishers, 1971.

While Chaucer used Deschamps' *Mir* as a model for the Wife of Bath, he developed her character far beyond what she was in the work of other writers. Until the twentieth century the *WBP* stood alone as a work of fiction that contains a detailed analysis of marriage from a female perspective (p 258). See **1132**.

520   Muscatine, Charles. *Chaucer and the French Tradition: A Study in*

Style and Meaning. Berkeley: University of California Press, 1957; rpt 1964.

Chaucer elaborated upon Jean de Meun's Duenna for his creation of Alisoun (p 205). While the scholarly learning of which the Duenna speaks seems artificial in its placement, Chaucer makes Alisoun's knowledge of authorities a realistic incorporation (p 207). He alters text to accommodate Alisoun's domestic and common origins (p 209) and attributes much of the Wife's acquired knowledge to hearsay (p 210). Chaucer also turns exemplum into autobiography.

521 Rockwell, K.A. '*Canterbury Tales*: *General Prologue*, 526, The *Wife of Bath's Prologue*, 435, "Spiced conscience."' *N&Q* 202(1957), 84.

The phrase *sweet spiced conscience* in the *WBP* recalls the similar *spiced conscience* found in the *GP*'s description of the Parson. Alisoun's words advocate a husband's possession of a docile temperament.

522 Slaughter, Eugene Edward. *Virtue According to Love, in Chaucer*. New York: Bookman Associates, 1957.

While the *WBP* satirizes women, it does provide a female's perspective on love in marriage. Alisoun feels that she is in accordance with religio-philosophical doctrine with respect to her views on the marriage debt. For her, a husband must not only satisfy her in bed but obey her will. It is not until Jankyn gives up his book and yields to his wife that their marriage flourishes (pp 204–5). See **310** and **1133**.

523 Baum, Paull F. *Chaucer: A Critical Appreciation*. Durham: Duke University Press, 1958.

See **1134**.

524 ———. 'Chaucer's Puns: A Supplementary List.' *PMLA* 73(1958), 167–70.

Notes the pun on *flower* / *flour* in III.113, 477–8. See **311**.

525 Donaldson, E. Talbot. *Chaucer's Poetry: An Anthology for the Modern Reader*. New York: Ronald Press, 1958/rev 1975.

A product of antifeminism, Alisoun forces a reader to compare the misogynistic tradition with real women (p 914). Ultimately, Alisoun is a symbol of human nature. See **1135**.

526 Mroczkowski, Przemyslaw. 'Mediaeval Art and Aesthetics in *The Canterbury Tales*.' *Spec* 33(1958), 204–21.

Certain pieces of medieval artwork reflect themes similar to the Wife's preoccupation with female sovereignty and with sex. *Luxuria* was personified as a scepter-wielding woman who has power over man. Thirteenth-century ivories depict a woman crowning her subservient lover with roses (p 210). Several cathedrals contain carvings in which a woman beats a man or in which partners struggle with one another for possession of a rod.

527   Owen, Charles A., Jr. 'The Development of the *Canterbury Tales*.' *JEGP* 57(1958), 449–76.

The *WBP* should be considered as linked to the Man of Law's *Epilogue*; initially, it was intended to introduce what is now the *ShT* (p 453). Around 1393, Chaucer removed the Wife from Fragment B and amplified the *WBP* for the development of the Marriage Group (p 455). Alisoun's desire to be first in church offering may have contributed to the Parson's discussion of pride (p 460).

528   Ackerman, Robert W. 'The English Rimed and Prose Romances.' In *Arthurian Literature in the Middle Ages: A Collaborative History*. Ed. Roger Sherman Loomis. Oxford: Clarendon Press, 1959; rpt 1961. Pp 480–519.

See **138**.

529   Pratt, Robert A. 'Chaucer and Isidore on Why Men Marry.' *MLN* 74(1959), 293–4.

See **139**.

530   Steadman, John M. 'The Book-Burning Episode in the *Wife of Bath's Prologue*: Some Additional Analogues.' *PMLA* 74(1959), 521–5.

See **140**.

⽯ The Wife of Bath's Prologue
1961-1970

531 Baum, Paull F. *Chaucer's Verse*. Durham: Duke University Press, 1961.
See **1140.**

532 Magoun, Francis P., Jr. *A Chaucer Gazetteer*. Chicago: University of
Chicago Press, 1961.
Definitions of locations in *WBP*, such as Bath, Crete, Dunmow, Essex,
Galilee, Oxford, Paris, and Samaria, are provided. See **314.**

533 Pratt, Robert A. 'The Development of the Wife of Bath.' In *Studies in
Medieval Literature in Honor of Professor Albert Croll Baugh*. Ed.
MacEdward Leach. Philadelphia: University of Pennsylvania Press,
1961. Pp 45–79.
Chaucer's conception of the Wife of Bath developed over time. In an
earlier plan for ordering the *CT*, Chaucer intended the Man of Law to
tell *Mel*. Alisoun, having been wearied by *Mel* and objecting to a tale
being told by the Parson, makes her voice heard in the *Endlink* and
proceeds to tell the *ShT* (pp 46–7). That the portion of the *WBP* that
concerns her marriages was written first is evinced by its appropriate
thematic ties to *MLT* and *ShT*. This quality is absent in the sermon on
marriage-vs-virginity of the *WBP*. This sermon, the Pardoner's
interruption, and Alisoun's rejoinder were composed later and focus on
the theme of woe in marriage. Alisoun's five marriages create a need
for her to defend sensuality, hence the sermon on marriage-vs-virginity.
Chaucer's decision to develop a Marriage Group occurred later, as did
his arranging a new tale for Alisoun.

534 Silverstein, Theodore. 'Wife of Bath and the Rhetoric of Enchantment:
Or, How to Make a Hero See in the Dark.' *MP* 58(1961), 153–73.
See **1142.**

535 Sullivan, Hazel. 'A Chaucerian Puzzle.' In *A Chaucerian Puzzle and Other Medieval Essays*. University of Miami Publications in English and American Literature, V. Ed. Natalie Grenis Lawrence and Jack A. Reynolds. Coral Gables: University of Miami Press, 1961. Pp 1–46.

The belief that Chaucer originally intended Alisoun to tell the *ShT* and that he forgot to alter the feminine pronouns when he changed his mind seems to have originated with Tyrwhitt. Critics have continued to build a house of straw out of this theory (p 14). The female philosophy expressed in the opening lines of the *ShT* does not fit Alisoun's personality. She is a much more independent woman than the wife of St. Denis. The *ShT* is a story 'of dependent woman and dominant man' (p 22), whereas Alisoun's philosophy maintains that women should dominate men. The opening lines of the *ShT* were rearranged by a scribe, leaving the female pronouns out of place in the mouth of the Shipman.

536 Baker, Donald C. 'The Bradshaw Order of the *Canterbury Tales*: A Dissent.' *NM* 63(1962), 245–61.

A primary reason for the Bradshaw Shift is that Bailly's reference in the prologue to *MkT* to Rochester geographically precedes the Summoner's reference to Sittingbourne in *WBP*. In the mss of *CT*, however, *WBT* follows *MLT* in all but five and it appears before *ShT* in all but six (p 248). The Marriage Group theory is not a thematic key to tale order, for each of the tales contains some sort of gender relationship (p 254).

537 Malone, Kemp. 'The *Wife of Bath's Tale*.' *MLR* 57(1962), 481–91. See **1145**.

538 Margulies, Cecile Stoller. 'The Marriages and the Wealth of the Wife of Bath.' *MS* 24(1962), 210–6.

Much of *WBP* is in accordance with the medieval laws regarding marriage and 'legal actions between husbands and wives' (p 210). According to tradition, husbands gave dowers to their wives during the church door ceremony. The church door is where Alisoun's betrothals took place. Pagan Roman and Teutonic law recognized a difference between betrothal and ceremonial marriage. The two practices were fused into one by the tenth century. As described in *Use of Sarum* husbands would give dowers to their wives at the church door with a priest's blessing. A religious service occurred afterwards, inside the church. By the twelfth century, the practice of giving the bride a dower became a legal requirement; however, since her 'husband had legal control over her body and her belongings during ... her life' (p 214) a wife would not truly possess her dower until her husband died. While Alisoun claims not to have been selective in choosing her husbands (III.622–6), her marriages to old men allowed her access to her dowers. Although in 'marrying a widow he deprived himself of the right to take orders in the Church' (p 215), Jankyn obtains control of Alisoun's extensive wealth. Through 'taking clever advantage of her legal position and of all her marital rights' (p 216) Alisoun manages to regain power over her possessions.

539 Pratt, Robert A. 'Chaucer's "Natal Jove" and "Seint Jerome ... Agayn Jovinian."' *JEGP* 61(1962), 244–8.

In his reading, Chaucer would at times come across 'a casual allusion to an ancient personage and to the idea of his having written on a subject of great interest' (p 246) and envision an actual text composed by that person. For example, Chaucer credits Lollius with having written a book on Troy in *HF*. The reference to *Crisippus* (III.677) as one of the contributors to Jankyn's book comes from a passage in Jerome's *Jov*. This same passage sheds light on an obscure reference to Jove in *TC*.

540 Robertson, D.W., Jr. *A Preface to Chaucer: Studies in Medieval Perspectives.* Princeton: Princeton University Press, 1962.

WBP is filled with exegetical and theological materials which Alisoun consistently distorts for her own purpose. Alisoun may be interpreted allegorically through her relationship to the Samaritan Woman by the Well and her reference to the Wedding Feast at Cana. The relationship of the Old and New Laws in Scripture, the topological interpretations that would have accompanied them in a medieval culture, and contemporary church teachings on the sacrament of marriage also play a significant role in determining Alisoun's character. Attention should also be given to the writings of Jerome, Paul, and Augustine.

541 Boyd, Beverly. 'The Wife of Bath's Gay *Lente*.' *AN&Q* 1(1963), 85–6.

The word *Lente*, found in III.543, 550, should be defined as the season of spring, not as the church season that precedes Easter. Support for this definition may be found in Alisoun's description of the time period in III.546 as the months of March, April, and May. The liturgical Lent never occurs in May because of the church's specific guidelines about when Easter should be celebrated. Also, the Wife attends both performances of miracle plays and weddings during this time. Miracle plays were enacted in 'the post-Paschal period' (p 86), and canon law prohibited the sacrament of marriage from being celebrated in Lent. Chaucer did not mean to depict Alisoun as one who violated the solemnity of the church's Lent, but as one who succumbed 'to spring fever' (p 86).

542 Cavalcanti, Leticia Niederauer Tavares. 'Sovereignty in Love or Obedience in Marriage: An Analysis of the Sovereignty-Obedience Theme and Its Relationship to the Characterization of Women in the Major Works of Geoffrey Chaucer.' *DA* 23(1963), 2522.

Chaucer reveals ideal, courteous marriages in *BD*, *KnT*, *WBP*, *WBT*, and *FranT*, and places the conflict between real and ideal marriages upon his female characters. Alisoun is a combination of an autocrat and a victim of love who can only gain freedom when Jankyn yields it to her.

543 Clemen, Wolfgang. *Chaucer's Early Poetry*. Trans. C.A.M. Sym. London: Hertford and Harlow, 1963.

Alisoun's tirade on marriage includes references to patristic doctrine and classical philosophy.

544 Hoffman, Richard L. 'The Wife of Bath and the Dunmow Bacon.' *N&Q* 208(1963), 9–11.

The mention of *bacon* (III.418) is a reference to the reward of bacon given to the couple who managed to live in domestic peace for one year. It does not refer to food of the common man, as Skeat has proposed (**4**), nor does it signify, as Robinson suggests, Alisoun's older husbands (**38**). III.419 emphasizes that the Wife neither prioritized marital harmony nor ever wished to win the Dunmow contest. The Dunmow bacon is mentioned specifically in III.217–8. The incorporation of this contest in *WBP* ties in with Alisoun's intention *To speke of wo that is in mariage* (III.3).

545 Nevo, Ruth. 'Chaucer: Motive and Mask in the "General Prologue."' *MLR* 58(1963), 1–9.

See **317**.

546 Payne, Robert O. *The Key of Remembrance: A Study of Chaucer's Poetics*. New Haven: Yale University Press, 1963.

Although Alisoun advocates a separation between experience and knowledge that contrasts with Saturn's call for a fusion of the two, both Alisoun and Saturn reject the literary tradition (p 66).

547 Pratt, Robert A. 'Saint Jerome in Jankyn's Book of Wikked Wyves.'

Criticism 5(1963), 316–22.

The portions of St. Jerome's work mentioned in Alisoun's description of Jankyn's book resemble selections of the saint's writing found in manuscripts, dating from the late- 12th, 13th, 14th and 15th centuries, that also contain Map's *Val*. Six of the manuscripts Pratt has examined incorporate excerpts from *Jov* that discuss both wicked and good wives and debase the status of married individuals. Two of the manuscripts include quotations from Solomon; five manuscripts contain the saint's qualification of virgins, good wives, and good widows. Alisoun, though, does not credit any clerk with praising the goodness of wives. 'The Jerome anecdotes described by Alice as part of Jankyn's book concern Xantippe, Pasiphäe, Clytemnestra and Eriphile' (p 318), all of whom are notoriously wicked. Alisoun's use of Jerome is two-fold. While she initially refers to him as a major source of antifeminist material, she later relies on his authority to establish herself as a truly good wife, one who was never as evil as the afore-mentioned women were. The burning of Jankyn's book signifies a triumph of women over men. Jerome's examples of good women that the Wife ignores appear in *FranT* in Dorigen's complaint. Dorigen, a noble wife, and her list of many good women make up part of the Franklin's counter-attack against the Wife.

548 Albertini, Vergil R. 'Chaucer's Artistic Accomplishment in Molding the *Wife of Bath's Tale.*' *Northwest Missouri State College Studies* 28(1964), 3–16.

See **144**.

548a Bowden, Muriel. *A Reader's Guide to Geoffrey Chaucer*. New York: Farrar, Straus, and Company, 1964; rpt Farrar, Straus, and Giroux, 1966 and 1970.

Chaucer has Alisoun state her views on the fourteenth-century church's valuing of virginity over marriage without expressing his own opinions (p 77). Alisoun credits much of her personal composition to her horoscope. Her performance offends the Clerk. Her personality is not suited to tell the *gentillesse* sermon. See **318** and **1163**.

549 Corsa, Helen Storm. *Chaucer: Poet of Mirth and Morality*. Notre Dame: University of Notre Dame Press, 1964.

Alisoun's comedy is that 'of tensions and conflicts kept in balance' (p 138). Her internal conflict adds significance and richness to her comedy. She displays as strong a talent for telling her tale as she does in arguing and rationalizing in the *WBP*. Alisoun uses her comic abilities to survive in a society that would traditionally condemn her (p 148).

550 Craik, T.W. *The Comic Tales of Chaucer*. London: Methuen, 1964.
See **1151**.

551 Harrington, David V. 'Chaucer's *Merchant's Tale*, 1427–28.' *N&Q*
209(1964), 166–7.
MerT IV.1427–8 resembles *WBP* III.44c–f, the key words being the
positive term *parfyt* and the negative term *sotile*. Because she is
antagonistic to clerkly antifeminism, it is not fitting that Alisoun would
either praise or align herself with clerks.

552 Hoffman, Richard L. 'The Wife of Bath as Student of Ovid.' *N&Q*
209(1964), 287–8.
See **319**.

553 Howard, Edwin J. *Geoffrey Chaucer*. New York: Twayne, 1964.
Alisoun may be defined as a truly feminine character through her desire
to be loved, her need to dominate her husbands, and her vanity (p 140).
WBP should not be termed as confessional literature, for confession
implies regret. Alisoun's candor in discussing her personal life is in
keeping with both her social status and the fact that she is talking to
complete strangers. See **1153**.

554 Huppé, Bernard F. *A Reading of the Canterbury Tales*. Albany: State
University Press of New York, 1964/rev 1967.
While there is no link between the authority of *MLT* and the experience
of *WBP*, Alisoun's abrupt entrance is a fitting reaction to *MLT* (p 107).
Glossing is an important concept in *WBP*, be it found in Alisoun's
interpretation of text or in a sexual sense (p 109). That Alisoun might
have children and that Jankyn may be dead are unanswered questions
which suggest Alisoun may be unconsciously writing her own past (p
110). Alisoun gives her assessment of marriage-vs-virginity (pp 111–7)
and of her married life (pp 118–29). Behind Alisoun's jocularity there is
a lost soul (p 135). See **146**.

555 Mahoney, John. 'Alice of Bath: Her "secte" and "gentil text."' *Criticism*
6(1964), 144–55.
Alisoun's defense of successive marriages is quite orthodox; she is not,
like the Samaritan woman, a bigamist (pp 145–6). Women preachers
belonged to some heretical groups of the fourteenth century, and their
beliefs in sexual freedom were supported by the 'wax and multiply'
phrase of Genesis which Alisoun quotes. While not a heretic, Alisoun
would have been attracted to the latter doctrine, and Chaucer may

have developed the first 88 lines of *WBP* with this thought in mind (p 154). The Clerk recognizes the heretical content of Alisoun's speech and the irony of Jankyn, with his antifeminist ideas, being united with her.

556 Donaldson, E.T. 'Chaucer, *Canterbury Tales*, D 117: A Critical Edition.' *Spec* 40(1965), 626–33.

Six different renditions of III.117 from various mss are provided for comparison with Manly and Rickert's edition of *CT* (p 626). Manly and Rickert (**29**) incorporated the Ellesmere ms variant, despite its differences from the other five versions, because of the ms's fine quality and because its line says what we want to hear Alisoun say (p 628).

557 Gillie, Christopher. *Character in English Literature*. London: Chatto & Windus, 1965. Pp 41–55.

Alisoun reveals her self-preoccupation in *WBP* (p 43). She is made a tragic figure through her need for a young spouse as she grows older, for with age she loses her ability to achieve mastery (p 47). Her carnality presents her as a daughter of Eve who yields to nature. Alisoun's widowhood increases her dangerousness to men as she seeks her next victim (p 55). Alisoun and Criseyde are two versions of Chaucer's Every-woman.

558 Haller, Robert S. 'The Wife of Bath and the Three Estates.' *AnM* 6(1965), 47–64.

Through her domination of her bourgeois and clerical husbands and the hag's power over the knight, Alisoun establishes female sovereignty and the bourgeois ethic over the three estates. She conquers her mercantile husbands by commodifying sex and marriage (pp 49–51), and she overturns Jankyn's clerical authority with her experience (pp 51–5). The hag appeals to the knight's sexual appetite in the marital dilemma, thereby illustrating how the nobility can lose its power (pp 55–60).

559 Hoffman, Richard L. 'Ovid's Argus and Chaucer.' *N&Q* 210(1965), 213–6.

See **147**.

560 Holbrook, David. *The Quest for Love*. University, AL: University of Alabama Press, 1965.

The character of the Wife of Bath serves as a means for Chaucer to explore the realm of human sexuality (p 94). Alisoun's frankness in discussing human genitalia and the drawbacks of virginity 'brings with it a touch of . . . poignancy of the human situation' (p 97). Alisoun is well aware of the disadvantages her age causes her in her quest to assuage her sexual appetite. It is ironic that Jankyn reads to a woman of her experience about the nature of women. In the couple's fight, Alisoun champions freedom for women. Like Falstaff, the Wife possesses a consciousness of morality that is infused with the practical reality of typical human actions.

561   Hussey, Maurice, A.C. Spearing, and James Winney. *An Introduction to Chaucer*. London: Cambridge University Press, 1965.
      The Wife's delight in sex, jovial society, and finery can be attributed to the influence of Venus in her horoscope. Her outspokenness and more 'masculine qualities' (p 168) come from the presence of Mars in her astrological chart. If Venus were her ascendant planet, the Wife would have been exceedingly feminine and physically beautiful.

562   Levy, Bernard S. 'Chaucer's Wife of Bath, the Loathly Lady, and Dante's Siren.' *Symposium* 19(1965), 359–73.
      See **1158**.

563   Loomis, Roger S. *A Mirror of Chaucer's World*. Princeton: Princeton University Press, 1965.
      In ms Bibl. de l'Arsenal, Paris, a miniature depicts Solomon in three different scenes: his judgment when two women each claim the same child as hers; his role as teacher; and his reception of the Queen of Sheba. A fourth scene details Adonis' death. The *Parables of Solomon* are part of the contents of Jankyn's book. See **320**.

564   Mulvey, Mina. *The Canterbury Tales: Analytic Notes and Review*. Woodbury, NY: Illustrated World Encyclopedia, 1965.
      Analysis of *WBP* shows the irony that Alisoun's woe in marriage is of her own making (pp 43–6). Alisoun presents a humanistic outlook. See **321** and **1161**.

565   Rowland, Beryl. 'Chaucer's the *Wife of Bath's Prologue*, D.389.' *Explicator* 24(1965), Item 14.
      Alisoun's reference to grain grinding at the mill in III.389 has a strong sexual undertone. This association may be found in the *Talmud*, Scripture, and classical writings.

566   Ruggiers, Paul G. *The Art of the Canterbury Tales*. Madison: University of Wisconsin Press, 1965.
      Alisoun's adherence to a philosophy of the generative process accounts for her indulging her instincts (pp 198–9), yet Alisoun is predominantly

interested in the act of sex. Chaucer's allowing Alisoun to tell a romance of transformation elaborates on another dimension of Alisoun's personality that is only subtly alluded to in *WBP*. See **1174**.

567 Silvia, Daniel S., Jr. 'Glosses to the *Canterbury Tales* from St. Jerome's *Epistola Adversus Jovinianum.*' *SP* 62(1965), 28–39.
See **151**.

568 Utley, Francis Lee. 'Some Implications of Chaucer's Folktales.' *Laographia* 22(1965), 588–99.
WBP has a definite literary source and not a folktale analogue (p 598). See **1162**.

569 Wood, Chauncey. 'Chaucer's the *Wife of Bath's Prologue*, D.576 and 583.' *Explicator* 23(1965), 19–33.
The identity of Alisoun's dame may be her gossip. In III.548, Alisoun refers to the woman as *my gossyb dame Alys*.

570 Biggins, Dennis. 'A Chaucerian Crux: *Spiced conscience*, I(A) 526, III(D) 435.' *ES* 47(1966), 169–80.
The Parson's not having a *spiced conscience* suggests that he does not possess a cynical or hard heart (p 174). A meaning quite opposite to the above is suggested in *WBP*. Alisoun implies an enduring or mellowed sensibility. While these meanings differ, they are both related to the proverb 'If you beat spice, it will smell the sweeter' (p 180).

571 Braddy, Haldeen. 'Chaucer's Bawdy Tongue.' *SFQ* 30(1966), 214–22.
Because of Alisoun's middle-class status, Chaucer does not make her speech as crude as that of the lower orders (p 217). While Alisoun uses euphemisms for sex, her language is fraught with an erotic theme.

572 Duncan, Edgar H. '"Bear on Hand" in the *Wife of Bath's Prologue*.' *TSL* 11(1966), 19–33.
Despite the familiar themes of his sources, Chaucer managed to present the antifeminist tradition in a fresh manner in *WBP*. One method for achieving this freshness is his varied usage of the phrase *bear on hand* for structural, thematic, and rhetorical purposes (pp 20–1). The phrase connotes mastery. Another cleverly manipulated phrase is *thou seyst* (pp 24–5).

573 Haskell, Ann S. 'The St. Joce Oath in the *Wife of Bath's Prologue*.' *ChauR* 1(1966), 85–7. Rpt in *Essays on Chaucer's Saints*. The Hague: Mouton, 1976. Pp 70–4.
Alisoun's swearing by St. Joce (III.483) during her discussion of her

unfaithful fourth husband is appropriate, because St. Joce's *burdoun* has phallic symbolism (p 86).

574 Hoffman, Richard L. *Ovid and the Canterbury Tales*. Philadelphia: University of Pennsylvania Press, 1966.

Ovid's *Ars Amatoria* influenced Alisoun's defense of adultery, her description of her drunkenness, her attending public functions, her finding a new husband at her old husband's funeral, and her reference to Pasiphäe. The *Met* contributed to Alisoun's references to the mad crow and to Argus. See **153** and **322**.

575 Howard, Donald R. *The Three Temptations: Medieval Man in Search of the World*. Princeton: Princeton University Press, 1966.

While the ascetic tradition advocated the ideal of a celibate life, medieval canon law was concerned with the more realistic concepts of marriage. Alisoun reveals an awareness of both the Church's ideal and its rules. While her several marriages were not against canon law, she is particularly defensive about the fact that she has neither preserved her virginity nor remained a widow (pp 89–90).

576 MacDonald, Donald. 'Proverbs, *Sententiae*, and *Exempla* in Chaucer's Comic Tales: The Function of Comic Misapplication.' *Spec* 41(1966), 453–65.

While *WBP* is full of proverbs, *sententiae*, and *exempla*, Alisoun's voicing of gnomic statements does not signify that she has the wisdom associated with them. In contrast with *Mel*'s Dame Prudence, the Wife uses monitory elements to support an argument with which her audience does not agree. If the Wife consciously misuses proverbs, she is a cleverly deceptive rhetorician; however, if her applications are unconsciously misapplied, she then appears to be quite foolish (p 457).

577 Muscatine, Charles. 'The *Canterbury Tales*: Style of the Man and Style of the Work.' In *Chaucer and Chaucerians: Critical Studies in Middle English Literature*. Ed. D.S. Brewer. London: Nelson, 1966. Pp 88–113.

Chaucer's 'doctrine and learned diction' (p 94) are artfully concealed beneath Alisoun's character. The concept of female sovereignty is symbolically displayed in the spurs Alisoun wears (p 47). Jankyn's fall during his fight with Alisoun is illustrated in the rhythm of III.790–3 (p 100).

578 Nist, John R. 'The Art of Chaucer's Poetry.' *TSL* 11(1966), 1–10.

Alisoun 'represents *unconditional* love' (p 8) fighting against authority

and the conditional love of patriarchal society. She is a 'secular —
almost profane' version of Mary (p 8). Alisoun is a self-proclaimed
nymphomaniac, not a congenital one.

579 Owst, G.R. *Literature and Pulpit in Medieval England: A Neglected
Chapter in the History of English Literature and of the English
People.* New York: Barnes and Noble; Oxford: Blackwell, 1966.
(Originally published by Cambridge: The University Press, 1933.)
Homilists who complained against women used antifeminist sentiments
similar to those in *WBP* (p 385).

580 Rogers, Katherine M. *The Troublesome Helpmate: A History of
Misogyny in Literature.* Seattle: University of Washington Press, 1966.
While the Clerk, the Merchant, and the Host feel that Griselda is the
ideal wife, their views are violated by the rebellious Alisoun (p 80).
WBP and *WBT* illustrate the point that marriage can work well if the
wife is allowed to rule the husband. Alisoun's arguments are so
convincing that it appears that Chaucer is challenging the traditional
conception of marriage through her (p 83).

581 Scholes, Robert, and Robert Kellogg. *The Nature of Narrative.* New
York: Oxford University Press, 1966.
For Chaucer, Alisoun is a realistic representative of human nature;
however, her character is conceivably more symbolic than that of her
forerunner, La Vieille (pp 92–3). Alisoun is an allegorical representation
of the carnal being. Her astrological chart symbolizes the challenge of
sin to God because it is indicative of the sensual, 'feminine' powers
which conquer reason (p 97).

582 Verbillion, June. 'Chaucer's *Wife of Bath's Prologue*, 175.' *Explicator*
24(1966), Item 58.
Alisoun's reference to herself as a whip in III.175 may have been
influenced by Dante's *Purgatorio*, where he provides lofty examples
of the virtue that is the opposite of a specific sin. Alisoun acts as both a
whip and rein for the Pardoner, discouraging him from marrying through
the examples of her own marriages.

583 Zimbardo, Rose A. 'Unity and Duality in the *Wife of Bath's Prologue
and Tale*.' *TSL* 11(1966), 11–18.
If *WBP* and *WBT* are considered together, *WBP* 'presents the theme as
dialectic' and *WBT* 'stands as an exemplum illustrating the conclusion
to which the dialectic has come' (p 11). In Chaucer's illustration of the
dialectic between authority and experience, Alisoun advocates a

synthesis of ideal concepts with reality (pp 12–3). This unity is exemplified by Alisoun and Jankyn's establishing marital peace. *WBT* continues the theme of 'reconciliation through love' (p 16) when the hag fuses spiritual and physical good (p 18).

584 Beichner, Paul E. 'The Allegorical Interpretation of Medieval Literature.' *PMLA* 82(1967), 33–8.

While allegorical readings of *CT* may be apt in some cases, such interpretations should not be levied on all of Chaucer's work. For example, Jankyn tells the Wife the story of a man whose three wives hang themselves on a tree. The man's friend requests a cutting of this tree so that he might cultivate it in his garden. While a version of this tale that appears in the *Gesta Romanorum* has a *significatio* in which the wives represent 'pride; lusts of the heart, and lusts of the eyes'(p 34) and are therefore rightly destroyed, Jankyn's storytelling is designed to aggravate his wife. In this case, an allegorical interpretation of Jankyn's story would defeat its point.

585 Cox, Lee Sheridan. 'A Question of Order in the *Canterbury Tales.*' *ChauR* 1(1967), 228–52.

Alisoun is the intended interrupter of the Man of Law's *Endlink. WBP* and *WBT* are strong responses to Constance's condition.

586 Curtis, Penelope. 'Chaucer's Wyf of Bath.' *CR* 10(1967), 33–45.

Alisoun is an illustration of Chaucer's view of the relationship between deception and self-deception (p 33). The *GP* description of Alisoun provides a balance to her contradictions that is absent in *WBP*. All that Alisoun relates in *WBP* has an impulse towards both truth and falsehood (p 43). While Alisoun is unable to resolve the contradictions of life in *WBP*, she manages this task in her fictional *WBT* (pp 35–6). Both Alisoun and the Pardoner have confessional prologues, tell two tales, and seek control over men.

587 Grose, M.W. *Chaucer: Literature in Perspective*. London: Evans Bros.; New York: Arco, 1967.

While *KnT* develops the effect of astrology on a daily basis, *WBP* provides an example of stellar influence on a person's life (p 57). Alisoun's faults are attributed to the planets. While Venus was the ruling planet at her birth, the effect of Mars roughened the finer Venusian qualities Alisoun should have received. See **228**.

588 Holland, Norman N. 'Meaning as Transformation: The *Wife of Bath's Tale.*' *CE* 28(1967), 279–90.

See **1172**.

589 Hussey, Maurice. *Chaucer's World: A Pictorial Companion.* Cambridge: Cambridge University Press, 1967.

Fig 76 presents a *misericord* of a wife beating her husband. Alisoun's horoscope is recalled by Fig 77, a picture from *Mittelalterliche Hausbuch*, which depicts an equestrian Venus riding in the sky between Libra and Taurus and over her revelling children. In Fig 78, Mars rides the sky between Aries and Scorpio above his violent children. Medieval art's Wheel of the Senses (Fig 79) is a drawing in which Reason stands tall behind a five-spoked wheel on which animals, which symbolize the senses, are depicted. It is representative of Alisoun's strongly sensual nature (p 115). See **326**.

590 Jordan, Robert M. *Chaucer and the Shape of Creation: The Aesthetic Possibilities of Inorganic Structure.* Cambridge: Harvard University Press, 1967.

While Alisoun is victorious over her husbands, on the whole, *WBP* is a triumph for the antifeminist tradition. Chaucer inorganically combines Alisoun's defense of marriage as opposed to virginity (pp 216–21), her deceptive relating of her husbands' accusations (pp 222–4), and her detailing of Jankyn's book (pp 225–6) to achieve a three-fold antifeminist argument.

591 Muscatine, Charles. 'The Wife of Bath and Gautier's *La Veuve.*' In *Romance Studies in Memory of Edward Billings Ham.* Ed. Urban T. Holmes. Hayward: California State College Press, 1967. Pp 109–14. See **158**.

592 Overbeck, Pat T. 'Chaucer's Good Woman.' *ChauR* 2(1967), 75–94.

Alisoun's disregard for authority, her manipulations in marriage, and her sexual drive make her a Good Woman (p 93). While the Good Woman of *LGW* often met with death, Alisoun finds a promise of salvation in *CT* (p 94).

593 Revard, Carter. 'The Lecher, the Legal Eagle, and the Papelard Priest: Middle English Confessional Satires in MS. Harley 2253 and Elsewhere.' In *His Firm Estate: Essays in Honor of Franklin James Eikenberry.* Ed. Donald E. Hayden. University of Tulsa Department of English Monograph Series, 2. Tulsa: The University of Tulsa, 1967. Pp 54–71.

Works such as *WBP*, *RvT*, and *PardP* are confessional satires because they reveal the flaws of their narrating personae (p 57).

594 Schaar, Claes. *The Golden Mirror: Studies in Chaucer's Descriptive*

Technique and Its Literary Background. Lund: C.W.K. Gleerup, 1967.
The primary emotional scene depicted in *WBP* is Alisoun's battle with
Jankyn (p 69). Minor portraits of the fourth husband and Jankyn, the
apprentice, are described in *WBP*. Jankyn, the clerk, receives the fullest
description (p 223). See **1175**.

595 Schmidt, A.V.C. 'The Wife of Bath's Marital State.' *N&Q* 212(1967),
230–1.
See **1176**.

596 Silvia, D.S. 'The Wife of Bath's Marital State.' *N&Q* 212(1967), 8–10.
Jankyn is alive at the time of Alisoun's Canterbury pilgrimage; however,
Alisoun is already looking for her sixth husband because she has lost
interest in her current relationship with Jankyn.

597 Baird, Joseph L. 'The "Secte" of the Wife of Bath.' *ChauR* 2(1968),
188–90.
While *secte* denotes both *sex* and *company*, it also means *suit at law*
(p 189). The Clerk's usage of *secte* along with *mayntene*, another legal
term, suggests that Chaucer intended a legal definition.

598 Braddy, Haldeen. 'Chaucer's Bilingual Idiom.' *SFQ* 32(1968), 1–6.
The *CT* contain much vernacular speech. Alisoun is 'multilingual, with
morphological entries that smack of French, Latin, and Anglo-Saxon'
(p 3).

599 Brookhouse, Christopher. 'The Confessions of Three Pilgrims.' *LauR*
8(1968), 49–56.
WBP 'is both a confession and an attack' (p 52). Alisoun is
subconsciously troubled by her failure to have children and is worried
about aging (p 53). See **1178**.

600 Hanning, Robert W. 'Uses of Names in Medieval Literature.' *Names*
16(1968), 325–38.
That the Wife of Bath shares her name with Alison of the *MilT* and
that both women have an Oxford clerk as a lover suggests a connection
between the two women (p 328).

601 Hira, Toshinori. 'Two Phases of Chaucer, Moral and Mortal.' In
*Maekawa Shunichi Ky ju Kanreki Kinen-ronbunsh: Essays and
Studies in Commemoration of Professor Shunichi Maekawa's 61st
Birthday*. Ed. Maekawa Shunichi. Tokyo: Eihosha, 1968. Pp 91–114.
Alisoun's awareness of her astrological chart is an example of the
medieval belief in planetary power, an ideology Chaucer may or may
not have believed in (p 108). See **329**.

602 Hoffman, Richard L. 'The *Canterbury Tales*.' In *Critical Approaches to Six Major English Works: Beowulf through Paradise Lost*. Ed. R.M. Lumiansky and Herschel Baker. Philadelphia: University of Pennsylvania Press, 1968; London: Oxford University Press, 1969. Pp 41–80.
Alisoun's knowledge of the *olde daunce* reflects the music of the sensual Venus (p 57).

603 Pulliam, Willene. 'The Relationship of Geoffrey Chaucer's Works to the Antifeminist Tradition.' *DA* 28(1968), 3646–7A.
While not an antifeminist himself, Chaucer incorporated much of the tradition into his writings. In the *CT*, the pillow lecture, the jealous husband, the vices of women, and the archwife are recurring motifs.

604 Rogers, P. Burwell. 'The Names of the Canterbury Pilgrims.' *Names* 16(1968), 339–46.
While the Wife of Bath is usually called *Alice*, Jankyn endearingly addresses her as *suster Alisoun* (III.804) after their fight. A common name has been given to Alisoun, 'a plain person' (p 393). That Alisoun's gossip is also named Alice is merely indicative of this name's popularity.

605 Sanders, Barry. 'Further Puns from the *Prologue* and *Tale* of the Wife of Bath.' *PLL* 4(1968), 192–5.
Nether purs (III.44), *flour* (III.113), *borel* (III.356), and the combination of *candle*, *light*, and *lantern* (III.333–5) all have sexual connotations.

606 Smith, Walter. 'Geoffrey Chaucer, Dramatist.' *Interpretations* 1(1968), 1–9; rpt 1(1985).
See **331**.

607 Wagenknecht, Edward. *The Personality of Chaucer*. Norman, OK: University of Oklahoma Press, 1968.
Evidence of Chaucer's preoccupation with the Wife of Bath is found in the length of *WBP*, which nearly rivals that of *GP* (p 95). To Chaucer, the cat symbolized passion, so Alisoun likens herself to one. The Wife finds it difficult to accept the aging process. While having been guilty of fornication, Alisoun denies committing adultery. Alisoun's advocacy of marriage is in accordance with Jerome (p 97). Chaucer describes Alisoun, her pride and lecherousness, from a Catholic perspective. See **1183**.

608 Whittock, Trevor. *A Reading of the Canterbury Tales*. Cambridge: Cambridge University Press, 1968.

WBP is told to counter *MLT*; it does not mark the beginning of a Marriage Group (p 118). Much of *WBP* is aimed against the medieval Church and its attitude towards women and sex. Alisoun's worst flaw is her desire for female sovereignty over men (p 125). See **1184**.

609 Bergeron, David M. 'The Wife of Bath and Shakespeare's *The Taming of the Shrew*.' *UR* 35(1969), 279–86.
Multiple allusions, phrasings, themes, and qualities of characters in Shakespeare's *Taming of the Shrew* suggest that Shakespeare was familiar with *WBP* and *WBT*.

610 Braddy, Haldeen. 'Chaucer — Realism or Obscenity?' *ArlQ* 2(1969), 121–38 [cited]. Rpt in *Geoffrey Chaucer: Literary and Historical Studies*. Port Washington: Kennikat, 1971. Pp 146–58.
Chaucer blended realism with obscenity when it was in keeping with his subject matter. An example of this practice would be his detailing of Alisoun's sex life in *WBP* (p 122).

611 Corrigen, Matthew. 'Chaucer's Failure with Women: The Inadequacy of Criseyde.' *WHR* 23(1969), 107–20.
Chaucer's Alisoun is an incomplete character who functions well as a literary depiction but not as a woman (p 109). Chaucer '*describes* her almost from hearsay .... He does not question his own psyche in search of her uniqueness' (p 111).

612 Cotter, James Finn. 'The Wife of Bath and the Conjugal Debt.' *ELN* 6(1969), 169–72.
While Alisoun is correct in her assertion that her husbands must pay her the conjugal debt, she ignores the portions of the teachings of Paul and Aquinas which explain that both husband and wife are to be responsible towards one another.

613 Duncan, Edgar H. 'Chaucer's "Wife of Bath's Prologue," Lines 193–828, and Geoffrey of Vinsauf's *Documentum*.' *MP* 66(1969), 199–211.
A portion of Vinsauf's *Documentum* provides unique guidelines for amplification in poetry which seem to have provided Chaucer with a means of organizing the wealth of antifeminist material he incorporated into *WBP*. Vinsauf's text might also have encouraged Chaucer to make Jankyn a clerk.

614 Guthrie, William Bowman. 'The Comic Celebrant of Life.' *DAI* 29(1969), 1098.
Alisoun embodies the sensuality and fertility of the Dionysian life-force.

She opposes the repressiveness of Scriptural authority and of her husbands.

615 Rowland, Beryl. 'The Mill in Popular Metaphor from Chaucer to the Present Day.' *SFQ* 33(1969), 69–79.

Alisoun's reference to grinding at the mill (III.384–90) reflects the long-standing sexual associations of woman as mill and man as miller, 'the procreative agent' (p 70).

616 Covella, Sister Francis Dolores. 'The Speaker of the Wife of Bath Stanza and Envoy.' *ChauR* 4(1970), 267–83.

Since many critics perceive an inconsistency between the Clerk's personality and the tone of his *Envoy*, it may be assumed that the *Envoy* is spoken by another pilgrim, such as the Pardoner (p 276) or the Host (pp 276–9) or even Alisoun herself (pp 279–82).

617 Donaldson, E. Talbot. 'The Ordering of the *Canterbury Tales*.' In *Medieval Literature and Folklore Studies: Essays in Honor of Francis Lee Utley*. Ed. Jerome Mandel and Bruce A. Rosenberg. New Brunswick: Rutgers University Press, 1970. Pp 193–204.

The major reason for rejecting the Ellesmere order of *CT* lies in geographical discrepancies between the Summoner's reference to Sittingbourne (III.847) and Harry Bailly's reference to Rochester (VII.1926). Pratt's (**533**) theory that *ShT* was initially intended for Alisoun is a likely supposition for the shift in tale order (p 201).

618 Levy, Bernard S. 'The Wife of Bath's *Queynte fantasye*.' *ChauR* 4(1970), 106–22.

See **1192**.

619 Mogan, Joseph J., Jr. 'Chaucer and the *Bona Matrimonii*.' *ChauR* 4(1970), 123–41.

Chaucer applies theological doctrine to *MilT*, *WBP*, *MerT*, and *ParsT* (p 123). In *WBP*, the concept of the *bona matrimonii* is subtle, because women's sovereignty and not human salvation is its theme (p 136). Peter Lombard recognized the *debitum*, a concept which Alisoun uses to make her husbands aware of what they owe her. It is rare that she acknowledges her husbands' power over her body. Alisoun's valuing the pleasure of sex is contrary to most theological views (p 139).

620 Mustanoja, Tauno F. 'The Suggestive Use of Christian Names in Middle English Poetry.' In *Medieval Literature and Folklore Studies: Essays in Honor of Francis Lee Utley*. Eds. Jerome Mandel and Bruce A. Rosenberg. New Brunswick: Rutgers University Press, 1970. Pp 51–

76.

The name *Jankyn* signifies a typical country boy in *Lutel Soth Serman*. There are two Jankyns in *WBP*. One is an apprentice whom Alisoun is accused of carrying on with by her husband; the other is her fifth husband, the Oxford clerk (pp 65–6). The name appears elsewhere in *CT*. The squire in *SumT* bears this name, and it is the negative label the Host ascribes to the Parson. The name *Alis* or *Alison* originates 'from the old Germanic name *Adalhaidis* through Old French *Aalis, Aélis*' (p 70); they are linked with flirting and love in Middle English verse. Appropriately, then, the wife in *MilT* and the Wife of Bath have this name.

621 Parker, David. 'Can We Trust the Wife of Bath?' *ChauR* 4(1970), 90–8.

While Alisoun advocates female sovereignty, she recounts Jankyn's mastery over her (III.503–24) as being the delight of her fifth marriage (pp 94–5). Alisoun also comments that Jankyn's withholding his love from her made her desire him more. Alisoun should be viewed as an individual whose contradictions indicate that she doesn't tell the truth. Her inconsistencies do not suit a reading of her as an iconographic figure.

622 Pearsall, Derek A. '*The Canterbury Tales.*' In *History of Literature in the English Language.* Volume 1, *The Middle Ages.* Ed. W.F. Bolton. London: Barrie and Jenkins, 1970. Pp 163–93.

WBP lends itself to the concept of a dramatic reading of *CT* (p 171).

623 Reid, David S. 'Crocodilian Humor: A Discussion of Chaucer's Wife of Bath.' *ChauR* 4(1970), 73–89.

'The Wife is a stock figure and an absurdity' (p 74). While readers are aware of Alisoun's faults, they find her humorous and human (p 75). Alisoun manifests human qualities because she represents a class of people, yet her character makes sense only when defined by comedy. Alisoun delivers a burlesque sermon in which any misogynistic satire is outdone by the farce of matrimony (p 80). There is seemingly no didactic purpose to *WBP* or *WBT*, yet Chaucer may have been exploiting the vanities of the world through Alisoun. See **1193**.

624 Silvia, D.S. 'Chaucer's *Canterbury Tales*, D.44a–f.' *Explicator* 28(1970), Item 44.

Lines 44a–f of *WBP* are charged with sexual imagery that should not be ignored. While it is uncertain whether or not Chaucer intended to keep them in *WBP*, the lines certainly fit Alisoun's carnality.

625 Spencer, William. 'Are Chaucer's Pilgrims Keyed to the Zodiac?' *ChauR* 4(1970), 147–70.

Alisoun announces her own Taurus/Venus/Mars horoscope. Mars has marred many of the finer Venusian qualities Alisoun has inherited. Alisoun shares her love of finery with the Taurus/Venus Squire and her propensity for travel with the Aries/Mars Knight (pp 162–3).

626 Wood, Chauncey. *Chaucer and the Country of the Stars*. Princeton: Princeton University Press, 1970.

Alisoun's horoscope is extremely simple. The combination of Venus and Mars in it suggests adultery and lechery. While people are not forced to adhere to their horoscopes, Alisoun is not to be swayed from planetary influence (p 173). Since astrology was viewed as false prophecy, the Wife's adherence to stellar predictions is in keeping with her inaccurate interpretation of text. The *Aphorisms* of Hermes Trismegistus and the work of Almansor support the notion that the presence of Mars in a house of Venus in a woman's stellar chart indicates her lecherousness (p 175). Guido Bonatti, Andalò, and Albohali confirm that Mars in Taurus indicates infidelity in both sex and loyalty. Curry (**454, 1085**) had assumed that Venus is the Wife's dominant planet. There is, however, no support for this assumption. While Curry also believes that Alisoun is penitent in her bemoaning of the fact that love is sin, Alisoun's remarks should be interpreted as vented irritation.

ᘓ The Wife of Bath's Prologue 1971-1980

627 Cotter, James Finn. 'The Wife of Bath's Lenten Observance.' *PLL* 7(1971), 293–7.

Alisoun behaves in a decidedly unorthodox manner during Lent. She confesses to following Venus in order to obtain grace and dresses in the non-penitential color red (p 295). In this season of fast and abstinence she cavorts with Jankyn while her husband is out of town.

628 Magee, Patricia Anne. 'The Wife of Bath and the Problem of Mastery.' *MSE* 3(1971), 40–5.

Alisoun's primary desire is not mastery. It is a subconscious yearning for the challenge of trying for the unattainable goal of female sovereignty (p 42). Alisoun's favorite husband was the one who was most difficult to subdue. Winning her challenge after her fight with Jankyn, Alisoun is content with the man. The taste for challenge is echoed in the hag's struggle with the knight (p 44). Alisoun obtains her aggressive tendencies from Mars's influence and desires a sensual expression of this aggressiveness because of Venus' power over her (p 45).

629 Murtaugh, Daniel M. 'Women and Geoffrey Chaucer.' *ELH* 38(1971), 473–92.

See **233** and **1199**.

630 Nichols, Nicholas Pete. 'Discretion and Marriage in the *Canterbury Tales*.' *DAI* 32(1971), 3263A.

Chaucer views marriage as a sacred institution and, in his writing, approves only of those marriages that discreetly maintain the obligations between the husband and his helpmate. In the *WBP*, the morally blind Alisoun reflects the indiscreet wives of the fabliaux. See **1200**.

631 Rowland, Beryl. *Blind Beasts: Chaucer's Animal World*. Kent: Kent

State University Press, 1971.

Animal imagery found in the *WBP* includes Alisoun's being associated with a lioness and a cat; her first three husbands are associated with mice and sheep. Jankyn aligns swine with women's lechery (p 78). Alisoun refers to her colt's tooth and makes reference to the proverbial horse Bayard (pp 126–7). While Alisoun admires Jankyn's virility as one would admire a horse, she herself is likened to a 'blundering horse' (p 139) when she is in love. Alisoun uses the spaniel in likening women's pursuit of men to a hunting dog's activities, and she recalls the lion of the Aesopic fable in her famed complaint. See **1201**.

632   Shapiro, Gloria K. 'Dame Alice as Deceptive Narrator.' *ChauR* 6(1971), 130–41.

Alisoun does not fully portray herself to her audience. She has a strong religious element in her which manifests itself in the sermon on *gentillesse* (p 131). Her prayer at the end of the *WBT* is an attempt to cover her inner nature as is her account of her fourth husband, in which she hides her suffering during the failed marriage. Despite her delight in sex, Alisoun does not believe in adultery (p 136). She also recognizes virginity as a higher state than married life. While Alisoun upholds experience over authority, she obviously recognizes the power of religious authority through her references to it (p 138).

633   Thomas, Mary Edith. *Medieval Skepticism and Chaucer*. New York: Cooper Square, 1971.

The depth of Chaucer's talent as a dramatic artist is seen in his depiction of Alisoun and his detailing of her argument in the *WBP*. See **273** and **1203**.

634   Delasanta, Rodney. '*Quoniam* and the Wife of Bath.' *PLL* 8(1972), 202–6.

Alisoun's usage of the word *quoniam* is more than a sexual euphemism. The word's ecclesiastical connotation of praising God allows Alisoun to equate her vagina with something divine that is to be worshipped.

635   Eliason, Norman. *The Language of Chaucer's Poetry: An Appraisal of the Verse, Style, and Structure. Anglistica*, Vol. 17. Copenhagen: Rosenkilde and Bagger, 1972.

Chaucer's colloquial writing is achieved in part by incorporating direct address, such as *WBP*'s *lordynges, sire, ye wise wyves, old kaynard, old lecchour*, and also by swearing (pp 114–5). Personal names in Chaucer undergo variation, such as Alys/Alisoun or Jankyn/Janakyn.

Name variation 'was commonplace in Chaucer's day' (p 33) and not merely for metrical or rhyming purposes. Alisoun's speech is marked with garrulousness and a frank vocabulary that contribute to her individuality as a character (p 90). See **1204**.

636 Fisher, John H. 'Chaucer's Last Revision of the *Canterbury Tales.*' *MLR* 67(1972), 241–51.
Before his death, Chaucer was working on a revision of Fragments I–V of the *CT* (p 243). Unity is provided for Fragments III–V by the marriage theme. Because the *ShT* was initially intended for the Wife of Bath, Fragment VII was once intended to follow Fragment II. In placing the antifeminist speech of the *WBP* into the mouth of a woman, Chaucer shocks his audience. See **1205**.

637 Gillmeister, Heiner. *Discrecioun: Chaucer und die Via Regia.* Bonn: Grundman, 1972. [In German.]
The concept of a lack of discretion, which Alisoun claims to maintain (III.622), is found throughout the *CT* (p 71).

638 Hamilton, Alice. 'Helowys and the Burning of Jankyn's Book.' *MS* 34(1972), 196–207.
Abelard's *Historia Calamitatum* is probably the work in Jankyn's book that deals with Heloise, because this work illustrates how woman is the cause of man's downfall. Both Abelard's work and the *WBP* contain personal experience for the edification of others (p 200). Abelard's lust parallels that of Alisoun, and the burning of Jankyn's book recalls Abelard's being forced to burn his own text. The sources of the *Historia Calamitatum* parallel those of the *WBP* (pp 202–3).

639 Harwood, Britton J. 'The Wife of Bath and the Dream of Innocence.' *MLQ* 33(1972), 257–73.
Since love has been a sin for Alisoun, she feels that she has been made unbeautiful through the guilt of using sex as a commodity. The hag, however, asserts that her innocence makes her lovable (p 265). Alisoun desires the innocence she lost in her moneyed marriage bed (pp 266–7). Both Jankyn and the knight yield to the honor of their wives. The rapist knight symbolizes the force enacted upon Alisoun's youthful innocence. The ugliness of Alisoun's guilt, which the hag represents, is erased by the knight's honor (p 273).

640 Haymes, Edward R. 'Chaucer and the Romantic Tradition.' *SAB* 37(1972), 35–43.
Chaucer made use of formulas in his narrative writing. Lines III.361,

532, 1215, 1271 illustrate his formulas which use *thee* (p 41). *Joy and bliss* is a frequently used formulaic phrase, often rhymed with *kiss*, as in III.830.

641 Higdon, David Leon. 'The Wife of Bath and Refreshment Sunday.' *PLL* 8(1972), 199–201.

Alisoun's likening of sex, Solomon's wives, and Christ's miracle of the loaves and fishes to refreshment recalls the church practice of Refreshment Sunday. On this day in mid-Lent, the Gospel reading was of Christ's miracle of the loaves, and Lenten restrictions were relieved. *Refection*, a fourteenth-century synonym for *refreshment*, had a sexual connotation.

642 Kean, Patricia Margaret. *The Art of Narrative: Chaucer and the Making of English Poetry*. Volume 2. London: Routledge and Kegan Paul, 1972.

Unlike La Vieille in the *RR*, Alisoun is a wealthy widow and her love-match with Jankyn is not disastrous. Alisoun is neither as vindictive nor as cynical as La Vieille (pp 154–5). While Alisoun achieves marital bliss in a manner highly different from that of Dorigen and Arveragus, her means suit her personality. See **1208**.

643 Kellogg, Alfred L. *Chaucer, Langland, Arthur: Essays in Middle English Literature*. New Brunswick: Rutgers University Press, 1972.

The attraction of Boccaccio, Chaucer, and Petrarch to Griselda's story substantiates Alisoun's lion-painting complaint (p 277). Alisoun's marriage to and triumph over Jankyn is bitter to the Clerk (p 292). He subsequently tells the *ClT* and addresses his *Envoy* to Alisoun. The Clerk requites Alisoun completely. She does not reply to his tale (p 315).

644 Muscatine, Charles. *Poetry and Crisis in the Age of Chaucer*. Notre Dame: University of Notre Dame Press, 1972.

While the *WBP* is convincing by itself, when Chaucer puts Alisoun into the perspective of the *CT*, her point of view does not provide an acceptable approach towards life (p 115). See **1210**.

645 Potter, Joyce Elizabeth. 'Chaucer's Use of the Pagan God Jove.' *DAI* 33(1972), 1147A.

When Chaucer refers to Jove, he portrays him in either the fictive light found in *HF* and *LGWP* or in a realistic manner such as in *KnT* and *TC*. In the *WBP*, Jove is presented in both modes.

646 Robinson, Ian. *Chaucer and the English Tradition*. Cambridge:

Cambridge University Press, 1972.

The *WBP* is filled with Alisoun's forceful personality and the importance of the *WBP* lies in Alisoun's applying realistic language to love. The two portions of the *WBP* belong to two contradictory segments of her personality (p 101). Alisoun's astrological chart causes her to be both loving and domineering. The *WBP* presents a comic view of love.

647 Ross, Thomas Wynne. *Chaucer's Bawdy*. New York: E.P. Dutton, 1972.

Chaucer employs suggestive language in order to heighten the comedy of some of his work. In Alisoun's case, her frank terminology reveals much about her character (p 3). A substantial glossary provides definitions of Chaucer's more colorful words and their locations in his work.

648 Rowland, Beryl. 'Chaucer's Dame Alys: Critics in Blunderland?' *NM* 73(1972), 381–95.

Alisoun is a tragic figure who possesses human qualities that are still recognizable today. Like the Pardoner, she seeks 'to find a place in an alien society' (p 385). Her rampant sexuality has caused Alisoun trauma; she now wants to revenge herself on men (p 391). Alisoun is unwilling to accept blame for her apparent nymphomania (p 393). See **1211**.

649 ———. 'On the Timely Death of the Wife of Bath's Fourth Husband.' *Archiv* 209(1972), 273–82.

Alisoun's account of her fourth husband contains references that lack the specific applications of those found in her discussion of her first three husbands. The references to Metellius' wife and to Darius concern violent deaths (p 281). Alisoun's dream and her telling Jankyn she would marry him if she were able suggest that she persuaded him to be her accomplice in murder. Jankyn's reading aloud about women who have killed their husbands provokes Alisoun's anger. Fear of exposure causes Jankyn to yield sovereignty to Alisoun.

650 ———. 'The Wife of Bath's "Unlawful Philtrum."' *Neophil* 56(1972), 201–6.

Alisoun's reference to barley bread is linked with the erotic folk magic of making bread in the form of human genitalia. The bread was given as a love token.

651 Talbot, C.H. 'Dame Trot and Her Progeny.' In *Essays and Studies in Honor of Beatrice White*. Ed. T.S. Dorsch. New York: Humanities Press, 1972. Pp 1–14.

The eleventh-century female doctor Trotula who is mentioned in Jankyn's book was not an isolated case. Many medical women served the medieval poor, simultaneously fighting against gender barriers.

652   Brewer, Derek S. *Chaucer*, 3rd ed. London: Longman, 1973. [First pub 1953, 1960.]

There is a distinct difference between Alisoun's rough personality and the delicate nature of the *WBT* (p 108). Alisoun's advocacy of sovereignty is in itself an antifeminist satire (p 139). Alisoun retains an audience's sympathy during her confession because of her appealing personality and because her victimized husbands were old and rich (p 186). While Alisoun's nearly organic speech is realistic, it is organized around antifeminist literature (p 187). See **1214**.

653   Eliason, Norman E. 'Personal Names in the *Canterbury Tales*.' *Names* 21(1973), 137–52.

While Chaucer uses both *Alice* and *Alison* twice in referring to the Wife of Bath and her gossip, he uses the variant *Alisoun* only for the *MilT* (p 142). The resemblance between the names suggests that the Wife of Bath and the wife of the *MilT* have many similarities (p 149). In giving his characters titles, Chaucer connects teller and tale (p 51).

654   Fleissner, Robert F. '*Innocent as a Bird* (X.40).' *AN&Q* 11(1973), 90.

The phrase *innocent as a bird* (III.232) is related to the Tell-Tale Bird. It implies the irony of the adulterous wife assuring her husband the bird is lying.

655   ———. 'The Wife of Bath's Five.' *ChauR* 8(1973), 128–32.

Chaucer may have given Alisoun five husbands because he knew in the Pythagorean system that five was symbolic of both carnal love and marriage (p 129). Alisoun's having had five husbands 'reflects back on the interrelationship of heavenly and earthly love as revealed in the pentad and pentagonal symmetry' (p 130).

656   Fox, Allan B. 'The *Traductio* on *Honde* in the *Wife of Bath's Prologue*.' *NDEJ* 9(1973), 3–8.

Chaucer adds *traductio* on the word *honde* to end-rhyme in order to chart differences in Alisoun's marriages in the *WBP* (p 3). The concept of giving one's hand in marriage is to be kept in mind when the word *honde* is used. When Alisoun discusses her first three husbands, *honde* is rhymed with *lond*, *understonde*, and *stonde*. The rhymes indicate the property she gained, the mastery she possessed, and the accusations she hurled in these marriages. The sexual connotations of *honde* are also present in Alisoun's reflections on the past (p 6). By the time of her fifth marriage, Alisoun's land is more attractive to Jankyn than her hand. After the couple's fight, Jankyn relinquishes his land and his hand into Alisoun's *honde*. Once again, she has achieved sovereignty in marriage.

657   Knight, Stephen. *The Poetry of the Canterbury Tales*. Sydney: Angus and Robertson, 1973. Rev 'The Poetry of the *Wife of Bath's Prologue* and *Tale*.' *Teaching of English* 25(1973), 3–17.

Despite her incorporation of authority into the *WBP*, Alisoun ultimately rejects it in her burning of Jankyn's book. Alisoun's usage of polysyllabic words, her skill in arguing, and her knowledge of Scripture underscore her intelligence. The poetry of the *WBP* is both 'vivid and forceful' (p 54). Chaucer uses his skill to capture a carping wife and a cowed husband in the lines of the *WBP* (pp 54-5). See **339** and **1216**.

658   Pittock, Malcolm. *The Prioress's Tale [and] the Wife of Bath's Tale*. Notes on English Literature. Oxford: Blackwell, 1973.

Alisoun's behavior toward and beliefs concerning marriage are viewed in light of church opinions on the sacrament (pp 46–59). Alisoun is a deceptive narrator, yet she maintains the reader's sympathy (pp 60–3). See **341** and **1217**.

659   Rutledge, Sheryl P. 'Chaucer's Zodiac of Tales.' *Costerus* 9(1973), 117–43.

The astrological signs can be associated with various Canterbury stories. Alisoun's discourse is linked with Scorpio, the house that governs the genitalia and is ruled by Mars. Reflective of the warrior god, Alisoun dresses like a knight on her pilgrimage. People born under Scorpio are often associated with the sin of lust and are partial to the color red. Both the Bible and Augustine equate lust with the scorpion's sting. There are references to poisoned husbands in Jankyn's book that may be tied to the scorpion's poison. The eighth house of the zodiac is also involved with men's legacies, and Alisoun has inherited much from her husbands.

660   Singh, Catherine. 'The Alliterative Ancestry of Dunbar's "The Tretis of the Tua Mariit Wemen and the Wedo."' *LeedsSE* 7(1973–4), 22–54.

Dunbar's poem may not have been influenced as much by Chaucer as has been supposed. Dunbar's skill at creating alliterative poetry exceeds Chaucer's (p 24). While the women of Dunbar's poem do resemble Alisoun, they are more sophisticated and less romantic than she is. The

Wedo is closer in character to La Vieille (p 34).

661 Item cancelled.

662 Utley, Francis Lee. 'Chaucer's Way with a Proverb: *Allas! Allas! That evere love was synne!' NCFJ* 21(1973), 98–104.

In medieval literature, the proverbial saying, 'Lechery is no sin,' comes from the disreputable mouths of *Piers*'s Lady Mede and *Mankind*'s New Gyre. Alisoun uses the more ambiguous term *love* instead of *lechery* (p 102). Alisoun's *Allas* suggests that she is aware of her faults, but that by nature she is not inclined to mend her ways.

662a Axelrod, Steven. 'The Wife of Bath and the Clerk.' *AnM* 15(1974), 109–24.

The Clerk and Alisoun have a courting relationship that develops the sexual motif of the *GP*, contrasts with the rivalries of other pilgrims, and suits Alisoun's personality (p 115). Alisoun's attacks against clerks in the *WBP* are a form of courtship. She is attracted to the Clerk because he resembles Jankyn (p 120) and because the *ClT* reveals that its teller will be a challenge to her (p 119).

663 Bennett, J.A.W. *Chaucer at Oxford and at Cambridge.* Oxford: Oxford University Press, 1974.

Many of the texts that are compiled in Jankyn's book may be found in the Merton catalogue (pp 80–1).

664 Biggins, Dennis. 'Chaucer's *Wife of Bath's Prologue*, D.608.' *Explicator* 32(1974), Item 44.

Chaucer uses the less crude term *quoniam* in III.608 for an anticlimactic effect. A listener expects Alisoun to repeat her usage of *queynte*. *Quoniam* is also related to *cunnus*.

665 ———. '"O Jankyn, be ye there?"' In *Chaucer and Middle English Studies in Honour of Rossell Hope Robbins.* Ed. Beryl Rowland. London: Allen and Unwin, 1974. Pp 249–54.

A catalogue of critics and their opinions as to whether or not Jankyn is dead at the time of Alisoun's Canterbury pilgrimage is provided. Chaucer's continual reference to Alisoun as a wife and Alisoun's lack of widow's weeds suggest that Jankyn is alive, yet no positive evidence may be found in the text.

665a Brewer, Derek S. 'Towards a Chaucerian Poetic.' *PBA* 60(1974), 219–52. Rpt in *Chaucer: The Poet as Storyteller.* London: Macmillan, 1984. Pp 54–79.

The confessional *WBP* may be analyzed under 'naturalistic premises' (p 78). See **1220a**.

666 Dillon, Bert. *A Chaucer Dictionary: Proper Names and Allusions*. Boston: G.K. Hall, 1974.

References to critical studies and spelling variations accompany alphabetized entries such as the name *Midas* and the work Ovid's *Ars Amatoria*. The entries are defined and also referenced throughout Chaucer's works.

667 Elliott, Ralph. *Chaucer's English*. London: André Deutsch, 1974.

In comparison with the precise language of the *PrT*, there is an abundance of common words in the *WBP* and *WBT* that suit Alisoun's rambling dialogue (p 109). Much of the imagery Alisoun employs is taken from her domestic surroundings (p 198). She is prone to circumlocution (p 224). While she uses bawdy puns and profanity, as do many of Chaucer's more middle-class characters, Alisoun is not given to colloquialism. Chaucer relied heavily on medieval physiognomy to describe characters such as Alisoun (pp 312–5).

668 Engelhardt, George J. 'The Lay Pilgrims of the *Canterbury Tales*: A Study in Ethology.' *MS* 36(1974), 278–330.

All of Alisoun's husbands have been 'derelict to the office of husbands' (p 323). See **343** and **1224**.

669 Hamlin, B.F. 'Astrology and the Wife of Bath: A Reinterpretation.' *ChauR* 9(1974), 153–65.

The specific details of planetary position at the time of Alisoun's birth indicate 'a ten-day period in early 1342' (p 158) and permit an astrological chart to be drawn for Alisoun. If the chart is read according to Ptolemaic beliefs, concepts with which Chaucer would have been familiar, Alisoun's 'martial and marital nature' (p 153) may be perceived. Alisoun's masculine side, her uncertain but profitable marriages, her gossiping tendencies, and her preoccupation with feet may be read from this chart.

670 Kernan, Anne. 'The Archwife and the Eunuch.' *ELH* 41(1974), 1–25.

The numerous parallels and contrasting elements between the portraits of the Wife of Bath and the Pardoner in the *GP*, their each telling a confessional sermon followed by an exemplary tale, and the cupidity of both characters suggest that Chaucer plays these two characters against one another. The mysterious, older characters of both their tales may be seen as reflections of the tellers (pp 7–9). Since both Alisoun and the Pardoner are 'exemplars ... of distorted and barren sexuality' (p

25), it is highly appropriate that it is the Pardoner who interrupts the *WBP*.

671 Matthews, William. 'The Wife of Bath and All Her Sect.' *Viator* 5(1974), 413–43.

While medieval literature tended to depict old men as either revered sages or humorous fools, old women were presented as garrulous, disobedient, and lecherous creatures. A woman was considered to be old at forty, whereas men were described as aged at sixty or seventy. Alisoun's marriages, her confessional prologue, and her behavior align her with the old woman tradition in literature.

672 Parr, Roger P. 'Chaucer's Art of Portraiture.' *SMC* 4(1974), 428–36. See **346**.

673 Reinicke, George F. 'Speculation, Intention, and the Teaching of Chaucer.' In *The Lerned and the Lewed: Studies in Chaucer and Medieval Literature*. Ed. Larry D. Benson. Cambridge: Harvard University Press, 1974. Pp 81–93.

Whiting conjectured that Alisoun looks to the Clerk for a sixth husband (pp 85–6).

674 Sanders, Barry. 'Chaucer's Dependence on Sermon Structure in the *Wife of Bath's Prologue* and *Tale*.' *SMC* 4(1974), 437–45.

The *WBP* is protest literature that takes the form of 'a burlesque sermon' (p 437), in which Alisoun uses authority in a comic manner. In this sermon, Alisoun, herself a product of pulpit satire, proves that the church does not realize that wives should be given mastery in order for there to be peace in marriage. Alisoun calls attention to her husbands' being inept preachers and violates the doctrine of confession in revealing her fourth husband's secrets. See **1227**.

675 Scott, A.F. *Who's Who in Chaucer*. London: Elm Tree Books; New York: Taplinger Publishing Co., Inc., 1974.

Definitions are provided for Abraham, Alisoun, *Dame Alys*, Appelles, Argus, Clytemnestra, Crisippus, Christ, Diana, Hercules, Heloise, Jankyn, Jerome, Jovinian, Lamech, Arrius Latumyus, Lucia, Mark, Minotaur, Ovid, Paul, Pasiphäe, Ptolomy, Solomon, Sampson, Socrates, Trotula, *Wylkyn*, and Xantippe in the context of the *WBP*. See **1228**.

676 Severs, J. Burke. 'Chaucer's Clerks.' In *Chaucer and Middle English Studies in Honour of Rossell Hope Robbins*. Ed. Beryl Rowland. London: Allen and Unwin, 1974. Pp 140–52.

The Clerk, offended by Alisoun's unorthodox views on female

sovereignty, her carnality, and her comparative evaluation of marriage and virginity, tells the tale of Griselda (p 149). Jankyn, like the Clerk, was schooled in the antifeminist tradition. Jankyn's book resembles numerous mss of the thirteenth and fourteenth centuries.

677 Boren, James L. 'Alysoun of Bath and the Vulgate "Perfect Wife."' *NM* 76(1975), 247–56.

The mentioning of Solomon's Proverbs in Jankyn's book may indicate that Chaucer intended to juxtapose Alisoun's character with that of the Vulgate's *mulier fortis*.

678 Brewer, Derek. 'Structure and Character Types of Chaucer's Popular Comic Tales.' In *Estudios sobre los generos literarios*. Eds. J. Coy and J. De Hoz. Salamanca, 1975. Pp 107–18. Rpt in *Chaucer: The Poet as Storyteller*. London: Macmillan, 1984. Pp 80–9.

The *WBP* 'is a comic tale in itself' (p 89). Despite her admission to every vice the antifeminists accuse women of committing, Alisoun is a beloved comic character.

679 Item cancelled.

680 Clogan, Paul M. 'Literary Criticism in William Godwin's *Life of Chaucer*.' *M&H* 6(1975), 89–98.

Godwin describes the *WBP* as 'licentious' (p 195).

681 Delany, Sheila. 'Sexual Economics, Chaucer's Wife of Bath, and *The Book of Margery Kempe*.' *MinnR* 5(1975), 104–15. Rpt in *Writing Woman*. New York: Shocken Books, 1983. Pp 76–92.

The lives of the Wife of Bath and Margery Kempe are compared and contrasted. Both women were of the middle class, well-traveled, and each had her own finances. While Alisoun delights in her sexuality, Margery strives to subdue her fleshly desires. Each woman was the property of her husband and equated sex with money. Margery's husband agreed to her desire for chastity when she paid his debts (p 112), while Alisoun used her sexuality for monetary gain.

682 Gallick, Susan. 'A Look at Chaucer and His Preachers.' *Spec* 50(1975), 456–76.

The *WBP* contains several elements of the sermon: a preacher who speaks from experience, a didactic tone, a frequently addressed sermon topic, and a division of the topic into elaborated parts (p 463). The Pardoner recognizes Alisoun as a skilled preacher who can gloss and provide *exempla*, Scripture, and lore in order to illustrate her point. He also sees the *WBP* as an antifeminist sermon. While Alisoun does use much material from the antifeminist tradition, she appears in a strong, feminist light.

683 Kelly, Henry Ansgar. *Love and Marriage in the Age of Chaucer.* Ithaca: Cornell University Press, 1975.

In both the *WBP* and *WBT*, Alisoun provides examples of mutuality in marriage (p 33n). Alisoun's intimations of marriage to Jankyn while her fourth husband is still alive (III.567–8) is an example of her taking measures towards the future (p 198). While she is aware of the potential to sin, Alisoun probably feels that marriage will legitimize her actions (p 271).

684 Mannucci, Loretta Valtz. *Fourteenth-Century England and the Canterbury Tales.* Milan: Coopli, 1975.

Alisoun's realistic approach to life makes her value experience in the *WBP*. Her analogies of gold and wooden vessels and white and brown breads do not overturn the traditional values placed upon virginity but establish that all sexual states have a proper function. That Alisoun consciously decides to act as the embodiment of the antifeminist tradition, not because it is simply in her nature to do so, is the striking feature about her (p 143). She uses the stereotype that man is the rational gender to promote female sovereignty in III.440–2 (p 144). Her experience is victorious over Jankyn's authority. See **351** and **1234**.

685 Miskimin, Alice S. *The Renaissance Chaucer.* New Haven: Yale University Press, 1975.

Alisoun becomes an 'ironic allegorical symbol' in the *Buk* (p 112). She is Chaucer's archetype of ironic authority and antitype of humility (p 126). Fifteenth-century misogynistic satires, particularly Dunbar's version of the Wife of Bath, show the intricacies of Alisoun's dramatic voice (p 129).

686 Palomo, Dolores. 'The Fate of the Wife of Bath's "Bad Husbands."' *ChauR* 9(1975), 303–19.

Alisoun is noticeably silent about the untimely deaths of her fourth husband and Jankyn. The *WBP* should be analyzed not as an attack against antifeminism but as a woman's personal history subtly interwoven into her complaint (p 304). Alisoun's defense of marriage reflects the profitable matches she was placed into as a youth. Alisoun may have returned the physical brutality of her third husband and thereby brought on his death (p 308). She almost reveals that she and Jankyn contrived the death of her fourth husband (pp 308–9). The Wife confesses to her gossip in III.534–8 that Jankyn is a murderer. Jankyn dies for his crime, and Alisoun must go on a pilgrimage to atone for her adultery with him (p 314). See **1236**.

687 Weissman, Hope Phyllis. 'Antifeminism and Chaucer's Characterizations of Women.' In *Geoffrey Chaucer: A Collection of Original Articles*. Ed. George D. Economou. New York: McGraw-Hill, 1975. Pp 93–110. Rpt in *Critical Essays on Chaucer's Canterbury Tales*. Ed. Malcolm Andrew. Toronto: University of Toronto Press, 1991. Pp 106–25 [cited].

Alisoun's *GP* portrait aligns her with Eve and parodic images of the Good Woman of Proverbs (p 106). In the *WBP* Chaucer shows how antifeminism has maligned women by having Alisoun fail in her attempts to justify herself as a sympathetic rendering of what the antifeminist perception of Eve does to woman's nature (p 121). Alisoun fails to express the essence of equality in marriage that occurs when Jankyn yields sovereignty to her (pp 122–3). See **1239**.

688 Caie, Graham D. 'The Significance of the Early Chaucer Manuscript Glosses (With Special References to the *Wife of Bath's Prologue*).' *ChauR* 10(1976), 350–60.

Glosses to the *WBP* not only provide sources for Chaucer's material, but they often comment seriously on the work in order to prevent readers from being too sympathetic towards Alisoun (p 351). They underscore patristic ideology and point out Alisoun's barren spirituality.

689 David, Alfred. *The Strumpet Muse: Art and Morals in Chaucer's Poetry*. Bloomington: Indiana University Press, 1976.

While Alisoun's argument for experience ultimately fails, 'her argument is the most persuasive case that can be made for' it (p 136). The three portions of the *WBP*: the sermon, her early marriages, and her later ones, contain humor, irony, and double-edged satire. As a product of patriarchal authority, Alisoun 'is not really a free agent' (p 153). See **1243**.

690 Donaldson, E. Talbot. 'Some Readings in the *Canterbury Tales*.' In *Medieval Studies in Honor of Lillian Herlands Hornstein*. Ed. Jess B. Bessinger, Jr., and Robert R. Raymo. New York: New York University Press, 1976. Pp 99–110.

Because of its absence in most mss, III.44a–f has been assumed by Manly and Rickert (**29**) 'to be a late Chaucerian addition' (p 105). A scribe most likely connected the *fyve* of III.44 with the *sixte* of III.45;

however, 44f also contains the word *fyve*. Editors should not hypothesize about revisions 'when there is an apparent scribal cause for omission' (p 105). In III.838 the word *pees* has been read as *pace* by Koch, although no ms supports this claim. Had Chaucer meant *pass*, a word still associated with *pace* in his day, he would have written *passe*. Manly and Rickert have not discussed the fact that 14 of the 50 mss interpret *pees* as a verb, not as a noun. One of 'the four independent lines of transmission from O¹' (p 106) that the editors used supports the idea that the intended word is *pisse*.

691   Hawkins, Harriett. *Poetic Freedom and Poetic Truth: Chaucer, Shakespeare, Marlowe, Milton*. Oxford: Clarendon Press, 1976.
The Wife of Bath's first three husbands fall into the category of frequently nameless characters whose apparent purpose is exploitation (pp 6–7). Our knowledge of the husbands is confined to 'age, number, and economic status' (p 20). Their similar fates fuse them into a single identity (p 11). Chaucer prompts the reader to side with Alisoun and share her victory over her husbands (p 18). See **353**.

692   Howard, Donald R. *The Idea of the Canterbury Tales*. Berkeley: University of California Press, 1976.
Alisoun exhibits the orthodox view that Christians should be obedient to church law, but she realizes that the perfection of virginity is not for all (p 248). She is troubled, though, by her belonging to the lowest grade of perfection. The Wife's radical position on female sovereignty generates the Marriage Group. See **1244**.

693   Justman, Stewart. 'Medieval Monism and Abuse of Authority in Chaucer.' *ChauR* 11(1976), 95–111.
The abuse of legal and moral codes in the *CT* is a thematic representative of disrespect for authority (p 109). Many Canterbury characters establish themselves as authorities, including Alisoun and Jankyn. These multiple authorities underscore the disunity of their world. Chaucer's treatment of authority stems from medieval formal disputation (p 96). Both Alisoun and Jerome recognize inconsistencies in the writings of Paul (p 102). Alisoun's fault of partial citation is a crime of which Jankyn is also guilty and Jerome himself reveals inconsistencies in his logic (p 104).

694   Lanham, Richard A. *The Motives of Eloquence: Literary Rhetoric in the Renaissance*. New Haven: Yale University Press, 1976.
Alisoun's game is not play but rhetoric and she beats the authoritative masters in this game. It is Alisoun's game, not its outcome, that is the

important thing (p 72).

695 Leyerle, John. 'Thematic Interlace in the *Canterbury Tales.*' *E&S* 29(1976), 107–21.

Alisoun's major regret is that she is growing old. The Parson's discussion of lechery addresses the *WBP* 'point by point' (p 112). See **240**.

696 Long, Charles. 'The Wife of Bath's Confessions and the Miller's True Story.' *Interpretations* 8(1976), 54–66.

While both the Miller and the Wife are dubious narrators, the *MilT*'s account of a young wife having an affair with a clerk resembles the Wife's early history. The Miller's Alison may be the Wife of Bath in her youth. Since Nicholas and Jankyn both are Oxford clerks, are called *hende*, and may be violent lovers, they may be the same person. Jankyn's references to being on a rooftop (III.778–9) and to woman's nakedness (III.782–4) suggest he was privy to the cuckolding and trick on Absolon in the *MilT*. Old John is not only the Reeve but Alisoun's fourth husband, who keeps silent out of shame (p 65).

697 Maguon, Francis P. 'The Dunmow Flitch: An Addendum and Adieu.' *NM* 77(1976), 253.

Couples swore the *Dunmow Oath* before receiving their prize of a flitch of bacon.

698 Oberembt, Kenneth J. 'Chaucer's Anti-Misogynist Wife of Bath.' *ChauR* 10(1976), 287–302.

Alisoun's anti-misogynist speech should not be branded as heretical. It is a comic exposure of human behavior and accepted sexual doctrine (p 290). Alisoun recognizes that men are as susceptible to sexuality as woman are, and she uses this fact to her advantage in her marriages (p 292). Her delight in sexuality is tempered, however, by her awareness of the *bona matrimonii* and her Christian call to avoid sin (p 298). See **1245**.

699 Renoir, Alain. 'The Impossible Dream: An Underside to the Wife of Bath.' *Moderna Språk* 70(1976), 311–22.

Because Chaucer often establishes a contrast between surface truths and those that run deeper, Alisoun's character should be viewed beyond the popular conception of her as a creature of rampant sexuality. Alisoun's euphemistic speech reveals that she is not as happy as she would have her audience believe and that she wishes for children (pp 321–2).

700 Ruggiers, Paul G. 'A Vocabulary for Chaucerian Comedy: A Preliminary

Sketch.' In *Medieval Studies in Honor of Lillian Herlands Hornstein*. Ed. Jess B. Bessinger, Jr., and Robert R. Raymo. New York: New York University Press, 1976. Pp 193–225.

Comic elements and characteristics found in the *WBP* include Alisoun's deceiving, interrogating, and debasing her husbands, the loose structure of Alisoun's garrulous performance (p 203), the attention given to authorities (p 205), and Alisoun's comparisons (p 216). See **354** and **1246**.

701 Tristram, Philippa. *Figures of Life and Death in Medieval English Literature*. London: Paul Elek, 1976.

Alisoun is a figure of Age; Jankyn a figure of Youth. Alisoun's fifth marriage represents a 'challenge to her vigour' (p 28). This union is a reversal of Alisoun's previous treatment of her first three marriages, in which she had the advantage of youth (p 224). Chaucer exposes the inconsistency of the medieval conception of fortune and its opposition to freedom through his construction of Alisoun. While she claims that planetary influence has made her what she is, Alisoun has played a strong role in shaping her own life.

702 Tuttle, Edward F. 'The *Trotula* and Old Dame Trot: A Note on the Lady of Salerno.' *Bulletin of the History of Medicine* 50(1976), 61–72.

That Trotula appears in Jankyn's book reveals both clerical and popular knowledge of this woman (p 69). One should hesitate before relating the figure of Dame Trot to Trotula.

703 Wenzel, Siegfried. 'Chaucer and the Language of Contemporary Preaching.' *SP* 73(1976), 138–61.

Alisoun, a 'long-winded advocate' (p 141) of her beliefs, possesses a preacher's tactics. Her preaching style is not opposed to authoritarian proof; rather, it follows authority (p 152). See **1249**.

704 Zacher, Christian K. *Curiosity and Pilgrimage: The Literature of Discovery in Fourteenth-Century England*. Baltimore: Johns Hopkins University Press, 1976.

The Wife of Bath is one of several of the Canterbury pilgrims 'more impelled toward the shrine of Venus than toward the shrine of Becket' (p 108). Saint Joce, patron saint of pilgrims, whom the Wife calls upon in III.483, is often represented carrying a *burdoun*. The phallic symbolism of the pilgrim staff underscores the dual purpose of the Wife's pilgrimage. Alisoun's sexuality and her marriage experiences qualify her to begin the marriage debate (p 110).

705 Ames, Ruth M. 'Prototypes and Parody in Chaucerian Exegesis.'In *The Fourteenth Century (Acta 4)*. Ed. Paul E. Szarmach and Bernard S. Levy. Binghamton: Center for Medieval & Early Renaissance Studies, 1977. Pp 87–105.

Chaucer maintained both a parodic and a pious attitude towards Scripture. The *WBP* is an example of the comedy and irony Chaucer could produce in creating scriptural parallels (p 88). Alisoun's license to interpret Scripture is reflective of the free thought of the fourteenth century (p 92). Alisoun adheres to the literal carnality of the Old Law, and her scriptural selections of the Samaritan woman and of Solomon complement her self-portrait (p 93).

706 Berggren, Ruth. 'Who *Really* Is the Advocate of Equality in the Marriage Group?' *MSE* 6(1977), 25–36.

Contrary to Kittredge's assertions, Alisoun does not seek domination in marriage but rather seeks equality. The humiliation Alisoun has suffered in marriage prompts her to deceive her first three husbands. The mastery she obtains through such deceit is 'dubious' (p 27). Alisoun does not abuse the sovereignty Jankyn yields to her. See **241** and **1250**.

707 Burlin, Robert B. *Chaucerian Fiction*. Princeton: Princeton University Press, 1977.

The contradictory *WBP* and *WBT* contain some consistency, for Alisoun is continually trying to assert feminine independence in a male-dominated society. In her early marriages Alisoun learned how to fashion the self into an entity that could provide for herself. The reality of her fourth marriage was one she could not rewrite; her recalled failure in this portion of the *WBP* causes Alisoun to lose her narrative focus (p 221). Her fifth marriage taught Alisoun how to use text as a weapon. Jankyn's book is a reminder of male oppression.

708 Diamond, Arlyn. 'Chaucer's Women and Women's Chaucer.' In *The Authority of Experience: Essays in Feminist Criticism*. Ed. Arlyn Diamond and Lee R. Edwards. Amherst: University of Massachusetts Press, 1977. Pp 60–83.

While Chaucer's creation of Alisoun has been lauded for its insightful presentation of woman, the Wife of Bath is a compilation 'of masculine insecurities and female vices as seen by misogynists' (p 68). While Alisoun has financial independence and potential for great success, her strengths suggest negative aggression. Chaucer uses Alisoun to formulate jokes about domineering women. Alisoun proves that the contents of Jankyn's book are correct (p 71). See **1251**.

709 Donaldson, E. Talbot. 'Designing a Camel: Or, Generalizing the Middle Ages.' *TSL* 22(1977), 1–16.

Students of the Middle Ages should not be quick to generalize the era. To assume that the medieval mind-set found woman to be inferior to men (p 2), that intelligence stems from holiness (p 4), that Alisoun has no children because she never discusses any (p 7), and that 'Christianity governed all men's lives' (p 8) is to oversimplify issues. The Wife of Bath exposes the inaccuracy of several of the church-oriented, antifeminist assumptions.

710 East, W.G. '"By preeve which that is demonstratif."' *ChauR* 12(1977), 78-82.

See **1252**.

711 Garbáty, Thomas J. 'Chaucer and Comedy.' In *Versions of Medieval Comedy*. Ed. Paul G. Ruggiers. Norman, OK: University of Oklahoma Press, 1977. Pp 173–90.

Chaucer derived his character type of the Wife of Bath from Roman comedy, yet he transformed her through his writing into a more humanized individual (p 174). We witness her humanity when she loses track of what she is saying in *WBP* III.585–6 (p 184). Chaucer became so involved with this character that she is referred to in the Clerk's *Envoy* and in the *MerT* as well as in *Buk*. Her appeal to Chaucer stems from his giving her an appreciation of the more serious aspects of life. Although she has suffered, she has an optimistic attitude. These qualities are a reflection of Chaucer's sympathetic nature and comic perception of life (p 178). The dialogue between Chaucer's characters establishes 'a human comedy of pilgrims' (p 184).

712 Gardner, John. *The Life and Times of Chaucer*. New York: Alfred A. Knopf, 1977.

The *WBP* contains one of Chaucer's five references throughout the *CT* to jealous men who try to imprison their women. Chaucer is sympathetic to the woman in all cases (p 165). Alice Perrers may have partially inspired Chaucer's creation of the Wife of Bath (p 182).

713 ———. *The Poetry of Chaucer*. Carbondale: Southern Illinois University Press, 1977.

Alisoun overthrows the Church's authoritative view of marriage that has been exemplified by Constance's life (p 274). The Friar's interruption

of the *WBP* extends the 'debate on government' (p 275). See **357** and
1254.

714 Hanning, Robert W. 'From *Eva* and *Ave* to Eglentyne and Alisoun:
Chaucer's Insight into the Roles Women Play.' *Signs* 2(1977), 580–99.
In his creation of the Prioress and Alisoun, Chaucer examines the roles
women were assigned in the Middle Ages. Alisoun's performance is
contradictory, deceptive, and confessional (p 592). Her contradictions
are a result of her attempt to reject her role, because in denying this
imposed identity, she must assume a masculine one and, subsequently,
hates herself for emulating her oppressors (p 599).

715 Haskell, Ann S. 'The Portrayal of Women by Chaucer and His Age.'
In *What Manner of Woman: Essays on English and American Life
and Literature*. Ed. Marlene Springer. New York: New York University
Press, 1977. Pp 1–14.
There is no consistent point of view on women in medieval literature.
Clerical antifeminism, a subject attacked in the *WBP*, represents one
perspective on the female (p 5). Chaucer depicts middle-class women
through his detailing of the Wife, the gildsmen's wives, and Simkyn's
wife. These women flaunt the economic success of their husbands (p
8). Alisoun's character exhibits female strength and sexuality (p 10).
While Alisoun feels a personal need to remarry, other widows in medieval
literature manifest no urgency to do so. This lack of internal or external
pressure is contrary to the actual condition of widows in the late Middle
Ages (p 9). See **1255**.

716 Knight, Stephen. 'Politics and Chaucer's Poetry.' In *The Radical
Reader*. Ed. Stephen Knight and Michael Wilding. Sydney: Wild and
Woolley, 1977. Pp 169–92.
See **1256**.

717 Long, Charles. 'The Clerk's Secret Shame: He Is Jankyn.'
Interpretations 9(1977), 22–33.
The similarities between Jankyn and the Clerk suggest they are the
same man. The Clerk's silent and shamed appearance adds credence
to this theory. His *Envoy* is a coded declaration of love for his wife (p
30).

718 Miller, Robert P., ed. *Chaucer: Sources and Backgrounds*. New York:
Oxford University Press, 1977.
See **174**.

719 Owen, Charles A., Jr. *Pilgrimage and Storytelling in the Canterbury*

Tales: The Dialectic of 'Ernest' and 'Game.' Norman, OK: University of Oklahoma Press, 1977.

The similarities between Alisoun and the wife of St. Denis, their mutual disregard for logic, and the acknowledgement of religious authority in the *WBP* and *ShT* strongly suggest that Alisoun was the initial teller of the *ShT* (p 16). Despite the comic nature of her presentation, Alisoun relates the human desires for sex and power (p 146). While Alisoun believes she gains power in her marriage with Jankyn, it is actually love that she receives (p 153). See **1258**.

720   Pichaske, David R. *The Movement of the Canterbury Tales: Chaucer's Literary Pilgrimage.* Norwood, PA: Norwood Editions, 1977; rpt Folcroft, PA: Folcroft Library Editions, 1978.

Fragments III–V of the *CT* focus on social order; marriage becomes the metaphor for this order. The *WBP* and *WBT* are so much a part of Alisoun that fiction and the self become fused (p 65). Alisoun responds to the *MLT* because it is not based on the world of experience. The theme of misinterpretation is found in the *WBP* not only in Alisoun's use of Scripture but also in the way Alisoun has been treated as an object and not as a person (p 67). Chaucer continually undermines Alisoun's argument, turning the *WBP* into a string of contradictions. Alisoun yields to the power of destiny and becomes its victim; she does not take the advice of the hag in the *WBT* and yield to God (p 69). While many of Alisoun's beliefs are embodied in the *ShT*, the romance she does tell reflects more of her character (p 134).

721   Schauber, Ellen, and Ellen Spolsky. 'The Consolation of Alison: The Speech Acts of the Wife of Bath.' *Centrum* 5(1977), 20–34.

Analysis of Alisoun's speech reveals that she 'argues, insists, challenges, and confides' (p 22) and proves that Alisoun is aware her audience will be resistant to her notions (p 26). The hag shares Alisoun's use of rhetorical questions, yet the content of her speech is more noble than Alisoun's. The hag may be compared to Boethius' Lady Philosophy and to Prudence, representatives of medieval ideals. Alisoun, a parody of Lady Philosophy, fails to achieve her goals (pp 30–1).

722   Brewer, Derek. *Chaucer and His World.* London: Eyre Methuen; New York: Dodd, Mead and Company, 1978/2nd ed, Cambridge: D.S. Brewer, 1992.

Despite Chaucer's acceptance and use of the antifeminist tradition in the *WBP*, he makes the reader sympathetic towards Alisoun (p 181).

The Wife's personality represents recklessness, triumphant womanhood, love, and freedom. See **1264**.

723 ――――, ed. *Chaucer: The Critical Heritage.* Volume 1, 1385–1837. Volume 2, 1837–1933. London: Routledge and Kegan Paul, 1978. See **362**.

724 Burton, T.L. 'The Wife of Bath's Fourth and Fifth Husbands and Her Ideal Sixth: The Growth of a Marital Philosophy.' *ChauR* 13(1978), 34–50.
Alisoun's account of her fourth husband reveals defeat despite her swearing to the contrary (pp 35–41). Her marriage to the sexually masterful Jankyn reveals Alisoun's desire to be a submissive wife (p 43). The relationship in the *WBT* reveals a marriage in which a wife may maintain her independence while wedded to a strongly sexual husband. See **1267**.

725 Cook, James W. '"That she was out of alle charitee": Point-Counterpoint in the *Wife of Bath's Prologue* and *Tale.*' *ChauR* 13(1978), 51–65.
Alisoun's participation in the sacrament of marriage with the intent of obtaining sexual gratification bars her from receiving sacramental grace (pp 52–4). She also counters church teaching with her doctrine of female sovereignty. Alisoun's negative personality traits reflect the state of her soul (p 55). Her inability to love in a Christian sense disassociates her from the moral hag of the *WBT* who saves her husband's soul.

726 Delasanta, Rodney. 'Alisoun and the Saved Harlots: A Cozening of Our Expectations.' *ChauR* 12(1978), 218–35.
Chaucer's having Alisoun be first to make church offering seems to be a play on the typological motif of the saved harlot who will enter heaven before many others will. The Wife's preoccupation with Jankyn's feet at her fourth husband's funeral parallels Mary Magdalene's anointing Christ's feet with her tears (pp 226–7). Alisoun's discussion of the fourth husband's tomb is a trivialized reflection of the Magdalene's presence at Christ's tomb as well as imagery from the *Song of Songs*.

727 Mendelson, Anne. 'Some Uses of the Bible and Biblical Authority in the *Wife of Bath's Prologue* and *Tale.*' *DAI* 39(1978), 2295A.
Using the verbal techniques she has learned from Jankyn, Alisoun attacks patriarchal authority. This form of questioning debate is alien to Alisoun's personality. In combination with Alisoun's ignorance of the material she is using, her debate tactics provide for the comedy of the *WBP*. See **1269**.

728 Palmer, Barbara D. '"To speke of wo that is in mariage": The Marital Arts in Medieval Literature.' In *Human Sexuality in the Middle Ages and Renaissance*. Ed. Douglas Radcliffe-Umstead. Pittsburgh: University of Pittsburgh Center for Medieval and Renaissance Studies, 1978. Pp 3–14.

For Alisoun, neither experience nor authority has been able to provide marital bliss (p 3). Like the *WBP*, the *RvT*, *SumT*, *MerT*, *ShT*, and *NPT* share the opinion that marriage can be expected to contain adultery, jealousy, arguments, and the like (p 8).

729 Roth, Elizabeth. 'On the Wife of Bath's "Embarrassing Question."' *AN&Q* 17(1978), 54–5.

Similar phrasing in Dorigen's question in V.868–72 aids in interpreting Alisoun's question concerning the genitalia as *And created by so wise a being* (III.117).

730 Rowland, Beryl. *Birds with Human Souls: A Guide to Bird Symbolism*. Knoxville: University of Tennessee Press, 1978.

The magpie (p 103) and the goose (p 69) appear in the *WBP* III.456 and III.269–70, respectively. See **1270**.

731 Sands, Donald B. 'The Non-Comic, Non-Tragic Wife: Chaucer's Dame Alys as Sociopath.' *ChauR* 12(1978), 171–82.

Alisoun may be diagnosed as a sociopath, a person who believes in herself but struggles with antisocial reactions and with addictions. The strain of evil in Alisoun belies her association with the comic Falstaff (p 174), and the absence of children in her life is not enough to render her a tragic figure (pp 175–6).

732 Spisak, James W. 'Medieval Marriage Concepts and Chaucer's Good Old Lovers.' In *Human Sexuality in the Middle Ages and Renaissance*. Ed. Douglas Radcliff-Umstead. Pittsburgh: University of Pittsburgh Center for Medieval and Renaissance Studies, 1978. Pp 15–26.

Chaucer uses several of the *CT* characters, including the Wife of Bath, to interpret the marriage laws set forth by Jerome, Augustine, Huguccio of Pisa, Lawrence of Spain, Peter Lombard, and the *Libri poenitentiales*. Alisoun represents Chaucer's view of a more realistic portrayal of marriage that is based on experience (pp 22–3).

733 Whitbread, L. 'Six Chaucer Notes.' *NM* 79(1978), 41–3.

See **365**.

734 Blake, N.F. 'The Relationship between the Hengwrt and the Ellesmere

Manuscripts of the *Canterbury Tales.*' *E&S* 32(1979), 1–18.
In the initial plan of the Hg ms, Fragment III was to have been placed between H and I (p 5). The *ManT* followed the *WBT* because of its tie to the *WBP* (pp 8–9). References to Alisoun in earlier tales helped the *WBP* and *WBT* move up further in the *CT* sequence (p 14).

735 Burnley, J.D. *Chaucer's Language and the Philosophers' Tradition.* Chaucer Studies, 2. Ed. D.S. Brewer. Totowa: Rowman and Littlefield, 1979.
Alisoun's call for female sovereignty makes her a tyrant (p 42). Her advocacy of the will above the reason goes against medieval ethics (p 85).

736 Carruthers, Mary. 'The Wife of Bath and the Painting of Lions.' *PMLA* 94(1979), 209–22.
The concepts the Wife attacks are ideals held by her class concerning women. In her time, books of conduct existed to teach wives how the patriarchy felt they should behave. These writings do not, however, accord with medieval practice. Experience taught people that marrying a wealthy widow was more advantageous than wedding a propertied virgin (p 213). Alisoun's experience has taught her that sex is a useful tool for acquiring property. Her definition of mastery is economic control (p 214). Once she has gained financial security, Alisoun is free to marry for love. Too young to realize the value of experience, Jankyn relies on the authority of his version of a deportment book to reform Alisoun (p 215). Granting Jankyn her property causes Alisoun to lose mastery in this marriage until she forces Jankyn to return her land to her. See **1272**.

737 Jordan, Robert M. 'The Wife of Bath.' *PMLA* 94 (1979), 950–1.
In 'The Wife of Bath and the Painting of Lions' (**736**), Carruthers' addition of historical materials to Chaucer's text provides limited information. She should have focused on Alisoun's speech and not on feminist hermeneutics.

738 Wimsatt, James I. 'The Wife of Bath.' *PMLA* 94(1979), 951–2.
While Carruthers argues that Chaucer criticizes Jerome by using Alisoun as his spokesperson (**736**), she does not consider that fourteenth-century men would have received *Jov* uncritically. Critical study of sources and medieval spirituality supersedes the historic-context approach.

739 Carruthers, Mary. 'The Wife of Bath.' *PMLA* 94(1979), 952–3.
In his criticism of Carruthers' work, Jordan is unaware of both Chaucer's

development of his character's personalities and his construction of a frame-space (**737**). Wimsatt disagrees with Carruthers' valuing of a historical framework in her criticism (**738**). There is no reason why a historical context cannot aid literary analysis.

740 David, Alfred. 'Chaucerian Comedy and Criseyde.' In *Essays on Troilus and Criseyde*. Ed. Mary Salu. Chaucer Studies, 3. Cambridge: D.S. Brewer, 1979; rpt Totowa: Rowman and Littlefield, 1980. Pp 90–104.

The brand of comedy Chaucer created around Criseyde is continued in the *CT* in the *WBP* and *WBT* (p 104). Alisoun and Criseyde share widowhood, practicality, romantic tendencies, skepticism, and joy in life.

741 Hamel, Mary. 'The Wife of Bath and a Contemporary Murder.' *ChauR* 14(1979), 132–9.

The account in Jankyn's book of a wife who murders her husband and then has sex with her lover in the husband's bed may be a reference to a similar occurrence in the 1300's chronicled by the Monk of Westminster. Neither Alisoun nor Jankyn is a murderer (p 135). It is the lust of the murderer and of Alisoun that Jankyn attacks through his reading (pp 138–9).

742 McCall, John P. *Chaucer among the Gods: The Poetics of Classical Myth*. University Park: Pennsylvania State University Press, 1979.

In her discussion of Venus, Mars, and Mercury, Alisoun over-simplifies their personalities (p 125). She manipulates classical references for her arguments (p 139). See **1275**.

743 Reisner, M.E. 'New Light on Judoc the Obscure.' *Chaucer Newsletter* 1(1979), 19–20.

Chaucer may have had Alisoun swear by St. Joce because the saint's relics were reported to have reposed at the New Minster in Winchester, a locale that bears strong ties to Arthurian legend. The Tabard also belonged to the Abbot of Hyde.

744 Rhodes, Jewell P. 'Female Stereotypes in Medieval Literature: Androgyny and the Wife of Bath.' *Journal of Women's Studies in Literature* 1(1979), 348–52.

While Alisoun is usually described as a feminist, it is more accurate to define her as an androgyne. Through her incorporation of the two gender systems into her life, Alisoun does liberate herself from societal restrictions, yet she becomes morally corrupt in both gender roles.

745 Rowland, Beryl. 'Exhuming Trotula, *Sapiens Matrona* of Salerno.'

Florilegium 1(1979), 42–57.

Trotula appears in Jankyn's book not because of her medical knowledge but more likely because of the connotations of the word *trot* that suggest an old woman who continues to dwell on her sexuality (pp 49–50).

746 Sato, Tsutomu. *Sentence and Solas: Thematic Development and Narrative Technique in the Canterbury Tales.* Tokyo: Kobundo, 1979.

The *WBP* details the equilibrium and tension of gender relations. Alisoun derives her existence from the war between the sexes (p 134). While Alisoun has accepted the way of the world, she has not ceased to contend with it. Sexuality is the key to her identity (p 137). See **1277**.

747 Schulenburg, Jane Tibbets. 'Clio's European Daughters: Myopic Modes of Perception.' In *The Prism of Sex: Essays in the Sociology of Knowledge.* Ed. Julia A. Sherman and Evelyn Torton Beck. Madison: University of Wisconsin Press, 1979. Pp 33–53.

Alisoun points out the clerical monopolization on preserving history and its subsequent distortion of women. Only female saints were cast in a positive light. Christine de Pisan was also aware of the biased presentation of women in history and was thus motivated to write her *City of Ladies.* While the Dark Ages acknowledged woman's role in history, the twelfth-century renaissance removed them from history (p 48).

748 West, Philip. 'The Perils of Pauline Theology: the *Wife of Bath's Prologue* and *Tale.*' *EAS* 8(1979), 7–16.

In the *WBP*, Alisoun 'reduce[s] glossing to absurdity' (p 9) through mimicking the glossators. Alisoun's performance may be divided into three segments: her two-part prologue and her tale. This organization of her performance contributes greatly to Alisoun's construction of a parody of Pauline text. Both the *WBP* and the *WBT* are highly reflexive.

749 Woolf, Rosemary. 'Moral Chaucer and Kindly Gower.' In *J.R.R. Tolkien, Scholar and Storyteller: Essays In Memoriam.* Ed. Mary Salu and Robert T. Farrell. Ithaca: Cornell University Press, 1979. Pp 221–45.

While some view the *WBP* as a reflection of Chaucer's beneficence towards women, Alisoun must see her sexuality as an economic tool. The Wife is not condemned for this practice because her multiple marriages make her seem unreal, and not because Chaucer renders her character in a human light (pp 243–4). Alisoun's use of sex as a commodity in marriage reflects the equation of money and sex in the *ShT*, the tale she was originally supposed to tell. By having the Wife ultimately tell a romance, Chaucer runs the risk of her being sentimentalized by the reader. Hints of the Wife having taken lovers, however, eliminate this tendency. Unlike Gower, who was overly indulgent towards his culpable characters, and unlike Dunbar, who manipulated his readers' view of his Alisoun-like characters, Chaucer successfully combines 'amused sympathy' (p 245) for Alisoun with an awareness of her faults.

750 Aers, David. *Chaucer, Langland and the Creative Imagination.* London: Routledge and Kegan Paul, 1980.

Alisoun exposes the fact that those who are strongly opposed to carnality, such as the apostle Paul, are very much involved with sexuality (p 85). Her fragmented interpretation of Scripture is a criticism of exegetical practices. Chaucer shows the difficulty of challenging traditional social norms through Alisoun's attack on and her acceptance of her culture. She advocates sexual pleasure, yet agrees that it is for the purpose of procreation (p 149). Although Alisoun marries Jankyn for love, she is still influenced by sexual economics and the patriarchal practice of dominance.

751 Benson, Robert G. *Medieval Body Language: A Study of the Use of Gesture in Chaucer's Poetry. Anglistica*, No. 21. Copenhagen: Rosenkilde and Bagger, 1980.

Expressive, demonstrative, and ceremonial gestures have been incorporated into the *WBP*. Significant examples include III.443, 588, 590, 672, 829, 830 (p 133). See **1280**.

752 Bolton, W.F. 'The Wife of Bath: Narrator as Victim.' In *Gender and Literary Voice*. Ed. Janet Todd. New York: Holmes and Meier Publishers, Inc., 1980. Pp 54–65.

See **1281**.

753 Carruthers, Mary J. 'On Making Students Relevant to Chaucer.' In *Approaches to Teaching Chaucer's Canterbury Tales*. Ed. Joseph Gibaldi. Consultant editor, Florence H. Ridley. New York: The Modern Language Association of America, 1980. Pp 76–80.

In order that students may grasp Alisoun's advocacy of experience over authority, the Wife of Bath should be taught in a historical context that includes contemporary writings as well as economic and social factors (p 78).

754 de Weever, Jacqueline. 'Chaucerian Onomastics: The Formation and Use of Personal Names in Chaucer's Works.' *Names* 28(1980), 1–31.

Two of the four Chaucerian characters named Jankyn are found in *WBP* as are two of Chaucer's Alisouns. Both the Wife of Bath and Alison of the *MilT* resemble the Alisoun of the Harley lyrics (p 18). Chaucer's extravagant and dramatic use of *exempla* is found in *WBP* (p 30). See **1283**.

755 Fritz, D.F. 'The Animus-Possessed Wife of Bath.' *Journal of Analytical Psychology* 25(1980), 163–80.
   See **1285**.

756 Gerke, Robert S. 'Fortitude and Sloth in the *Wife of Bath's Tale* and the *Clerk's Tale.*' *PPMRC* 5(1980), 119–35.
   The tension between the *WBP* and *WBT* and the *ClT* is a result of Chaucer's use of the vice-and-virtue tradition. The Clerk responds to Alisoun's sloth and her ignoring of realism. He asserts the benefits of fortitude in one's existence. Alisoun does acknowledge the Christian call to be virtuous, yet she realizes that the ideal, aesthetic life is beyond the endurance of most people.

757 Holloway, Julia Bolton. 'Medieval Pilgrimage.' In *Approaches to Teaching Chaucer's Canterbury Tales*. Ed. Joseph Gibaldi. Consultant editor, Florence H. Ridley. New York: The Modern Language Association of America, 1980. Pp 143–8.
   The Samaritan woman's well is Jacob's well, not only a popular pilgrimage site but, in Scripture, the location where Jacob met Ruth and where his daughter Dinah, like the *WBT*'s maiden, was raped (p 146). See **368**.

758 Howard, Donald R. *Writers and Pilgrims: Medieval Pilgrimage Narratives and Their Posterity*. Berkeley: University of California Press, 1980.
   Medieval authors who composed works about their pilgrimages valued experience over authority, much as the Wife of Bath does (p 89).

759 Klene, Jean, C.S.C. 'Chaucer's Contributions to a Popular Topos: The World Turned Upside-Down.' *Viator* 11(1980), 321–34.
   The role reversals in Alisoun's marriages are examples of an upside-down world.

760 Lawler, Traugott. *The One and the Many in the Canterbury Tales*. Hamden, CT: Archon Books, 1980.
   Chaucer incorporates 'diversity within a larger unity' (p 17) into his *CT*. Alisoun knows that all people are different, while St. Paul believes all should be virgins. Difficulty in achieving synthesis is the basis of the

WBP as well as several other tales (p 26). While Alisoun's individuality is asserted by her dress, Jankyn is a stereotypical poor clerk. Alisoun is a professional wife complete with a professional rivalry with the Clerk. The contrast between men and women throughout the *CT* begins with the Wife and Parson in the *GP* (pp 64–5).

761 Morse, Charlotte C. 'The Politics of Marriage: Power in Paradise?' *BForum* 5(1980), 265–9.

Chaucer explores the paradisal dream of a peaceful marriage in the *CT*. While Alisoun views marriage as a power struggle, she is loath to reject the possibility of marital bliss. The stories of Constance and Griselda expose a political dimension of marriage in which rulers treat subjects as they treat their wives (p 269). Alisoun advocates a reversal of the power-structure in marriage, not an elimination of it. The *ClT* offers a strong medieval view of the politics and blissful nature of marriage. See **1289**.

762 Robertson, D.W., Jr. '"And for my land thus hastow mordred me?": Land, Tenure, the Cloth Industry, and the Wife of Bath.' *ChauR* 14(1980), 403–20.

That Alisoun is a bondswoman and a rural textile merchant is consistent with an iconographic reading of her character. Were she a free tenant, Alisoun would have had legal problems in maintaining her inherited acquisitions. Chaucer uses Alisoun's character to satirize the negative aspects of the growth of the textile industry.

763 Spisak, James. 'Anti-Feminism Bridled: Two Rhetorical Contexts.' *NM* 81(1980), 150–60.

Chaucer incorporates portions of *Jov* into the *WBP* in order that he might parody Jerome's work by placing it in the mouth of a woman like Alisoun.

ℰℴ The Wife of Bath's Prologue 1981-1990

764 Allen, Judson Boyce, and Theresa Anne Moritz. *A Distinction of Stories: The Medieval Unity of Chaucer's Fair Chain of Narratives for Canterbury*. Columbus: Ohio State University Press, 1981.
   See **1293**.

765 Berry, Reginald. 'Absurder Projects: Scriblerus, Chaucer, and the Discommodities of Marriage.' *ESC* 7(1981), 141–55.
   John Gay produced a play based on the Wife of Bath in 1712–13 that reflects Restoration marriage comedies yet focuses on the foolishness of man and woman instead of attacking marriage itself. The *WBP* proved to be one of Chaucer's most influential works for the Scriblerus Club (p 147), members of which included Gay, Pope, and Swift.

766 Blake, Norman 'Chaucer's Text and the Web of Words.' In *New Perspectives in Chaucer Criticism*. Ed. Donald M. Rose. Norman, OK: Pilgrim Books, Inc., 1981. Pp 223–40.
   In the *NPT*, Pertelote has 'the herte in hoold' (VII.2846) of Chauntecleer. This line may also be found in a lyric, which may have been known to Chaucer, recorded in a fifteenth-century ms. A parallel line appears as well in the *WBP* III.589 (pp 238–9). See **1295**.

767 Chamberlain, David. 'Musical Signs and Symbols in Chaucer: Convention and Originality.' In *Signs and Symbols in Chaucer's Poetry*. Ed. John P. Hermann and John J. Burke, Jr. University, AL: University of Alabama Press, 1981. Pp 43–80.
   See **1296**.

768 Coletti, Theresa. 'The *Mulier Fortis* and Chaucer's *Shipman's Tale*.' *ChauR* 15 (1981), 236–49.
   Had Chaucer kept Alisoun as the narrator of the *ShT*, another level of

irony would have been found in the *ShT*'s allusions to the *mulier fortis*. Alisoun's occupations of wife and weaver connect her to this Good Woman of Proverbs (245–6).

769 Davenant, John. 'Chaucer's View of the Proper Treatment of Women.' *Maledicta* 5(1981), 153–61.

The answer to the knight's question indicts all women as having unnatural desires to dominate their husbands. While Alisoun has triumphed over her husbands, she is not to be viewed in a positive light. Because he attempts to subdue Alisoun, Jankyn is the sole sympathetic character for Chaucer's male audience. He is 'a reference point of normality' (p 160). Chaucer uses Alisoun to show that impassioned women must be dominated physically.

770 Fries, Maureen. 'The "Other" Voice: Woman's Song, Its Satire and Its Transcendence in Late Medieval British Literature.' In *Vox Feminae: Studies in Medieval Woman's Song*. Ed. John F. Plummer. Kalamazoo: Medieval Institute Publications, 1981. Pp 155–78.

The widow in Dunbar's *Tua Mariit Wemen and the Wedo* resembles the Wife of Bath in her quest for mastery over her husband. She uses her spouse's finances for her own gain and to cuckold him. Unlike Alisoun, however, she doesn't anticipate any further marriages (pp 169–70).

771 Gardner, John. 'Signs, Symbols, and Cancellations.' In *Signs and Symbols in Chaucer's Poetry*. Ed. John P. Hermann and John J. Burke, Jr. University, AL: University of Alabama Press, 1981. Pp 195–207.

While Robertson (**540**) argues that Alisoun is not a feminist because as a cloth maker she exploited women laborers, Chaucer never mentions such actions on Alisoun's part. There was no awareness of such exploitation at that time, and feminism was a historical reality of Chaucer's day (pp 197–8).

772 Neuss, Paula. 'Images of Writing and the Book in Chaucer's Poetry.' *RES* 32(1981), 385–97.

The theme that text needs experience to support it is found in both *TC* and *WBP*. By referring to the *mark of Adam* (III.696) Alisoun alludes to writing as well as to race (p 394). Alisoun destroys Jankyn's book, in part, because it is cheating her of sexual experience by preoccupying her husband.

773 Orme, Nicholas. 'Chaucer and Education.' *ChauR* 16(1981), 38–59.

Chaucer was only marginally concerned about the education of youths, but the theme does emerge in the *SqT* and *WBT*. The role of oral education in the home, particularly through maternal teaching, is seen in the *PardT*, *ManT*, and in Alisoun's recounting of her mother's advice regarding men (pp 40–1). Chaucer's interest in higher learning is reflected by the presence of seven clerks in his work, one of whom is Jankyn. See **1298**.

774 Owen, Charles A., Jr. 'A certein nombre of conclusiouns: The Nature and Nurture of Children in Chaucer.' *ChauR* 16(1981), 60–75.
Alisoun's marrying at twelve indicates that medieval childhood passed swiftly into adulthood (p 61). A more humorous vision of childhood may be found in Alisoun's recounting the lessons concerning men that her mother taught her (pp 66–7).

775 Puhvel, Martin. 'The Wyf of Bath and Alice Kytele: A Web of Parallelism.' *SN* 53(1981), 101–6.
If there was a human model for Alisoun, it may be Alice Kytele. Her name, her multiple marriages, her acquisition of wealth, her carnality, and the accusations that she practiced magic and killed her husbands, all suggest that she is the source for Chaucer's character.

776 Robertson, D.W., Jr. 'Simple Signs from Everyday Life in Chaucer.' In *Signs and Symbols in Chaucer's Poetry*. Ed. John P. Hermann and John J. Burke, Jr. University, AL: University of Alabama Press, 1981. Pp 12–26.
Some of Chaucer's references were commonly represented in art. The Wedding Feast at Cana is detailed on a stained-glass window at Canterbury, and a *gat-tothed* wife is one of the illustrations for *RR* (pp 15–6). The details of her portrait and the events of the *WBP* expose Alisoun as a carnal figure who defies tradition and embodies the newly evolving, exploitative capitalist ethos (pp 25–6).

777 Rowland, Beryl. 'Thwarted Sexuality in Chaucer's Works.' *Florilegium* 3(1981), Part II, 239–67.
The Wife of Bath's bewailing the equation of love with sin reflects the medieval conception of sex outside the sanctity of marriage (p 250). Alisoun, who makes no secret of the sexual shortcomings of several of her husbands, is one example of how Chaucer incorporates the concept of thwarted sexuality into his writings. In the *WBP*, Alisoun admits that her continual trips to the altar are spurred by sexual frustration. That the Wife has never found delight in *bacon* (III.418) indicates she hasn't been satisfied by intercourse with any of her husbands. This lack of

pleasure, coupled with Alisoun's promiscuity, indicates that she is a nymphomaniac. Unwilling to take responsibility for her actions, she blames astrological influences for her behavior (p 253).

778 Rudat, Wolfgang E.H. 'Chaucer's Spring of Comedy: The *Merchant's Tale* and Other "Games" with Augustinian Theology.' *AnM* 21(1981), 111–20.

Alisoun's defense of the joys of postlapsarian sex is in conflict with Augustine's opinions in *De Civitate Dei* (pp 117–8).

779 Singer, Margaret. 'The *Wife of Bath's Prologue* and *Tale*.' In *Studies in Chaucer*. Ed. G.A. Wilkes and A.P. Riemer. Sydney Studies in English. Sydney: University of Sydney, 1981. Pp 28–37.

Chaucer constructs the *WBP* with both a realistic narrative and an argument based on ideals (p 29). This process makes Alisoun appear at times to be drawn from the occurrences she relates, but sometimes she is an exemplar of abstractions. The theme of sovereignty links the *WBP* with the *WBT* (p 33). See **1299**.

780 Storm, Melvin. 'Alisoun's Ear.' *MLQ* 42(1981), 219–26.

See **377**.

781 Allen, Judson Boyce. *The Ethical Poetic of the Later Middle Ages: A Decorum of Convenient Distinction*. Toronto: University of Toronto Press, 1982.

Alisoun begins the *WBP* by announcing her topic of marital woe (p 136). Her argument divides into four parts: a defense of marriage, autobiography, the *WBT*, and the *gentillesse* sermon (p 155). See **1300**.

782 Ando, Shinsuke. 'Chaucer no Joseitachi [Women in Chaucer's Works].' In *Eikoku Renaissance Bungaku no Joseizo*. [*Images of Women in Renaissance Literature*.] Ed. P. Milward and S. Ishii. Tokyo: Aratake, 1982. Pp 51–75. [In Japanese.]

While the female characters of Chaucer's early career are rather stereotypical, the women of *CT*, such as Alisoun, reveal his creative genius. Through Alisoun and her performance, intimations of Chaucer's perceptions of marriage, feminism, and irony can be perceived.

783 Barney, Stephen A. 'Chaucer's Lists.' In *The Wisdom of Poetry: Essays in Early English Literature in Honor of Morton W. Bloomfield*. Ed. Larry D. Benson and Siegfried Wenzel. Kalamazoo: Medieval Institute Publications, 1982. Pp 189–223.

Alisoun has acquired some of her wisdom from her mother's experience and most of it from the authority of Jankyn's book (p 195). Alisoun's quoting Jankyn (III.655–8) is Chaucer's sole construction of a priamel, a metered listing of wisdom (p 198). See **1301**.

784　Blake, N.F. 'The Wife of Bath and Her Tale.' *LeedsSE* 13(1982), 42–55.

Chaucer did not associate Alisoun with the *ShT* nor did he intend to have her function in any of the tale links (p 44). There were four developmental stages of the *WBP*: the *GP* portrait, a short version of the *WBP*, references to Alisoun outside her tale and beyond the *CT*, and an elaborated *WBP* (p 47). See **1302**.

785　Gallacher, Patrick J. 'Dame Alice and the Nobility of Pleasure.' *Viator* 13(1982), 275–93.

See **1303**.

786　Luecke, Janemarie, O.S.B. 'Three Faces of Cecilia: Chaucer's *Second Nun's Tale*.' *ABR* 33(1982), 335–48.

Although the Second Nun shares a similar 'recourse to power ideology' (p 347) with Alisoun, her tale of female power is accepted while Alisoun's is not because the Second Nun and Cecilia represent the feminine ideal of virginity.

787　Owen, Charles A., Jr. 'The Alternative Reading of the *Canterbury Tales*: Chaucer's Text and the Early Manuscripts.' *PMLA* 97(1982), 237–50.

The Hengwrt and Ellesmere mss share glossings of III.110, 115–6, and 705. The glossators concentrated on the Wife's marriage lecture, her account of her first three husbands, and her discussion of Jankyn's book (p 241). Sources for the glosses include Jerome, Valerius, *Almansoris Propositiones*, and *Alexandreis*. See **179**.

788　Rex, Richard. '"Spiced conscience" in the *Canterbury Tales*.' *MP* 80(1982), 53–4.

In the *WBP*, Alisoun uses the concept of a *spiced conscience* ironically, informing her husbands that she wants them to be as patient and docile as sheep.

789　Rhodes, James F. 'Motivation in Chaucer's *Pardoner's Tale*: Winner Take Nothing.' *ChauR* 17(1982), 40–61.

The Pardoner is in sympathy with Alisoun because both deal with marginalization in their lives (p 42). Their performances are similar in structure.

790　Wasserman, Julian N. 'The Ideal and the Actual: The Philosophical Unity of the *Canterbury Tales*, MS Group III.' *Allegorica* 7(1982),

65–99.

Fragment III is unified by the philosophical theme of the tensions between the concrete and the abstract. Alisoun and the Summoner advocate the truth of the real world while the Friar is a proponent of symbolic representation of higher ideals (p 66). Alisoun recommends the subjective truth of experience, denying a universal truth and establishing experience as the 'formulative principle of art' (p 69). As an Aristotelian, she attacks the Platonic ideal of chastity (p 71). The *WBT* is also an affront to Platonism, for it is the knight's personal experience that convinces him of the hag's non-universal truth (pp 72–5).

791 Alkalay-Gut, Karen. 'Problems in Literary Herstory: Chaucerian MSConceptions.' *RCEI* 6(1983), 73–8.

There is a tendency in feminist criticism to project current opinions onto Chaucer and his world. Diamond (**708, 1251**) bases her belief that Chaucer has separate criteria for morally evaluating his male and female characters because Alisoun is both intelligent and morally corrupt. Diamond neglects to notice that the Pardoner, the Friar, and the Miller also possess these characteristics (p 75). An accurate point that both Diamond and the Wife of Bath make is that since medieval literature was produced by men, it is difficult to obtain a truly representative, contemporary depiction of women (p 76).

792 Costigan, Edward. '"Privetee" in the *Canterbury Tales*.' *Studies in English Literature* 60(1983), 217–30.

The word *private* and its variants appear most often in *WBT*, *ShT*, and *MilT*, stories which focus on marriage and sexuality. Alisoun manifests the dichotomy between the private world and the public one by unabashedly announcing that her body bears the mark of Mars not only on her face, but also in a *privee place* (III.620) (pp 220–1). She candidly reveals her private life to her audience, as she has shared her fourth husband's secrets with her gossips. See **1307**.

793 Finke, Laurie A. 'Falstaff, the Wife of Bath, and the Sweet Smoke of Rhetoric.' In *Chaucerian Shakespeare: Adaptation and Transformation*. Medieval and Renaissance Monograph Series, 2. Ed. E. Talbot Donaldson and Judith J. Kollmann. Ann Arbor: Michigan Consortium for Medieval and Early Modern Studies, 1983. Pp 7–24.

Both Alisoun and Falstaff manipulate language in an attempt to recreate their worlds. Alisoun challenges marital order and the rhetorical traditions of the ordered world. Alisoun uses repetition and climax to present an ironic depiction of antifeminism (p 12). She becomes an actor who wears many masks. When she loses control, Alisoun is reduced to an almost silent voice (p 18).

794 Gussenhoven, Sister Frances, RSHM. 'Shakespeare's *Taming of the Shrew* and Chaucer's Wife of Bath: The Struggle for Marital Mastery.' In *Chaucerian Shakespeare: Adaptation and Transformation.* Medieval and Renaissance Monograph Series, 2. Ed. E. Talbot Donaldson and Judith J. Kollmann. Ann Arbor: Michigan Consortium for Medieval and Early Modern Studies, 1983. Pp 69–79.

The *WBP*, *WBT*, and *The Taming of the Shrew* share the theme of mastery in marriage. Images they share include the word *shrew* (pp 69–70), references to model and wicked wives (pp 70–1), and 'falconry, education, and clothes' (p 71). These last images concern themselves with the issue of mastery. The works conclude with a blissful relationship.

795 Harris, Jocelyn. 'Anne Elliot, the Wife of Bath, and Other Friends.' *W&L* 3(1983), 273–93.

See **1309**.

796 Kirkpatrick, Robin. 'The Wake of the *Commedia*: Chaucer's *Canterbury Tales* and Boccaccio's *Decameron*.' In *Chaucer and the Italian Trecento*. Ed. Piero Boitani. Cambridge: Cambridge University Press, 1983. Pp 201–30.

While Alisoun initially seems to be a Boccaccian character of Dionysiac force, she lacks the wit of the Italian writer's heroine (p 219). The comedy of the *WBP* relies on Chaucer's ability to blend words with precise definitions with vague expressions of experience (p 215). Alisoun challenges not only authority but also the confines of ordered narrative (p 217). See **1311**.

797 Kollmann, Judith J. '"Ther is noon oother incubus but he": the *Canterbury Tales, Merry Wives of Windsor*, and Falstaff.' In *Chaucerian Shakespeare: Adaptation and Transformation*. Medieval and Renaissance Monograph Series, 2. Ed. E. Talbot Donaldson and Judith J. Kollmann. Ann Arbor: Michigan Consortium for Medieval and Early Modern Studies, 1983. Pp 43–68.

Parallels between the *GP*, *WBP*, and *WBT* and *The Merry Wives of Windsor* suggest Shakespeare's familiarity with Chaucer. The *CT* and Shakespeare's play both have similar character types (p 46). The clever and deceptive Wives of Windsor resemble Alisoun and the hag, although the Wives are of a more ethical nature than Alisoun (p 48). Shakespeare's play treats themes found within the Marriage Group (p 50). The primary theme of *The Merry Wives of Windsor* and the *WBT* is the edification of the knight (p 56). Falstaff's association with the devil and his lechery recall Alisoun's insulting of the Friar (pp 62–3).

798 Leslie, Nancy T. 'The Worthy Wife and Virtuous Knight: Survival of the Wittiest.' In *Chaucerian Shakespeare: Adaptation and Transformation*. Medieval and Renaissance Monograph Series, 2. Ed. E. Talbot Donaldson and Judith J. Kollmann. Ann Arbor: Michigan Consortium for Medieval and Early Modern Studies, 1983. Pp 25–41.

Alisoun and Falstaff are both consummate actors who embody 'man's protean capabilities' (p 26). Both use Scripture for their own designs, exhibiting a twisted form of logic, and they also use inconclusive arguments and proverbs. They reveal their personalities by using puns (p 35).

799 Malvern, Marjorie M. '"Who peyntede the leon, tel me who?": Rhetorical and Didactic Roles Played by an Aesopic Fable in the *Wife of Bath's Prologue*.' *SP* 80(1983), 238–52.

Alisoun's lion-painting speech is the unifying *sentence* of her satire. In a rhetorical sense, it functions much like those devices in classical and medieval satire (p 240) and focuses on antifeminist clerks (p 242). Alisoun's obscenities reflect the antifeminist debasing of love. Alisoun moves from using caricature in discussing her first three husbands to employing digression in her accounting of her last two marriages (p 248). Just as the lion of Aesop's fable proves himself a threat to man, so too does Alisoun illustrate the truth of women to Jankyn (pp 251–2).

800 Mann, Jill. 'Satisfaction and Payment in Middle English Literature.' *SAC* 5(1983), 17–48.

The notion that light can be repeatedly and endlessly given away without being diminished, which is used in *Pearl* to explain the inexhaustible joys of heaven, is applied by the Wife in III.329–36 to the inexhaustible nature of sexual pleasure.

801 Patterson, Lee. '"For the Wyves love of Bathe": Feminine Rhetoric and Poetic Resolution in the *Roman de la Rose* and the *Canterbury Tales*.' *Spec* 58(1983), 656–95.

In the antifeminist literary tradition, woman's voice was aligned with carnality (p 662) and widows became feared, sexual creatures who were therefore mocked (p 663). Alisoun is a combination of two antifeminist type characters: the carnal widow and the meddling go-between, drawn from Jean le Fèvre's *La Vieille*, Guillaume de Lorris and Jean de Meun's *RR*, and de Collerye's *Sermon pour une nopce*. In the *WBP*, Alisoun uses exegetical intertextuality to highlight the carnality of language (p 677), a tactic that fits her sermon-like discourse. In the first two sections of the *WBP*, Alisoun provides 'a characteristically ambivalent self-image' (p 678). In the final portion of this performance, Alisoun exposes her sensitivity about Jankyn and becomes a victim of antifeminism (p 679). Unlike the earlier, overly sexual representative of woman in the *WBP*, Alisoun is here rendered human. See **1313**.

802 Pearsall, Derek. 'Chaucer's Pardoner: The Death of a Salesman.' *ChauR* 17(1983), 358–65.
While Alisoun's performance follows the movement of her mind through her emotions, the Pardoner is devoid of feeling and is therefore a creature of will (p 361).

803 Shoaf, R.A. *Dante, Chaucer, and the Currency of the Word: Money, Images and Reference in Late Medieval Poetry*. Norman, OK: Pilgrim Books, 1983.
Incidents of both horizontal, or between-tale, and vertical, or within-a-tale, 'quiting' occur in the *CT*. Alisoun horizontally rebukes the Man of Law and vertically challenges men and marriage (pp 169–70). Alisoun envies the Pardoner's oratorical skills and the Pardoner covets her sexual exploits. Alisoun's primary commodity is herself (p 225).

804 Sturges, Robert S. 'The *Canterbury Tales'* Women Narrators: Three Traditions of Female Authority.' *MLS* 13(1983), 41–51.
While the Canterbury stories that are told by men about women depict heroines who submit to male authority and are removed from any female tradition, the Wife, the Prioress, and the Second Nun 'create ... a whole female tradition of authority, in which powerful women are involved to pass their authority on to other women, including the narrator herself' (p 41). The Wife differs from the other women in that she wishes to overthrow, not provide an alternative to, male authority. Alisoun bases her female tradition on what she has been taught by her mother and her application of these teachings to her own life. She shares her learning with her gossip and thereby undercuts both her husband's and clerical authority (p 44). Alisoun counsels her female audience to learn from her life. In the *Who peynted the leon* portion of the *WBP*, Alisoun expresses a desire for a 'female poetic tradition' (p 45) to be used as a device with which women might acquire power. See **1315**.

805   Traversi, Derek Antona. *The Canterbury Tales: A Reading*. London: Bodley Head; Newark: University of Delaware Press, 1983.

As a Christian, Chaucer probably would not have supported Alisoun's powerful upholding of Jovinian's arguments against those of Jerome. The discussion of Alisoun's married life may originally have been Alisoun's tale (p 95). While Alisoun claims to discuss marital woe, she recounts the marital pleasures she has obtained and hides the woes of her experience. Alisoun dismisses authoritative texts that will not support her lifestyle and moves on to ones she can manipulate. Her views on virginity and marriage show awareness of human nature. Alisoun's discourse reveals a disappointment with herself for having no children and an attempt to justify her failed existence (pp 100–1). The struggles in Alisoun's later marriages reflect Alisoun's fight to hold on to her youth (p 105). Her lust for Jankyn at her fourth husband's funeral exposes this conflict of life and death within her. The *WBT* sheds light on the marital bliss Alisoun claims to have established with Jankyn. See **1316**.

806   Vasavari, Louise O. 'An Example of "Parodia Sacra" in the *Libro De Buen Amor*: "Quoniam" "Pudenda."' *La Corónica* 12(1983–84), 195–203.

The *quoniam* pun in *WBP* dates back to classical Latin (p 197).

807   Wurtele, Douglas. 'The Predicament of Chaucer's Wife of Bath: St. Jerome on Virginity.' *Florilegium* 5(1983), 208–36.

Alisoun's protests against Jerome are in keeping with her need to be first. Jerome, having placed virgins above married women, denies Alisoun the chance to be first in heaven. It is from Jankyn that Alisoun has learned of Jerome's beliefs (p 209). Jovinian believes that married women and virgins are equal in God's eyes. Since Jovinian allows Alisoun to have control over her afterlife, the Wife views Jerome's attack against Jovinian as an injustice against herself. Jerome, however, does not devalue marriage but rather places virginity on a higher level than the married state. Alisoun's harangue contrasts with Jerome's logic. Both use St. Paul either to denounce or support Jovinian (p 214). Alisoun and Jerome also make use of Genesis, Proverbs, Matthew, and John. Few of Alisoun's references deal with the marriage-vs-virginity debate, while Jerome's do.

808   Adams, Roberta E. 'Chaucer's Wife of Bath and Marriage in Fourteenth-Century England.' *DAI* 44(1984), 3069A.

Critics tend to ignore the influence of marriage in the fourteenth century when analyzing the Wife of Bath. Alisoun's marriages to wealthy, older husbands conform to social standards of acceptability, while the love-matches that she willingly entered into after gaining economic security do not. The *WBP* exposes the conflict between the canonical view of marriages and the realities of such relationships. See **1318**.

809 Alford, John A. 'Scriptural Testament in the *Canterbury Tales*: The Letter Takes Its Revenge.' In *Chaucer and Scriptural Tradition*. Ed. David Lyle Jeffrey. Ottawa: University of Ottawa Press, 1984. Pp 197–203.

Alisoun initiates not only a debate on marriage but one on exegetical interpretation that is taken up by the Friar and the Summoner, creating a unity within Fragment III.

810 Baird-Lange, Lorrayne Y. 'Trotula's Fourteenth-Century Reputation, Jankyn's Book, and Chaucer's Trot.' *SAC Proceedings* 1(1984), 245–56.

Trotula is present in Jankyn's book because she is a '*type* of the Wife of Bath' and is a personification of clerical and medical antifeminism (p 246). Chaucer probably was unfamiliar with the medical treatises of Trotula and drew from the Old French *trot*, a word that suggests prostitutes, witches, and hags.

811 Benson, Larry D. 'The "Queynte" Punnings of Chaucer's Critics.' *SAC Proceedings* 1(1984), 23–47.

Junius' belief that *queynte* is the English version of the French *bel chose*, based on their close association in the *WBP*, is correct (p 36). The absence of scribal editing of *queynte* suggests that it was not an obscenity (p 40) but rather a euphemism for the female genitalia.

812 Besserman, Lawrence. '*Glosynge is a glorious thyng*: Chaucer's Biblical Exegesis.' In *Chaucer and Scriptural Tradition*. Ed. David Lyle Jeffrey. Ottawa: University of Ottawa Press, 1984. Pp 65–73.

Alisoun's scriptural interpretation may be criticized if one consults the scriptural commentaries of the late fourteenth century, specifically the *Glossa ordinaria* (p 66).

813 Brewer, Derek. *An Introduction to Chaucer*. London: Longman, 1984. The sympathetic nature of Alisoun's confession is in conflict with her failure to realize her moral flaws. Another 'comic duality' (p 205) of the *WBP* is Chaucer's usage of both intensification and selected details. They provide realistic and unrealistic qualities. See **1321**.

814 ———. 'The Rationalism of Chaucer.' In *Chaucer: The Poet as*

Storyteller. London: Macmillan, 1984. Pp 120–9.

Chaucer's skepticism of women and of clerks is manifested in the *WBP* (p 127). See **1322**.

815 Caie, Graham D. 'The Significance of Marginal Glosses in the Earliest Manuscripts of the *Canterbury Tales*.' In *Chaucer and Scriptural Tradition*. Ed. David Lyle Jeffrey. Ottawa: University of Ottawa Press, 1984. Pp 75–88.

The Wife of Bath, the Pardoner, and the Summoner are the fake exegetes of the *CT*. Alisoun interprets texts literally and provides either erroneous or partial quotations of Scripture and patristic authority (p 75). Since his audience was familiar with the Bible, Chaucer could use characters like Alisoun for intertextual humor. Since much of the glossing in the *WBP* comes from patristic writings, not Scripture, an emphasis should be placed on who it is that interprets the text (p 77). Certain scribal glosses on the *WBP* comment on specific word choice; others comment upon the content of Alisoun's speech. Some glosses that contain Chaucer's sources are misquoted by the scribe.

816 Eade, J.C. *The Forgotten Sky: A Guide to Astrology in English Literature*. Oxford: Clarendon Press, 1984.

In *WBP* (III.697–705) Chaucer offers a standard pairing of opposites when he discusses the positions of Venus and Mercury. Ptolemy understood this positioning to have a seasonal base (p 144–5).

817 Fleming, John V. 'Gospel Asceticism: Some Chaucerian Images of Perfection.' In *Chaucer and Scriptural Tradition*. Ed. David Lyle Jeffrey. Ottawa: University of Ottawa Press, 1984. Pp 183–95.

Alisoun's commentary on Matthew 19 and its topic of perfection reveals that while she considers perfection to be a church precept, her interpretation of perfection as a church counsel is quite unorthodox.

818 Glasser, Marc. '*He nedes moste hire wedde*: The Forced Marriage in the *Wife of Bath's Tale* and Its Middle English Analogues.' *NM* 85(1984), 239–41.

In contrast to parallel scenes in the British analogues, the knight's forced marriage in the *WBT* contains a stronger element of 'forced consent' (p 240). This coersion reflects the dynamics of Alisoun's own marriages, in which there have been struggles for sovereignty.

819 Hanning, Robert W. 'Chaucer and the Dangers of Poetry.' *CEA* 46(1984), 17–26.

Chaucer frequently examines the delights and the dangers of human power over words. Alisoun, the stereotypical gregarious female, functions as an illustration of the conflict between speech and privacy (p 23). In relating that she has revealed her husband's confidences to her gossip, she inhibits the Host from disclosing his own wife's secrets. In the Merchant's *Endlink*, Bailly fears that Alisoun will report his remarks to Goodelief. Alisoun is 'an embodiment of the storytelling impulse' (p 25).

820 Iwasaki, Haruo. '"Not worth a straw" and Similar Idioms.' *Key-Word Studies in Chaucer* 1(1984), 33–49.
In Chaucer's work, the phrase *not worth a straw* is most frequently found in *CT*. The words usually stem from the voices of Alisoun, the Host, and Pandarus.

821 Kane, George. *Chaucer*. Oxford: Oxford University Press, 1984.
The details of Alisoun's elaborate and comic self-portrait give life to Alisoun (p 98).

822 Leicester, H. Marshall, Jr. 'The Wife of Bath as Chaucerian Subject.' *SAC Proceedings* 1(1984), 201–10.
The *WBP* is a dramatic presentation of the self as subject. Alisoun uses astrology to define herself, but emotional expressions in the passage where she recounts the stars reveal her resistance to relying solely on stellar definition (p 205). Alisoun reveals that she does make independent choices and conforms to her horoscope only when it is convenient (p 206). Alisoun becomes a constructed subject of patriarchal astrology when she adheres to her horoscope. Jankyn's book, reflective of the relationship between Venus and Mars, symbolizes Alisoun and Jankyn's love of arguing in their relationship. Alisoun's recalling the book recalls her love for Jankyn.

823 Murphy, Ann B. 'The Process of Personality in Chaucer's *Wife of Bath's Tale.*' *Centennial Review* 28(1984), 204–22.
The *WBP* expands the 'sexual and materialistic' details found in the *GP* (p 207). While Alisoun's views of female sovereignty may be disturbing, they prompt an audience to question male mastery. The tension between authority and experience broadens into conflicts between spirituality and materialism and between language and meaning (p 209). Alisoun associates sex with money and love with power (p 215). See **381** and **1325**.

824 Peck, Russell A. 'Biblical Interpretation: St. Paul and the *Canterbury Tales.*' In *Chaucer and Scriptural Tradition*. Ed. David Lyle Jeffrey.

184 / *Wife of Bath's Prologue and Tale*

Ottawa: University of Ottawa Press, 1984. Pp 143–70.

Alisoun and Paul have shared interests: man's sovereign rights, the nature of inheritance and possessions, the proper use of the flesh, marriage, and making the old into the new (p 158). While Alisoun is in opposition to Paul on most issues, her discussions are illuminating and more accessible than the saint's. While Alisoun is not fond of stellar influence in her life, she prefers it to Paul's call for her to be controlled by her husband (p 160). See **1326**.

825 Reiss, Edmund. 'Biblical Parody: Chaucer's "Distortions" of Scripture.' In *Chaucer and Scriptural Tradition*. Ed. David Lyle Jeffrey. Ottawa: University of Ottawa Press, 1984. Pp 47–61.

Chaucer often mixes Scripture with classical works. Jankyn's book contains both biblical and classical wicked wives (p 50). The Wife of Bath, Man of Law, Monk, and Merchant all misuse Scripture (p 57). Alisoun misinterprets Paul, misquotes the Gospels, expresses disdain for Ecclesiasticus, and is selective in her acceptance of the Bible's bigamists. Alisoun cannot perceive the spirit of the Word and prefers the Old Testament to the New.

826 Ridley, Florence H. 'The Literary Relations of William Dunbar.' In *Medieval Studies Conference, Aachen 1983: Language and Literature*. Ed. Wolf-Dietrich Bald and Horst Weinstock. Frankfurt: Peter Lang, 1984. Pp 169–84.

Dunbar was familiar with Chaucer's work, and parallels to the Wife of Bath may be found in his *Tua Mariit Wemen and the Wedo*. Dunbar's female characters, however, are much more cold and polished than the robust Alisoun (p 170).

827 Robertson, D.W., Jr. 'The Wife of Bath and Midas.' *SAC* 6(1984), 1–20.

In Ovid, Apollo curses Midas with 'the ears of a "slow stepping ass"' (p 8). The Friar accuses Alisoun of telling a plodding tale (III.831), and she rides an ambler. The ass has been noted for its deafness and lechery, two characteristics which Alisoun shares. Alisoun's life resembles that of Midas. She initially desires wealth and later appreciates carnality. See **1328**.

828 Ruggiers, Paul. *Editing Chaucer: The Great Tradition*. Norman, OK: Pilgrim Books, 1984.

Tyrwhitt (**2**) placed the *WBP* after the *MLT* and believed the contested passages belonged in the *WBP*, regardless of their authorship. Manly and Rickert (**29**) believed the contested passages were authorial revisions (p 225). See **1329**.

829 Wurtele, Douglas. 'Chaucer's *Canterbury Tales* and Nicholas of Lyre's *Postillae literalis et moralis super totam Bibliam.*' In *Chaucer and Scriptural Tradition*. Ed. David Lyle Jeffrey. Ottawa: University of Ottawa Press, 1984. Pp 89–107.

Because his audience was familiar with the Bible, Chaucer has Alisoun misuse Scripture for the purpose of creating comedy and ironically undercutting her. Alisoun's character is revealed as being very complex when compared with the work of Nicholas of Lyre (p 104). Her literal interpretations contrast sharply with Nicholas' enlightened glossing.

830 Blake, N.F. *The Textual Tradition of the Canterbury Tales*. London: Edward Arnold, 1985.

The *WBP* and *WBT* replaced the *SqT*'s position after the Man of Law's *Endlink* in Harley 7334 and the new order became fixed (pp 111–2).

831 Brewer, Derek. 'The International Medieval Popular Comic Tale in England.' In *The Popular Literature of Medieval England*. Tennessee Studies in Literature, 28. Ed. Thomas J. Heffernan. Knoxville: University of Tennessee Press, 1985. Pp 131–47.

While Chaucer has some sympathy for the domineering Alisoun, he does not portray her as a successfully subversive woman. Jankyn's beating Alisoun reaffirms the social structure of Chaucer's day (pp 144–5).

832 Carruthers, Mary. '*Clerk Jankyn at hom to bord / with my gossib.*' *ELN* 22(1985), 11–20.

Careful historical word study suggests III.527–30 means that Jankyn returned from Oxford to live in his family's home. A member of his family was not only Alisoun's good friend but a baptismal sponsor for one of her children (p 13).

833 Item cancelled.

834 Collins, Marie. 'Feminine Response to Masculine Attractiveness in Middle English Literature.' *E&S* 38(1985), 12–28.

Alisoun's assessment of Jankyn's legs during her fourth husband's funeral is an atypical response of woman to man's attractiveness in medieval literature (p 12). She is direct in describing his body, despite the fact that she is past her prime, and she does not belong to the courtly tradition.

835 Donaldson, E. Talbot. *The Swan at the Well: Shakespeare Reading*

Chaucer. New Haven: Yale University Press, 1985.

While it will never be certain that Shakespeare had Alisoun in mind when creating Falstaff, both characters are 'supremely self-confident in their idiosyncrasy' (p 129), misuse Scripture, rely on their wits, and create their own realities. Both characters are morally corrupt.

836 Ferster, Judith. *Chaucer on Interpretation*. Cambridge: Cambridge University Press, 1985.

Alisoun is aware that interpretation forms literary meaning and identity. The antifeminist tradition is self-interested and has shaped the way Alisoun and women in general are viewed. What Alisoun does not see is how she interprets others through her own self-interest. Alisoun uses antifeminism to describe her first three husbands. Jankyn's book is a tangible focus for Alisoun's rage (p 126). Alisoun does not admit that the self has a role in forming its own identity and chooses to blame the stars for the way she is (p 128). Her need for self-justification prompts Alisoun to confide in Jankyn about her fourth husband (p 132). Jankyn's awareness of Alisoun's past explains why he seeks refuge in books. See **1334**.

837 Fisher, John H. 'Chaucer and the Written Language.' In *The Popular Literature of Medieval England*. Tennessee Studies in Literature, 28. Ed. Thomas J. Heffernan. Knoxville: University of Tennessee Press, 1985. Pp 237–51.

While the *WBP* contains much colloquial speech, it also includes words that are associated with some formal literary works (p 247).

838 Gottfried, Barbara. 'Conflict and Relationship, Sovereignty and Survival: Parables of Power in the *Wife of Bath's Prologue*.' *ChauR* 19(1985), 202–24.

Alisoun is aware of the challenge of speaking of private, female experience to a public, patriarchal society. Her deconstruction of authority is hindered because she can define herself only through patriarchal language. She strives to survive against suffering through her 'humor, brilliance, and resiliency' (p 204) despite her ambivalent relationship to authority (p 206). In her marriage to Jankyn, Alisoun strongly enjoys marital experience (p 218). Love destroys sovereignty and leaves Alisoun vulnerable. Jankyn's involvement with text prompts Alisoun to embrace experience again (p 223). See **383**.

839 Hanning, R. W. 'Roasting a Friar, Mis-taking a Wife, and Other Acts of Textual Harassment in Chaucer's *Canterbury Tales*.' *SAC* 7(1985),

3–21.

The friar of the *SumT* and Alisoun are glossators who misuse text and manipulate people as if they were text. In turn, they are glossed by others (p 9). As a human text, Alisoun struggles against antifeminist glosses, yet she embodies the antifeminist conception of woman. Jankyn's prowess in bed is likened to glossing (pp 19–20). He is able to manipulate Alisoun into a willing partner despite their animosity. Through his book, Jankyn is able to make Alisoun an example of antifeminist projections.

840 Hyman, Eric J. '"Thy verray lewednesse": From the *Canterbury Tales* Toward a Theory of Comedy.' *DAI* 45(1985), 2111.

The *WBP* offers a war-between-the-sexes brand of comedy. It is the logic of association that holds its comic nature together. Alisoun is both the satirical carping wife and a valiant woman who undermines the patristic tradition.

841 Ikegami, Tadahiro. 'The Wife of Bath's Pseudo-Scholastic Discussion of Marriage.' In *Symposium on the Wife of Bath*. Medieval English Studies Symposia 2. Ed. Hishashi Shigeo, Hisao Tsuru, Isamu Saito, and Tadahiro Ikegami. Tokyo: Gaku Shobo, 1985. Pp 101–22. [In Japanese.]

WBP is a satire drawn from the antifeminist and antimatrimonialist sentiments found in authoritarian literature. Alisoun's pseudo-scholarly ability is comic.

842 Kawasaki, Masatoshi. 'From Conflict to Harmony — in Case of the Wife of Bath.' In *Symposium on the Wife of Bath*. Medieval English Studies Symposia 2. Ed. Hisashi Shigeo, Hisao Tsuru, Isamu Saito, and Tadahiro Ikegami. Tokyo: Gaku Shobo, 1985. Pp 123–42. [In Japanese.]

The concepts of authority and experience move from conflict to harmony not only in *WBP* and *WBT* but through *CT* as a whole.

843 Lindskoog, Verna de Jong. 'Chaucer's Wife of Bath: Critical Approaches in the Twentieth Century.' *DAI* 45(1985), 2520A.

See **384**.

844 Massó, Pedro Guardia. 'Tensión astrológica y la Comadre de Bath [Astrological Tension and the Wife of Bath].' In *Estudios literarios ingleses: Edad Media*. Ed J.F. Galván Reula. Madrid: Catedra, 1985. Pp 107–19. [In Spanish.]

An analysis of Alisoun's horoscope reveals the 'tension' that results from her having been born under the conflicting influence of both Mars (aggression) and Venus (passion), and with conflicting inclinations of Mercury (wisdom) and Venus (passion). The *chambre of Venus* is intentionally ambiguous, referring at once to both anatomy and astronomy. 'The astrological influences of Venus and Mars dominate her appetite, but she does not consider herself the victim of chance or a slave of astrology. ... The destiny of the Wife of Bath does not demonstrate astrological fatalism. Just as the passionate Chanticleer defies his dreams and consciously gives in to the enchantments of Pertelote, the Wife of Bath lets herself be carried forward by her own inclinations. ... Just as in the middle ages the planetary system was geocentric, in the private world of the Wife of Bath all of her husbands are planets who revolve around her' (pp 118–9 — translation).

845 Pearsall, Derek. *The Canterbury Tales*. London: George Allen and Unwin, 1985.

Chaucer adds life to antifeminist writings in the *WBP* and humanizes the antifeminist shrew by his creation of Alisoun. He removes her from the inconographic tradition by giving her a contemporary location and social status and by having her continually engage the thoughts of his readers (p 81). The *WBP* functions much like a dramatic monologue (pp 77-8). See **1338**.

846 Rex, Richard. 'Old French *Bacon* and the Wife of Bath.' *MSE* 10(1985), 132–7.

Robinson's association of *bacon* with Alisoun's first three husbands is the most accurate interpretation of the word (**38**). In Old and Middle French, *bacon* is slang for *cunnus* (p 133). *Bacon* is used in this sense in the fabliaux *Le meunier et les deux clercs*; *De Barat, Haimet et Travers*; and *D'Estormi*. It is also used in a fifteenth-century riddle. Alisoun uses *bacon* in order to emphasize her husbands' deficiencies in bed (p 136).

847 Robertson, D.W., Jr. 'Who Were "The People?"' In *The Popular Literature of Medieval England*. Tennessee Studies in Literature, 28. Ed. Thomas J. Heffernan. Knoxville: University of Tennessee Press, 1985. Pp 3–29.

Alisoun's festive lifestyle is reflective of the opportunities for pleasure that the wives of successful middle-class merchants enjoyed (p 16).

848 Sekimoto, Eiichi. 'Women Portraits in Dunbar.' In *Symposium on the Wife of Bath*. Medieval English Studies Symposia 2. Ed. Hisashi Shigeo, Hisao Tsuru, Isamu Saito, and Tadahiro Ikegami. Tokyo: Gaku Shobo,

1985. Pp 79–100. [In Japanese.]
Alisoun's discussion of marriage is more realistic and contains more vitality than that of the women in Dunbar's work.

849 Spearing, A.C. *Medieval to Renaissance in English Poetry.* Cambridge: Cambridge University Press, 1985.
See **1341**.

850 Takamiya, Toshiyuki. 'Margery Kempe and the Wife of Bath.' In *Symposium on the Wife of Bath*. Medieval Studies Symposia 2. Ed. Hisashi Shigeo, Hisao Tsuru, Isamu Saito, and Tadahiro Ikegami. Tokyo: Gaku Shobo, 1985. Pp 101–22. [In Japanese.]
Margery Kempe and Alisoun share similar class origins, strong voices, preoccupations with sex, and passions for pilgrimages.

851 Tsuru, Hisao. 'Alison's Sorrow — Her Old Age and Marriages.' In *Symposium on the Wife of Bath*. Medieval Studies Symposia 2. Ed. Hisashi Shigeo, Hisao Tsuru, Isamu Saito, and Tadahiro Ikegami. Tokyo: Gaku Shobo, 1985. Pp 143–65. [In Japanese.]
Old age in relation to marriage is the focus of both *WBP* and *WBT*.

852 Williams, Michael E. 'Three Metaphors of Criticism and the *Wife of Bath's Tale.' ChauR* 20(1985), 144–57.
Barring the theories of deconstruction, most critics view text in one of three ways. Those critics who see text as having an overall function usually view the *WBT* as an exemplum of the *WBP* (pp 146–8). Those critics who see the text as an entity with multiple systems perceive intricacies within the *WBP* and view how various parts of the *WBP* and *WBT* play off against one another (pp 148–51). Those critics who believe in exclusive hypotheses that pertain to a text examine the tensions within that text. For example, the *WBT* contains both strongly religious and strongly anti-religious facets (pp 152–3).

853 Wilson, Katharina M. 'Chaucer and St. Jerome: The Use of "Barley" in the *Wife of Bath's Prologue.' ChauR* 19(1985), 245–51.
While the source of Alisoun's associations of barley bread with wives and wheat bread with virgins has been attached to *Jov*, Jerome's letter to Pammachius contains a fuller discussion of arguments for celibacy. Jerome intended his bread analogy to establish a hierarchy between virginity and matrimony; however, barley has had negative connotations associated with it. Jerome's equation of marriage with barley bread is thus debasing. Roman soldiers were rationed barley bread for displaying cowardice (p 248). Barley also connotes sexuality, pompous speech,

and low intellect.

854 ———. '*Figmenta vs. Veritas*: Dame Alice and the Medieval Literary Depiction of Women by Women.' *TSWL* 4(1985), 17–32.

Contrary to Alisoun's lion-painting complaint, the writings of Hrotsvit of Gandersheim depict strong heroines and non-threatening Christian men. Her work poses no affront to the Christian patriarchy. The writings of Christine de Pizan do share Alisoun's sentiments. They attack clerics and misogyny.

855 Aers, David. *Chaucer*. Harvester New Readings. Atlantic Highlands: Humanities Press, 1986.

The relation of money and sex in the *ShT* and *WBT* show how the increasing capitalism of the Middle Ages affected language and human relationships. While Alisoun rejects authority, she accepts commodification of her body (p 70).

856 Benson, C. David. 'The *Canterbury Tales*: Personal Drama or Experiments in Poetic Variety.' In *The Cambridge Chaucer Companion*. Ed. Piero Boitani and Jill Mann. Cambridge: Cambridge University Press, 1986. Pp 93–108.

The Falstaff-like Wife of Bath grew so much in popularity that Chaucer refers to her in *Buk* and *MerT*. Alisoun's dramatic voice does not undermine orthodox teachings on marriage (p 100). Just as Alisoun is a skilled manipulator of words, so too is Chaucer a clever designer of character. See **1344**.

857 Disbrow, Sarah. 'The Wife of Bath's Old Wives' Tale.' *SAC* 8(1986), 59–71.

See **1348**.

858 Erzgräber, Willi. '*Auctorite* and *Experience* in Chaucer.' In *Intellectuals and Writers in Fourteenth-Century Europe: The J.A.W. Bennett Memorial Lectures*. Ed. Piero Boitani and Anna Torti. Tübingen: Gunter Narr Verlag, 1986. Pp 67–87.

Alisoun challenges traditional doctrine through her own experience (p 82). Relying on her manipulative glossing of Scripture and her common sense, she notes the values of marriage and equates its worth with that of virginity. Alisoun does not want to eliminate dominance in marriage. Rather, she wants to grant dominance to women.

859 Fleming, Martha. 'Repetition and Design in the *Wife of Bath's Tale*.' In *Chaucer in the Eighties*. Ed. Julian N. Wasserman and Robert J. Blanch. Syracuse: Syracuse University Press, 1986. Pp 151–61.

See **1349**.

860 Fradenburg, Louise O. 'The Wife of Bath's Passing Fancy.' *SAC* 8(1986), 31–58.

See **1350**.

861 Green, Donald C. 'The Semantics of Power: *Maistrie* and *Soveraynetee* in the *Canterbury Tales*.' *MP* 84(1986), 18–23.

By focusing on the usage and connotations of the words *maistrie, soveraynetee, servage, servyse, governance,* and *assent,* Chaucer's audience may note very strong ties between the Marriage Group tales. The Clerk's acknowledgement of the Host's *governance* over the pilgrims (IV.23) reflects Jankyn's and the knight's yielding power to the Wife (III.814) and to the hag (III.1231) and at the same time anticipates Walter's empowerment in the *ClT*. Walter's subjects maintain the difference in meaning between *soveraynetee* and *servyse* (IV.114) of man to woman because the state of matrimony provides a husband with sovereignty over his wife, while courtly love requires a man to serve his lady (p 20). The *FranT* merges these two conditions of marriage and courtly love. Arveragus willingly gives Dorigen power but insists that he have sovereignty in name. The Wife of Bath, however, promotes woman's sovereignty over man whether he be her lover or husband. The Wife uses the term *soveraynetee* in close connection with *maistrie* three times. The *FranT, ParsT,* and *Mel* all claim that a wife's mastery is not a natural condition of marriage. The Clerk's sole mention of the word *maistrie*, which occurs in his *Envoy*, is an ironic praising of the Wife's notions.

862 Hanna, Ralph, III. 'Jankyn's Book.' *PCP* 21(1986), 30–6.

To Alisoun, experience is part of an oral tradition, whereas authority comes from books. Jankyn's book reveals that Heloise 'was not only a creation of books for males but a creator of them' (p 33). While Jean de Meun viewed Heloise as having renounced her gender in order to become an authority, Alisoun glories in her femininity and her adherence to her oral power.

863 Knapp, Peggy A. 'Alisoun Weaves a Text.' *PQ* 65(1986), 387–401.

If the *WBP* falls into the genre of apologia, it may be perceived either as a defense of a new, entrepreneurial woman (pp 389–91) or a burdened feminist's attack against the patriarchy (pp 391–2). If it falls into the genre of a confession, the *WBP* is either a patristic exemplum (pp 392–5) or the revelation of a sociopath (pp 395–7). III.575–82 presents

Alisoun as belonging to all of these categories.

864 Knight, Stephen. *Geoffrey Chaucer*. Oxford: Basil Blackwell, 1986.
Through the revelations of the *WBP*, Alisoun is seen as a bold, self-aware woman who escapes patriarchal and clerical repression in both the domestic and economic arenas (p 100). See **1353**.

865 Lee, B.S. 'Chaucer's Handling of a Medieval Feminist Hierarchy.' *UES* 24(1986), 1–6.
Chaucer uses Alisoun to reveal that women seldom receive what patristic stereotypes suggest they will.

866 Long, Walter C. 'The Wife as Moral Revolutionary.' *ChauR* 20(1986), 273–84.
Alisoun is both a Dionysian figure who undermines tradition and an Apollonian figure, 'a constructive moral agent' (p 275). She argues for gender equality. This serious issue reconciles the inconsistencies between the *WBP* and *WBT*.

867 Mehl, Dieter. *Geoffrey Chaucer: An Introduction to His Narrative Poetry*. Cambridge: Cambridge University Press, 1986.
The *WBP* is inconsistent with Alisoun's psychological make-up. It is a satirical, condensed representation of the antifeminist tradition of literature, not a personal revelation (p 147). In the final portion of the *WBP*, Alisoun's violence underscores the antifeminist depiction of women. The Wife is more a dramatic personification of antifeminist views than an individual (p 148). See **1355**.

868 Olson, Paul A. *The Canterbury Tales and the Good Society*. Princeton: Princeton University Press, 1986.
Through his use of comic satire, Chaucer creates for Alisoun an Epicurean sect that includes the Friar, the Summoner, the Pardoner, the Merchant, and the Franklin. The sect is ruled by carnality and twisted reason. The *FranT* and *MerT* further explore both the capitalistic attitudes found in the *WBP* and the hag's 'promise of an Epicurean garden' (p 257). Only divine love and the laughter of Jankyn can transform Alisoun's materialistic world.

869 Payne, Robert O. *Geoffrey Chaucer*, 2nd ed. Boston: Twayne, 1986. See **248**.

870 Puhvel, Martin. 'The Wife of Bath's "Remedies of Love."' *ChauR* 20(1986), 307–12.
See **392**.

871 Robertson, D.W., Jr. 'Chaucer and the Economic and Social

Consequences of the Plague.' In *Social Unrest in the Late Middle Ages*. Ed. Francis X. Newman. Binghamton: Center for Medieval and Early Renaissance Studies, 1986. Pp 49–74.

Alisoun's monetary gains from the textile industry and her husbands, her vanity, and her social prominence make her a representation of the absence of steadfastness in society, one of Chaucer's concerns (pp 64–5).

872 Schibanoff, Susan. 'Taking the Gold Out of Egypt: The Art of Reading as a Woman.' In *Gender and Reading: Essays on Readers, Texts, and Contexts*. Ed. Elizabeth A. Flynn and Patrocino P. Schweickart. Baltimore: Johns Hopkins University Press, 1986. Pp 83–106.

Unlike Christine de Pisan, whose self-confidence was shaken through her reading of antifeminist literature, Alisoun heard this literature read to her. Alisoun does not recognize the fixedness of text. She clings to oral tradition and its practice of repeating, or rereading, text (p 89). Christine de Pisan would eventually learn this art.

873 Scott, William O. 'Chaucer, Shakespeare, and the Paradoxes of Dream and Fable.' *CEA* 49(1986-87), 25–32.

Alisoun's performance is fraught with 'the transparency of deception' (p 29).

874 Amsler, Mark. 'The Wife of Bath and Women's Power.' *Assays* 4(1987), 67–83.

As a wealthy widow, Alisoun possesses power, yet Chaucer's text reveals the irony that such power 'is contradictory and self-destructing for her as a female' (p 68). Alisoun's gain of sovereignty over Jankyn is countered by the economic replacement of love by sex (pp 77–9). The *WBT* merely inverts the hierarchical structure of power and does not criticize the concept of mastery (p 80).

875 Bishop, Ian. *The Narrative Art of the Canterbury Tales: A Critical Study of the Major Poems*. London: Everyman's University Library; Dent, 1987.

While the *WBP* is comic, it assumes a form of dialectic where woman's primary weapon is her tongue (pp 120–1). Of all her husbands, Alisoun loves Jankyn most, because he is her most challenging opponent. Jankyn knows both that he can infuriate Alisoun with antifeminist tracts and that his wife's weakness is her appetite for sex. In keeping with many medieval literary debates, the battle of words between Alisoun and Jankyn is reduced to a physical fight (p 124). See **1358**.

876 Blamires, Alcuin, and Michael Scott, eds. *The Canterbury Tales.* Atlantic Highlands: Humanities Press International, 1987.

While Alisoun attacks the patriarchy, her actions are limited because she is a product of antifeminism (pp 32–3). The inconsistencies of Alisoun's personality make psychological analysis of the *WBP* and *WBT* difficult. The *WBP* should be read with respect towards its sources, but it should not be allegorized (p 49). Alisoun's lion-painting complaint illustrates the problem of subjectivity in writing (pp 52–3). See **1359**.

877 Creigh, Geoffrey, and Jane Belfield, eds. *The Cobler of Caunterburie and Tarltons Newes out of Purgatorie.* Medieval and Renaissance Texts, 3. Leider: E.J. Brill, 1987.

The *WBP* and *WBT* provided influence for the sovereignty debate in 'The Gentleman's Tale' in *The Cobler of Caunterburie* (p 13).

878 Delany, Sheila. 'Notes on Experience, Authority and Desire in the Wife of Bath's Recital.' *HUSL* 15(1987), 27–35.

While Alisoun does not discuss her work and travel, these modern aspects of her life are internalized in her consciousness. Sex is described commercially and Alisoun is continually in motion (p 28). Had Chaucer incorporated such realistic detail into the *WBP*, Alisoun would have been too much of an individual and not enough of an exemplum. See **1363**.

879 Erzgräber, Willi. 'The Origins of Comicality in Chaucer.' In *Chaucer's Frame Tales: The Physical and the Metaphysical.* Ed. Joerg O. Fichte. Tübingen: Gunter Narr Verlag; Cambridge: D.S. Brewer, 1987. Pp 11–33.

Alisoun aggressively attacks clerical culture in the *WBP*, using its own rhetorical tactics against it and employing common sense (pp 27–8). Alisoun's battle with Jankyn recalls the mystery play conflicts between Noah and his wife. Despite her criticism of the patriarchy, Alisoun does not step away from tradition. She merely wishes to transform male sovereignty into female sovereignty.

880 Ganim, John M. 'Carnival Voices and the *Envoy* to the *Clerk's Tale.*' *ChauR* 22(1987), 112–27.

If the Clerk's *Envoy* is read as being separate from the *ClT*, it becomes a lyric addressed to wives, specifically the Wife of Bath (p 114). The Clerk's commentary on Alisoun's *lyf* gives this word a hagiographic connotation and puts Alisoun on par with the authorities against whom she has argued (p 120). In his attempt to put Alisoun in her place with his *Envoy*, the Clerk proves that Alisoun's complaints about clerks are true (p 121).

881 Gillam, D. 'Some Sidelights on Chaucer's Alice of Bath.' *Names* 35(1987), 64–73.

Alisoun's reference to herself as *Alys* is rhymed with *talys* (III.319–20, 547–8) and suggests an association between these two words. When *Alisoun* is used (III.530, 804) a close, personal relationship is indicated (p 36). A subtle pun between *Alisoun* and *eleison* may also be present when this name is used. The popularity of the name *Alice* stems from the heroine of French dance-songs. Alisoun's love for and knowledge of dancing ties in with this association. The reputation of Alice Perrers may have influenced Chaucer in his name choice for his Wife of Bath (p 68).

882 Hanning, Robert W. '"I shall finde it in a maner glose": Versions of Textual Harassment in Medieval Literature.' In *Medieval Texts and Contemporary Readers*. Ed. Laurie A. Finke and Martin B. Shichtman. Ithaca: Cornell University Press, 1987. Pp 27–50.

The concept of glossing provides a thematic unity for Fragment III (p 44). While she is a proponent of experience, Alisoun devotes much of the *WBP* to manipulating authoritative texts. She must exist in a world of patriarchal text, having been glossed as an antifeminist stereotype.

883 Hendricks, Thomas J. 'Astrology in the *Canterbury Tales*.' *DAI* 48(1987), 1199A.

The pilgrims unconsciously analyze the power of fate as opposed to that of free will when they incorrectly incorporate astrology into their narratives for the purpose of explaining cause and effect. This use of astrology exposes the pilgrims' materialism and irresponsibility, as well as the gulf between them and the Divine.

884 Howard, Donald R. *Chaucer: His Life, His Works, His World*. New York: E.P. Dutton, 1987. Pp 428–49.

Alisoun's nostalgic, regretful tone in the *WBP* may reflect Chaucer's reaction to his wife's death (p 429).

885 Knapp, Peggy A. 'Wandrynge by the weye: On Alisoun and Augustine.' In *Medieval Texts and Contemporary Readers*. Ed. Laurie A. Finke and Martin B. Shichtman. Ithaca: Cornell University Press, 1987. Pp 142–57.

Alisoun's textual glossings establish her as 'a theorist of interpretation' (p 142). Augustine's *On Christian Doctrine* was the foundation for allegorical interpretation and its influence works directly on Alisoun. It cannot, however, serve as the ultimate authoritative source for glossing because of its historical treatment.

886 Leicester, H. Marshall, Jr. 'Oure Tonges *Différance*: Textuality and Deconstruction in Chaucer.' In *Medieval Texts and Contemporary Readers*. Ed. Laurie A. Finke and Martin B. Shichtman. Ithaca: Cornell University Press, 1987. Pp 15–26.

Alisoun's and the Pardoner's performances are not well received by the pilgrims, yet they succeed in revealing their tellers (p 24).

887 Mertens-Fonck, Paule. 'Art and Symmetry in the *General Prologue* to the *Canterbury Tales.*' In *Actes du Congrès d'Amiens, 1982*. Ed. Société des Anglicistes de l'Enseignement Supérieur. Paris: Didier, 1987. Pp 41–51.

See **395**.

888 ———. 'Tradition and Feminism in Middle English Literature: Source-Hunting in the Wife of Bath's Portrait and in *The Owl and the Nightingale.*' In *Multiple Worlds, Multiple Words: Essays in Honour of Irène Simon*. Ed. Hena Maes-Jelinek, Pierre Michel, and Paulette Michel-Michot. Liège: Université de Liège, 1987. Pp 175–92.

See **396**.

889 Quinn, William A. 'Chaucer's Janglerye.' *Viator* 18(1987), 309–20.

While Alisoun is aware of the moral flaws of gossiping, she in unrepentant of her garrulous practice. Alisoun's *janglerye* is of an 'ambiguous nature' (p 315) and her immorality is of a less serious nature than that of the hypocritical Pardoner.

890 Stone, Brian. *Chaucer*. Penguin Critical Studies. London: Penguin Books, 1987.

The rambling *WBP* contains authoritative sources that have been tailored to suit the world of a fourteenth-century woman. It is a rich presentation of a feminine character (p 88). See **252** and **1366**.

891 Storm, Melvin. 'Uxor and Alison: Noah's Wife in the Flood Plays and Chaucer's Wife of Bath.' *MLQ* 48(1987), 303–19.

While Chaucer derived Alisoun's character from the scholarly antifeminist tradition, her character bears a resemblance to Noah's wife in the mystery plays. The relationship between these two character reveals Alisoun's inverse association with the medieval ideal of womanhood, the Virgin Mary.

892 Taylor, Paul B. 'Wife of Bath, Pardoner, and *Sir Thopas*: Pre-Texts and Para-Texts.' In *The Structure of Texts*. Ed. Udo Fries. Tübingen:

Gunter Narr Verlag, 1987. Pp 123–32.

Alisoun's performance serves as a 'pre-text' (p 124) for the *PardP* and *PardT*, which in turn does the same for Chaucer's *Thop*. *Thop* is a distortion of Alisoun's and the Pardoner's prologues and tales and may be interpreted through them.

893 Williams, David. *The Canterbury Tales: A Literary Pilgrimage.* Twayne's Masterwork Studies. Boston: Twayne, 1987.

Alisoun's definition of experience, that it consists of sex and power, removes her from the present and makes her both desire the past and anticipate the future (p 66). See **1368**.

894 Besserman, Lawrence. *Chaucer and the Bible: A Critical Review of Research, Indexes and Bibliography.* New York: Garland Publishing, 1988.

Annotations reveal which editions of Chaucer's work offer commentary on scriptural references. They add to the catalogue of biblical quotations found in the *WBP* (pp 80–90). See **1371**.

895 Bowden, Betsy. 'The Oral Life of the Written Ballad of *The Wanton Wife of Bath.*' *NCFJ* 35(1988), 40–77.

The *WBP* served as a direct source for the ballad *The Wanton Wife of Bath*. The ballad emphasizes 'the source's textuality' (p 41).

896 Brewer, Derek. 'Orality and Literacy in Chaucer.' In *Mündlichkeit und Schriftlichkeit im englischen Mittelalter.* Ed. Willi Erzgräber and Sabine Volk. Tübingen: Gunter Narr Verlag, 1988. Pp 85–119.

Chaucer mimics Alisoun's garrulousness in the *WBP* (p 103).

897 Crane, Susan. 'Alison of Bath Accused of Murder: Case Dismissed.' *ELN* 25(1988), 10–15.

There is little evidence to conclude that Alisoun murdered her fourth husband. Because she is a fictional character, Alisoun cannot be analyzed psychologically. Since Chaucer created Alisoun in order to undermine the antifeminist tradition, he would not have made her such an unscrupulous woman that she would commit murder.

898 Delany, Sheila. 'Difference and the Difference It Makes: Sex and Gender in Chaucer's Poetry.' *Florilegium* 10(1988–91), 83–92 [cited]. Rpt in *A Wyf Ther Was: Essays in Honor of Paule Mertens-Fonck*. Ed. Juliette Dor. Liège: Université de Liègè, 1992. Pp 103–11.

Alisoun's lion-painting complaint negates itself through its own rhetoric.

899 de Weever, Jacqueline. *Chaucer Name Dictionary: A Guide to Astrological, Biblical, Historical, Literary, and Mythological Names*

in the Works of Geoffrey Chaucer. New York: Garland, 1988.
Entries are listed alphabetically and have substantial definitions. For example, *Clitermystra* is not only defined, but her reference in Jerome's *Jov* is cited as is Chaucer's reference to her in the *WBP*. Variant spellings and titles of critical articles are also found under individual listings (p 93).

900 Diekstra, F.N.M. 'Chaucer and the Romance of the Rose.' *ES* 69(1988), 12–26.
Alisoun's recounting of her husband's speeches is influenced by the Jealous Husband of *RR*. That antifeminist sentiments come from a woman's mouth in Chaucer produces a more striking effect than that found in Jean de Meun's work (p 20). Like Alisoun, the *RR*'s Dame Nature advocates copulation in conjunction with the 'increase and multiply' injunction of Genesis (p 25).

901 Fichte, Joerg O. 'Hearing and Reading the *Canterbury Tales*.' In *Mündlichkeit und Schriftlichkeit im englischen Mittelalter*. Ed. Willi Erzgräber and Sabine Volk. Tübingen: Gunter Narr Verlag, 1988. Pp 121–31.
The marginal glosses of the *CT* in the Ellesmere and Hengwrt mss fall into nine categories. An illustration of the fifth type, in which specific words clarify textual arrangement, is found in the Ellesmere ms *questio* in III.115. The eighth type includes the subdivision found in the *WBP* and the ninth type, Latin quotations from Chaucer's sources, is present in the *WBP* as well (pp 128–9).

902 Fisher, Sheila. *Chaucer's Poetic Alchemy: A Study of Value and Its Transformation in the Canterbury Tales*. New York: Garland Publishing, Inc., 1988.
See **1374**.

903 Hamaguchi, Keiko. 'The Wife of Bath's Deafness and the Antifeminist Tradition.' In *Essays Presented to Professor Sachio Tanaka on the Occasion of His Retirement from Gifu University*. Tokyo: Kirihara Shoten, 1988. Pp 107–21. [In Japanese.]
Tracing the meaning of deafness within the antifeminist tradition reveals why Chaucer made Alisoun an ideal wife after her hearing was damaged in her fight with Jankyn.

904 Hansen, Elaine Tuttle. 'The Wife of Bath and the Mark of Adam.' *Women's Studies* 15(1988), 399–416. Rpt in *Chaucer and the Fictions of Gender*. Berkeley: University of California Press, 1992. Pp 26–57.

While Alisoun plays an important part in feminist criticism, she must not be unconditionally accepted as truly representative of women in Chaucer's day (p 400). While Alisoun seems to be a victorious opponent of antifeminism, she is limited by having to use male authority in order to support her claims. She 'endorses the antifeminist stereotypes she cites' (p 404). The hag's transformation into a submissive wife discloses Alisoun's lack of faith in the power of woman's speech (p 405). The lion-painting speech calls attention to the fact that Alisoun is the product of a male author. It is difficult to differentiate between the voice of the poet and that of the character, yet both are similar, marginalized entities (p 409). Alisoun's belief in language, which Chaucer does not share, underscores her subjection to male authority (p 410). While Chaucer appears to be sympathetic to the condition of woman, his female characters are still subject to the patriarchy. Male Chaucerian characters, however, are also limited by their gender.

905 Hill, Archibald A. 'Chaucer and the Pun-Hunters: Some Points of Caution.' In *On Language: Rhetorica, Phonologica, Syntactica: Festschrift for Robert P. Stockwell from His Friends and Colleagues*. Ed. Caroline Duncan-Rose and Theo Vennemann. London: Routledge, 1988. Pp 66–78.

Alisoun's use of the word *queynte* is not a pun because to accept it as such would 'change the total context' (p 72).

906 Hudson, Anne. *The Premature Reformation: Wycliffite Texts and Lollard History*. Oxford: Clarendon Press, 1988.

Alisoun's argument against authority reflects the language of Wyclif (p 393).

907 Johnston, Alexandra F. 'Chaucer's Records of Early English Drama.' *Records of Early English Drama* 13(1988), 13–20.

Chaucer's references to Biblical drama in the *MilT* and *WBP* are important because they are some of the earliest evidence that such drama took place in the fourteenth century (p 14).

908 Koff, Leonard Michael. *Chaucer and the Art of Storytelling*. Berkeley: University of California Press, 1988.

While the reference to Alisoun in *MerT* cannot serve as a tale-ordering device, it does suggest that Alisoun was a well-known Chaucerian character (p 115). Alisoun is unable to argue in 'clerkly fashion' (p 120). *WBP* and *WBT* reflect 'the sexual and intellectual complexities of our nature' (p 127). The gender of whoever performs Alisoun's words does influence interpretation of and emphasis within the text.

909 Lammers, John H. 'The Archetypal Molly Bloom, Joyce's Frail Wife of Bath.' *James Joyce Quarterly* 25(1988), 487–502.
Molly Bloom is most often compared with Alisoun because 'they are the same archetypal character' (p 488).

910 North, J.D. *Chaucer's Universe*. Oxford: Clarendon Press, 1988; rpt 1990.
Of the three historical and astrological possibilities for determining the year of Alisoun's birth, 1342 is the most probable (p 302). According to the stars, Alisoun is destined to marry a clerk in her fortieth year. Her anniversary horoscope is 6 February 1382.

911 Roberts, Ruth Marshall. 'Chaucer, An Androgynous Personality.' *POMPA* (1988), 137–42.
See **398**.

912 Salter, Elizabeth. *English and International: Studies in the Literature, Art and Patronage of Medieval England*. Ed. Derek Pearsall and Nicolette Zeeman. Cambridge: Cambridge University Press, 1988. Pp 245–55.
Chaucer's experimentation with frame-space lends complexity to Alisoun's character in the *WBP* (pp 245–55).

913 Schibanoff, Susan. 'The New Reader and Female Textuality in Two Early Commentaries on Chaucer.' *SAC* 10(1988), 71–108.
While the glossator of the Egerton ms condemns Alisoun and creates a conflict between the genders over authority, the glossator of the Ellesmere ms is sympathetic towards Alisoun. The difference between the glossators indicates the different possibilities for interpretation of text among individuals. Early editions of Chaucer chose to omit glosses because they were aware of the new, private reading style that was emerging in their culture (p 107).

914 Sleeth, Charles R. '"My dames loore" in the *Canterbury Tales*.' *NM* 89(1988), 174–84.
Alisoun's mother is her authority figure. Maternal authority is also found in the *PardT* and *ManT*. In all three works, maternal advice is susceptible to misinterpretation. That Alisoun's mother has taught her to deceive and trick men does not support the antifeminist tradition but displays Alisoun as a robust woman.

915 Straus, Barrie Ruth. 'The Subversive Discourse of the Wife of Bath: Phallocentric Discourse and the Imprisonment of Criticism.' *ELH*

55(1988), 527–54.

While Alisoun's subversive discourse becomes 'enclosed within masculine discourse' (p 527) in *WBP*, Alisoun undermines this confinement by challenging the qualities upon which masculine discourse depends. This task is repeated in *WBT* through Alisoun's adding a 'structure of secrets and "truth"' (p 528) into her story. These additions expose how Alisoun and her performance are incorporated into phallocentricism. Alisoun also poses a threat to literary critics because she shows that critics cannot master texts.

916 Wurtele, D.J. 'Chaucer's Wife of Bath and the Problem of the Fifth Husband.' *ChauR* 23(1988), 117–28.

Alisoun is concerned with the issue of bigamy because Jankyn has left her. For her to marry again would be unlawful (p 118). That Jankyn aided Alisoun in murdering her fourth husband provides a motive for his departure.

917 Ashley, Kathleen M. 'Renaming the Sins: A Homiletic Topos of Linguistic Instability in the *Canterbury Tales*.' In *Sign, Sentence, and Discourse: Language in Medieval Thought and Literature*. Ed. Julian N. Wasserman and Lois Roney. Syracuse: Syracuse University Press, 1989. Pp 272–93.

Alisoun's naturalistic defense of sexual pleasure is in keeping with the concept of making lechery seem less distasteful (pp 285–6).

918 Blamires, Alcuin. 'The Wife of Bath and Lollardy.' *MÆ* 58(1989), 224–42.

Contrary to Knight's opinion (**864**), Alisoun cannot be associated with Lollardy. While Chaucer and Alisoun are concerned with the issue of authority, a central concern for Lollards, Alisoun's love of pilgrimages and her penchant for swearing are against Lollard principles.

919 Canfield, J. Douglas. *Word as Bond in English Literature from the Middle Ages to the Restoration*. Philadelphia: University of Pennsylvania Press, 1989.

Alisoun undermines the chivalric upholding of word as bond and chivalry's valuing of chastity. Both Alisoun and the hag turn patriarchal logic against itself (p 19). Risking damnation, Alisoun also defies the Word of God. She redefines language.

920 Cohen, Jeremy. *'Be Fertile and Increase: Fill the Earth and Master It': The Ancient and Medieval Career of a Biblical Text*. Ithaca: Cornell University Press, 1989.

Alisoun's reference to the call of Genesis to increase and multiply (III.28–9) demonstrates her awareness of medieval attention to God's natural order (p 272). She uses this passage to legitimize her sexual activity, and it exposes the tension between patriarchal religion and the goddess *Natura* (pp 301–3).

921 Cooper, Helen. *Oxford Guides to Chaucer: The Canterbury Tales.* Oxford: Clarendon, 1989/rev 1996.

An analysis of *WBP*'s date, text, genre, structure, themes, style, and its context within *CT* complements a thorough examination of the sources of this work. See **1381**.

922 Dinshaw, Carolyn. *Chaucer's Sexual Poetics.* Madison: University of Wisconsin Press, 1989.

In the Man of Law's *Endlink* and in the *WBP*, Alisoun takes a stand against glossing and establishes her body as text, thus linking literal interpretations and carnality with women (p 113). Going against the concept of silent, passive femininity, Alisoun speaks out as the literal text. Her body speaking as the Other, Alisoun 'mimics patriarchal discourse' in order to transform misogynistic hermeneutics into sexualized hermeneutics. This transformation is what Chaucer is trying to establish in his creation of Alisoun. In speaking of her financial gains through marriage, Alisoun acknowledges that women are treated as commodities (p 118). Alisoun's questioning, her flawed logic, and her Scriptural misquotation are reflective of glossators. While she exposes the misogynistic elements of glossators, Alisoun revels in Jankyn's ability to gloss her body, an illustration of the carnality of glossing. In this relationship, Jankyn's glossing is acceptable because it recognizes and appeases feminine desire. See **1382**.

923 Elliott, Ralph. 'Chaucer's Garrulous Heroine: Alice of Bath.' *SMELL* 4(1989), 1–29.

The *WBP* is filled with the pronoun *I*, proverbs, and oaths. In the dialogue between Alisoun and her husbands, variations of *thou seyst* appear frequently. Alisoun's discourse is reflective of her class and her rural environment (p 14). Her horoscope is a convenient excuse for the way she acts (p 16). See **399** and **1383**.

924 Fisher, John H. 'Assertion of the Self in the Works of Chaucer.' *MedPers* 4–5(1989–90), 1–24.

The Marriage Debate represents the tension between 'autocratic overlordship and local husbandry interfaced in the manor and the town' (p 4). Significantly, Alisoun, the strongest voice against authority, is an artisan from a small town (p 5). Through the sermon on *gentillesse*, Alisoun rejects the principle of Munt, the concept that a ruler oversees his subjects as a husband does his wife. It is the ideal of 'wifehood' that conveys universality to the Wife of Bath (p 14). Chaucer's pilgrims are primarily identified by occupation, not by personal names. It is not until the *WBP* that Alisoun's name is given. Chaucer's female characters reveal themselves and their desires through dramatic monologues and debate.

925 Frank, Robert Worth, Jr. 'Inept Chaucer.' *SAC* 11(1989), 5–14.
The notion that Alisoun murdered her fourth husband is both misleading and absurd, since it makes a mockery of the structural artistry of the *WBP* and the consistency of character in the Wife of Bath. If scholars who propose that she is a murderer are correct, then the *WBP* is 'perversely flawed' (p 8).

926 Fyler, John. 'Love and the Declining World: Ovid, Genesis, and Chaucer.' *Mediaevalia* 13(1989), 295–307.
Both Chaucer and Ovid were aware that the Golden Age was not as ideal as it was purported to be. That Alisoun places herself well above Lamech's bigamy is an example of Chaucer's frank perception of the past (pp 304–5).

927 Griffiths, Jeremy, and Derek Pearsall, ed. *Book Production and Publishing in Britain 1375-1475*. Cambridge: Cambridge University Press, 1989.
Jankyn's book was most likely valued at several pounds (p 7).

928 Hallissy, Margaret. 'Widow-To-Be: May in Chaucer's *Merchant's Tale*.' *SSF* 26(1989), 295–304.
May's marriage resembles Alisoun's first three unions; however, May is too blinded by lust to manage her affairs as well as Alisoun does.

929 Hanna, Ralph, III. '*Compilatio* and the Wife of Bath: Latin Backgrounds, Ricardian Texts.' In *Latin and Vernacular: Studies in Late-Medieval Texts and Manuscripts*. York Manuscript Conferences: Proceedings Series, University of York, Centre for Medieval Studies 1. Ed. A.J. Minnis. Woodbridge, Suffolk; Wolfeboro, NH: Brewer, 1989. Pp 1–11.
The *WBP* may be labeled as a compilation because most of it has been taken directly from its sources (p 1). While the compilation tradition features depersonalized rhetoric, Jankyn, in his recitation of his book, adds personality to the text and subsequently weakens its claim to

universal truth (p 6). Alisoun as well gives voice to compiled text, and, while she is still trapped by patriarchal language (p 7), she exposes the antifeminist tradition as a human, not a divine, creation (p 8).

930 ———. 'The Hengwrt Manuscript and the Canon of the *Canterbury Tales.*' In *English Manuscript Studies 1100—1700*, volume 1. Ed. Peter Beal and Jeremy Griffiths. Oxford: Basil Blackwell 1989. Pp 64–84.

The absence of the contested passages in *WBP* from the Hengwrt ms indicates these passages are most likely Chaucerian revisions made after the tales had been collected for compilation in the Hengwrt (p 78).

931 Hilberry, Jane Elizabeth. 'The Silent Woman: Speech, Gender, and Authority in Chaucer and Shakespeare.' *DAI* 50(1989), 953A.

Both Chaucer and Shakespeare explore the interrelations of speech, gender, and authority through the Wife of Bath and Kate in *The Taming of the Shrew*. Female speech and silence are both connected to male authority.

932 Knapp, Peggy A. 'Alisoun of Bathe and the Reappropriation of Tradition.' *ChauR* 24(1989), 45–52.

In her use of the antifeminist tradition in *WBP* and the genre of romance in *WBT*, Alisoun sets out to redefine literature that defines women according to masculine desire. Alisoun turns antifeminist authority into a theatrical performance (p 47). *WBT* stresses the point that men must not only learn from women but also learn to view them as partners (p 49). Alisoun is both a new and a traditional female (p 51).

933 Prescott, Ann Worthington. 'Chaucer and Music and Song.' *Chaucer Newsletter* 11(1989), 1, 6–7.

Roger Nixon and Prescott have composed several choral selections based on Chaucer's works. One of the five songs based on the *CT* is an amusing rendition of Alisoun's personal life.

934 Richman, Gerald. 'Rape and Desire in the *Wife of Bath's Tale.*' *SN* 61(1989), 161–5.

See **1388**.

935 Simmons-O'Neill, Elizabeth. '"Sires, by youre leve, that am nat I": Romance and Pilgrimage in Chaucer and the "Gawain/Morgne"-Poet.' *DAI* 50(1989), 135A.

See **1389**.

936 Strohm, Paul. *Social Chaucer*. Cambridge: Harvard University Press,

1989.

Chaucer presents multiple versions of the truth that are challenged by various pilgrims. Alisoun's advocacy of female sovereignty is attacked by the Clerk's view of the traditional power structure (p 171). Patterson's (**1065**) point that the voice of the peasantry is underrepresented is reinforced by the fact that the Miller and the Wife do not truly belong to this class (p 174).

937 Wetherbee, Winthrop. *Geoffrey Chaucer: The Canterbury Tales.* Landmarks of World Literature. Cambridge: Cambridge University Press, 1989.

The *WBP* is a history of Alisoun's body that initially views marriage as power (p 84). While she can adeptly wield masculine tools of language and literature, Alisoun's need to use them demonstrates her entrapment within the patriarchy. While the glossing of exegetes is initially seen as misogynistic, glossing later becomes a pleasurable, physical experience for Alisoun. See **1390**.

938 Bloch, R. Howard. 'Critical Communities and the Shape of the Medievalist's Desire: A Response to Judith Ferster and Louise Fradenburg.' *Exemplaria 2* (1990), 203–20.

Judith Ferster's article ['"Your Praise is Performed by Men and Children": Language and Gender in the *Prioress's Prologue* and *Tale.*' *Exemplaria* 2(1990), 149–68] would provide an intriguing interpretation of the *WBP*. The question of whose voice is speaking in the *WBP* is complex, and Ferster does not acknowledge that answering such a question may entail 'denying ... the very principle of constant appropriation and reappropriation of power each time someone speaks or represents speech' (207).

939 Delany, Sheila. 'Strategies of Silence in the Wife of Bath's Recital.' *Exemplaria* 2(1990), 49–69.

The concept of silence within Alisoun's text and how we interpret this silence is a focal issue for the consideration of how medieval ideologies are present in Alisoun's performance and how modern ideologies examine this literature. Alisoun's lion-painting complaint creates much irony in the *WBP* (pp 50–6). The silence in Alisoun's performance undermines both Alisoun and her text (pp 56–62). The knight's riddle can only be answered if women are perceived as an excluded group (pp 62–6).

940 Farrell, Thomas J. 'The *Envoy de Chaucer* and the *Clerk's Tale.*'

ChauR 24(1990), 329–36.

While the standard interpretation of the relationship of the Clerk's *Envoy* to the *ClT* views this piece as the Clerk's response to the Wife of Bath, the rubric *Lenvoy de Chaucer* provides us with the direction to see the *Envoy* as independent from the Clerk's performance.

941 Fradenburg, Louise O. '"Voice Memorial": Loss and Reparation in Chaucer's Poetry.' *Exemplaria* 2(1990), 169–202.

D.W. Robertson's criticism of the Wife of Bath as a self-serving reader of text (**540**) is applicable both to Robertson himself regarding his views of Alisoun and to other Chaucerian critics who try to find modern concepts in medieval literature. Robertson's maintaining that contemporary readers still see Alisoun as stereotypically feminine continues the tradition of perceiving woman as Other (p 177).

942 Ganim, John M. *Chaucerian Theatricality*. Princeton: Princeton University Press, 1990.

The *WBP* can be viewed as a 'rewriting' (p 47) of the *ShT*. In the *WBP* the equation of sex and commerce is replaced by dialectics (p 50). While the *ShT* presents a disturbing view of language and experience, Alisoun provides a parody of this view.

943 Georgianna, Linda. 'Love So Dearly Bought: The Terms of Redemption in the *Canterbury Tales*.' *SAC* 12(1990), 85–116.

Alisoun's remark that Christ *bought us with his herte blood* (III.718) is an example of Chaucer's numerous references to Christ's salvation of humanity 'in English commercial terms' (87). Her reason for going on pilgrimages — to search for lovers — is not ideal (97).

944 Hansen, Elaine Tuttle. 'Fearing for Chaucer's Good Name.' *Exemplaria* 2(1990), 23–36.

Not until the 1970's did critical attention to Chaucer's 'alleged empathy with women' (p 24) truly emerge and the 'female monster' (p 25) become a 'heroine' (p 25). Yet 'through the construction of notorious, ambiguous, "lifelike" female characters like the Wife, the problems and anxieties of (masculine) identity are strategically displaced onto Woman' (p 33). While Chaucer does align himself with characters of both genders, he ultimately depicts woman as the Other.

945 Knapp, Peggy. *Chaucer and the Social Contest*. New York: Routledge, 1990.

Alisoun is a 'theorist of interpretation' (p 114) whose consideration of glossing and reading underscores the importance of female speech.

Through her use of learning and authority, she develops an 'apologia for the emerging estate of pragmatic, worldly entrepreneur[s]' (p 118). Alisoun embodies the roles of a feminist (pp 118–20) and of Eve (pp 120–2). She may be viewed as a sociopath (pp 122–4). Alisoun manipulates Jankyn by presenting herself as a victim both in her dream and after their fight. *WBT* acts as a *exemplum* for *WBP*.

946 Laird, Edgar S. 'Mars in Taurus at the Nativity of the Wife of Bath.' *ELN* 28(1990), 16.
The thirteenth-century *Compilatio de astorum scientia* of Leopold of Austria predicts that women born when Mars is in Taurus, as Alisoun is, will become whores.

947 Laskaya, Catherine Anne. 'Representing Gender in the *Canterbury Tales*.' *DAI* 50(1990), 2484A.
In the *CT* Chaucer does not subscribe to the distinct gender roles of the Middle Ages. His Christ-like characters are female. Through his characterization of Alisoun, Chaucer protests conventional gender ideology. He demonstrates his disregard for cultural convention in outlining Alisoun's refusal to comply with standard gender roles. 'In the Wife of Bath's prologue, tale, voice, and body, boundaries become amorphous' (2484).

948 Leicester, H. Marshall, Jr. *The Disenchanted Self: Representing the Subject in the Canterbury Tales*. Berkeley: University of California Press, 1990.
Chapters 2–5 focus on Alisoun. Chapter 2 highlights Alisoun's presentation of self as an authority figure. Alisoun makes herself an *exemplum* because she dislikes the *exempla* of established authorities. Alisoun's life is in accord with the *WBT*'s conclusion that sovereignty is a necessity. Both Alisoun's words and what she omits from her performance show her attitudes toward her role. In Chapter 3, attention is given to retrospective revision, the main characteristic of Alisoun's performance. A struggle is present in *WBP* between Alisoun's need for control of her self-presentation and her desire to elaborate on her memories. The brevity of her account of her fourth husband discloses her discomfort with his memory. Alisoun makes use of her horoscope for self-definition. Chapter 4 contains an assessment of Alisoun's fifth marriage. She and Jankyn are compatible because of their lack of interest in marital harmony. The couple loves to fight and each of them takes delight in Jankyn's reading from his book. The text undermines the

concepts of Venus and eros in conflict with Mars and aggression in Alisoun's horoscope by a fusion of these qualities. Chapter 5 focuses mainly on the *WBT*. While Alisoun's performance is highly personal, she adheres to her public goals. The Midas digression reflects elements of the *WBP*. Midas can serve as a parallel to Alisoun's fourth or fifth husband. Midas' wife, then, is Alisoun, yet she also resembles Arthur's queen. The hag is Alisoun's worst envisioning of herself in the future. Alisoun is critical of the romance genre because it fails to incorporate the realities of experience. Alisoun's character is a role, and Alisoun maintains the choice of whether or not she will perform this role.

949 Mann, Jill. 'Anger and "Glosynge" in the *Canterbury Tales.' PBA* 76(1990), 203–23.
See **1398**.

950 ———. *Apologies to Women: Inaugural Lecture Delivered 20th Nov. 1990.* Cambridge: Cambridge University Press, 1990.
In his *Dialogue with a Friend*, Hoccleve attempts to 'create a Chaucerian atmosphere' (p 21). The friend cites Alisoun as an authority on women's distaste for criticism.

951 Martin, Carol A.N. 'Alys as Allegory: The Ambivalent Heretic.' *Comitatus* 21(1990), 52–71.
Through her textile skills, her multiple marriages, and her resemblance to a renegade preacher, Alisoun does link herself with heretical Lollardy. The accusation of Lollardy against the Parson in the Man of Law's *Endlink* and the presence of two Jankyns, a name tied to Lollardy, in the *WBP* underscore the above association. Chaucer adds Lollard imagery to Alisoun's character so that he might investigate the differences between Lollards and standard Christianity (p 53). Alisoun's penchant for pilgrimages, her offerings in church, and her confessional style of speaking go against Lollard practice. D.W. Robertson condemns the Wife for her literal methods of interpreting Scripture (**540**), but he bases his opinion on the 'very textual authorities which Alys says she knows nothing about and in an interpretive tradition which Augustine's own principles do not endorse' (p 59). Christian allegory saw that textual meaning might be found on many levels, and Alisoun does arrive at significant meaning, despite her inept handling of Scripture.

952 Martin, Priscilla. *Chaucer's Women: Nuns, Wives, and Amazons.* Iowa City: University of Iowa Press, 1990.
Alisoun's struggles are less concerned with her husbands than with the

antifeminist tradition. The fight she has with Jankyn manifests the destructive effects of patriarchal language (p 12). Alisoun's dual roles of wife and soldier, inspired by her horoscope, lead to contradictions in her nature (pp 93–102). The garrulous Alisoun may be compared with the more silent Prioress. It is Alisoun's ability to speak well that, ironically, condemns her (p 220). See **1399**.

953   Nolan, Edward Peter. *Now Through a Glass Darkly: Specular Images of Being and Knowing from Virgil to Chaucer.* Ann Arbor: University of Michigan Press, 1990.
      See **193**.

954   Nyquist, Mary. 'Ever (Wo)Man's Friend: A Response to John Fyler and Elaine Tuttle Hansen.' *Exemplaria* 2(1990), 37–47.
      Fyler's (**926**) argument cannot reconcile the assumptions that the 'generic and gendered' (p 38) connotations of *man* are both possible in any usage of the term and that such ambiguity is controlled by authorial intent. Hansen's (**944**) awareness of the fallible critical practice of assuming a 'transhistorical solidarity' (p 42) between the genders of medieval and modern audiences is a valid concern, because history cannot be ignored in analyzing sexual politics.

955   O'Brien, Dennis. 'Academic Study in a Deconstructive Age, or What If the Wife of Bath Had Read Harold Bloom?' *CEA* 52(1990), 2–9.
      Alisoun is adept at textual deconstruction (p 3). She establishes opposition between men and women and between text and experience. See **1400**.

956   Patterson, Lee. '"No man his reson herde": Peasant Consciousness, Chaucer's Miller, and the Structure of the *Canterbury Tales*.' In *Literary Practice and Social Change in Britain, 1380–1530*. Ed. Lee Patterson. Berkeley: University of California Press, 1990. Pp 113–55.
      The threat of the peasantry to the aristocracy, represented by the Miller's requiting the Knight, is dispersed by Alisoun, the Friar, and the Summoner (p 123). Alisoun advocates her personal rights in the *WBP* and does not pose any political threat to the nobility (p 150).

957   Robinson, Peter M.W. 'The Oxford Computer and Manuscripts Project.' *Chaucer Newsletter* 12(1990), 6–7.
      Computer study of the Chaucerian manuscripts may reveal 'the textual tradition' (p 6) of *WBP*.

958   Taylor, Paul Beekman. 'Alisoun in Iceland: An Image of the Wife of

210 / Wife of Bath's Prologue and Tale

Bath in Nordic Myth.' *Journal of Popular Culture* 24(1990), 75–80. Alisoun's attraction to Jankyn's feet (III.595–9) has a parallel in the Icelandic *Skáldskaparmál*. Alisoun's character resembles that of the Norse goddess Skadi. The two uses of the word *scathe* in *CT* (I.446, IV.1170) both refer to Alisoun.

959 Wallace, David. 'Chaucer's Body Politic: Social and Narrative Self-Regulation.' *Exemplaria* 2(1990), 221–40.

Alisoun's performance inspires an anger that motivates the male speakers in Fragment III (p 223). The friction between the Summoner and the Friar is introduced in the *WBP* (III.829–56). That this antagonism must be silent during the remainder of Alisoun's performance leads to the build-up of anger, a pervasive emotion in Fragment III (p 222).

960 ———. '"Whan she translated was": A Chaucerian Critique of the Petrarchan Academy.' In *Literary Practice and Social Change in Britain, 1380–1530*. Ed. Lee Patterson. Berkeley: University of California Press, 1990. Pp 156–215.

Chaucer's ending of the *ClT* shares the sexual economics found in Boccaccio's version of this story. The fusion of sex and trade reflects back to Alisoun (p 205).

961 Wilson, Katharina, and Elizabeth M. Makowski. *Wykked Wyves and the Woes of Marriage: Misogamous Literature from Juvenal to Chaucer*. Albany: State University of New York Press, 1990.

Through her ironic incorporation of the antifeminist tradition into her argument, Alisoun satirizes misogyny and 'ridicules the arguments of the misogamous canon' (p 152). While *WBP* appears to be a *persuasio* on marriage, it is actually a *dissuasio* on the subject.

❧ The Wife of Bath's Prologue 1991–1995

962 Andrew, Malcolm, ed. *Critical Essays on Chaucer's Canterbury Tales*. Toronto: University of Toronto Press, 1991.
This book is a compilation of twenty-one critical essays that span from 1809 to 1987 and include early landmark criticism such as Kittredge's 'Chaucer's Discussion of Marriage' (**210**) as well as poststructural articles.

963 Astell, Ann W. 'Job's Wife, Walter's Wife, and the Wife of Bath.' In *Old Testament Women in Western Literature*. Ed. Raymond-Jean Frontain and Jan Wojciky. Conway: University of Central Arkansas Press, 1991. Pp 92–107.
Gregory's misogynistic presentation of Job's wife in his *Moralia in Iob* receives Chaucerian treatment in the characters of Alisoun and Griselda. Alisoun's reactions to antifeminism reflect 'the ambivalence he [Chaucer] feels as a male artist burdened with the *translatio* of an established, but morally limited and limiting genre' (p 96).

964 Biscoglio, Frances Minetti. 'The Wives of the *Canterbury Tales* and the Tradition of the Valiant Woman of Proverbs 31:10–31.' *DAI* 52(1991), 1321.
The polarized medieval view of women was influenced by Proverbs 31.10–31 and its presentation of the *mulier fortis*. Chaucer incorporates ironic reflections of the *mulier fortis* in his depictions of good and wicked wives. The Wife of Bath, a wicked wife, receives such treatment.

965 Bott, Robin L. 'The Wife of Bath and the Revelour: Power Struggles and Failure in a Marriage of Peers.' *MedPers* 6(1991), 154–61.
That the Wife of Bath's fourth marriage was one 'of equals, which resulted in savage power struggles and marital failure' (p 154) can be

discovered through an analysis of her silence and digressions in the *WBP*. Because Alisoun does not reveal her fourth husband's economic worth, it may be assumed that he possessed wealth that equalled Alisoun's. Alisoun provides no explanation for her fourth marriage. She also neglects to discuss any inheritance she might have received from this man. The elite burial location of this husband indicates his strong economic power; Alisoun could not control where he was buried (p 156). Alisoun doesn't mention any age difference or relate her sex life with the fourth husband. 'Unable to use age or wealth as a lever, the Wife attempts ... to make him jealous' (p 157). Alisoun's husband grants her freedom so that he, in turn, might have his: 'What she really desired was independence for herself and thralldom for her husband' (p 159).

966 Brown, Peter, and Andrew Butcher. *The Age of Saturn: Literature and History in the Canterbury Tales*. Oxford: Basil Blackwell, 1991. If we view Chaucer's sources for the *WBP* as works that 'share sexual and matrimonial themes' (p 25), Alisoun's opinions on marriage 'express issues of perennial interest' (p 25). We must also consider social attitudes towards marriage in Chaucer's time when considering Alisoun's performance. The *WBP* reveals the kinship among women that resulted from their exclusion from the world of men (pp 27–9), man's flawed representation of women in text (pp 29–33), and the power of nature in conflict with that of institutionalized authority (pp 34–6). Other noteworthy topics in Alisoun's performance include the world of faery as an 'alternative authority' (p 37) to the church and the naturalness of sex and its proper use between a man and woman (pp 37–42). We may also learn of the medieval rituals surrounding marriage, as well as both Chaucer's concern with the need for an altered view of marriage in a post-plague era and the need to emphasize spirituality over the temporal in marriage.

967 Felch, Susan M. 'Rehearsing *Everich a word*: Chaucer's Linguistic Investigation in the *Canterbury Tales*.' *MedPers* 6(1991), 144–53. The Friar's rebuke of Alisoun's performance marks a confusion of 'language with reality' (p 147).

968 Fineman, Joel. *The Subjectivity Effect in Western Literary Tradition: Essays Toward the Release of Shakespeare's Will*. Cambridge: MIT Press, 1991. The authorities that Alisoun draws upon for her prologue and tale are placed into the context of the sexual hierarchy exemplified in the *GP*'s male April that pierces the female March (p 13).

969 Frese, Dolores Warwick. *An Ars Legendi for Chaucer's Canterbury Tales: Re-Constructive Reading*. Gainesville: University of Florida Press, 1991.

See **405**.

970 Gittes, Katharine S. *Framing the Canterbury Tales: Chaucer and the Medieval Frame Narrative Tradition*. New York: Greenwood Press, 1991.

Alisoun's quotation from Gerard of Cremona's translation of the *Almagest* suggests the fondness of medieval writers for Arabic wisdom (p 67). While Kittredge (**210**) feels that Alisoun's performance belongs to the Marriage Group, Ruggiers (**566**) groups it with other chivalric stories in the *CT* (p 112). The Pardoner gains intelligence on marriage from Alisoun's performance. Alisoun reveals her philosophy on marriage through her performance (p 131).

971 Hagen, Susan K. 'The Wife of Bath: Chaucer's Inchoate Experiment in Feminist Hermeneutics.' In *Rebels and Rivals: The Contestive Spirit in the Canterbury Tales*. Studies in Medieval Culture, 29. Ed. Susanna Greer Fein, David Raybin, and Peter C. Braeger. Kalamazoo: Medieval Institute Publications, 1991. Pp 105–24.

While Chaucer shows his awareness that married life might not fulfill a woman through his portrayal of Alisoun, his *WBT* ends with a satisfying marriage. The endings of both the *WBP* and the *WBT* seem unsatisfactory (p 116). Chaucer was limited in his attempt to portray female experience by the medieval authoritarian view that there was no female experience outside of relations with God and man (p 107). He could not ultimately overturn the patriarchal hierarchy of his day (p 118). Alisoun recognizes a distinction between God's and man's authority and challenges the latter. She 'offers a new hermeneutics based on experience rather than the received authority of the exegete' (p 110). Her non-linear style of presentation, reactionary gynocentrism, counters traditional male hermeneutics. While Alisoun seems to be obsessed with her sexuality, it should be remembered that she is a male's creation.

972 Hill, John M. *Chaucerian Belief: The Poetics of Reverence and Delight*. New Haven: Yale University Press, 1991.

Chaucer's thematic pairing of experience and authority, exemplified directly in the *WBP*, is more substantial than his coupling of the terms *sentence* and *solas* in the *CT* (pp 12–13). Kittredge's (**210**) dramatic reading of the *CT* applies only partially to the three confessional prologues of the Pardoner, the Wife, and the Canon's Yeoman (p 18). The concept of organicism can prove helpful when studying a self-revealing prologue such as Alisoun's (p 25).

973 Johnson, Dawn. 'Some Views of Love in Chaucer.' *Pleiades* 12(1991), 59–63.

While Alisoun and the knight of the *WBT* initially represent the irreligious practices of multiple marriages and rape, they later espouse 'a more Christian attitude of love and marriage' (p 59).

974 Kiser, Lisa. *Truth and Textuality in Chaucer's Poetry*. Hanover: University Press of New England, 1991.

Alisoun is presented as a woman 'knowing more about how to exploit the uncertain boundary between truth and fiction than she is usually credited with' (p 137). Alisoun places her arguments in the mouths of specific speakers. Throughout her performance, Alisoun demonstrates that human speech does not resemble truth so much as it does fictional narrative (p 142).

975 Mann, Jill. 'Chaucer and the "Woman Question."' In *This Noble Craft: Proceedings of the Xth Research Symposium of the Dutch and Belgian University Teachers of Old and Middle English and Historical Linguistics, Utrecht, 19–20 January, 1989*. Ed. Erik Kooper. *Costerus*, n.s. 80. Amsterdam: Rodopi, 1991. Pp 173–88. Article based on *Geoffrey Chaucer*. Feminist Readings. Atlantic Highlands: Humanities Press International, Inc., 1991.

The second portion of the *WBP* contains a dual structure. The Wife repeats what her first three husbands allegedly said to her, speeches steeped in antifeminism, as a counter-attack against men. Alisoun's consistent reference to wives and women in the plural transforms her individual marriages into a general condition of women 'and acts as a constant reminder of the anti-feminist commonplaces on which she draws' (p 184). While Alisoun justifies her arguments by exposing the antifeminist tradition, she ironically reinforces the misogynistic view of women because she is so vocal. The Wife's specific involvement with gender stereotypes promotes her individuality (pp 184–5). The third portion of the *WBP* contains a single female perspective. Again, antifeminist writings create the angry woman they claim only to observe. Chaucer chose not to ignore gender stereotypes but to expose them so that it might be seen how they affect individual lives (pp 186–7).

976 ———. *Geoffrey Chaucer*. Feminist Readings. Atlantic Highlands: Humanities Press International, 1991.

In *MerT* and *WBP*, Chaucer sets antifeminism and 'wommanly pitee' within dynamic structures that enable him to avoid the risk of stasis in the polarization of male treachery and female suffering that marks *LGW* (pp 48-9). He incorporates antifeminist material into *WBP*, plotting speaker against speech (p 70). In her struggle against the stereotypes of her gender, Alisoun establishes herself as a new authority and 'male discourse passes into female control' (p 73). Alisoun reveals the symbiosis of 'female bullying and masculine oppression' (p 79). Her individual engagement with antifeminist stereotypes creates a sense that she is a real person. Her account of Jankyn's readings from his book forces us to listen to antifeminist satire from the position of a woman. Her victory over Jankyn is not accomplished through her aggressiveness but by pathos (p 85). See **197** and **1413**.

977 ———. 'The Authority of the Audience in Chaucer.' In *Poetics, Theory and Practice in Medieval English Literature*. Ed. Piero Boitani and Anna Torti. Suffolk: Brewer, 1991. Pp 1–12.

While Jerome composed *Jov* in order to promote celibacy and not in order that men 'torment their wives' (p 7), Jankyn does use Jerome's work to annoy Alisoun. Alisoun may thus feel that literature is unpleasant. While a man's 'creative exegesis' (p 8) was credible, society would not accept the same creativity in women. Alisoun and Jerome interpret exegetically in the same manner.

978 Mertens-Fonck, Paule. 'The Indebtedness of the *Canterbury Tales* to the Clerk-Knight Debates.' In *This Noble Craft: Proceedings of the Xth Research Symposium of the Dutch and Belgian University Teachers of Old and Middle English and Historical Linguistics, Utrecht, 19–20 January, 1989*. Ed. Erik Kooper. *Costerus*, n.s., 80. Amsterdam: Rodopi, 1991. Pp 189–99.

Chaucer uses the theme of the clerk-knight debates in Alisoun's performance. Alisoun, as a knight, and Jankyn, as clerk, exhibit rivalry. The motif of the 'choice of a lover from a woman's point of view' (p 190) is found in the happy endings of the *WBP* and the *WBT*.

979 ———. 'Life and Fiction in the *Canterbury Tales*: A New Perspective.' In *Poetics: Theory and Practice in Medieval English Literature*. Ed. Piero Boitani and Anna Torti. Suffolk: Brewer, 1991. Pp 105–15.

While Alisoun's *GP* portrait does not establish her as a heroine of romance, some details recall the courtly knight. At the end of the *WBP*, Alisoun literally does battle against antifeminism. Because her immediate opponent is the Oxford clerk, Jankyn, the ending of the *WBP* is 'a burlesque comment on the clerk-knight rivalry' (p 108). Through her performance, Alisoun provides answers to the primary question of the clerk-knight debates: 'Who is the best lover, the clerk or the knight?' (p 109). The *WBP* and the *WBT* reveal what changes clerks and knights should undergo in order to make women happy.

980 Osberg, Richard H. 'Clerkly Allusiveness: Griselda, Xanthippe, and the Woman of Samaria.' *Allegorica* 12(1991), 17–27.

Griselda's leaving her water pot on the threshold when Walter comes to her home represents both her abandoning the Old Law and her willingness to be an obedient wife. This action is in strong contrast with the actions of Alisoun, who adheres to the Old Law and is not an obedient spouse.

981 Owen, Charles A., Jr. 'Fictions Living Fictions: The Poetics of Voice and Genre in Fragment D of the *Canterbury Tales*.' In *Poetics: Theory and Practice in Medieval English Literature*. Ed. Piero Boitani and Anna Torti. Suffolk: Brewer, 1991. Pp 37–56.

The interruptions and digressions within Fragment III form 'a dialectic of voice and genre' (p 39). Chaucer's absence as narrator in the fragment allows his audience to perceive the fiction as if they were experiencing it first hand. Alisoun's dominant presence permeates both 'the scene described and the scene of the Wife describing' (p 40). Her fiction becomes the identity she presents to her audience. 'Her passion brings the past into the present' (p 41). While the peaceful resolution of the *WBP* contradicts the events of Alisoun's life, it does serve to establish Alisoun as a romance heroine and thereby unite her with her tale. Alisoun 'is clearly a fiction living fictions' (p 42).

982 Sherman, Gail Berkeley. 'Saints, Nuns, and Speech in the *Canterbury Tales*.' In *Images of Sainthood in Medieval Europe*. Ed. Renate Blumenfeld-Kosinski, Timea Szell, and Brigitte Cazelles. Ithaca: Cornell University Press, 1991. Pp 136–60.

Perhaps critics do not comment upon gender issues of the Prioress and the Second Nun as they do with the Wife of Bath because the *PrT* and the *SNT* do not treat the theme of Alisoun's lion-painting complaint (pp 139–40).

983 Storm, Melvin. 'The Miller, the Virgin, and the Wife of Bath.' *Neophil* 75(1991), 291–303.

The parallels Chaucer draws between Alison of the *MilT* and Alisoun of Bath enable him to apply 'the moral and spiritual implications of the scriptural allusions' (p 291) of the *MilT* to the *WBP*. Some of the most striking parallels are the women's lustful natures and the animal imagery that is applied to them (pp 294–5). Alisoun's adherence to the Old Law juxtaposes her with the Virgin Mary, Mother of the New Law. It is through the *MilT*'s Alison and its Annunciation motif that the contrast between the Wife of Bath and the Blessed Mother is highlighted.

984 Sturges, Robert S. *Medieval Interpretation: Models of Reading in Literary Narrative, 1100–1500*. Carbondale: Southern Illinois University Press, 1991.

Alisoun's perception of John's Gospel account of the Samaritan woman is comparable to the Samaritan woman's perception of Christ. Both women are unsure of Christ's meaning (p 163). While the Samaritan woman was able to question Christ's meaning, Alisoun cannot derive such a response from text. She therefore uses her own interpretation of divine teachings. Alisoun's burning of Jankyn's book restores direct communication in her marriage. Conversely, it is only through the indirect discourse of tale-telling that the pilgrims can communicate with one another (p 170).

985 Wurtele, Douglas J. 'Treachery in Chaucer's Poetry.' *FCS* 18(1991), 315–43.

During the reign of Richard II there was so much tension created by suspicions of treason that the evils of betrayal became a frequent theme in Chaucer's work. In the *WBP*, this theme is very subtle. As Beryl Rowland has shown, Alisoun and Jankyn may have conspired to murder the Wife's fourth husband (**649**). Alisoun's calling Jankyn a *false theef* (III.800) suggests that the man is treacherous (p 329). There are several incidents of wives murdering their husbands in Jankyn's book.

986 Bisson, Lillian M. 'In the Labyrinth: Reading the *Canterbury Tales* through *The Name of the Rose*.' *MedPers* 7(1992), 19–33.

While the Host has an orderly plan for the story context, factors such as Alisoun's and the Pardoner's relating 'personal histories that threaten to overwhelm their tales' (p 28) mar the balance between the tales and their framework.

987 Bowers, John M., ed. *The Canterbury Tales: Fifteenth-Century*

Continuations and Additions. Kalamazoo: Medieval Institute Publications, 1992.

Textual notes (pp 51–3) accompany the Squire-Wife of Bath link from the BL Lansdowne 851 ms (pp 43–4) and the Merchant-Wife of Bath link from the BL Royal 18.c.ii.ms.

988 Breuer, Horst. 'Narrative Voices in Chaucer's *Wife of Bath's Prologue.*' In *Anglistentag 1991 Düsseldorf: Proceedings.* Ed. Wilhelm G. Busse. Tübingen: Niemeyer, 1992. Version of 'Die erzählerische Vermittlung in Chaucers *Wife of Bath's Prologue.' GRM* 42(1992), 28–47.

Although the *WBP* is delivered in first-person narration, it contains dialogical discourse. The masculine voices of Alisoun's husbands, Christ and his disciples, and members of the antifeminist tradition are present along with the Wife's voice (p 418). This male discourse seems to act as a 'counter-balance to the Wife of Bath's first-person point of view' (p 420). It subverts her argument and exposes her fallibility. Chaucer makes use of nine rhetorical devices in order to incorporate the masculine voices and comment on Alisoun's reliability as narrator: blasphemy, animal imagery, twisted quotations and pseudo-syllogisms, self-betrayal and intrinsic contradictions, allegorizing, male speech, belated restoration of figural viewpoint, and proverbs and contamination (pp 421–5). By diluting the Wife's argument with multiple male voices, Chaucer added elements upon which her unreasonableness and the comedy of the *WBP* might be contrasted. Despite the manifold incorporations in the *WBP*, Alisoun's voice remains dominant; it is what the reader most appreciates. 'Her own "experience" gets the upper hand against "auctoritee"' (p 426).

989 ———. 'Die erzählerische Vermittlung in Chaucer's *Wife of Bath's Prologue.' GRM* 42(1992), 28–47. [In German.]

There is still room for particular inquiries concerning the narrative arrangement of the *WBP*. Alisoun makes use of blasphemy, animal metaphors, false citations, pseudo-syllogism, self-betrayal, insults, and allegory in her performance. Through her rebellious '*topsy-turvydom*' (p 45) Alisoun promotes wifely experience over authoritative texts.

990 Brown, George H. 'The (Ab)use of the Bible by Medieval Writers.' In *The Idea of Medieval Literature: New Essays on Chaucer and Medieval Culture in Honor of Donald R. Howard.* Ed. James M. Dean and Christian Zacher. Newark: University of Delaware Press,

1992. Pp 285–300.

Chaucer's 'clipped well-chosen biblical reference[s] and allusion[s]' (p 286) in the *WBP* as well as other Canterbury stories mark his artistic and unique use of Scripture.

991 Calabrese, Michael Anthony. 'Meretricious Mixtures: Chaucer's Ovid and the Poetry of Love and Exile.' *DAI* 53(1992), 804A.

In her function as an Ovidian rhetorician, Alisoun manipulates both identities and realities in her struggle with convention.

992 Carruthers, Leo. '*No womman of no clerk is preysed*: Attitudes to Women in Medieval English Religious Literature.' In *A Wyf Ther Was: Essays in Honour of Paule Mertens-Fonck.* Ed. Juliette Dor. Liège: Université de Liège, 1992. Pp 49–60.

Chaucer uses the Wife to express his awareness of the injustice of the antifeminist school towards women. Alisoun provides numerous examples of antifeminist religious writers and their work in order to expose this unfairness. The Wife does expose the human tendency to flatter one's self, though, when she notes how gender portrayal would have been reversed if women had had the opportunity to write (pp 49–50). Unfortunately, the theological writers in Chaucer's day were not able to overcome their human tendencies and espouse more Christian sentiments in their depictions of women. Despite the antifeminism of Theophrastus and Jerome, there are some elements of Christianity that are egalitarian and even reverential towards women. In *Jacob's Well*, men are indicted for their faults and the human soul is not only given female attributes but also depicted as the Samaritan Woman. While Alisoun chooses to avoid acknowledging Christ's message against widows' remarrying, she is unaware that Jesus reveals his identity as Savior to this woman. Alisoun has been exposed to neither the truly Christian way of perceiving woman nor to the medieval clerks who adhered to Christ's message (p 60).

993 Crane, Susan. 'The Writing Lesson of 1381.' In *Chaucer's England: Literature in Historical Context.* Medieval Studies at Minnesota, volume 4. Ed. Barbara A. Hanawalt. Minneapolis: University of Minnesota Press, 1992. Pp 201–21.

The book-burning incident in the *WBP* evinces an undermining of authority that is reflective of the third estates' inability to access communication (pp 213–4). Alisoun's stance against authority aligns her with the marginalized illiterate, and the incidents of the *WBP* share characteristics of the uprising of 1381.

994 Delany, Sheila. 'Difference and the Difference It Makes: Sex and Gender in Chaucer's Poetry.' In *A Wyf Ther Was: Essays in Honour of Paule Mertens-Fonck.* Ed. Juliette Dor. Liège: Université de Liège, 1992. Pp 103–11.

Despite Chaucer's sympathies toward the condition of women in his day, his society's ambivalence towards women acted as a barrier that he could not cross. Such duality may be found in the *WBP.* While Alisoun's *Who peyntede the leon* speech initially seems to be a strong protest against the absence of woman in the writing field, it is actually a reinforcement of cultural norms. Marie de France's lion fable outlines the hierarchical relationship of man to the lion. Lions cannot create narrative; they are dangerous beasts; man must control the beast. Alisoun's symbolic equation of woman with the lion, then, firmly places the female in subservience to the male (pp 109–10).

995 Donaldson, Kara Virginia. 'Alisoun's Language: Body, Text and Glossing in Chaucer's *The Miller's Tale.*' *PQ* 71(1992), 139–53.

While Alisoun literally attacks a misogynistic text and then relates her actions to her listeners in order to expose 'the effects and implications of patriarchal glossing of women' (p 142), Alison of the *MilT* has no voice and is glossed by John, Nicholas, and Absolon.

996 Ellis, Roger. 'Persona and Voice: Plain Speaking in Three Canterbury Tales.' *BJRL* 74(1992), 121–39.

The *WBP* contains a strong 'sense of voicing' (p 131) that is immediate and grows out of personal experience. 'The voicing of the narrative and the voice of the narrative are thus more directly and immediately related' (p 131). A portion of the *WBP*'s voices come from Alisoun's immediate past and the other voices are 'from book time' (p 131). Because Alisoun has listened to the voices of her husbands and has heard text being read, the *WBP* is a compilation of reported and direct speech. Until the book-burning fight, Jankyn speaks only from his book. Since his language comes to us through Alisoun's reporting, we cannot be sure of the accuracy with which he is being quoted. Alisoun's 'voicing is primarily a matter of response to what someone has actually said to her' (p 134). Alisoun both voices the text she has heard and creates complex irony with it.

997 Fisher, John H. *The Importance of Chaucer.* Carbondale: Southern Illinois University Press, 1992.

Alisoun's performance and *ClT* protest the patriarchal hierarchy (p 102). The depth of Chaucer's artistry is revealed in his ability to create a highly realistic character such as Alisoun from a 'pastiche of passages taken directly from antifeminist anthologies' (p 134).

998   Fowler, Elizabeth. 'Misogyny and Economic Person in Skelton, Langland, and Chaucer.' *Spenser Studies* 10(1992), 245–73.
Alisoun and Skelton's Elynour Rummynge 'share a boisterous self-assertion ... that is ... economic' (p 245) and are products of antifeminism. While Elynour is a grotesque character in the fabliaux tradition, Alisoun has sympathetic, psychological depth. Both women have an economic independence that is united with their sexual assertiveness. A character named Alice in Skelton's poem boasts of her pilgrimages (p 256).

999   Ganim, John M. 'The Literary Uses of the New History.' In *The Idea of Medieval Literature: New Essays on Chaucer and Medieval Culture in Honor of Donald R. Howard.* Ed. James M. Dean and Christian K. Zacher. Newark: University of Delaware Press, 1992. Pp 209–26.
Alisoun 'is an example of transvestite poetics' (p 222).

1000   Hahn, Thomas. 'Teaching the Resistant Woman: The Wife of Bath and the Academy.' *Exemplaria* 4(1992), 431–40.
As a product of the misogynist tradition, Alisoun can claim her text to be her own only within the realm of patriarchal discourse. Since woman has no text of her own, 'she is *the* text' (p 438). Woman becomes the Other that is either lacking or excessive in the binary, gender-coded language of the patriarchy (pp 437–9).

1001   ———. 'Postscript.' *Exemplaria* 4(1992), 481–3.
Alisoun's ability to move 'through her various texts bears upon questions of subjectivity and the production of literary discourse' (p 481). This concept is related directly to the evolving concept of self in the later Middle Ages. See **1000, 1002,** and **1421.**

1002   Engel, Lars. 'Reply.' *Exemplaria* 4(1992), 485–8.
Neuse's response to Hahn's article is humanist in nature (**1421** and **1000**). Hahn examines the *WBP* through the social condition of medieval women, a context that is, in part, textual (p 486).

1003   Hanning, R.W. 'Telling the Private Parts: "Pryvetee" and Poetry in Chaucer's *Canterbury Tales.*' In *The Idea of Medieval Literature: New Essays on Chaucer and Medieval Culture in Honor of Donald R. Howard.* Ed. James M. Dean and Christian K. Zacher. Newark:

University of Delaware Press, 1992. Pp 108–25.

The *WBP* is composed of confessions that stem from both Alisoun's personal life and generic revelations of women (p 117). Alisoun's practice of gossiping is related to oral tradition. For something to survive in a non-literate world, it cannot be kept private. Alisoun's penchant for lying counters her gossiping tendency 'with its subversion of *privetee*' (p 122). The combination of the private truths with fiction makes one's secrets more socially acceptable.

1004 Lindley, Arthur. '"Vanysshed was this daunce, he nyste where": Alisoun's Absence in the *Wife of Bath's Prologue* and *Tale*.' *ELH* 59(1992), 1–21.

The disappearances that occur during Alisoun's performance, those of the dancing ladies, the hag, and Jankyn, serve to underscore the concept that the antifeminist tradition portrays Alisoun as an evil parody of what woman really is. As the product of a male author, Alisoun is actually absent from her performance. This incompleteness of her presence is 'Chaucer's intricately ironized protest' (p 17) against authority's stifling the female voice.

1005 Mandel, Jerome. *Geoffrey Chaucer: Building the Fragments of the Canterbury Tales*. Rutherford: Fairleigh Dickenson University Press, 1992.

Not only do the tales of Fragment III share several minor elements, they also have strong structural and thematic similarities. The introductions of *WBP, WBT, FrT, SumT* usually contain a portrait and an attack against another pilgrim. The narratives are interrupted, each involves a quest, and all have a double conclusion that results in anger. In each of these works, the Host cries for peace (pp 109–18). The shared themes include wandering, acquisition, mastery or control, and a contract of obligation (pp 118–27).

1006 Martin, Priscilla. 'Chaucer and Feminism: A Magpie View.' In *A Wyf Ther Was: Essays in Honour of Paule Mertens-Fonck*. Ed. Juliette Dor. Liège: Université de Liège, 1992. Pp 235–46.
See **410**.

1007 Miller, Clarence H. 'Three Phrases in the *Canterbury Tales*: 'youre dyvynytee, (*FrT* III–D 1512), 'youre gentillesse' (*SqT* V–F 695), 'Goode lief' (*Pro WBT* III–D 431).' *N&Q* 237(1992), 152–5.

The interpretation of Alisoun's use of *Goode lief* becomes problematic when it is considered to be either an endearment directed at one of her husbands or as an interjection. A more logical interpretation suggests that Alisoun uses the endearment to address a third party whom she is regaling with tales of her marriages (pp 154–5).

1008 O'Brien, Timothy. 'Troubling Waters: The Feminine and the Wife of Bath's Performance.' *MLQ* 53(1992), 377–91.

That Alisoun comes from Bath aligns her with the medieval topos of the bath. The archetypal association of women with water is echoed in imagery of 'water, wells, and refreshment' (p 378). The ties to water in the *WBP* criticize the misogynistic mutating of archetypal feminine power into a threatening element. See **1422**.

1009 Owen, Charles A., Jr. 'The *Canterbury Tales*: Beginnings (3) and Endings (2).' *Chaucer Yearbook* 1(1992), 189–212.

Textual evidence suggests that Chaucer altered 'an early sequence — Man of Law's Introduction — Melibeus — Epilogue — first 162 lines of the Wife of Bath's Prologue — Shipman's Tale' (p 195).

1010 Patterson, Lee. 'Feminine Rhetoric and the Politics of Subjectivity: La Vieille and the Wife of Bath.' In *Rethinking the Romance of the Rose: Text, Image, Reception*. Ed. Kevin Brownlee and Sylvia Huot. Philadelphia: University of Pennsylvania Press, 1992. Pp 316–58.

While Jehan Le Fèvre's *La Vieille* motivated Chaucer's thematic concepts of youth and beauty in opposition with age and wisdom, Jean de Meun's *RR* 'provided Chaucer with a rhetorical structure, a *disposition*, that organizes' (p 317) the *WBP* and the *WBT* as well as much of the *CT*. While Alisoun's version of the Midas story aligns a woman's speech with her carnal urges, her strategy is to prompt her audience to recall Ovid's version of the tale, which reveals flaws in men, specifically the inability to listen. Alisoun's association of her body with text reflects the medieval view of poetic language as being sexual and feminine. Through her carnal rhetoric, Alisoun promotes readings of text that are alternative to medieval hermeneutics.

1011 Richmond, Velma Bourgeois. *Geoffrey Chaucer*. New York: Continuum, 1992.

The Wife of Bath and the Pardoner both have prologues in which they 'confess' their sins (p 55). Chaucer uses both of these characters to address problems in organized religion. The thematic woe of the *WBP* is illustrated in the *ShT*. The wife in the *ShT* echoes Alisoun's beliefs regarding sex and money (p 89). The theme appears along with a reference to the Wife in *Buk* (p 195). See **1424**.

1012 Ridley, Florence H. 'The Friar and the Critics.' In *The Idea of Medieval Literature: New Essays on Chaucer and Medieval Culture in Honor of Donald R. Howard*. Ed. James M. Dean and Christian Zacher. Newark: University of Delaware Press, 1992. Pp 160–72.

Alisoun, the Friar, and the Pardoner are not related so much by the thematic content of their tales as in their manner of developing them (p 165).

1013 Smith, Macklin. '*Sith* and *Syn* in Chaucer's *Troilus*.' *ChauR* 26(1992), 266–82.

Chaucer makes use of the pun on the word *syn* in both the *CT* and *TC*. In the *WBP*, Alisoun's use of *sith* and *syn* in III.434–7 places a moral evaluation on her husbands' preaching. Likewise, the loathly lady employs *syn* three times (III.1217–8, 1236–7, 1242–4) for multiple meanings (p 273).

1014 Strohm, Paul. *Hochon's Arrow: The Social Imagination of Fourteenth-Century Texts*. Princeton: Princeton University Press, 1992.

Alisoun's ability to be economically independent is established in the *GP* and this quality is figured through sexuality in the *WBP* (p 40). Sex is a profitable commodity for Alisoun in her first three marriages and, while her value decreases with time, Alisoun still resolves to sell her *bren* (III.478). Through sexual economics, Alisoun is fighting to gain sovereignty. She is a treasonous wife, rebelling against her lord and reflecting actual middle-class female struggles with the patriarchy.

1015 Wilson, Janet. 'Margery and Alisoun: Women on Top.' In *Margery Kempe: A Book of Essays*. Ed. Sandra McEntire. New York: Garland, 1992. Pp 225–37.

Alisoun and Margery Kempe both tend toward excess, refuse to be silenced, establish control of their husbands, and disturb social norms. Both women reveal the difficulties of having the female voice authenticated. Their bodies are described with the 'grotesque realism' (p 227) of the Bakhtinian carnival, and they acquire attention through their manners of dress. Margery is accused of Lollardy and the Wife preaches like a Lollard. That the *Book of Margery Kempe* was transcribed by a clerk connects with Jankyn and the antifeminist tradition.

1016 Wimsatt, James I. 'The Wife of Bath, the Franklin, and the Rhetoric of St. Jerome.' In *A Wyf Ther Was: Essays in Honour of Paule Mertens-Fonck*. Ed. Juliette Dor. Liège: Université de Liège, 1992. Pp 275–81.

While the fourteenth century considered Jerome to be of the antifeminist tradition, his *Jov* is more a 'pro-ascetic' (p 275) tract than an antifeminist or antimatrimonial work. Jerome's extreme writing style and the insults he directs at Jovinian stem from his study of Roman rhetoric and Latin satirists (pp 276–7). Alisoun is also a Ciceronian rhetorician. She saves her untraditional theme for the end of the *WBP*, making sure her listeners have been primed to receive her ideas. Much of what the Wife draws from Jerome is the saint's incorporation of Theophrastus into his work. Alisoun's late reference to Jerome (III.673–5) gives rise to the premise that she may not have known she was misquoting him earlier in the *WBP*. There is dialogical discourse in the *WBP*. Alisoun's and Jerome's voices give conflicting views on virginity and sexuality. It is the reader's choice to decide which voice speaks the truth (p 281).

016a Wurtele, Douglas. 'The "Double Sorwe" of the Wife of Bath: Chaucer and the Misogynist Tradition.' *Florilegium* 11(1992), 179-205.

Alisoun's protests against clerks and the Church are not merely personal resentment but an outcry against the injustices done to her sex. In addition to the works in Jankyn's book, she has met with 'the admonitions of preachers versed in the rigorist tradition' (p 182) that even denounced sex in marriage. While the writings of Innocent III, St. Raymund of Pennaforte, and John Bromyard are highly antimatrimonial, those of Hugh of St. Victor, Alan of Lille, and Bartholomew Anglicus contain a more liberal attitude towards the sexual aspect of marriage. It is unfortunate that Alisoun was not exposed to the works of these less stringent authors.

1017 Wynne-Davies, Marion. '"He conquered al the regne of femenye": Feminist Criticism and Chaucer.' *CrSurv* 4(1992), 107–13.

While feminist critics find Alisoun and her performance to be attractive topics for discussion, they should also devote their studies to 'female characters who do not coincide so readily with twentieth-century feminist ideals' (p 110). As scholars formulate theories concerning medieval literature, they must note that Chaucer's *CT* 'is constructed like a kaleidoscope' (p 112). 'For every dominant Wife' there is 'a docile Griselda' (p 112).

1018 Zauner, Erich. 'The Wife of Bath aus Chaucers *Canterbury Tales*: Ein Frauenbild aus der frühen englischen Literatur.' *Moderne Sprachen* 36(1992), 7–14. [In German.]
See **1428**.

1019 Bowman, Mary R. '"Half as she were mad": Dorigen in the Male

World of the *Franklin's Tale.' ChauR* 27(1993), 239–51.
Chaucer displays his awareness of the difficulty a male author has in
representing a female character through Alisoun's lion-painting
complaint. The 'masculine wish-fulfillment' (p 241) displayed in the
resolution of the *WBT* shows Chaucer's inability to represent fully female
perspectives and desires.

1020 Cox, Catherine. 'Holy Erotica and the Virgin Word: Promiscuous
Glossing in the *Wife of Bath's Prologue.' Exemplaria* 5(1993), 207–
37.
While Alisoun is the product of masculine discourse, her performance
does contain an 'ambivalent feminine poetics' (p 208) to which we may
connect Alisoun's references to glossing. Alisoun links sexual love and
language and glosses 'one in terms of the other' (p 212). She appears
to enjoy talking about sex more than participating in the act itself. Through
her appetite for glossing, Alisoun seeks to satisfy her desire for filling a
void in her life. This appetite adds to Alisoun's 'carnal excess' (p 217),
her need to consume both 'sexually and textually' (p 218). Despite the
attention given to 'the feminine utility of poetic polysemy' (p 237) in
Alisoun's performance, the *WBP* provides no solutions to the interrelation
of 'gender, language, and society' (p 237). While this lack of resolution
creates a sense of ambivalence within this anti-anti-feminist prologue,
it fosters debate among critics.

1021 David, Alfred. 'Old, New, and Yong in Chaucer.' *SAC* 15(1993), 5–21.
Alisoun maintains contempt for all old things, including her own advancing
age (p 16). See **412** and **1430**.

1022 Dickson, Lynne. 'Deflection in the Mirror: Feminine Discourse in the
Wife of Bath's Prologue and *Tale.' SAC* 15(1993), 61–90.
Alisoun is not the embodiment of antifeminist material. Rather, her
performance defies patristic misogyny in two ways. The first defiance
is carried out through Chaucer's 'juxtaposing and layering both feminine
and masculine responses to misogynist discourse' and thereby both
revealing 'the inadequacies of a purely masculine response' and
encouraging 'readers to respond instead as complex sexual beings' (p
62). The second defiance entails outlining the 'tyranny of a purely
patriarchal mode of understanding by dramatizing the degree to which
Alison's efforts to articulate a feminine position are threatened and
constrained by the weight of this culturally sanctioned tradition' (p 62).
The *WBP* and *WBT* do not merely resist patriarchal domination but

move towards promoting feminine discourse and cultivating a female audience.

1023 Dillon, Janette. *Geoffrey Chaucer*. New York: St. Martin's Press, 1993. Through his characterization of the Wife of Bath, Chaucer presents his audience with the dual perspective of a woman who is aware that she is the embodiment of the antifeminist tradition and a woman who speaks out against it. Alisoun's debasement of authority and her views on marriage place her in direct conflict with the clergy. Her insistence that she too, and not the Church alone, may interpret Biblical text marks a further challenge to the clergy and to patriarchal society as well. Because the Pardoner and the Friar both view the Wife as preaching during the *WBP*, they see her adopting a role denied to both women and the uneducated. Chaucer may have developed Alisoun's character with Lollard imagery, for the heretical group advocated the practices of using English, as opposed to Latin texts, and of promoting female education; however, Alisoun's goals are more radical than those of the Lollards. In her fifth marriage, Alisoun is directly challenged by a book of clerkly compilation and she retaliates physically against both Jankyn and the text. Her own wickedness does not dissolve the antifeminist tradition, but it exposes the truths about humankind.

1024 Hallissy, Margaret. *Clean Maids, True Wives, and Steadfast Widows: Chaucer's Women and Medieval Codes of Conduct*. Westport: Greenwood, 1993. Chaucer respects the association between Alisoun and her gossip, a female relationship that symbolizes an affront to masculine authority (p 78). Alisoun has many strong alliances with women that outlast her marriages. Chaucer also grants Alisoun spatial mobility; she has the freedom to go on pilgrimages (p 100). The Wife's occupation of weaver not only indicates her economic independence but also is symbolic of her ability to create the *WBP* and the *WBT*. Her rhetorical abilities reveal an acquisition of a male power (p 164) and Alisoun uses speech to gain mastery. She moves from the private discourse of the gossip to public speech, the masculine realm (p 173). Her multiple marriages and demands for the marriage debt go against the norms for widows and wives (p 168). That Alisoun does not speak of children does not mean she has none. Alisoun and Jankyn are equal in their knowledge of authority (p 174), yet Alisoun manages to conquer him and to regain her wealth. See **413** and **1432**.

1025 Kamowski, William. 'The Sinner against the Scoundrels: The Ills of Doctrine and *Shrift* in the Wife of Bath's, Friar's and Summoner's Narratives.' *R&L* 25(1993), 1–18.

Alisoun's performance introduces several religious topics that are echoed in the *FrT* and *SumT*. Chaucer has the Friar, the Summoner, and the Pardoner, 'Parasites who pervert the concept of Penance' (p 2), interrupt Alisoun. Her performance includes 'an attack on the doctrine that supported the practices of the three' (p 2). The *WBT* demonstrates the proper practice of Penance through its emphasis on charity and mercy as opposed to doctrine (p 6).

1026 Kelly, H. Ansgar. 'Sacraments, Sacramentals, and Lay Piety in Chaucer's England.' *ChauR* 28(1993), 5–22.

If Jankyn were a parish clerk, he would not have been able to continue this duty once he married Alisoun (p 6). Alisoun's remark that her gossip knew more of her secrets than did her priest is an indication of the frequency of confession among Chaucer's characters (p 8).

1027 Morsberger, Katharine M. 'Voices of Translation: Poet's Voice and Woman's Voice.' *PCP* 28(1993), 3–19.

In translating the *WBP* Pope was exposed to the imaginings and language of the Other. While his poetic talents were already honed, in this exercise Pope was able to better understand his own word-choice and poetic process. See **1434**.

1028 Odegard, Margaret. '"Alas, alas, that ever love was sin!": Marriages Moral and Immoral in Chaucer.' In *Censored Books: Critical Viewpoints*. Ed. Nicholas J. Karolides, Lee Burress, and John M. Kean. Metuchen: Scarecrow, 1993. Pp 144–58.

The 1987 censoring of the *CT* in a Florida public school district displays a failure to perceive the ethical issues Chaucer raises in his writing. While the *MilT*, *WBP*, and *WBT* 'have been charged with obscenity and immorality' (p 146), they are frequently anthologized and are considered to be Chaucerian masterpieces. Through his creation of Alisoun and her performance, Chaucer recognizes the middle class and gives a female character a strong voice which is both revolutionary and ethical. Alisoun's battle with antifeminism is a major twentieth-century issue. Her frank discussion of sexuality reveals that 'creation is good' (p 151) and Alisoun shows us that women can be successful. The *WBT* is a statement against 'the blindness of notions of chivalry in its implicit attitudes toward other classes and toward women' (p 154). The tale should not be considered immoral because it briefly outlines a rape. Rather, the tale upholds the just treatment of women.

1029 Patterson, Lee. 'Perpetual Motion: Alchemy and the Technology of the Self.' *SAC* 15(1993), 25–57.
Both Alisoun's and the Pardoner's performances assist critical study of the *CYP* and *CYT*. Alisoun's reworking of antifeminist tracts for her feminist argument reflects the Canon's Yeoman's means of self-representation through 'unstable' (p 34) alchemical terminology.

1030 Rudat, Wolfgang E.H. *Earnest Exuberance in Chaucer's Poetics: Textual Games in the Canterbury Tales.* Lewiston: Mellen, 1993.
We may find in III.371, where Alisoun says that her husband compares a woman's love to hell, a thinly-veiled reference to Proverbs 30:20. In that proverb Agur refers to a woman who after adultery wipes her mouth clean and claims to have done no wrong (pp 96-8). The 'mouth' here refers to the woman's 'lower' lips or labia, and the reference carries over as well to the Prioress's supposedly delicate table manners. Justinus's reference to the Wife of Bath in the *MerT* is part of an interior monologue in which the Merchant consults his personified reason (p 230). Alisoun goes against the theories of Augustine and asserts that post-lapsarian intercourse is just as pleasurable as pre-lapsarian sex was (p 231).

1031 Schildgen, Brenda Deen. 'Jerome's Prefatory Epistles to the Bible and the *Canterbury Tales*.' *SAC* 15(1993), 111–30.
Alisoun's manipulative quoting of Scripture substantiates Jerome's concern regarding the misrepresentation of the Bible (p 117). Jerome's concerns were echoed by those who were against the Lollard call for a vernacular Bible.

1032 Vance, Sidney. 'Contending with the Masculinist Traditions: *Sundiata*'s Sogolon and the Wife of Bath.' In *Global Perspectives on Teaching Literature: Shared Visions and Distinctive Visions.* Ed. Sandra Ward Lott, Maureen S.G. Hawkins, and Norman McMillan. Urbana: National Council of Teachers of English, 1993. Pp 101–8.
See **1437**.

1033 Andreas, James R. '"Wordes betwene": The Rhetoric of the Canterbury Links.' *ChauR* 29(1994), 45–64.
Chaucer creates an interruption of Alisoun's performance in order to make it 'open, honest, and above all interesting' (p 52).

1034 Blamires, Alcuin. 'Questions of Gender in Chaucer, from *Anelida* to

Troilus.' LeedsSE 25(1994), 83–110.

While Chaucer derived the convention of a suitor relating a dream from Jean de Meun, who had in turn been inspired by Ovid, Chaucer has Alisoun tell her dream to Jankyn. The other two authors used the convention in order to have a man seduce a woman (p 87). Alisoun and Arcite demonstrate that both sexes desire what they cannot have (p 89). Chaucer also plays with the gender roles when he has the knight behave like a virginal bride on his wedding night (p 94).

1034a Bloom, Harold. *The Western Canon: The Books and School of the Ages.* New York: Harcourt, 1994.

Chaucer's pleasure in his creation of Alisoun is reflected in the *Buk.* In spite of her colorful portrait in the *GP*, her 'Falstaffian wit, her feminism (as we might now say), above all her fantastic way to live are not yet truly in evidence' (p 114). Alisoun's frankness, especially in regards to sex, 'has appalled many of the male scholars who have defamed the Wife' (p 115).

1035 Daileader, Celia R. 'The *Thopas-Melibee* Sequence and the Defeat of Antifeminism.' *ChauR* 29(1994), 26–39.

Dame Prudence is just as concerned with certain feminist points as Alisoun is. The patriarchal abuses of female speech and woman's body of which Alisoun complains are righted in the *Thop-Mel* sequence. The poor quality of *Thop* exposes the weakness of the male authority, the Chaucer persona, who tells the tale. Thus the tale serves to elevate the upcoming wisdom of Prudence. *Mel*, *WBP*, and *WBT* all contain elements of male violence against women: Sophie's wounding, Alisoun's combat with Jankyn and her dream of his slaying her, and the maiden's rape. Alisoun's glossing of her dream is a glossing of her body (p 31). Just as the Wife offers her body as text, so too do Sophie's wounds tell a truth that is glossed by her mother. The allegorical relation of the daughter's wounds to her father's lack of protection of his house indicts Melibeus for assaulting his child. Both Alisoun and Prudence are versed in Scripture and antifeminist texts and both speak the phrase, *That am nat I* in response to patriarchal conceptions of women (p 35). These women both say *no* to the antifeminist tradition. Alisoun accomplishes this *no* by declaring the injustice of the tradition, and Prudence follows with a discourse that results in re-establishing peace (p 38).

1036 Fisher, John H. 'Historical and Methodological Consideration for Adopting "Best Text" or "Usus Scribendi" for Textual Criticism of

Chaucer's Poems.' *Text* 6(1994), 165–80.

A comparison of excerpts of the *WBP* (III.278–89) taken from the Hengwrt, Corpus 198, Harley 7334, Lansdowne, Cambridge Dd 4.24, Cambridge Gg 4.27, Ellesmere, and Cambridge Peterhouse 71.1 manuscripts illustrate the *usus scribendi* editorial technique.

1037 Gallacher, Patrick J. 'Chaucer and the Rhetoric of the Body.' *ChauR* 28(1994), 216–36.

Chaucer constructs an 'interaction of agitated bodily movement and philosophical quiet' at various points in the *CT*. Alisoun's account of the dynamics between Xantippa and Socrates (III.729–32) provides contrast for the actions of the uneasy knight before he hears the *gentillesse* sermon.

1038 Hirsh, John C. '*General Prologue* 526: "A Spiced Conscience."' *ChauR* 28(1994), 414–7.

There is differing commentary on I.526, the reference to the Parson's *spiced conscience*. The appearance of the phrase in *WBP* III.435 is different in meaning from its earlier usage because Alisoun adds the adverb *sweete* to it (p 414). This addition undercuts the word *spiced*. Alisoun uses the phrase to inform her husband that she desires him to be instantaneously obedient. The phrase as it applies to the Parson in the *GP* refers to an abruptly and strongly roused soul (p 416).

1039 Justman, Stewart. 'Trade as Pudendum: Chaucer's Wife of Bath.' *ChauR* 28(1994), 344–52.

Chaucer allows the brunt of his exposure of the bourgeoise to fall on Alisoun and leaves his Guildsmen rather untouched. Alisoun's carnality is also a reflection of the aggressiveness of the middle class. She reveals her commercial drive in her views on marriage and sex. She 'is evidently a consumer of men' (p 348).

1040 Minnis, Alastair J. 'Repainting the Lion: Chaucer's Profeminist Narratives.' In *Contexts of Pre-Novel Narrative: The European Tradition*. Ed. Roy Eriksen. Berlin: Mouton de Gruyer, 1994. Pp 153–83.

In *LGW* Chaucer works to correct Alisoun's lion-painting complaint by depicting women as 'morally ... stronger and more constant' (p 167) than men.

1041 Nilsen, Don L.F. 'Geoffrey Chaucer's Humor.' *InG* 15(1994), 77–84.

Among the variety of critical opinions concerning Chaucer's humor, Hugh Walker (**460**) finds Alisoun's performance to be a 'satire on lascivious women' (p 79) and Alisoun herself to be one of literature's most humorous women.

1042 Parks, Ward. 'Oral Tradition and the *Canterbury Tales.*' In *Oral Poetics in Middle English Poetry*. Ed. Mark C. Amodio with Sarah Gray. New York: Garland, 1994. Pp 149–79.

The late fourteenth-century questioning of 'scripture, text, *auctoritas*' (p 172) is reflected in the *WBP* and the *NPT*.

1043 Root, Jerry. '"Space to speke": The Wife of Bath and the Discourse of Confession.' *ChauR* 28(1994), 252–74.

Through the genre of confessional poetry the *WBP* may be viewed with a Foucauldian sense of cultural unity and interpreted in a new way. While the *ParsT* conforms more to sacramental confession, confession for Chaucer goes beyond its institutionalized form. He saw a distinction between 'the institutionalization of a discourse of the self ... and "tales" of the self' (p 253). In keeping with her disdain for authority, Alisoun uses the concept of Church confession for her own agenda. She carves out her own space to speak and discloses her private life. She gains power over 'the conditions of representation' (p 255), thereby accessing a means of interpretation denied to medieval women. When she decides to speak, Alisoun replaces the Parson and offers a confession instead of a penitential treatise; she uses words to become her own author of self. Opposing standard medieval rhetorical form, Alisoun's discourse begins with a discussion of marriage and virginity in abstract and flows into the specifics of both her and her husbands' genitalia. She focuses on the literal body just as she literally interprets text. This point of view underscores her carnal and fallen nature. Her tactics represent the unfair position in which the female body has been placed. Medieval exegetes gloss women as flesh. Jankyn's support of such clerical writings combined with his literal glossing of Alisoun's body in bed associates the Wife's body with authoritative text. In her case the text has been abused. Alisoun's voicing her own form of confession provides her with power to attain some salvation. She will not be forced to abuse her body by begetting virgins, a practice that Jerome and St. Paul advocated for fallen woman to atone for her sins. The Wife will not let her sexuality be empowered by 'an economy of reproduction' (p 259). After the Pardoner interrupts Alisoun, she explains that she is not only the physical representation of the antifeminist view of women, but also that she is using this tradition, specifically through the power of words, against her husbands. A dialogue is suggested by Alisoun's repetition of the words of her husbands and her own scolding voice. The carping wife may be seen as a product of the complaining husband. Her knowledge of her fourth husband's secrets places her in the position of the confessor or priest (p 265). Another mark of Alisoun's assumption of power is her threat to make her spouse's confessions public. Alisoun chooses her gossip, another female, for her confessor and doesn't seek any representative of the antifeminist tradition.

1044 Shynne, Gwanghyun. 'Chaucerian Textuality: The Politics of Allegory in the *Canterbury Tales.' DAI* 54(1994), 3047A.
Confessional prologues such as those of the Wife of Bath, the Pardoner, and the Canon's Yeoman reveal Chaucer's awareness of meta-textuality.

1045 Spearman, Alan. '"How he Symplicius Gallus ...": Alison of Bath's Name-Calling or "The Taming of the Shrewed."' *ChauR* 29(1994), 149–62.
Chaucer's using the variant *Symplicius* as opposed to the more common *Sulpicius Gallus* allows Alisoun to imply that this figure from Jankyn's book is simple in the negative sense. Having this feminine power over the names of authorities, Alisoun is able to familiarize her opponents and defeat them on her own territory.

1046 Van, Thomas A. 'False Texts and Disappearing Women in the *Wife of Bath's Prologue* and *Tale.' ChauR* 29(1994), 179–93.
The *WBP* and *WBT* reach beyond the subject of combative gender relations and touch upon 'the theme of how to love well' (p 180). Alisoun exposes some inconsistencies in antifeminist arguments: while women are considered to be of little value, their actions are monitored and while women cannot gloss, they are often the subject of texts (p 181). Antifeminism's reduction of Alisoun as a woman to mere genitalia is parodied by her (p 184).

1047 Winick, Stephen D. 'Proverbial Wisdom in the *Canterbury Tales.' Proverbium* 11(1994), 259–81.
Whiting's (**472, 1097**) concept of what a proverb is differs from Chaucer's. For example, Chaucer would label Alisoun's reference to Ptolemy (III.324–7) as a proverb while Whiting would categorize it as *sententia* (p 261). Alisoun justifies her actions through self-valorization, stigmatization, and assigning blame to others (pp 268–9).

1048 Chance, Jane. *The Mythographic Chaucer: The Fabulation of Sexual*

Politics. Minneapolis: University of Minnesota Press, 1995.

Alisoun assumes the traditionally male role of schoolmaster to teach her lessons of experience from the school of marriage (p 21). It is from Jankyn that Alisoun has learned how to use medieval mythography for her own design. Alisoun uses Venus and Mars, Venus without Bacchus and Ceres, and the children of Venus to illustrate her powerful desires and refers to the children of Mercury, Hermaphroditus, and Argus to depict negative images of her husbands. Alisoun selectively describes some of the wives in Jankyn's book in order to make herself look better and also to have the reader recall the actions of the mythological husbands that motivated these wives to be wicked. See **1445a**.

1049　Chickering, Howell. 'Form and Interpretation in the *Envoy* to the *Clerk's Tale*.' *ChauR* 29(1995), 352–72.

While the Clerk's *Envoy* is traditionally viewed as the Clerk's direct rejoinder to Alisoun's performance, its rubric, *Lenvoy de Chaucer*, confuses the issue of who is actually speaking. The *Envoy* can be seen as an elaborate piece of poetry in which Chaucer sees the multiple dimensions of a single issue.

1050　Dinshaw, Carolyn. 'Chaucer's Queer Touches / A Queer Touches Chaucer.' *Exemplaria* 7(1995), 75–92.

The Pardoner's interruption of the *WBP* highlights Alisoun's heterosexual subjectivity (pp 84–5). Alisoun's female behavior and desire are made up of exegetical discourse.

1050a　Eadie, John. 'The Wife of Bath's Non-Hengwrt Lines: Chaucerian Revisions or Editorial Meddling?' *NM* 96(1996), 169–76.

The five variant or contested passages in the *WBT* not only contradict other passages in the prologue but lend an intensely antifeminist tone to the piece, a tone far less in evidence without the passages. Since the passages are not in the authoritative Hengwrt ms, they are most likely the work of a 'meddling editor' rather than Chaucerian revisions.

1051　Fields, Peter John. 'Craft in the *Canterbury Tales*: Rhetoric and Survival.' *DAI* 55(1995), 2821A.

Chaucer employs the word *craft* to signify a character's struggle to control his or her world. Strong speakers such as Alisoun do not align themselves with the Bakhtinian category of timid speakers who prefer 'interiorized discourse to that of open debate.' (p 2821). Powerful speakers such as Alisoun, the Canon's Yeoman, and the stranger-knight in the *SqT* should be aligned with the metaphysics of Emanuel Levinas.

1052 Hallissy, Margaret. *A Companion to Chaucer's Canterbury Tales.* Westport: Greenwood Press, 1995.

Alisoun defies authority by not wearing widow's weeds. To Alisoun, the concept of unquestionable authority signifies the patriarchy. Her attempt to correct male misrepresentations of women serves to redefine 'the nature of authority' (p 106). Alisoun goes against church authority through her multiple marriages, and she champions an individual's right to choose (something medieval people, especially women, were not encouraged to do). Alisoun's personalized use of Scripture and the value she places on experience are the means by which she confronts church authority. Alisoun's language reflects dominance and her views concerning sex contain economic overtones. Chaucer highlights the importance of female relationships by giving the Wife of Bath and her gossip the same name, a tactic that shows they are 'so close that they are virtually identical' (p 118). See **1446**.

1053 Heinrichs, Katherine. 'Tropological Woman in Chaucer: Literary Elaborations of an Exegetical Tradition.' *ES* 76(1995), 209–14.

Chaucer's awareness of Augustine's allegorical interpretation of the Fall of Man manifests itself in several of the Canterbury stories. The *WBP* contains some subtle references to Augustinian ideology. Alisoun's sensual nature reflects Eve's, and the falls that Jankyn and Alisoun sustain during their fight recall the Fall of Man (p 212). Both antifeminist writers and Alisoun misinterpret the early exegetical treatment of Adam and Eve when they insist that the purpose of the allegory is to associate all women with carnality (p 213).

1054 Kennedy, Beverly. 'The Variant Passages in the *Wife of Bath's Prologue* and the Textual Transmission of the *Canterbury Tales*: The "Great Tradition" Revisited.' In *Women, the Book and the Worldly.* Ed. Lesley Smith and Jane H.M. Taylor. Cambridge: D.S. Brewer, 1995. Pp 85–101.

The six contested passages of the *WBP* cause this work to vary greatly in critical editions of Chaucer. Each of the passages is misogynistic in nature and subsequently transforms Alisoun's character from a woman who repeatedly marries to a sexually promiscuous one. Because they are clumsily written and do not maintain Chaucer's typical style of textual ambiguity, they should be viewed as scribal additions. Relying on the practices of their predecessors, many editors unquestioningly include the contested passages as authentic in their editions (p 91–6). The

Victorian emphasis on a woman's purity and its accompanying stigma against remarrying has led critics away from the medieval view of remarriage and has aided in perpetuating the acceptance of the contested passages as authentic (p 97–101).

1054a Robinson, Peter M.W. 'An Approach to the Manuscripts of the Wife of Bath's Prologue.' *Computer-based Chaucer Studies.* Ed. Ian Lancashire. Toronto: University of Toronto Press, 1995. Pp 17-47.

Through the *Collate* program, computerized transcriptions will eventually provide scholars with easy access to viewing the variety of discrepancies among the 57 mss of the *WBP*, particularly the widely-used HG and El mss. 'We can read what the early scribes wrote, and with these new methods we can go some way towards reconstructing what they read. The gap between what they read and what they wrote opens new perspectives for our understanding of Chaucer's masterpiece' (p 45).

1055 Ryan, Francis X., S.J. 'Sir Thomas More's Use of Chaucer.' *Studies in English Literature* 35(1995), 1–17.

While the *ClT* seems to have been the Chaucerian work that most influenced Sir Thomas More, Alisoun's cry against the equation of love with sin (III.614) is reflected in More's *Heresies*.

1056 Taylor, Paul Beekman. 'Time in the *Canterbury Tales*.' *Exemplaria* 7(1995), 371–93.

While certain Chaucerian characters marry at the best prescribed times, Alisoun's marriages occur when she is either too young or too old for her partners (pp 386–7). See **1449**.

1057 Weli, Susanne. 'Freedom through Association? Chaucer's Psychology of Argumentation in the *Wife of Bath's Prologue*.' *PCP* 30(1995), 27–41.

While critics debate whether Alisoun is a proto-feminist or an embodiment of antifeminism, they should take note of her honesty and humor. Chaucer may have employed humor to alleviate the tension created by the issues he raises in Alisoun's argument. He may also have drawn from Aristotle's conception of the psychology of argument in order to create a realistic and vitally human character.

1058 Beidler, Peter G. 'A Critical History of the *Wife of Bath's Prologue and Tale*.' In *The Wife of Bath*. Case Studies in Contemporary Criticism Series. Ed. Peter G. Beidler. Boston: Bedford Books of St. Martin's Press, 1996. Pp 89–114.

This history of the criticism on the Wife of Bath contains sections on the date and development of the Wife of Bath and her tale; manuscripts and editing; source relationships; and historical, New Critical, new historicist, Marxist, psychological, dramatic, and feminist approaches to the text.

1059   Finke, Laurie, '"All is for to selle": Breeding Capital in the *Wife of Bath's Prologue* and *Tale*.' In *The Wife of Bath*. Case Studies in Contemporary Criticism Series. Ed. Peter G. Beidler. Boston: Bedford Books of St. Martin's Press, 1996. Pp 171–88.

The *WBP* and *WBT* can be viewed through the values, practices, and beliefs of Chaucer's contemporary culture. Alisoun perceived marriage in economic terms. Her role in her first three marriages was to produce not children but capital that she would spend to acquire her later husbands. This practice undermines the feudal basis of gender relations. In *WBT*, the practice fashions a world in which women are almost totally in control of men.

1060   Fradenburg, Louise O. '"Fulfild of fairye": The Social Meaning of Fantasy in the *Wife of Bath's Prologue* and *Tale*.' In *The Wife of Bath*. Case Studies in Contemporary Criticism Series. Ed. Peter G. Beidler. Boston: Bedford Books of St. Martin's Press, 1996. Pp 205–20.

Freud and Lacan illuminate the fantasy world revealed in *WBP* and *WBT*. In *WBP* Alisoun reveals the nature of the fantasies that give her the license to enjoy her world without dwelling on the realities of old age and death. In *WBT* Alisoun takes herself and her audience into an older world in which the ennui of daily life is replaced by passion and adventure. Autobiography and psychoanalysis are similar experiences that use language to reveal the appetites, pleasures, and pains of a subject.

1061   Hansen, Elaine Tuttle. '"Of his love daungerous to me": Liberation, Subversion, and Domestic Violence in the *Wife of Bath's Prologue* and *Tale*.' In *The Wife of Bath*. Case Studies in Contemporary Criticism Series. Ed. Peter G. Beidler. Boston: Bedford Books of St. Martin's Press, 1996. Pp 273–90.

Contradictory camps of feminist critics see Alisoun as an advocate of women's rights or a subversive revolutionary who desires to change woman's condition. Alisoun is actually a male author's construction of women. This construction is troubling to women because they seek their own voice and do not desire someone who can only approximate their feelings to speak for them. Other troubling issues of Alisoun's performance include the fact that Alisoun loves Jankyn and his sexual skills despite the fact that he beats her and that the rapist is rewarded with a beautiful, submissive wife.

1062 Leicester, H. Marshall, Jr. '"My bed was ful of verray blood": Subject, Dream, and Rape in the *Wife of Bath's Prologue* and *Tale*.' In *The Wife of Bath*. Case Studies in Contemporary Criticism Series. Ed. Peter G. Beidler. Boston: Bedford Books of St. Martin's Press, 1996. Pp 234–54.

While Alisoun claims that she lies when she reveals her dream about being murdered in her bed, a deconstructionist may suspect the lie itself might be a lie, concealing the fact that she did have such a dream. Alisoun may have her own reasons for not wishing her audience to think she had this dream. Critics should neither perceive a literary character as having an existence outside the text nor attempt to pin the character down to one set of meanings or readings.

1063 Morrison, Susan Signe. 'Don't Ask, Don't Tell: The Wife of Bath and Vernacular Tradition.' *Exemplaria* 8(1996), 97–123.

The Friar's admonition to Alisoun about preaching reflects the church's stance against women preachers and the Lollard movement. Chaucer uses the *WBP* and *WBT* in support of 'vernacular translations of authoritative texts' (p 98). Alisoun's euphemisms for her genitalia and her body as text, reflect the 'tri-lingual nature of translation in late fourteenth-century England, from Latin and/or French into the vernacular' (p 104–5). Alisoun promotes the autonomy of readers in that we must interpret these many translations (p 109). Alisoun's references to Trotula and Heloise, women writers whose work was translated into the vernacular, support the need for texts for women in the vernacular. Alisoun's metaphors appeal to women. As Midas' wife reveals his secret, so too do women like Alisoun and her gossip share the power of secrets. Likewise, vernacular texts reveal the 'secrets' of the Latin authorities. The *WBT* deals with 'limitation and boundary' (p 119) through Alisoun's wordplay with variations of the term *lymytour* and through the rape of the maiden. The loathly lady promotes vernacular text when she attacks social preference for people who are high born and things that go with high society.

1064 Parry, Joseph D. 'Dorigen, Narration, and Coming Home in the

Franklin's Tale.' ChauR 30(1996), 262–93.

In contrast to Alisoun's rejection of the definition of woman found in patriarchal *exempla*, Dorigen accepts and defines herself according to Jerome's writing.

1065 Patterson, Lee. '"Experience woot wel it is noght so": Marriage and the Pursuit of Happiness in the *Wife of Bath's Prologue* and *Tale*.' In *The Wife of Bath*. Case Studies in Contemporary Criticism Series. Ed. Peter G. Beidler. Boston: Bedford Books of St. Martin's Press, 1996. Pp 133–54.

Alisoun should be viewed not as a weaver or a pilgrim, but as a wife, a woman who defines herself through the financial and romantic connections with a series of husbands. To understand what marriage means to Alisoun, we must understand what it meant to the culture of Chaucer's time. Alisoun neither questions nor undermines marriage. She desires to use marriage for her own financial and emotional advantage. In a patriarchal society, Alisoun uses what avenues are open to her in order to better her situation.

1066 Slover, Judith. 'A good wive was ther of biside Bath.' In *Chaucer's Pilgrims: An Historical Guide to the Pilgrims in the Canterbury Tales*. Ed. Laura C. Lambdin and Robert T. Lambdin. Westport, CT: Greenwood, 1996. Pp 243–55.

See **416** and **1458**.

❧ The Wife of Bath's Tale 1900-1930

1067 Lounsbury, Thomas R. *Studies in Chaucer: His Life and Writings.* Volume 3. New York: Harper and Brothers, 1892; rpt New York: Russell and Russell, 1962.

Chaucer's disbelief in King Arthur is evident in the *WBT* (p 496). 'Poetic treatment is allowed its full sway' in the *WBT* (p 340). See **420**.

1068 Brink, Bernard ten. *History of English Literature.* Volume 2. Trans. William Clarke Robinson. New York: Henry Holt, 1893; London: George Bell, 1901.

The *WBT* is summarized on pp 162–3. See **421**.

1069 Braithwait, Richard B. *A Comment upon the Two Tales of Our Ancient, Renouuned, and Ever Living Poet Sir Jeffray Chaucer, Knight.* London: W. Godbid, 1665. Text quoted from *Richard Braithwait's Comments in 1665 upon Chaucer's Tales of the Miller and the Wife of Bath.* Ed. C.F.E. Spurgeon. Chaucer Society Publications, 2nd ser, 33. London: Kegan Paul, Trench, Trübner, 1901.

There is a sharp juxtaposition of beauty and ugliness when the dancing ladies vanish and the hag remains (p 81). The voices of the queen, the hag, and the knight are heard in seventeenth-century speech. The hag reveals her inner beauty through the *gentillesse* sermon (p 90). See **423**.

1070 Root, Robert Kilburn. *The Poetry of Chaucer: A Guide to Its Study and Appreciation.* Boston: Houghton-Mifflin, 1906/rev 1922; rpt 1934; rpt Gloucester, Mass.: Peter Smith, 1950, 1957.

See **92** and **427**.

1071 Schofield, William Henry. *English Literature from the Norman Conquest to Chaucer.* London: Macmillan, 1906; rpt 1914, 1921; New York: Haskell House, 1968; Phaeton Press, 1969.

The concept of the incubus begetting children upon women, much like

Alisoun's reference in the *WBT*, seems to have been a popular euphemistic explanation of why unmarried women and nuns became pregnant (p 189).

1072 Hinckley, Henry Barrett. *Notes on Chaucer: A Commentary on the Prolog and Six Canterbury Tales.* Northhampton: Nonotuck Press, 1907; rpt New York: Haskell House, 1964, 1970.
The explanatory note for *SqT fairye* (V. 96) contains a reference to the *WBT* (p 220). See **281**.

1073 Canby, Henry Seidel. *The Short Story in English.* New York: Holt & Co., 1909; rpt 1926.
The plot of Chaucer's *WBT* is less credible than that of Gower's *Flor*, and the pillow lecture is an 'incongruity' (p 63). Chaucer's narrative, however, exhibits a richness of 'comment,' 'humor,' and 'pathos' (p 63) that is not found in Gower's writing. The *WBT* may be defined as a lai with Celtic analogues (p 67). Works that have been influenced by *WBT* include Dunbar's *The Tua Mariit Wemen and the Wedo* and *Advice to an Old Gentleman who Wished for a Young Wife*.

1074 Mackail, John William. *The Springs of Helicon.* London: Longmans, Green, 1909. Excerpted in *Chaucer: The Critical Heritage.* Volume 2. Ed. Derek Brewer. London: Routledge and Kegan Paul, 1978.
The *WBT* is 'a slight thing pleasantly told' (p 53), the initial lines of which are reflected in the opening of Keats' *Lamia*. See **433**.

1075 Lawrence, William W. 'The Marriage Group in the *Canterbury Tales*.' *MP* 11(1913), 247–58.
See **211**.

1076 Legouis, Emile. *Geoffrey Chaucer.* Trans. L. Lailavoix. New York: Dutton, 1913; rpt New York: Russell and Russell, 1961. Originally published in French as *Geoffroy Chaucer*. Paris: Bloud, 1910.
Chaucer uses Alisoun's character to discourage marriage in *Buk* (p 69). Her insulting of the Friar is 'maliciously roguish' (p 196).

1077 Edmunds, E.W. *Chaucer and His Poetry.* London: Harrap, 1914; rpt New York: AMS, 1971.
See **441**.

1078 Tupper, Frederick. 'Chaucer and the Seven Deadly Sins.' *PMLA* 29(1914), 93–128.
Pride in the form of inobedience appears in the *WBT* (p 99). The pillow lecture acts as a sermon against the knight's sin. Fittingly, Alisoun is full of pride and disobedience, and therefore exemplifies this sin. The *WBT*

begins Chaucer's set of 'sins stories' (p 121). The *SNT* counters the *WBT* with its motif of love.

1079 Lowes, John Livingston. 'Chaucer and the Seven Deadly Sins.' *PMLA* 30(1915), 237–371.

Chaucer treats the Seven Deadly Sins in certain tales through indirect association. A tale represents a sin through 'branches, concrete faults, or antitypes' (p 241). Tupper (**1078**) should have noted that the *WBT* deals both directly with pride and through its branch of inobedience (pp 342–57). *Gentillesse* is a characteristic of prowess, an antitype of sloth, that is an essential quality for a knight. The *WBT*'s knight lacks this quality. The pillow lecture exposes Alisoun's pride of birth and riches as well as her contempt for the poor. A medieval audience would see the connection between *gentillesse* and sloth as well as the wrath and lechery found within the *WBP*. Alisoun does not embody one sin. She is a compilation of all seven.

1080 ———. 'Chaucer and Dante's *Convivio*.' *MP* 13(1915), 19–33.

See **102**.

1081 Tupper, Frederick. 'Chaucer's Sinners and Sins.' *JEGP* 15(1916), 56–106.

Alisoun is *unbuxom* (p 96) and her disobedient character is suitable for a tale that deals with marital sovereignty. The purpose of *WBT* is underscored by *WBP*. Being unbuxom is a subdivision of the sin of pride. The concept of *gentillesse* counters the sins of pride and sloth (p 100). Chaucer ironically has Alisoun speak about *gentillesse*.

1082 Jefferson, Bernard L. *Chaucer and the Consolation of Philosophy of Boethius*. New York: Gordian Press 1917; rpt 1968; rpt New York: Haskell House, 1965.

See **259**.

1083 Lowes, John Livingston. 'The Second Nun's Prologue, Alanus, and Macrobius.' *MP* 15(1917), 193–202.

See **105**.

1084 Ayers, Harry M. 'Chaucer and Seneca.' *RomR* 10(1919), 1–15.

See **106**.

1085 Curry, Walter Clyde. 'More about Chaucer's Wife of Bath.' *PMLA* 37(1922), 30–51 [cited]. Rev in *Chaucer and the Medieval Sciences*. Oxford: Oxford UP, 1926/rev New York: Barnes and Noble, 1960.

The influence of Venus in the Wife's horoscope enables Alisoun 'to tell a story of the most delicate beauty and grace' (p 49) despite the coarse

244 / Wife of Bath's Prologue and Tale

attributes the influence of Mars had inflicted upon her. See **454**.

1086 Vogt, G.M. 'The *Wife of Bath's Tale, Woman Pleased*, and *La Fée Urgele*: A Study in the Transformation of Folk-Lore Themes in Drama.' *MLN* 37(1922), 339–42.

The *WBT* is reflected in two eighteenth-century plays, Fletcher's *Woman Pleased* and Favart's *La Fée Urgele*. Both plays contain a knight's quest to answer a riddle or face death, but not because he has committed rape. In Fletcher, the knight's lover disguises herself as a hag to give him the answer and the pair is eventually married. In Favart, the knight encounters dancing women and an old hag who, after demanding marriage for solving the knight's riddle, transforms herself into a look-alike of the knight's true love after he has renounced this love. While Chaucer's maiden is a passive victim, these plays offer a more fully-developed and active female character.

1087 Looten, Chanoine G. 'Chaucer et Dante.' *Revue de litterature comparee* 5(1925), 545–71. [In French.]

A brief discussion leads into a plot summary of *WBT*, which introduces a French translation of III.1125–30 in the pillow lecture which refers to Dante's *Purgatorio* (pp 665–6).

1088 Spurgeon, Caroline F.E. *Five Hundred Years of Chaucer Criticism and Allusion 1357–1900*. 3 volumes and a supplement. Cambridge: Cambridge University Press, 1925; rpt New York: Russell & Russell, 1960.

The *WBT* has been translated into French and German. Dryden also translated this work and Johnson retells the story. The *WBT* has influenced Hoccleve and appears in *The Institucion of a Gentleman*. References to *WBT* appear in *The Pilgrim's Tale* and in works by Reginald Scot, Harsnet, Ritson, and Hunt. Both Braithwait and Sir Walter Scott have commented upon the *WBT*. See **459**.

1089 Manly, John M. *Chaucer and the Rhetoricians*. Wharton lecture on English Poetry. Oxford: Milford, 1926.

If the *CT* can be evaluated according to rhetoric, fifty percent of the *WBT* has large rhetorical devices in it (p 107). Its main, dramatic, rhetorical devices are the *gentillesse* and Midas digressions (p 111).

1090 Snell, F.J. *The Age of Chaucer*. London: G. Bell and Sons, Ltd., 1926.

The *WBT* is related to the *WBP* in its theme of a wife's establishing sovereignty over her husband and in the similar age discrepancy between Alisoun and Jankyn and the hag and the knight. The *WBT* is inferior to

Gower's *Flor*, which avoids the 'burdensome digression' (p 209) of the pillow lecture.

1091 Cowling, George. *Chaucer*. London: Methuen, 1927; rpt Freeport, NY: Books for Libraries Press, 1971.

The *WBT* plays on a popular medieval story concept of a required marriage to an ugly, enchanted character. Chaucer uses the story to expand his theory of *gentillesse*, words that an aristocratic society were not ready to hear. The tale also conforms to the Wife's beliefs about marriage. See **461**.

The Wife of Bath's Tale 1931-1960

1092   Baldwin, Charles Sears. *Three Medieval Centuries of Literature in England 1100–1400*. Boston: Little Brown, 1932; rpt New York: Phaeton, 1968.

Of the romances in the *CT*, the *WBT* is most typical of the genre (pp 207–8). See **464**.

1093   Dempster, Germaine. *Dramatic Irony in Chaucer*. Stanford: Stanford University Press, 1932; rpt New York: Humanities Press, 1959.

See **112**.

1094   Brown, Carleton. 'The Evolution of the Canterbury "Marriage Group."' *PMLA* 48(1933), 1041–59.

Since a large group of the *CT* mss contain no reference to the Wife in the *ClT*'s *Envoy*, Chaucer probably added the stanza in order to connect the two.

1095   Lowes, John Livingston. *Geoffrey Chaucer and the Development of His Genius*. Boston: Houghton Mifflin, 1934 [cited]; rpt (with different pagination) Bloomington: Indiana University Press, 1958; rpt through 1962.

The distinctly feminine dialogue spoken by the Shipman marks his tale as being originally intended for the Wife of Bath and also shows how the *CT* was 'still in its plastic state when Chaucer left it' (p 206). Chaucer's extensive reading is seen in the hag's sermon on *gentillesse*, which is enriched by the works of Boethius, Jean de Meun, and Dante. The influences of Jerome and Deschamps are also present. See **469**.

1096   McCormick, Sir William. *The Manuscripts of Chaucer's Canterbury Tales: A Critical Description of their Contents*. With the assistance of Janet E. Heseltine. Oxford: Clarendon, 1933.

The *WBT*'s link with the *FrT* is found in all but 6 mss. These mss have missing pages. Only in the Holkham ms is Fragment III divided and the link placed after the *MerT.* See **466**.

1097 Whiting, Bartlett J. *Chaucer's Use of Proverbs.* Cambridge: Harvard University Press, 1934.
The seven sententious statements in the *WBT* are found in the pillow lecture (pp 99–100). See **472**.

1098 Train, Lilla. 'Chaucer's *Ladyes Foure and Twenty.*' *MLN* 50(1935), 85–7.
See **115**.

1099 Mersand, Joseph. *Chaucer's Romance Vocabulary.* Brooklyn: Comet Press, 1937/2nd ed, 1939.
The *WBT* contains six words used for the first time by Chaucer. See **478**.

1099a Patch, Howard Rollin. *On Rereading Chaucer.* Cambridge:Harvard University Press, 1939.
The queen's sympathy for the knight adds to the impression that Alisoun does not consider rape to be a heinous crime. The irony of the knight's valuing chastity on his wedding night magnifies Alisoun's sense of humor (p 221). See **479**.

1100 Shelly, Percy Van Dyke. *The Living Chaucer.* Philadelphia: University of Pennsylvania Press, 1940.
Alisoun's character carries over to the *WBT.* See **482**.

1101 Whiting, Bartlett J. 'The *Wife of Bath's Tale.*' In *Sources and Analogues of Chaucer's Canterbury Tales.* Ed. W.F. Bryan and Germaine Dempster. Chicago: University of Chicago Press, 1941; rpt New York: Humanities Press, 1958. Pp 223–68.
See **118**.

1102 Brown, Arthur C.L. *The Origin of the Grail Legend.* Cambridge: Harvard University Press, 1943.
As is exhibited in the *WBT*, Chaucer was aware that Arthur's Britain was the equivalent of the otherworld (p 349). See **119**.

1103 Coffman, George R. 'Another Analogue for the Violation of the Maiden in the *Wife of Bath's Tale.*' *MLN* 59(1944), 271–74.
The rape scene in the *WBT* III.882–9 bears a strong resemblance in its phrasing to a similar incident in the *Northern Metrical Life of St. Cuthbert.* Chaucer's usage of *oppressioun* in III.889 to define rape corresponds to the Latin *oppressio* found in *Libellus de Nativitate Sancti Cuthberti de Historiis Hybernensium*, which relates the violent

conception of St. Cuthbert.

1104 Whiting, B.J. 'Some Chaucer Allusions, 1923–1942.' *N&Q* 187(1944), 288–91.

The first five lines of the *WBT* are quoted in Llewelyn Powys' 1935 *Dorset Essays* (p 288). See **486**.

1105 Coffman, George R. 'Chaucer and Courtly Love Once More — The *Wife of Bath's Tale.*' *Spec* 20(1945), 43–50.

Employment of the courtly love tradition can provide the reader with a better interpretation of the *WBT*. The second book of Andreas Capellanus's *De amore* 'has two chapters that seem pertinent' (p 45) to the *WBT*. Chapter seven contains a female (perhaps Eleanor of Aquitaine or Marie de Champagne) judge's sentences at a Court of Love; chapter eight details a knight's securing 'the rules or code of love from Arthur's palace' (p 45) with the aid of a lady. While the knight's punishment should be death, the Court of Love provides him with a conditional reprieve. Another tie-in concerns the hag's discourse on gentillesse. While she is ineligible to receive courtly love because of her ugliness and old age, the hag clings to the one criterion she does possess: true gentility. Andreas and the hag agree upon all points of the origins of gentility, except poverty. Chaucer's having the hag undercut the knight's 'feudal concept of social orders based on property' exposes 'the incongruity of the whole concept of feudal society' (p 49). Likewise, his establishing a happy marriage between the knight and lady negates the importance of courtly love.

1106 Schlauch, Margaret. 'The Marital Dilemma in the *Wife of Bath's Tale.*' *PMLA* 61(1946), 416–30.

The choice of when their spouses will appear beautiful that Florent, Gawain, and, possibly, the hero of *Hen* face has its origins in folklore. In the *WBT*, the fidelity-choice the knight must make comes from 'Roman social satire and patristic denunciations of marriage' (p 418). Ovid and Juvenal both considered the hazards of having a beautiful or a virtuous wife. Theophrastus, John of Salisbury, and Alexander Neckham all elaborated on this theme, but it was extensively employed by Jehan le Fèvre in his *Lamentations de Matheolus*. This work not only provides Alisoun with fuel for her arguments but might also have contributed to the hag's description (p 420). Chaucer's decision to make use of the fidelity-choice aligns the *WBT* more closely with the *WBP*. The antifeminist dilemma, not a supernatural one, must be dealt with here.

Having the *WBT* dilemma rooted in patristic writings distinguishes the *WBT* from the Irish analogues and adds a unifying element to an expanded Marriage Group. The *MerT* begins a debate on marriage that alludes to Roman satire. The *WBT*, then, continues in such a vein as does the *ClT*.

1107   Bennett, H.S. *Chaucer and the Fifteenth Century*. Volume 2, Part 1 of the Oxford History of English Literature. Oxford: Clarendon Press, 1947; rpt with corrections, 1965.

The anti-mendicant material of the *WBT* is much sharper in its irony than Langland's treatment of friars (p 21). Chaucer shows his skill with verse in the opening lines of the *WBT*, maintaining a single sentence for the first 26 lines (p 93). See **490**.

1108   Huppé, Bernard F. 'Rape and Woman's Sovereignty in the *Wife of Bath's Tale*.' *MLN* 63(1948), 378–81.

Chaucer's innovative incorporation of rape in the *WBT* strengthens its structure (p 878). The queen's reaction to the knight is understandable if we accept, as evidence in the *WBT* suggests, that the ravished maiden is a peasant. As a judge in a Court of Love, the queen recognizes that the knight's actions, despite their sanction according to Andreas Capellanus, are not courtly and that they violate the Christian conception of love. The rape scene lends itself to the unification of the riddle quest motif with the marital dilemma story.

1109   Coghill, Nevill. *The Poet Chaucer*. London: Oxford University Press, 1949/2nd ed, 1967.

The *WBT* 'is an *exemplum* of all she preached and practised' (p 149). Alisoun's skill as a storyteller is seen in her ability to blend a depiction of Arthurian England with her desire to insult the Friar and have this beginning flow into the central action of her tale: the rape. Chaucer gave the Loathly Lady story to the Wife because it reflects her own life. See **298** and **495**.

1110   Kane, George. *Middle English Literature: A Critical Study of the Romances, the Religious Lyrics, Piers Plowman*. London: Methuen, 1951; rpt New York: Barnes and Noble, 1970.

While the *WBT* is artistically superior to other romances, it fails as a representation of this genre because of its teller (pp 24–5). See **130**.

1111   Malone, Kemp. *Chapters on Chaucer*. Baltimore: Johns Hopkins Press, 1951; rpt 1961.

The outcome of the *WBP*, domestic harmony after Jankyn yields sovereignty, is repeated in the *WBT*. The hag, however, chooses to use verbal persuasion as opposed to Alisoun's physical coercion (pp 215–6). The *WBT* is not suited to Alisoun's character, but the theme of marital harmony makes the *WBT* appropriate for its teller. Alisoun's insulting of the Friar and her discussion of what women most desire are two portions of the *WBT* that do reflect her personality. The *ShT* was originally intended for Alisoun. Since the story contains a wife who is deceived by a monk, the tale was given to the Shipman and Alisoun was given a tale with more powerful female figures in it (pp 217–8). See **299** and **500**.

1111a Carruthers, Mary. Afterward to 'The Wife of Bath and the Painting of Lions.' *Feminist Readings in Middle English Literature: The Wife of Bath and All Her Sect.* Ed. Ruth Evans and Lesley Johnson. New York: Routledge, 1994. Pp 39-44.

In the years following the publication of Carruthers' lion-painting article (**736** and **1272**) academic inquiry has analyzed the nature of Alisoun's feminism and has often concluded that the Wife is 'negative and disruptive' (p 40). Many scholars apparently wish 'to deny or restrain the one quality which Chaucer deliberately gave to this character in abundance, and that is power' (pp 40-1). Because we are unaccustomed to the presence of female power in public spheres, we 'continue to try to constrain her, to close her off either negatively or positively' (p 44).

1112 Pratt, Robert A. 'The Order of the *Canterbury Tales*.' *PMLA* 66(1951), 1141–67.

References to the Wife of Bath in Fragments IV and V support the placing of these fragments shortly after Fragment III (p 1143). Initially, the Man of Law's *Endlink* was to have been interrupted by Alisoun and followed by Alisoun's rendering of what is now the *ShT*.

1113 Roppolo, Joseph P. 'The Converted Knight in Chaucer's *Wife of Bath's Tale*.' *CE* 12(1951), 263–9.

The *WBT* is not only the story of a hag who transforms herself into a beautiful maiden, but it is also 'the story of the change which occurs in a selfish, proud, and morally blind knight who is taught to find beauty and worth in wisdom and purity' (p 263). If the reader focuses on the knight, certain scenes assume a greater relevance in the tale. The rape scene exposes the knight's true character. Many of the changes that Chaucer made from the analogues of the *WBT* in creating his own story pertain to 'the character and motivation of the knight' (p 265). It is desire for self-preservation that motivates the knight to go on his quest. In the analogues, the knight sets out with chivalrous intent. The knight both resists marrying the hag and is rude to her; however, the hag's sermon on gentillesse transforms the knight into a better person. 'It is the turning point of the story' (p 268), and it expresses the moral 'that true gentilesse comes from God alone' (p 269). Alisoun's incorporation of her own version of the Midas story is not a digression; it is a demonstration of her ability to mold stories 'to suit her own purposes' (p 268). She molds her own tale as well, emphasizing the theme of women's sovereignty 'in the rape scene, through the Queen's actions, and through the Loathly Lady' (p 269) and slighting the moral of gentillesse. 'We should not fail to note the ironic fact that the Wife of Bath cannot qualify under her own definition of gentilesse' (p 269).

1114 Speirs, John. *Chaucer the Maker*. London: Faber and Faber, 1951, 1954/2nd ed 1960, 1962; rpt 1964, 1967, 1972.

The beginning of the *WBT* shows 'the Wife's sympathy is with old nature cults' (p 148) that have been pushed aside by the church. The *WBT* is an extension of Alisoun's personality; it emphasizes her theme 'that a wife should be free' (p 149). See **502**.

1115 Gerould, Gordon Hall. 'Some Dominant Ideas of the Wife of Bath.' In *Chaucerian Essays*. Princeton: Princeton University Press, 1952. Pp 72–80.

The *WBT* is a fusion of two motifs: the riddle quest and the transforming hag (p 74). It is doubtful that the raped maiden was of the lower classes (p 75). Because Alisoun is preoccupied with sex, it is fitting that the knight commit rape. She seems oblivious to the irony of an Arthurian knight being so unchivalrous (p 79). See **504**.

1116 Preston, Raymond. *Chaucer*. New York: Sheed and Ward, 1952; rpt New York: Greenwood Press, 1969.

The pillow lecture on gentillesse 'is an elaboration indebted to Dante of Chaucer's *ballade* on the same subject' (p 247). In the *WBT*, unlike its analogues, the hag's transformation occurs at the story's end. See **507**.

1117 Schlauch, Margaret. 'Chaucer's Colloquial English: Its Structural Traits.' *PMLA* 67(1952), 1103–16.

WBT (III.975f) provides an example of delaying essential clauses (p 1108). See **508**.

1118 Greenfield, Stanley B. 'Sittingbourne and the Order of the *Canterbury Tales*.' *MLR* 48(1953), 51–2.

The Ellesmere ms order has the *SumT* come before the *MkT*. Many critics have discussed the Sittingbourne-Rochester conflict in ordering the tales. The Summoner's words never indicate that the pilgrims have arrived at Sittingbourne. In III.844–7, the Summoner vows to tell several stories about friars before the pilgrims reach Sittingbourne. His reference in III.2294 to having nearly arrived at a town after telling only one tale does not indicate Sittingbourne. It could refer to one of several communities before Rochester.

119   Makarewicz, Sister Mary Raynelda. *The Patristic Influence on Chaucer*. Washington, D.C.: Catholic University of America Press, 1953.
While the *WBT* acts as an illustration of the *WBP*, it is also a tale about educating a sinner (pp 217–8). See **300** and **509**.

120   Williams, Arnold. 'Chaucer and the Friars.' *Spec* 28(1953), 499–513.
Alisoun's insulting of friars reflects Chaucer's contemporary belief that friars should adhere to their vows of chastity and their vows of poverty (p 511).

121   Brewer, D.S. 'Love and Marriage in Chaucer's Poetry.' *MLR* 49(1954), 461–4.
While love and marriage are incompatible in Chaucer's *TC*, the opposite is true in *BD*, *KnT*, *LGW*, *SqT*, *WBT*, *ClT*, and other of his writings (p 461).

122   Kökeritz, Helge. 'Rhetorical Word-Play in Chaucer.' *PMLA* 69(1954), 937–52.
The repetition of rhyme words in *WBT* III.886–8 evinces Chaucer's rhetorical skill. See **510**.

123   Lumiansky, R.M. 'Aspects of the Relationship of Boccaccio's *Il Filostrato* with Benoit's *Roman De Troie* and Chaucer's *Wife of Bath's Tale*.' *Italica* 31(1954), 1–7.
Chaucer may have had in mind Troilo's speech on gentillesse, found in part seven of Boccaccio's *Il Filostrato*, when he composed the pillow lecture. In Boccaccio's work, Cassandra mocks 'Creseida's lowly station' (p 4) and Troilo responds 'that there is "gentilezza dovunque è virtute," and that it does not necessarily accompany high rank' (p 5). The speeches of both Troilo and the hag take place in bedrooms and occur between 'an unhappy young knight and an unattractive woman' (p 6) who possesses supernatural powers.

124   Salter, F.M. 'The Tragic Figure of the Wyf of Bath.' *Proceedings and Transactions of the Royal Society of Canada* 48(1954), 1–13.

Chaucer begins the *WBT* with the rape scene in order to emphasize the knight's transformation into a true gentleman. The fact that the hag does not refer specifically to the knight's crime in her sermon on gentillesse exposes 'her beauty of character' (p 9). See **511**.

1125   Townsend, Francis G. 'Chaucer's Nameless Knight.' *MLR* 49(1954), 1–4.
The *WBT*'s knight should be viewed as a serious character, not as a mere 'stock character' (p 1) of Arthurian romance. When compared to Gower's Florent, Chaucer's knight 'emerges as a very clear and a very strong character' (p 2). Townsend's interpretation of III.1159 relies on the shrewdness of the knight's character: he knows the hag wants to marry him, but he'll avoid this dilemma after he has secured his life. 'If we read the story in light of this interpretation of the knight's character, every incident falls into place naturally and consistently, even down to the loathly lady's accompanying the knight to the court' (p 2). The *WBT* is a fulfillment of the *WBP*; 'the knight is Dame Alice's vision of masculine perfection' (p 3). The *WBT* provides revelation of Alisoun's character up to its conclusion.

1126   Frost, William. *Dryden and the Art of Translation*. New Haven: Yale University Press, 1955.
Twentieth-century criticism of Dryden's translation of the *WBT* has not been overly favorable. The criticism stems from opinions that Chaucer's poetry cannot be translated into a better verse form and that Dryden's abilities as a translator are marginal.

1127   Lumiansky, R.M. *Of Sondry Folk: The Dramatic Principle in the Canterbury Tales*. Austen: University of Texas Press, 1955.
The *WBT* is a continuation of the aims Alisoun has in the *WBP*, for the answer to the riddle is that women desire mastery. In relinquishing sovereignty to the hag, the knight is rewarded with a marriage free from woe (p 126). The knight reforms after the *gentillesse* sermon and before he knows of his reward. He escapes woe because he has grown, not because he yields sovereignty (p 128). There is a striking contrast between Alisoun's behavior to Jankyn and the hag's treatment of the knight. Alisoun unwittingly exposes more of her nature to her audience than she intends (p 129). See **306** and **513**.

1128   Baum, Paull F. 'Chaucer's Puns.' *PMLA* 71(1956), 225–46.
In the *WBT*, there are puns made on the words *array* (III.902), *business* (1196), *head* (887f), *pursuit* (889f), and *worldly* (1033). The pun

connecting *sing* with *poverty* (1191) is extended through Chaucer's repeating the word *poverty* 11 times in 30 lines (p 244). See **307** and **516**.

1129 Bradley, Sister Ritamary, C.H.M. 'The *Wife of Bath's Tale* and the Mirror Tradition.' *JEGP* 55(1956), 624–30.
See **517**.

1130 Chapman, Robert L. 'The *Shipman's Tale* Was Meant for the Shipman.' *MLN* 71(1956), 4–5.
The presence of feminine pronouns in VII.12–19 coupled with the immoral theme of the *ShT* lead scholars to believe that Chaucer intended the *ShT* for the Wife of Bath (p 4). Since VII.5–10 contains a masculine opinion on marriage, it seems fitting that 12–19 would offer the feminine perspective on the same subject. The Shipman mimics a woman's voice (p 5). Because the Shipman deals with merchants, he tells a tale against one. The triumph of the monk over the wife in the *ShT* suggests that Alisoun would not have told this tale.

1131 Owen, Charles A., Jr. 'The Crucial Passages in Five of the *Canterbury Tales*: A Study in Irony and Symbol.' *JEGP* 55(1956), 294–311. Rpt in *Critical Essays on Chaucer's Canterbury Tales.* Ed. Malcolm Andrew. Buckingham: Open University Press, 1991. Pp 51–66.
Various passages within the *CT* 'expose the limited vision of created character and creating narrator' (p 244). The *FranT* V.988–98, *MerT* IV.1319–36, *WBT* III.1062–6, *PardT* VI.772, and *NPT* VII.3157–71 provide a unifying effect within each tale through the subtle presentation of symbolic meaning. The hag's request for the knight's love (III.1066) 'suggests that the real dilemma in the second part of the story is the wife's rather than the husband's' (p 302) and brings to light the theme of searching for love. This request reveals that a woman's chief desire is not for sovereignty alone, but for a husband's love as well. The hag achieves her desire through magical transformation. Just as the *WBT* deals with 'a problem, a theoretical solution, and a modification of theory in practice' (p 302), the Wife's character as well represents the discrepancy between theory and reality. The marriages in which she had sovereignty did not provide her with love, and those which gave her sovereignty denied her love.

1132 Schlauch, Margaret. *English Medieval Literature and Its Social Foundations.* Warsaw: Panstowowe Wydawnictwo Naukowe, 1956, 1967; rpt New York: Cooper Square Publishers, 1971.

Chaucer's alteration of the cause of the knight's journey as it is found in the analogues to the *WBT* and the additional choice regarding fidelity in the hag's proposition bring the tale into conformity with Alisoun's views of female sovereignty in marriage (p 262). See **519**.

1133 Slaughter, Eugene Edward. *Virtue According to Love, in Chaucer*. New York: Bookman Associates, 1957.

Whether or not the knight learns the lesson of *gentillesse* during the pillow lecture is unclear. His surrender of power to his wife results in his reward of an ideal bride. While absent prior to the wedding, ardor is present after the hag's transformation. See **310** and **522**.

1134 Baum, Paull F. *Chaucer: A Critical Appreciation*. Durham: Duke University Press, 1958.

The *WBT* serves as an *exemplum* for Alisoun's arguments in the *WBP*. Chaucer intended to present not a rational tale but one based in the otherworld (p 133).

1135 Donaldson, E. Talbot. *Chaucer's Poetry: An Anthology for the Modern Reader*. New York: Ronald Press, 1958/rev 1975.

The rapist/knight's transformation is a compliment to the power of women to do good (p 916). The *WBT* has been tailored to suit Alisoun's character. See **525**.

1136 Lawrence, William W. 'Chaucer's *Shipman's Tale*.' *Spec* 33(1958), 56–68.

Feminine pronouns, hints of lost youth, the list of what married women desire, and the philosophical tone of the *ShT* lead scholars to believe that the story was originally intended for Alisoun (p 58). Tupper's (**289**) opposing view is provided (pp 61–3). Chaucer altered the ending of the tale and omitted negative remarks concerning the wife of St. Denis from the fabliau source because of its initial teller. Chaucer later decided to place Alisoun in the Marriage Group and assigned her a version of the loathly lady tale (p 64). The Oxford order of the *CT* heightens the drama of the Marriage Group and places the *ShT* after the *MLT*. The link after the *ShT* shows the changes Chaucer made to adjust to a second teller of the story (p 67).

1137 Ackerman, Robert W. 'The English Rimed and Prose Romances.' In *Arthurian Literature in the Middle Ages: A Collaborative History*. Ed. Roger Sherman Loomis. Oxford: Clarendon Press, 1959; rpt 1961. Pp 480–519.

See **138**.

1138 Item cancelled

1139 Bronson, Bertrand H. *In Search of Chaucer*. Toronto: University of Toronto Press, 1960; rpt 1965.

There is a subtle rivalry among the Friar, the Summoner, and the Pardoner. All three are competing for Alisoun's fortune (p 63). Analysis of teller and tale should not be carried out from a modern perspective. The *WBT* was not intended to be a story of wish-fulfillment with regards to recapturing one's youth (p 78).

❧ The Wife of Bath's Tale 1961-1970

1140 Baum, Paull F. *Chaucer's Verse*. Durham: Duke University Press, 1961.
Both the structure and the satirical nature of the first 25 lines of the
WBT are analyzed (pp 94–6), as are the hag's discourse on poverty and
the four stresses of III.655–8 of the *WBP*.

1141 Mroczkowski, Przemyslaw. 'Incubi and Friars.' *KN* 8(1961), 191–2.
Alisoun's predilection for 'alluding *à rebours* to claims advanced by
the party with whom she had a quarrel' (p 191) is manifested in III.872–
81. A fourteenth-century exemplum found in ms Royal 7 D I supports
the claim of friars to have expelled incubi from the land. The exemplum
contains a complaint of the expelled demons against the friars' 'invasion'
(p 191). This incorporation may be a satirical barb that equates certain
actions of the clergy with some of the evil habits of incubi. The parallel
between this exemplum and the Wife's insulting of friars underscores
'Chaucer's familiarity with mendicant literature' (p 192).

1142 Silverstein, Theodore. 'Wife of Bath and the Rhetoric of Enchantment;
Or, How to Make a Hero See in the Dark.' *MP* 58(1961), 153–73.
The interruptions and digressions in the *WBP* and *WBT*, such as the
Pardoner's protest, the Friar and Summoner's argument, and Alisoun's
insulting of the Friar, further Alisoun's point of female sovereignty and
add realism to the texts. Alisoun's assertion that death was the
punishment for rape in Arthur's day is not historically accurate (p 157).
It is important that the knight face death so that he may experience
female mercy (p 159). While the heroes of the analogues to the *WBT*
have to choose the time of day their wives will be beautiful, the knight
has a fidelity clause added to his marital dilemma. The hag focuses on
issues of nobility rather than of beauty (pp 169–70). The hag's
transformation is not a manifestation of Alisoun's wish-fulfillment. She
is well aware of Eleanor of Aquitaine's belief that young men gratify

passion more readily with older women.

1143 Baker, Donald C. 'The Bradshaw Order of the *Canterbury Tales*: A Dissent.' *NM* 63(1962), 245–61.

See **536**.

1144 ———. 'Chaucer's Clerk and the Wife of Bath on the Subject of *Gentilesse*.' *SP* 59(1962), 631–40.

See **267**.

1145 Malone, Kemp. 'The *Wife of Bath's Tale*.' *MLR* 57(1962), 481–91.

According to the courtly love tradition, a woman could hold sovereignty over her lover but not over her husband (p 482). In Gower's *Flor*, the married woman has sovereignty extended to her, while Chaucer's hag yields to her mate. Chaucer's ending seemingly contradicts what the Wife has promoted in the *WBP*. The hag's power to make the knight her husband is rooted in law and honor. The pillow lecture serves to reveal her mental and moral superiority over the knight. In reward for his submission, the knight regains all he has given away. The Wife incorporates a fairy element into her story in order to wreak verbal vengeance on the Friar. The passage on what women like most is expanded in Chaucer's version of this tale because it is in keeping with Alisoun's personality. That the knight commits rape in the *WBT* most likely follows a version of the loathly lady tale that existed before the Arthurian elements were added to it (p 487). The hag is not to be construed as a reflection of the Wife. Each female has a distinctly different way of acquiring and treating a husband. While the *WBT* is escapist literature, Alisoun reveals her acceptance of the aging process in the *WBP*. Alisoun does not understand the finer points of her own tale (p 490).

1146 Wilks, Michael. 'Chaucer and the Mystical Marriage in Medieval Political Thought.' *Bul* 44(1962), 489–530.

Chaucer wrote the *WBT* as a statement on political sovereignty. In Irish analogues of the *WBT*, the hag, representative of the land, grants sovereignty to the future king. The writings of John of Salisbury indicate that in medieval political thought, the king wedded the kingdom (pp 501–2). This concept stemmed from the papacy, for in the theological realm, the Pope spiritually marries Christ to gain his divine right. When the ruler marries his kingdom, the kingdom is symbolically reborn (p 509). Chaucer's incorporation of rape in the *WBT* shows the evil of a ruler attempting to take the land by force without any legal sanction of marriage (pp 515–6). More specifically, Chaucer had in mind the tyranny of Richard II (p 518). A tyrannous ruler risked death if he didn't reform. While the knight is condemned, he is given a chance to redeem himself. Thus his reformation is central to the *WBT* (p 520). The hag symbolizes the supernatural or Christian element of kingship; the fair wife represents the governed populace.

1147 Brewer, Derek. *Chaucer in His Time*. London: Nelson, 1963; Longman, 1973; rpt through 1977.

While often disputed, the concept of gentility as a virtue and not a trait of noble inheritance illustrated in the *WBT* was a standard Christian concept of the Middle Ages (p 50). Chaucer evinces a respect for poverty in the hag's sermon.

1148 Albertini, Vergil R. 'Chaucer's Artistic Accomplishment in Molding the *Wife of Bath's Tale.' Northwest Missouri State College Studies* 28(1964), 3–16.

See **144**.

1149 Broadbent, John Barclay. *Poetic Love*. London: Chatto and Windus, 1964.

Told by members of the middle class, the Marriage Group tales treat realistic marital dilemmas. While the courtly love tradition did not belong to the middle class, Alisoun does marry Jankyn for love and she delights in his sexual power over her (p 53). While the *WBT* allegedly deals with female mastery, it reveals Alisoun's desire to be loved so erotically by a man that she will become beautiful. 'Chaucer spoils the story' with the pillow lecture (p 53). A woman wants her man to allow her to be both wife and mistress to him.

1150 Corsa, Helen Storm. *Chaucer: Poet of Mirth and Morality*. Notre Dame: University of Notre Dame Press, 1964.

See **549**.

1151 Craik, T.W. *The Comic Tales of Chaucer*. London: Methuen, 1964.

The punning and many of the speeches of the wife of St. Denis suggest that Alisoun was originally the intended teller of the *ShT* (p 68). The *WBT* is more suited to Alisoun because women have more power in this story. The *WBT* intriguingly contrasts with the *WBP*. Pluto and Proserpine argue as Alisoun and Jankyn would (p 150).

1152 Fisher, John H. *John Gower: Moral Philosopher and Friend of Chaucer*. New York: New York University Press, 1964.

See **145** and **225**.

1153 Howard, Edwin J. *Geoffrey Chaucer*. New York: Twayne, 1964.
The *WBT* is well-suited to its teller. A summary of the *WBT* is provided (pp 142–3). See **553**.

1154 Huppé, Bernard F. *A Reading of the Canterbury Tales*. Albany: State University Press of New York, 1964/rev 1967.
See **146** and **554**.

1155 Steinberg, Aaron. 'The *Wife of Bath's Tale* and Her Fantasy of Fulfillment.' *CE* 26(1964), 187–91.
Alisoun's digressions remind the reader of her presence and draw the story away from fairy and toward the real world (p 190). Unlike his counterparts in the *WBT*'s analogues, the knight is unaware of the hag's beauty and powers when he yields to her. That the rash-acting knight does not seize the choice of having his wife beautiful and perhaps unfaithful is hard to believe. If the knight is an 'unconscious projection of the Wife' (p 191), his actions are in accord with what Alisoun would desire.

1156 Haller, Robert S. 'The Wife of Bath and the Three Estates.' *AnM* 6(1965), 47–64.
See **558**.

1157 Hoffman, Richard L. 'Ovid and the "Marital Dilemma" in the *Wife of Bath's Tale*.' *AN&Q* 3(1965), 101–2.
See **148**.

1158 Levy, Bernard S. 'Chaucer's Wife of Bath, the Loathly Lady, and Dante's Siren.' *Symposium* 19(1965), 359–73.
While Alisoun's purpose in telling the *WBT* is to illustrate the benefits of female sovereignty in marriage, she unwittingly presents the opposite view as well. Chaucer's marital dilemma has an analogue in the Siren of Dante's *Purgatorio* (pp 368–9). The hag's transformation reduces the concept of marriage to fleshly pleasure (p 369). The *WBP* and the *gentillesse* sermon are analogues to the persuasive Siren's song (p 371).

1159 Miller, Robert P. 'The *Wife of Bath's Tale* and Mediaeval Exempla.' *ELH* 32(1965), 442–56.
See **150**.

1160 Moorman, Charles. 'The Philosophical Knights of the *Canterbury Tales*.' *SAQ* 64(1965), 87–99.
The knight's transformation from rapist to philosopher exemplifies the 'process of becoming the ideal' (p 97).

1161 Mulvey, Mina. *The Canterbury Tales: Analytic Notes and Review.* Woodbury, NY: Illustrated World Encyclopedia, 1965.

The *WBT* is analyzed (pp 46–8). Attention is given to interaction between the pilgrims, exhibited in Alisoun's insulting the Friar, and to parallels between Alisoun and Jankyn found in the hag and the knight. See **321** and **564.**

1162 Utley, Francis Lee. 'Some Implications of Chaucer's Folktales.' *Laographia* 22(1965), 588–99.

While the *WBT* contains numerous folk motifs, it should not be considered as having folktale analogues but as having literary ones. See **568.**

1163 Bowden, Muriel. *A Reader's Guide to Geoffrey Chaucer.* New York: Farrar, Strauss, and Giroux, 1964; 1966; rpt 1970.

Among its analogues, the *WBT* bears closest resemblance to *Flor* (p 39). That emphasis is placed on the chivalric code in the *WBT* is seen in the riddle's answer, the knight's choice, the *gentillesse* sermon, and the focus on keeping one's *trouthe* (p 40). See **318** and **548a.**

1164 Friedman, John Block. 'Eurydice, Heurodis, and the Noon-Day Demon.' *Spec* 41(1966), 22–9.

In the medieval period, evil supernatural creatures were viewed as offspring of the fallen angels. Belief in the lustful nature of fairies is illustrated in the *WBT* (p 27). *Incubus*, a spirit who takes the shape of a man in order to seduce, is a more fitting term than *fairy* for the friars.

1165 Hatton, Thomas Jenison. 'The *Canterbury Tales* and Late Fourteenth-Century Chivalry: Literary Stylization and Historical Idealism.' *DAI* 27(1966), 456A.

The *WBT* shows how chivalry may be employed for private gain as opposed to public service.

1166 Hoffman, Richard L. 'Ovid and the Wife of Bath's Tale of Midas.' *N&Q* 211(1966), 48–50.

See **152.**

1167 Rogers, Katharine M. *The Troublesome Helpmate: A History of Misogyny in Literature.* Seattle: University of Washington Press, 1966.

See **580.**

1168 Zimbardo, Rose A. 'Unity and Duality in the *Wife of Bath's Prologue* and *Tale.*' *TSL* 11(1966), 11–8.

See **583.**

1169 Cox, Lee Sheridan. 'A Question of Order in the *Canterbury Tales.*' *ChauR* 1(1967), 228–52.

See **585**.

1170 Curtis, Penelope. 'Chaucer's Wyf of Bath.' *CR* 10(1967), 33–45.
See **586**.

1171 Gardner, John. 'The Case against the "Bradshaw Shift"; or, the Mystery of the Manuscript in the Trunk.' *PLL* supplement 3(1967), 80–106.
A very early ordering of the *CT* had the initial *WBT*, not the *ShT*, follow the original *MLT*, now *Mel* (p 84). Chaucer later took the tale of Melibee and Prudence from the Man of Law and gave it to his own persona. This produced the order of *PrT*, *Thop*, *Mel*, *MkT*, and *NPT* and a debate on power and position (p 89). Seeking another debate for the *CT*, Chaucer developed the *WBT* for the Marriage Group.

1172 Holland, Norman N. 'Meaning as Transformation: The *Wife of Bath's Tale*.' *CE* 28(1967), 279–90.
The *WBT* 'starts with phallic, aggressive sexuality, regresses to a more primitive relation between taboo mother and passive son, and finally progresses to genital mutuality' (p 283). Alisoun tells this tale and behaves the way she does to her husbands because she has no phallus. Other interpretive meanings of the *WBT* include the Christian allegorical reading of man succumbing to his appetite for the world of the flesh and a mythic reading of the regenerative powers of the female (p 288).

1173 Miner, Earl. 'Chaucer in Dryden's *Fables*.' In *Studies in Criticism and Aesthetics, 1660-1800. Essays in Honor of Samuel Holt Monk*. Ed. Howard Anderson and John S. Shea. Minneapolis: University of Minnesota, 1967. Pp 58–65.
Because the seventeenth century viewed Chaucer's work as lacking in moral standards, Dryden could not excuse the more raucous tales of Chaucer (p 58). Dryden's translation of the *WBT* highlights the fabulous. While he heightens the effect of magic and fairy with his additions to the *WBT* (p 61), Dryden also distances the reader further from the story.

1174 Ruggiers, Paul G. *The Art of the Canterbury Tales*. Madison: University of Wisconsin Press, 1967. [First printing, 1965.]
The *WBT* expands Alisoun's character more than the *ShT* would have. That the hag uses authority to support her discourse shows how Alisoun has benefitted from Jankyn's teaching (p 213). See **566**.

1175 Schaar, Claes. *The Golden Mirror: Studies in Chaucer's Descriptive Technique and Its Literary Background*. Lund: C.W.K. Gleerup, 1967.
The *WBT* is more condensed than its analogues. It is nearly devoid of

character description. Single lines of detail are given to the knight, hag, and fair wife. Gower's *Flor* contains much fuller descriptions, as do *Wed* and *Mar* (pp 223–4). Chaucer's knight displays sadness when the queen pronounces her sentence and while he searches in vain for the riddle's answer. He expresses fear and torment on the wedding night. His sighs, which resemble Florent's in the analogue, are followed by joy when the hag transforms into a beauty. Other descriptive emotion is in the Midas digression when the heart of Midas' wife burns to tell his secret (pp 69–70). See **594**.

1176   Schmidt, A.V.C. 'The Wife of Bath's Marital State.' *N&Q* 212(1967), 230–1.

If one looks to the moral of the *WBT* as well as to the *WBP*, Silvia's reasoning **(596)** as to why Jankyn is alive may be disproved.

1177   Brewer, D.S. 'Class Distinction in Chaucer.' *Spec* 43(1968), 290–305. Rpt in *Tradition and Innovation in Chaucer*. Baltimore: Macmillan, 1982. Pp 54–72.

While the *gentillessse* sermond does not suit the Wife, it does reveal Chaucer's conception of class. Whether one is a *gentil* or a *churl* is not determined exclusively by social rank, but rather by how one acts. The knight is labeled a *cherl* (III.1158) for committing rape. The Wife also connects the term *vileyn* with the knight in light of his actions. Chaucer's usage of this word always carries a moral connotation, not a social one (p 300).

1178   Brookhouse, Christopher. 'The Confessions of Three Pilgrims.' *LauR* 8(1968), 49–56.

The *WBT* reveals Alisoun's class pretensions and her desire for her lost youth (p 54). See **599**.

1179   Hoffman, Richard L. 'The *Canterbury Tales*.' In *Critical Approaches to Six Major English Works: Beowulf through Paradise Lost*. Ed. R.M. Lumiansky and Herschel Baker. Philadelphia: University of Pennsylvania Press, 1968; London: Oxford University Press, 1969. Pp 41–80.

See **602**.

1180   Holland, Norman N. *The Dynamics of Literary Response*. New York: Oxford University Press, 1968; rpt New York: Columbia University Press, 1989.

While the *WBT* begins with rape, a taboo manifestation of aggressive sexuality, it later exhibits 'a more primitive relation between taboo mother and passive son' (p 16). The threatened beheading of the knight, his loss of control of the self, and the hag's implying that he may have lost his sanity (III.1095) imply castration (p 15). Alisoun's tale establishes the oppositions of paganism and Christianity and men and women, which are subsets of the larger contrast between experience and authority. Midas' ears may symbolize cuckolding or a defense against castration (pp 17–18). On an archetypal level, the *WBT* may be seen as an examination of the authoritative 'repulsive woman and powerless man' and the submissive 'Persephone and the ruler' (p 26). Psychoanalytic criticism reveals the contrast between 'phallic wounding' and 'oral submission' (p 26).

1181 Pulliam, Willene. 'The Relationship of Geoffrey Chaucer's Works to the Antifeminist Tradition.' *DAI* 28(1968), 3646–7A.
See **603**.

1182 Severs, J. Burke. 'The Tales of Romance.' In *Companion to Chaucer Studies*. Ed. Beryl Rowland. New York: Oxford University Press, 1968/ rev 1979. Pp 229–46/271–95.
That the *WBT* deals with 'knightly life and love' (p 271) categorizes it as a romance. Chaucer improves the plot of the loathly lady tale and, by having the knight commit rape, he emphasizes the meaning of the riddle's answer and the content of the *gentillesse* sermon (p 277). The majority of Chaucerian alterations to the loathly lady tale were incorporated in order to suit the tale to Alisoun. Critics have paid less attention to the *WBT* than they have to Alisoun herself. When the *WBT* is considered critically, it is usually related to Alisoun's personality (p 283).

1183 Wagenknecht, Edward. *The Personality of Chaucer*. Norman, OK: University of Oklahoma Press, 1968.
Contrary to the ethos of courtly love, marital love may be found in the *WBT* and *FranT* (p 94). In *TC*, *Anel*, *HF*, *LGW*, *SqT*, *WBT*, and *ClT*, Chaucer advocates devotion to one's lady (p 107). See **607**.

1184 Whittock, Trevor. *A Reading of the Canterbury Tales*. Cambridge: Cambridge University Press, 1968.
Recognition of another's will is the true moral of the *WBT*; it is not, as Alisoun assumes, obtaining mastery over another. The choices given to the knight are of a selfish nature; he wisely yields his choice to the hag. See **608**.

1185 Bergeron, David M. 'The Wife of Bath and Shakespeare's *The Taming of the Shrew*.' *UR* 35(1969), 279–86.

See **609**.
1186 Cary, Meredith. 'Sovereignty and Old Wife.' *PLL* 5(1969), 375–88.
See **162**.
1187 Mogan, Joseph J., Jr. *Chaucer and the Theme of Mutability*. The Hague: Mouton, 1969.
In the *WBT*, *gentillesse* stands in contrast to the transitory things of this world (pp 173–4).
1188 Slade, Tony. 'Irony in the *Wife of Bath's Tale*.' *MLR* 64(1969), 241–7.
The *WBT* should be viewed in terms of Alisoun's personality, not as a romance. Alisoun's common sense and preoccupation with sex are reflected in her matter-of-fact relation of sexual incidents. Chaucer adds an ironic element to the *gentillesse* sermon that neither the hag nor Alisoun perceives. Alisoun thinks the knight yields sovereignty to the hag because of her convincing discourse; however, the knight relinquishes his power because he is wearied by the lengthy harangue (p 247).
1189 Alderson, William L., and Arnold C. Henderson. *Chaucer and Augustan Scholarship*. Berkeley: University of California Press, 1970.
Dryden's translation of the *WBT* was based on Speght's 1598 text (p 57). Both Morell and Upton credited Dryden as a Chaucerian authority (p 58). While Morell cites Dryden for his use of *gap-tothed* (I.468), Dryden drew this expression from Speght (p 61).
1190 Allen, Judson Boyce, and Patrick Gallacher. 'Alisoun Through the Looking Glass: Or, Every Man His Own Midas.' *ChauR* 4(1970), 99–105.
Through the mirror tradition, the Wife of Bath and her words may be viewed at many levels of irony. Alisoun's distortion of the plot and moral of the Midas story exposes her as a bad judge (p 101). She wishes to be judged as readers judge the hag, yet those who grant sovereignty to Alisoun are themselves bad judges (p 103). Alisoun doesn't fit the image of herself that she projects (p 104).
1191 Gillam, D. '"Cast up the curtyn": A Tentative Exploration into the Meaning of the *Wife of Bath's Tale*.' In *Australasian Universities Language and Literature Association: Proceedings and Papers of the Twelfth Congress Held at the University of Western Australia, 5–11 February, 1969*. Ed. A.P. Treweek. Sydney: AULLA, 1970. Pp 435–55.
The *WBT* advocates cupidity and advises its audience to yield to its

carnal appetites, symbolized by the transformed bride, despite the true ugliness of carnal nature, symbolized by the hag (p 449). The hag's call to *cast up the curtyn* suggests an additional meaning to the *WBT*. An allegory of a sinner who faces death receiving the aid of Divine Mercy and Grace which lead him to enlightened salvation may be found in the knight, queen, and hag (p 451).

1192 Levy, Bernard S. 'The Wife of Bath's *Queynte fantasye.' ChauR* 4(1970), 106–22.

The knight's vision is transformed on the wedding night. Through the hag's sermon on *gentillesse*, he learns to see the hag as she truly is, as a *gentil* woman (p 109). The hag's definition of *gentil*, however, connotes physical love. She is persuasive because her husband withholds the marital debt from her (p 118). Contrary to the baptismal references Chaucer has incorporated in the *WBT*, the knight is not a sinner reformed but a sinner being seduced once again by the flesh (pp 118–9). While Alisoun promotes female sovereignty for happiness in marriage, her examples of the yielding husbands in the *WBP* and *WBT* reveal that the husband loses his virility when dominated (p 115). Alisoun strongly desires Jankyn's physical love because he often withholds it from her. Ironically, in gaining the upper hand in marriage, she loses the forbidden edge of her desire.

1193 Reid, David S. 'Crocodilian Humor: A Discussion of Chaucer's Wife of Bath.' *ChauR* 4(1970), 73–89.

The *WBT* is a mock-romance that finds the answer to the problems it poses in female sovereignty (p 82). Feminine dominance overcomes initial masculine dominance. While the subject matter of the pillow lecture is a common romance concept, it also suits Alisoun's aspirations. See **623**.

1194 Schlauch, Margaret. 'The Doctrine of "Vera Nobilitas" as Developed after Chaucer.' *KN* 17(1970), 119–27.

The hag's pillow lecture anticipates several literary works of the fifteenth century.

❧ The Wife of Bath's Tale 1971-1980

1195 Coghill, Nevill. *Chaucer's Idea of What Is Noble*. Oxford: Oxford University Press, 1971.
See **272**.

1196 Gardner, Averil. 'Chaucer and Boethius: Some Illustrations of Indebtedness.' *University of Cape Town Studies in English* 2(1971), 31–8.
Boethian elements are intriguingly woven into the *WBT*'s plot 'and become the central theme' (p 31). Boethius' conception of *gentillesse* is found in Book III of the *Consol*.

1197 Koban, Charles. 'Hearing Chaucer Out: The Art of Persuasion in the *Wife of Bath's Tale*.' *ChauR* 5(1971), 225–39.
In order to convince his audience of his ideals, Chaucer uses plot, *exempla*, and thought to heighten the persuasive power of the *WBT*. His deliberate phrasing emphasizes the willfulness of the rapist, the assigning of the riddle, the knight's entrapment in the marriage, and the hag's promise of obedience (pp 230–1). The wording prompts a listener to contemplate the ethical questions to which these situations give rise. Chaucer incorporated the more personalized elements of Alison's tale in order to make Alisoun a thought-provoking character (p 232), and the digressions strengthen the *WBT*'s unity (p 234). Hearing the *gentillesse* sermon in the context of the *WBT* causes an audience to examine the concepts of personal dignity.

1198 Magee, Patricia Anne. 'The Wife of Bath and the Problem of Mastery.' *MSE* 3(1971), 40–5.
See **628**.

1199 Murtaugh, Daniel M. 'Women and Geoffrey Chaucer.' *ELH* 38(1971), 473–92.
Alisoun, victim of time and men, refutes both of her enemies in the

hag's transformation. The choice given the knight echoes the antifeminist belief that a fair woman will be unchaste (mentioned in the *WBP*). The knight frees himself, the hag, and Alisoun from antifeminism by yielding his choice. See **233**.

1200 Nichols, Nicholas Pete. 'Discretion and Marriage in the *Canterbury Tales*.' *DAI* 32(1971), 3263A.

The *WBT*, *ClT*, *MLT*, and *Mel* serve to show that a wife's helping her husband to correct his faults should not result in her mastery of the marriage. The woman will return to her submissive role after the husband gains his wisdom. See **630**.

1201 Rowland, Beryl. *Blind Beasts: Chaucer's Animal World*. Kent: Kent State University Press, 1971.

Alisoun refers to the bittern when emphasizing woman's inability to keep secrets. See **631**.

1202 Shapiro, Gloria K. 'Dame Alice as Deceptive Narrator.' *ChauR* 6(1971), 130-41.

See **632**.

1203 Thomas, Mary Edith. *Medieval Skepticism and Chaucer*. New York: Cooper Square, 1971.

Chaucer's disdain of fairy tales is witnessed by the emphasis he places on the fictive nature of elves, and even of Arthur, in the *WBT*. See **273** and **633**.

1204 Eliason, Norman. *The Language of Chaucer's Poetry: An Appraisal of the Verse, Style, and Structure*. *Anglistica*, Vol. 17. Copenhagen: Rosenkilde and Bagger, 1972.

In order to prevent an audience's disbelief, the *WBT*'s opening lines admit this story lies in the genre of romance and contains elements of the fantastic (p 154). Structurally, the *WBT* focusses on one event, a knight's quest for an answer, yet digresses at the pillow lecture. This tangent serves to heighten the suspense before the hag's transformation (p 158). While the *WBT* and teller don't precisely fit one another, Chaucer incorporates remarks into the tale that clearly denote Alisoun's personality. The *gentillesse* sermon 'is one that nobody but the Wife could possibly take seriously' (p 171). The *WBT*'s being half the size of the *WBP* is a structural discrepancy. See **635**.

1205 Fisher, John H. 'Chaucer's Last Revision of the *Canterbury Tales*.' *MLR* 67(1972), 241–51.

The hag's sermon on *gentillesse* and Chaucer's changing the knight's choice from an issue of beauty to one of fidelity make the *WBT* particularly suitable both to its teller and as a Marriage Group tale. See **636**.

1206 Harwood, Britton J. 'The Wife of Bath and the Dream of Innocence.' *MLQ* 33(1972), 257–73.
See **639**.

1207 Haymes, Edward R. 'Chaucer and the Romantic Tradition.' *SAB* 37(1972), 35–43.
See **640**.

1208 Kean, Patricia Margaret. *The Art of Narrative: Chaucer and the Making of English Poetry.* Volume 2. London: Routledge and Kegan Paul, 1972.
While Alisoun is unable to recapture her youth, she allows the hag to do so (p 152). The ending of the *WBT* may be similar to that of the *KnT*, but Alisoun's definition of joy differs markedly from that of Theseus. See **642**.

1209 Kiessling, Nicholas K. 'The *Wife of Bath's Tale*: D 878–881.' *ChauR* 7(1972), 113–7.
While Alisoun does abuse the Friar, she is in sympathy with many of his personality traits. Her remark, while barbed, 'is also gentle and teasing' (p 117).

1210 Muscatine, Charles. *Poetry and Crisis in the Age of Chaucer.* Notre Dame: University of Notre Dame Press, 1972.
While a magical transformation does occur in the *WBT*, Chaucer does not emphasize Celtic fairy lore in the tale (p 127). See **644**.

1211 Rowland, Beryl. 'Chaucer's Dame Alys: Critics in Blunderland?' *NM* 73(1972), 381–95.
While early twentieth-century critics appreciated Alisoun as a 'vital creation' (p 381) of Chaucer's, later critics have worked to 'dehumanize' (p 381) her by reducing her to an iconographic figure. Alisoun's performance can, however, be equated 'with a modern case history' (p 395) because various elements of the human condition remain constant. Alisoun reveals her desire for both everlasting love and her youth in the *WBT*. 'That the protagonists should be a rapist and a hag enhances our awareness of the tragic irony of the human condition' (p 394). See **648**.

1212 Spearing, A.C. *Criticism and Medieval Poetry,* 2nd ed. London: Edward Arnold; New York: Barnes and Noble, 1972.
The *WBT* 'changes shape and focus halfway through, the beginning

apparently being forgotten by the time the end is reached' (p 26). The focus on the pillow lecture and the sovereignty issue draws the reader away from the knight's punishment for committing rape. The tendency of fourteenth-century writers to use concrete imagery is not always maintained by translators. Chaucer's *Be war, and keep thy nekke-boon from iren* (III.906) is contrasted with Dryden's rendering it as 'Beware, for in thy Wit depends thy Life!' (p 47). Chaucer employs repetition in the pillow lecture to enable the hag to enlighten the knight: 'the words *gentil, gentillesse,* and *genterye* are repeated 21 times in 68 lines' (pp 91–2).

1213 Bloomfield, Morton W. 'Chaucer and Reason.' *UES* 11(1973), 1–3.
Alisoun employs scholastic reasoning in *WBT.* This reasoning leads to the knight's transformation.

1214 Brewer, Derek S. *Chaucer,* 3rd ed. London: Longman, 1973. First pub 1953, 1960.
While the *WBT* begins with Alisoun's satire, it moves to issues of the doctrine of love and *gentillesse* (pp 140–1). The addition of rape to this loathly lady tale is a piece of Chaucerian extremism. Chaucer moves away from the simplicity of the traditional folktale and further into the moral aspects of human relationships. See **652**.

1215 Colmer, Dorothy. 'Chaucer and Class in the *Wife of Bath's Tale.*' *JEGP* 72(1973), 329–39.
The *WBT* is appropriate to its teller because Alisoun uses it to stake her claim against the old moneyed class. The pillow lecture manifests the tension between Alisoun's newly emerged class and the established privileges of the courtly aristocracy (pp 334–6). Chaucer should not be identified with either Alisoun or his audience. He removes himself from the tale through his incorporation of irony (p 338).

1216 Knight, Stephen. *The Poetry of the Canterbury Tales.* Sydney: Angus and Robertson, 1973. Rev 'The Poetry of the *Wife of Bath's Prologue* and *Tale.*' *Teaching English* 25(1973), 3–17.
When Alisoun tells the main plot of the *WBT,* the audience loses sight of the teller (p 60). The narrative is dramatic and moves quickly. See **339** and **657**.

1217 Pittock, Malcolm. *The Prioress's Tale [and] the Wife of Bath's Tale.* Notes on English Literature. Oxford: Blackwell, 1973.
The *WBT* lacks coherence in both narrative and morality (pp 70–9), and it does not present a static tone (pp 79–81). It has been styled to

suit the *WBP* and Alisoun's personality (pp 82–9). See **341** and **658**.

1218 Stevens, John. *Medieval Romance: Themes and Approaches*. New York: Hillary House; London: Hutchinson, 1973; rpt New York: Norton, 1974.

While medieval romance deals with aristocratic themes, the *WBT* includes the sermon on *gentillesse* which asserts that noble qualities are not restricted to one class. Alisoun, however, does not understand the nature of *gentillesse* herself. Courtly virtues are found in the knight's submission to the hag (p 58). The *WBT* works as a parable to illustrate its points on courtly behavior. The knight must learn the courtly practice of denying the self for the lover. The story does not center on its primary character; the knight doesn't even have a name.

1219 Brewer, Derek S. 'Chaucer and Chrétien and Arthurian Romance.' In *Chaucer and Middle English Studies in Honour of Rossell Hope Robbins*. Ed. Beryl Rowland. London: George Allen and Unwin, Ltd., 1974, Pp 255–9.

Chaucer himself, not one of his personae, debases Arthurian romance in the *WBT* (p 258). It is plausible that Chaucer was attracted to romances in his youth but grew to abhor them in his adult years.

1220 ———. 'Some Metonymic Relationships in Chaucer's Poetry.' *Poetica* 1(1974), 1–20. Rpt in his *Chaucer: The Poet as Storyteller*. London: Macmillan, 1984. Pp 37–53.

Chaucer employs the *amplificatio* of metonymy in the digression on patience in the *FranT*, Dorigen's complaint, the pillow lecture in the *WBT*, and in the description of Simkin and his wife in the *RvT* (pp 81–2).

1220a ———. 'Towards a Chaucerian Poetic.' *PBA* 60(1974), 219–52. Rpt in his *Chaucer: The Poet as Storyteller*. London: Macmillan, 1984. Pp 54–79.

Chaucer creates tension between tale and teller. The *gentillesse* sermon does not suit Alisoun's character (p 70). See **665a**.

1221 Carpenter, Ann. 'The Loathly Lady in Texas Lore.' *JASAT* 5(1974), 48–53.

The loathly lady of Texas folklore is most often not transformed as is the hag of *WBT*. She is ugly, possesses power, and comforts men.

1222 Crampton, Georgia Ronan. *The Condition of Creatures: Suffering and Action in Chaucer and Spenser*. New Haven and London: Yale University Press, 1974.

The Wife exhibits 'speculation, docility, and initiative' (p 180) in relation to fate and fortune. Chaucer's stories of love contain some type of bargaining. In the *WBT* as well as in the *SNT*, the bargain takes the form of agreement (p 196).

1223 Elliott, Ralph. *Chaucer's English.* London: André Deutsch, 1974. See **667**.

1224 Engelhardt, George J. 'The Lay Pilgrims of the *Canterbury Tales*: A Study in Ethology.' *MS* 36(1974), 278–330.

In *WBT*, Alisoun uses reason to discipline the knight. Through the character of the raped maiden, Alisoun reflects the exploitation she experienced in her youth. Through the hag, Alisoun represents the hopes she has for acquiring a sixth husband (p 324). See **343** and **668**.

1225 Jordan, Robert M. 'Chaucerian Romance?' *YFS* 51(1974), 223–34.

While *TC*, *KnT*, and *FranT* are more structurally complex than *WBT*, Alisoun's story has a more lucid plot than those of *SqT* and *Thop*. The *WBT* 'is based upon an additive principle of composition' (p 229). The inorganic composition of *WBT* lends itself to Chaucer's insertion of conspicuous digressions.

1226 Kernan, Anne. 'The Archwife and the Eunuch.' *ELH* 41(1974), 1–25. See **670**.

1227 Sanders, Barry. 'Chaucer's Dependence on Sermon Structure in the *Wife of Bath's Prologue* and *Tale*.' *SMC* 4(1974), 437–45.

The romance qualities of the *WBT* are comparable to the romantic elements found in medieval sermons (p 443). Unlike Alisoun, the hag uses feminine psychology, not 'cold Scriptural logic' (p 444), to establish her arguments. See **674**.

1228 Scott, A.F. *Who's Who in Chaucer.* London: Elm Tree Books; New York, Taplinger Publishing Co., Inc., 1974.

Definitions are given of *Arthour*, *Boece*, *Dant*, *Juvenal*, *Mida*, *Ovide*, *Senek*, *Tullius Hostilius*, and *Valerius* as they pertain to the *WBT*. See **675**.

1229 Thorpe, James. *A Noble Heritage: The Ellesmere Manuscript of Chaucer's Canterbury Tales.* San Marino: The Huntingdon Library, 1974.

Among the variety of tale types found in the *CT* is the feminist *WBT*. A summary of the *WBT* is given (p 5). See **348**.

1230 Item cancelled.

1231 Elbow, Peter. *Oppositions in Chaucer.* Middletown, CT: Wesleyan

University Press, 1975.

Chaucer envisioned human love and marriage as a simultaneous state of freedom and restriction. Chaucer employs magic and human yielding to illustrate this condition. The transformation in the *WBT* is an example of mutual yielding in love (pp 125–6).

1232 Jordan, Robert M. 'The Question of Genre: Five Chaucerian Romances.' In *Chaucer at Albany*. Ed. Rossell Hope Robbins. New York: Burt Franklin, 1975. Pp 77-103 [cited]. A condensed version of this article appears in *YFS* 51(1975), 223-34.

In comparison with the romances of the *SqT* and *Thop*, the *WBT* has a coherent plot. It shares a 'mode of narrative procedure' with *TC* and *KnT* and has 'a binary relationship between *conte* and superstructure' (pp 86–7). Much of the tale's expository material is barely related to the *conte*.

1233 Kelly, Henry Ansgar. *Love and Marriage in the Age of Chaucer*. Ithaca: Cornell University Press, 1975.

See **683**.

1234 Mannucci, Loretta Valtz. *Fourteenth-Century England and the Canterbury Tales*. Milan: Coopli, 1975.

Honor in one's behavior is a major theme of the *WBT* (p 137). The story resembles 'clerkish tales of dream-visions and magic' (p 146). The answer to the queen's riddle is what Arveragus yields to Dorigen in the *FranT*. See **351** and **684**.

1235 Mason, Tom A. 'Dryden's Version of the *Wife of Bath's Tale*.' *CQ* 6(1975), 240–56.

Dryden's enthusiasm for *WBT* has seldom been matched. He moves 'from the gentle to the severe' (p 244) in his treatment of Alisoun's insulting the Friar, and he captures the shock and brutality of the rape. Dryden provides a rapid and 'comically grotesque' (p 247) account of the many answers to his riddle that the knight receives. In his emphasis that the hag herself is the knight's punishment, Dryden aids the reader in focusing on the importance of the pillow lecture (p 250).

1236 Palomo, Dolores. 'The Fate of the Wife of Bath's "Bad Husbands."' *ChauR* 9(1975), 303–19.

The virile knight is in sharp contrast with the old husband who took Alisoun's virginity (p 305). The rape is not a product of sexual economics. The Midas digression underscores Alisoun's own inability to keep secrets, specifically Jankyn's guilt as a murderer (pp 312–3).

See **686**.

1237 Scheps, Walter. '"Up roos oure Hoost, and was oure aller cok": Harry Bailly's Tale-Telling Competition.' *ChauR* 10(1975), 113–28.

Harry Bailly does not comment upon the *WBT*. It is the Friar who offers criticism of Alisoun's discussion of matters best left to clerics. Bailly's reticence stems from his reluctance to argue with a woman who could gossip to Goodelief about him (V.2433–40). The Host's view of Alisoun would prejudice him against judging her story as the winning tale (p 121).

1238 Szittya, Penn R. 'The Green Yeoman as Loathly Lady: The Friar's Parody of the *Wife of Bath's Tale*.' *PMLA* 90(1975), 386–94.

The Friar aims to ridicule Alisoun by telling a version of her tale 'in a totally new moral environment' (p 391). Not only is the shape-shifting devil a parallel to the hag but the introduction of this character (III.1379–80) echoes that of the hag (III.989–90). The Friar's summoner pledges his *trouthe* to the yeoman as does the knight to the hag (p 388). Other parallels include references to hawks, dancing, transformations of magical characters who gain mastery over others, and structural similarity. See **239**.

1239 Weissman, Hope Phyllis. 'Antifeminism and Chaucer's Characterizations of Women.' In *Geoffrey Chaucer: A Collection of Original Articles*. Ed. George D. Economou. New York: McGraw-Hill, 1975. Pp 93–110. Rpt in *Critical Essays on Chaucer's Canterbury Tales*. Ed. Malcolm Andrew. Toronto: University of Toronto Press, 1991. Pp 106-25 [cited].

The absence of charity in Alisoun's life is detailed in the *WBT*. The knight's awareness that he will be rewarded motivates him to yield to the hag. The hag, then, does not bring the knight to a state of human awareness with her speech. She remains unliberated. See **687**.

1240 Braswell, Laurel. 'Chaucer and the Legendaries: New Sources for Anti-Mendicant Satire.' *ESC* 2(1976), 373–80.

See **171**.

1241 Brown, Carol K., and Marion F. Egge. 'The *Friar's Tale* and the *Wife of Bath's Tale*.' *PMLA* 91(1976), 291–2.

While Szittya (**1238**) suggests the *FrT* contains a morality different from that of the *WBT*, the author's statement may be furthered by the supposition that the Friar reverses the morality Alisoun expresses. The hag speaks of traditional goodness; the yeoman discusses the orthodox conception of evil. Subsequently, the knight's character improves while the summoner's deteriorates.

1242 Brown, Eric D. 'Transformation and the *Wife of Bath's Tale*: A Jungian Discussion.' *ChauR* 10(1976), 303–15.
The archetypal, seasonal fertility myth lends itself to viewing the hag's transformation as a renewal in which the winter of the unconsciousness evolves into the spring of consciousness (p 311).

1243 David, Alfred. *The Strumpet Muse: Art and Morals in Chaucer's Poetry*. Bloomington: Indiana University Press, 1976.
Because Alisoun and Jankyn cannot 'live happily ever after' (p 153), Alisoun tells a tale that can fulfill her fantasies for her real life. While the virtues in the pillow lecture are not what Alisoun has valued in life, fiction permits her to value them (p 155). Alisoun believes that the hag gains sovereignty over the knight, but the hag actually gains 'sovereignty over herself' (p 156). As the hag represents Alisoun, so too does Alisoun represent Chaucer. See **689**.

1244 Howard, Donald R. *The Idea of the Canterbury Tales*. Berkeley: University of California Press, 1976.
Contrary to Alisoun's insistence upon female sovereignty, the *WBT* illustrates Alisoun's wish-fulfillment and reveals that 'women want most what they cannot have' (p 253). See **692**.

1245 Oberembt, Kenneth J. 'Chaucer's Anti-Misogynist Wife of Bath.' *ChauR* 10(1976), 287–302.
Alisoun's attack on misogyny is furthered by the reasonable nature of the hag whose wise discourse undermines antifeminist concepts. See **698**.

1246 Ruggiers, Paul G. 'A Vocabulary for Chaucerian Comedy: A Preliminary Sketch.' In *Medieval Studies in Honor of Lillian Herlands Hornstein*. Ed. Jess B. Bessinger, Jr., and Robert R. Raymo. New York: New York University Press, 1976. Pp 193–225.
The *WBT* has comic elements, but its mixed literary form makes it difficult to define it specifically as a comedy (p 194). The hag's speech is an example of comic *agon* (p 201). The knight's decision to yield to his wife is a movement away from comedy towards the higher ideals that are characteristic of romance (p 218). See **354** and **700**.

1247 Szittya, Penn R. 'Reply.' *PMLA* 91(1976), 292–3.
Brown and Egge (**1241**) quote Szittya (**1238**) out of context and do not perceive that his intent is to establish the *FrT* as a retelling of the

WBT in a different moral context.

1248 Verdonk, P. '"Sir knyght, heer forth ne lith no wey": A Reading of Chaucer's the *Wife of Bath's Tale.*' *Neophil* 60(1976), 297–308.

The knight is a static character who, knowing his appeal to women, makes the most of opportunity (p 307). He is a product of Alisoun's wish-fulfillment.

1249 Wenzel, Siegfried. 'Chaucer and the Language of Contemporary Preaching.' *SP* 73(1976), 138–61.

The pillow lecture is indebted to the rhetoric of professional preachers. See **703**.

1250 Berggren, Ruth. 'Who *Really* Is the Advocate of Equality in the Marriage Group?' *MSE* 6(1977), 25–36.

As Jankyn yields to Alisoun, so too does the knight yield to the hag. Sovereignty may be defined as a woman's independence (p 28). The themes of courtly love and *gentillesse* aid the hag in her quest for sovereignty. See **241** and **706**.

1251 Diamond, Arlyn. 'Chaucer's Women and Women's Chaucer.' In *The Authority of Experience: Essays in Feminist Criticism.* Ed. Arlyn Diamond and Lee R. Edwards. Amherst: University of Massachusetts Press, 1977. Pp 60–83.

The *WBT* may be seen as a male fantasy in which a rapist is rewarded with a beautiful wife (p 72). See **708**.

1252 East, W.G. '"By preeve which that is demonstratif."' *ChauR* 12(1977), 78–82.

While Kittredge (**210**) excludes the *FrT* and *SumT* from the Marriage Group, the stories within the D-Fragment form a different debate, one that analyzes academic debate and the value of experience and authority in debate. Alisoun discusses the marriage-vs-virginity debate by combining the authority of Jerome and various Biblical texts with her personal experiences. In the *WBT*, the hag also relies on the authority of classical writers. The *FrT* and *SumT* continue the debate and, as the questions discussed become increasingly abstract, the importance of experience waxes while that of authority wanes.

1253 Evans, Gillian Rosemary. *Chaucer.* Glasgow: Blackie, 1977.

The *WBT* differs from its analogues in that the hag has not been placed under a spell. That Alisoun tells a tale in which a hag has power over a knight shows that she relates a story that is significant to her private life and her own interests (p 83). See **356**.

1254 Gardner, John. *The Poetry of Chaucer*. Carbondale: Southern Illinois University Press, 1977.

Although the hag does make use of classical wisdom to convince the knight that he should be happy with her, authority is continually overthrown in the *WBT* (p 278). The dancing ladies signify the ancient dance of the hours (p 277). See **357** and **713**.

1255 Haskell, Ann S. 'The Portrayal of Women by Chaucer and His Age.' In *What Manner of Woman: Essays on English and American Life and Literature*. Ed. Marlene Springer. New York: New York University Press, 1977. Pp 1–14.

The Wife acts as Chaucer's mouthpiece for many of his social views concerning women. The *WBT* twists the standard gender roles found in the romance. While a woman is raped, her rapist is stripped of power by women. The hag undercuts the conventional importance placed on class and beauty in her pillow lecture. Masculine superiority is also undermined when the knight must rely on the hag for his salvation. The hag's receiving the knight from the queen reverses the tradition of rewarding the hero with a woman. This forced marriage contains a sense of poetic justice for the knight who has committed rape (p 12). Through Chaucer's debasing the knight, the focal character of the romance, and by his reversing the romance's depiction of women, it may be seen that the romance was a dying genre in the fourteenth century. See **715**.

1256 Knight, Stephen. 'Politics and Chaucer's Poetry.' In *The Radical Reader*. Ed. Stephen Knight and Michael Wilding. Sydney: Wild and Woolley, 1977. Pp 169–92.

Chaucer often combined moral and comic themes. The serious mode of the pillow lecture is in conflict with the rollicking tone and content of *WBP* (p 176). Chaucer's worldly characters are more individualistic than his moral ones, who appear more as types (p 180).

1257 Miller, Robert P., ed. *Chaucer: Sources and Backgrounds*. New York: Oxford University Press, 1977.

See **174**.

1258 Owen, Charles A., Jr. *Pilgrimage and Storytelling in the Canterbury Tales: The Dialectic of 'Ernest' and 'Game.'* Norman, OK: University of Oklahoma Press, 1977.

The *WBT* echoes portions of the *WBP*. It allows Alisoun to further illustrate issues of desire and *gentillesse* (p 155). The tales of Fragment

III are united by drama and by the aggressive personalities of their narrators (p 168). See **719**.

1259   Pichaske, David R. *The Movement of the Canterbury Tales: Chaucer's Literary Pilgrimage*. Norwood, PA: Norwood Editions, 1977; rpt Folcroft, PA: Folcroft Library Editions, 1978.
See **720**.

1260   Pison, Thomas. 'Liminality in the *Canterbury Tales*.' *Genre* 10(1977), 157–71.
The term *cherl* does not have class connotations in Chaucer. In the *WBT*, the knight is considered a churl until he redeems himself by giving his wife mastery over him. It is through action as well that one can prove he is a true *gentil* (p 167).

1261   Schauber, Ellen, and Ellen Spolsky. 'The Consolation of Alison: The Speech Acts of the Wife of Bath.' *Centrum* 5(1977), 20–34.
See **721**.

1262   Tripp, Raymond P., Jr. *Beyond Canterbury: Chaucer, Humanism, and Literature*. Church Stretton, Shropshire: Onny Press, 1977.
The *WBT* follows conventional romance beginnings in its reference to the by-gone days of Arthur's court.

1263   Breslin, Carol Ann. 'Justice and Law in Chaucer's *Canterbury Tales*.' *DAI* 39(1978), 2246A.
The *WBT*, along with the *MLT* and *PhyT*, is directly involved with the administration of medieval justice in its trial scene.

1264   Brewer, Derek. *Chaucer and His World*. London: Eyre Methuen; New York: Dodd, Mead and Company, 1978 / 2nd ed Cambridge: D.S. Brewer, 1992.
Despite Alisoun's views on sovereignty, she ends the *WBT* with a marriage of mutual feelings and harmony. See **722**.

1265   ———, ed. *Chaucer: The Critical Heritage*. Volume 1, 1385–1837. Volume 2, 1837–1933. London: Routledge and Kegan Paul, 1978.
See **362**.

1266   Brown, Eric. D. 'Symbols of Transformation: A Specific Archetypal Examination of the *Wife of Bath's Tale*.' *ChauR* 12(1978), 202–17.
The hag and transformed bride reflect duality in Jung's concept of the mother archetype. The hag represents the terrible mother and the bride the good mother or anima (p 204). The transformation symbolizes a human's evolving away from the sensory world and into a higher state of psychic consciousness. The knight's committing rape signifies that

he initially operates at the instinctive level. Through the course of the *WBT* he moves toward the anima or intellect. The dancing ladies are a projection of the knight's unconscious that leads him to the hag, who represents his brutal crime (pp 212–3).

1267 Burton, T.L. 'The Wife of Bath's Fourth and Fifth Husbands and Her Ideal Sixth: The Growth of a Marital Philosophy.' *ChauR* 13(1978), 34–50.
That the knight is both a violent rapist and Alisoun's concept of the ideal man is a contradiction that stems from Alisoun (p 44). Her desire is for independence outside of the marriage bed, where she wants her husband to dominate (p 46). See **724**.

1268 Cook, James W. '"That she was out of alle charitee": Point-Counterpoint in the *Wife of Bath's Prologue* and *Tale*.' *ChauR* 13(1978), 51–65. See **725**.

1269 Mendelson, Anne. 'Some Uses of the Bible and Biblical Authority in the *Wife of Bath's Prologue* and *Tale*.' *DAI* 39(1978), 2295A.
The question motif emerges in the *WBT* in the forms of the riddle and the marital dilemma. The hag uses the questioning method to gain sovereignty. See **727**.

1270 Rowland, Beryl. *Birds with Human Souls: A Guide to Bird Symbolism*. Knoxville: University of Tennessee Press, 1978.
The bittern's call, 'a symbol of impending calamity' (p 9), is heard in the *WBT* III.972. See **730**.

1271 Blake, N.F. 'The Relationship between the Hengwrt and the Ellesmere Manuscripts of the *Canterbury Tales*.' *E&S* 32(1979), 1–18. See **734**.

1272 Carruthers, Mary. 'The Wife of Bath and the Painting of Lions.' *PMLA* 94(1979), 209–22.
Alisoun gets her chance to paint the lion in her telling of the *WBT*. While the *WBT* is sentimental, its legendary setting undercuts this emotion. Creating her own version of a medieval deportment book, Alisoun shows that wives should be sovereign (p 217). Unlike the solemn instructional books, the Wife adds the humor of life's experience to the *WBT*. While the knight views *gentillesse* as a class-oriented trait, the hag displays the refined notions that *gentillesse* is a virtue and poverty is not a disgrace. Alisoun should not be identified with the hag. See **736**.

1273 David, Alfred. 'Chaucerian Comedy and Criseyde.' In *Essays on Troilus and Criseyde*. Ed. Mary Salu. Chaucer Studies, 3. Cambridge:

D.S. Brewer, 1979; rpt Totowa: Rowman and Littlefield, 1980. Pp 90–104.
See **740**.

1274 Fyler, John M. *Chaucer and Ovid*. New Haven: Yale University Press, 1979.
Ovid's heroines, like Alisoun, are stereotypes (p 109). Following Ovid's practice, Chaucer would, at times, have a narrator place a version of him/herself into his/her tale. Alisoun does this through the hag in the *WBT* (p 127).

1275 McCall, John P. *Chaucer among the Gods: The Poetics of Classical Myth*. University Park: Pennsylvania State University Press, 1979.
Alisoun's Midas digression does not portray a positive view of women (pp 137–8). See **742**.

1276 Reisner, M.E. 'New Light on Judoc the Obscure.' *Chaucer Newsletter* 1(1979), 19–20.
See **743**.

1277 Sato, Tsutomu. *Sentence and Solas: Thematic Development and Narrative Technique in the Canterbury Tales*. Tokyo: Kobundo, 1979.
The *WBT* is well suited to Alisoun's personality (p 143). Alisoun is the hag and the hag's transformation is wish-fulfillment. While the knight charges the hag with being old, poor, and ignoble, it is the third quality with which the hag, or Alisoun, is most concerned. Such concern adds an idealistic dimension to Alisoun's personality (p 147). See **746**.

1278 West, Philip. 'The Perils of Pauline Theology: The *Wife of Bath's Prologue* and *Tale*.' *EAS* 8(1979), 7–16.
See **748**.

1279 Atkinson, Michael. 'Soul's Time and Transformations: The *Wife of Bath's Tale*.' *SR* 13(1980), 72–8.
The knight's relation to his psyche is seen through the soul's symbolic transformation from the raped maiden to the compassionate queen. The dancing ladies symbolize 'the doubleness of anima's time' (p 76). Their transformation into the hag is the reversal of the hag's evolution into the bride. The knight undergoes an internal transformation, a reconciliation with his feminine side, on his wedding night.

1280 Benson, Robert G. *Medieval Body Language: A Study of the Use of Gesture in Chaucer's Poetry*. Anglistica, No. 21. Copenhagen: Rosenkilde and Bagger, 1980.
The expressive and demonstrative gestures of the *WBT* may be found

in III.913, 1085, 1086, 1228, 1252, and 1254 (pp 133–4). See **751**.

1281 Bolton, W.F. 'The Wife of Bath: Narrator as Victim.' In *Gender and Literary Voice*. Ed. Janet Todd. New York: Holmes and Meier Publishers, Inc., 1980. Pp 54–65.

Chaucer gives Alisoun a uniquely female voice in order to expose woman's experience with misogyny. Alisoun's consistent voice and continual digressions make the *WBT* a 'realistic apologia' (p 54) of the *WBP*. The *gentillesse* sermon is the focal point of the *WBT*. Its value system contrasts with Alisoun's (p 59). That both Alisoun and the hag assume the masculine role of a clerk contradicts their doctrine of female sovereignty.

1282 Brewer, Derek. *Symbolic Stories: Traditional Narratives of the Family Drama in English Literature*. Cambridge: D.S. Brewer, 1980.

The *WBT* falls between Chaucer's fabliaux and his traditional tales. The loathly lady tales contain no father-figures and present a transformed mother-image (p 98).

1283 de Weever, Jacqueline. 'Chaucerian Onomastics: The Formation and Use of Personal Names in Chaucer's Works.' *Names* 28(1980), 1–31.

WBT is noteworthy for the namelessness of its characters (p 22). See **754**.

1284 Finlayson, John. 'Definitions of Middle English Romance.' *ChauR* 15(1980), 44–62, 168–81.

Chaucer added Arthurian elements to a folktale in order to produce the *WBT* (p 177). The *WBT* fails as a romance because it doesn't contain a knight's trial and self-discovery through chivalric adventure and because it lacks an atmosphere of *courtoisie* (p 178). Alisoun's romance fails because she is of the pretentious middle-class and therefore does not truly know about the life of the class above her.

1285 Fritz, D.F. 'The Animus-Possessed Wife of Bath.' *Journal of Analytical Psychology* 25(1980), 163–80.

Alisoun's warlike nature can be attributed to an internal conflict between her consciousness and her unconscious animus. Alisoun identifies with masculine qualities, yet in her personality, these traits are found to be negative (p 167). The hag's transformation represents an attainment of a polarity of 'male and female components' (p 173) that results in a whole individual. Alisoun's wish-fulfillment for wholeness remains unsatisfied in her antifeminist world.

1286 Gerke, Robert S. 'Fortitude and Sloth in the *Wife of Bath's Tale* and

the *Clerk's Tale.' PPMRC* 5(1980), 119–35.
See **756**.

1287 Holloway, Julia Bolton. 'Medieval Pilgrimage.' In *Approaches to Teaching Chaucer's Canterbury Tales*. Ed. Joseph Gibaldi. Consultant editor, Florence H. Ridley. New York: The Modern Language Association of America, 1980. Pp 143–8.
See **368** and **757**.

1288 Kern, Edith. *The Absolute Comic.* New York: Columbia University Press, 1980.
The issue of female sovereignty, found in the *WBT*, is part of the absolute comic because efforts to overturn the hierarchy involve the carnival spirit (p 41).

1289 Morse, Charlotte C. 'The Politics of Marriage: Power in Paradise?' *Forum* 5(1980), 265–9.
While the Wife of Bath enjoys the pleasures of matrimony, her focus on the issue of sovereignty indicates her recognition of marriage as a struggle for power (pp 266–7). Alisoun's promise to reward the husband who would yield to her is not a realistic answer to the dilemma of the unequal power division in medieval marriage. She merely wishes to reverse the imbalance. See **761**.

1290 Runde, Joseph. 'Magic and Meaning: The Poetics of Romance.' *DAI* 41(1980), 2128A.
If one seeks to provide a definition for the literary genre of romance, an examination of the *WBT* and *Sir Gawain and the Green Knight* would lead one to presume that the presence of magic as a guiding power for the hero is an important element of the definition.

1291 Schibanoff, Susan. 'The Crooked Rib: Women in Medieval Literature.' In *Approaches to Teaching Chaucer's Canterbury Tales*. Ed. Joseph Gibaldi. Consultant editor, Florence H. Ridley. New York: The Modern Language Association of America, 1980. Pp 121–8.
In teaching a course that focuses on representations of women in medieval literature, Schibanoff finds that Alisoun's performance facilitates students in determining if the *CT* reveal 'evidence of Chaucer's earlier interest in redefining women's literary roles' (p 126). While the traditional closure of the *WBT* reflects Chaucer's initial efforts 'to redefine women's literary images by changing only a few rules in the game' (p 127), the autobiographical portion of Alisoun's performance indicates 'Chaucer's new direction of changing the game all together'

(p 127).

1292 West, Michael. 'Teaching Chaucer in a Historical Survey of British
      Literature.' In *Approaches to Teaching Chaucer's Canterbury Tales*.
      Ed. Joseph Gibaldi. Consultant editor, Florence H. Ridley. New York:
      The Modern Language Association of America, 1980. Pp 110–5.
      The wish-fulfillment element of the *WBT* illustrates the transforming
      power of literature (p 114).

✌ The Wife of Bath's Tale 1981-1990

1293 Allen, Judson Boyce, and Theresa Anne Moritz. *A Distinction of Stories: The Medieval Unity of Chaucer's Fair Chain of Narratives for Canterbury.* Columbus: Ohio State University Press, 1981.

The theme of love's magical effects on one's perception runs through the *WBT, SqT, MerT*, and *FranT* (p 102). While Alisoun is a proponent of experience, she rejects the hag's experienced wisdom by having her transform herself into a young beauty (p 142). Resembling the Pardoner's rioters, Alisoun expresses a wish to conquer Death. The *WBP* and *WBT* underscore several woes of marriage: loss of virginity, loss of harmony, addition of pain, and frustration of designs for nobility (p 152).

1294 Barney, Stephen A. 'Suddenness and Process in Chaucer.' *ChauR* 16 (1981), 18–37.

The brief and abrupt mention of the rape (III.83) reflects the 'suddenness of the thing told' (p 24).

1295 Blake, Norman. 'Chaucer's Text and the Web of Words.' In *New Perspectives in Chaucer Criticism.* Ed. Donald M. Rose. Norman, OK: Pilgrim Books, Inc., 1981. Pp 223–40.

Chaucerian mss evince scribal concern with the feminine pronouns of the *ShT*, the story often regarded as the initial tale for Alisoun (pp 235–6). Dempster (**263**) has determined the second-person-singular pronouns in the hag's sermon to be addressing all of humanity. See **766**.

1296 Chamberlain, David. 'Musical Signs and Symbols in Chaucer: Convention and Originality.' In *Signs and Symbols in Chaucer's Poetry.* Ed. John P. Hermann and John J. Burke, Jr. University, AL: University of Alabama Press, 1981. Pp 43–80.

As an iconographic symbol, music may be a standard for examining the tradition and innovation in Chaucer's writing. Alisoun's knowledge of the *olde daunce* and the dancing ladies of the *WBT* represent cupidity (p 62). The Midas digression reflects Alisoun's deafness to the music of heaven (p 65). The elf queen of the *WBT* is contrasted with the widow of the *FrT*, who is compared to a stringed instrument, a symbol of being in God's service (p 73).

1297 Davenant, John. 'Chaucer's View of the Proper Treatment of Women.' *Maledicta* 5(1981), 153–61.
See **769**.

1298 Orme, Nicholas. 'Chaucer and Education.' *ChauR* 16(1981), 38–59.
The primary theme of the *WBT* is the education of the knight, not within the academic realm but in a humanizing sense. See **773**.

1299 Singer, Margaret. 'The *Wife of Bath's Prologue* and *Tale*.' In *Studies in Chaucer*. Ed. G.A. Wilkes and A.P. Riemer. Sydney Studies in English. Sydney: University of Sydney, 1981. Pp 28–37.
The pillow lecture is independent of the *WBT*, yet it tests the assertions of both the *WBP* and *WBT*. The hag's unified argument contrasts with Alisoun's string of analogies (p 34). Alisoun herself and the discrepancies between the *WBP* and *WBT* represent the relationship of 'precept and exempla' (p 37). See **779**.

1300 Allen, Judson Boyce. *The Ethical Poetic of the Later Middle Ages: A Decorum of Convenient Distinction*. Toronto: University of Toronto Press, 1982.
The Midas digression within the *WBT* is an illustration of the 'distinction of moral orders' (p 104) found in the *CT*. See **781**.

1301 Barney, Stephen A. 'Chaucer's Lists.' In *The Wisdom of Poetry: Essays in Early English Literature in Honor of Morton W. Bloomfield*. Ed. Larry D. Benson and Siegfried Wenzel. Kalamazoo: Medieval Institute Publications, 1982. Pp 189–223.
Chaucer's Theseus, Melibee, Chauntecleer, and Arthur all reconsider their opinions after listening to female counsel (p 196). See **783**.

1302 Blake, N.F. 'The Wife of Bath and Her Tale.' *LeedsSE* 13(1982), 42–55.
The *WBT* is an *exemplum* that is unconcerned with action and narrative. It continues the theme of marital harmony found in the *WBP* (p 52). The tales of Fragment III are unified by the theme of tyranny. See **784**.

1303 Gallacher, Patrick J. 'Dame Alice and the Nobility of Pleasure.' *Viator* 13(1982), 275–93.
In the *WBT* Chaucer connects Dante's views of *gentillesse* and those

on the need for pleasure in virtue found in the *Conv*. The pleasure principles of the *WBP* and *WBT* include 'pleasure as the perfection of an activity; the possibility of pleasure in spite of pain; and the conclusive effect of bodily pleasure' (p 279). The concept that different things have varying perfections in the *WBT* discloses the 'nobility of authentic pleasure' (p 283), and bodily and mental pleasure fulfill the virtue of *gentillesse*. Alisoun's speech about Job in the *WBP* (III.431–7) mocks the concept of the joy in pain that is pleasure (pp 285–7), yet she uses this idea when she reveals her dream to Jankyn and later comes to enjoy his abuse.

1304 Wasserman, Julian N. 'The Ideal and the Actual: The Philosophical Unity of the *Canterbury Tales*, MS Group III.' *Allegorica* 7(1982), 65–99.

See **790**.

1305 Bishop, Ian. 'Chaucer and the Rhetoric of Consolation.' *MA* 52(1983), 38–50.

Because of Chaucer's awareness of the delicate nature of consolation, he at time treats the handling of grief with irony. The hag's consolation of the knight on their wedding night is a comic presentation of *amplificatio* and *abbreviatio* (p 48). The hag chooses not to discuss her ugliness or her age but focuses on her lack of *gentillesse*, her least-offensive category to the knight. The hag works to have the knight's choice yielded to herself by wearying him with her lengthy speech.

1306 Cooper, Helen. *The Structure of the Canterbury Tales*. London: Duckworth, 1983.

While there is a Marriage Group, Chaucer did not textually unite these thematic tales. The structure of Fragment III resembles that of Fragment I: a romance, a parody of a romance, and a tale that relates to the second story (p 125). Fragment III contains much dramatic interaction. The *WBT* fits its teller both psychologically and rhetorically, and presents Alisoun's romantic, idealistic side. The Friar attacks Alisoun's idealism and the *FrT* contains parallels to the *WBT*. The Summoner responds to the Friar's personal attack by creating a character who resembles the Friar.

1307 Costigan, Edward. '"Privetee" in the *Canterbury Tales*.' *Studies in English Literature* 60(1983), 217–30.

The phrase *Privee and apart* (III.1114) connotes a positive synthesis between 'personal honour and public reputation' (p 218) with respect to *gentillesse*. Ideally, marriage represents a union of private lives in a public light. The knight does not want to make his marriage to the hag public and weds her in private. See **792**.

1308 Gussenhoven, Sister Frances, RSHM. 'Shakespeare's *Taming of the Shrew* and Chaucer's Wife of Bath: The Struggle for Marital Mastery.' In *Chaucerian Shakespeare: Adaptation and Transformation*. Medieval and Renaissance Monograph Series, 2. Ed. E. Talbot Donaldson and Judith J. Kollmann. Ann Arbor: Michigan Consortium for Medieval and Early Modern Studies, 1983. Pp 69–79.
See **794**.

1309 Harris, Jocelyn. 'Anne Elliot, the Wife of Bath, and Other Friends.' *W&L* 3(1983), 273–93.
Anne Elliot's opinion of the unfairness of books being the tools of men suggests that Jane Austen was familiar with Chaucer's works. Anne, like the hag, changes from a loathly creature into a beautiful woman, albeit through the return of her health and not through magic (p 275). The theme of *gentillesse* is also found in *Persuasion*. The mastery of one spouse over the other is seen as negative in Austen's novel and female constancy is upheld.

1310 Havely, Nicholas. 'Chaucer, Boccaccio, and the Friars.' In *Chaucer and the Italian Trecento*. Ed. Piero Boitani. Cambridge: Cambridge University Press, 1983. Pp 249–68.
The Summoner and the Wife of Bath compare friars to flies, dust, and bees. Through his characters, Chaucer aligns friars with hectic activity, as does Boccaccio (p 249).

1311 Kirkpatrick, Robin. 'The Wake of the *Commedia*: Chaucer's *Canterbury Tales* and Boccaccio's *Decameron*.' In *Chaucer and the Italian Trecento*. Ed. Piero Boitani. Cambridge: Cambridge University Press, 1983. Pp 201–30.
Both the *WBP* and the *WBT* contain an examination of the commingling of the language of authority and experience. Dante's *Conv*, which contains the hag's philosophy on nobility, questions the nature of authority (p 215). See **796**.

1312 Kollmann, Judith J. '"Ther is noon oother incubus but he": The *Canterbury Tales, Merry Wives of Windsor*, and Falstaff.' In *Chaucerian Shakespeare: Adaptation and Transformation*. Medieval and Renaissance Monograph Series, 2. Ed. E. Talbot Donaldson and Judith J. Kollmann. Ann Arbor: Michigan Consortium for Medieval and

Early Modern Studies, 1983. Pp 43–68.
See **797**.

1313 Patterson, Lee. '"For the Wyves love of Bathe": Feminine Rhetoric and Poetic Resolution in the *Roman de la Rose* and the *Canterbury Tales.*' *Spec* 58(1983), 656–95.
In the *WBT* what is base is elevated and cleansed (p 681). Alisoun is aware, though, of the unrealistic perfection of her tale. While antifeminism is used by the female voice of the *WBP* to expound feminine truths, the feminine Arthurian romance of the *WBT* and its teller's voice undermines the patriarchal practices of 'property and inheritance' (p 682). Alisoun is limited by her dependence on masculine language for the expression of her ideas, and feminine desire is ultimately dependent on masculine desire. See **801**.

1314 Roney, Lois. 'The Theme of Protagonist's Intention Versus Actual Outcome in the *Canterbury Tales.*' *ES* 64(1983), 193–200.
The knight intends to save his life with the riddle's answer, but finds that his promise gains him an undesirable wife. In the *WBT*'s analogues, the male knows he must marry the hag in order to save himself.

1315 Sturges, Robert S. 'The *Canterbury Tales*' Women Narrators: Three Traditions of Female Authority.' *MLS* 13(1983), 41–51.
Female authority is found in the *WBT* when the knight falls under the judgment of the queen and her ladies. The hag, in addition to these women, focuses on the task of educating the knight in understanding how the sexes should relate to each other (p 45). In telling this tale where women use power justly, Alisoun becomes a fulfillment of her own wish for a female poetic tradition that will endow women with power. See **804**.

1316 Traversi, Derek Antona. *The Canterbury Tales: A Reading.* London: Bodley Head; Newark: University of Delaware Press, 1983.
The friar's replacement of the incubus represents the imposition of the Christian view of sexuality on the *olde daunce* of pagan times (pp 111–3). Despite her advocacy of female sovereignty, Alisoun is aware of the true condition of her gender. The hag represents Alisoun's concern with her advancing age and the knight is reflective of Jankyn. It is through the fantasy of the *WBT* that Alisoun can still win a youthful husband (p 117). The *gentillesse* sermon reflects the *CT* theme of pilgrimage and advocates acceptance and patience. The reconciliation between the knight and the hag provides a harmony beyond the uneasy

292 / *Wife of Bath's Prologue and Tale*

truce Alisoun establishes with Jankyn. See **805**.

1317 Waterhouse, Ruth, and John Stephens. 'The Backward Look: Retrospectivity in Medieval Literature.' *SoRA* 16(1983), 356–73. See **185**.

1318 Adams, Roberta E. 'Chaucer's Wife of Bath and Marriage in Fourteenth-Century England.' *DAI* 44(1984), 3069A.

Two fourteenth-century books of conduct, *Le livre du chevalier de la Tour Landry* and *Le Menagier de Paris*, outlined the medieval definition of a good wife and were used to instruct women as to how they should behave. Through the *WBT*, Alisoun creates a code of conduct for husbands and shows the need for bliss and equality in marriage. See **808**.

1319 Ando, Shinsuki. 'A Note on Line 1196 of the *Wife of Bath's Tale.*' *Poetica* 15/16(1984), 154–9.

Bryngere out of bisynesse (III.1196) is best translated as 'remover of worries.'

1320 Arthur, Ross G. 'A Head for a Head: A Testamental Template for *Sir Gawain and the Green Knight* and the *Wife of Bath's Tale.*' *Florilegium* 6(1984), 178–94.

In the *WBT*, the knight is faced with the Old Testament justice of losing his head for taking a maidenhead. His quest leads him to fulfill the letter of the law and discover what women want (p 189). His yielding sovereignty to the hag fulfills the spirit of the law. The hag's transformation, which is not explained as it is in the analogues, is a true gift of mercy.

1321 Brewer, Derek. *An Introduction to Chaucer*. London: Longman, 1984. Chaucer alters the loathly lady tale so that the *WBT* may suit Alisoun's personality (p 207). He adds the fidelity clause to the marital dilemma because he wishes to highlight the realities of human relationships. The *WBT* supports marriages in which the ego yields to trust and love. See **813**.

1322 ———. 'The Rationalism of Chaucer.' In *Chaucer: The Poet as Storyteller*. London: Macmillan, 1984. Pp 120–9.

Chaucer makes fun of Arthurian romance in *WBT* and *Thop* (p 127). See **814**.

1323 Leicester, H. Marshall, Jr. 'Of a Fire in the Dark: Public and Private Feminism in the *Wife of Bath's Tale.*' *Women's Studies* 11(1984), 157–78.

The moral and feminist thoughts of the *WBT* belong to the public form of feminism. Alisoun takes a public stand and redefines the traditional, male-dominated tale (pp 159–60). The differences between the *WBT* and its analogues are evidence of this movement. In the Midas digression, Alisoun details the realistic struggles of woman's 'submission to and manipulation of masculine egos' (p 164). That no woman in the tale actually claims that the knight has the correct answer suggests that Alisoun is aware of the private nature of the question. By telling her tale Alisoun comes to realize that her vitality and spirit have not abandoned her with the passing of her youth (p 172).

1324 Meyer, Robert J. 'Chaucer's Tandem Romances: A Generic Approach to the *Wife of Bath's Tale* as Palinode.' *ChauR* 18(1984), 221–38.
Chaucer has fashioned the *WBT* so that it might challenge and rise above its premise of female sovereignty. The genre of romance provides Chaucer with the means of illustrating Alisoun's divided personality (p 229). The *WBT* consists of two romances. The first, or the mock romance, concludes with the knight's answer to the queen's riddle. The hero has not grown during his quest. The knight's attitude towards the chivalric code reflects Alisoun's association with matrimony. The hag's request for marriage begins the second romance (p 231). Alisoun's regret for her lost virginity is seen in the knight's passive behavior on his wedding night. The *gentillesse* sermon treats what men most desire and challenges the knight's conception of love and marriage (p 232). Through the telling of her tale, Alisoun realizes the vanity of most love and finds in fiction a healing love, something her life has lacked (p 233).

1325 Murphy, Ann B. 'The Process of Personality in Chaucer's *Wife of Bath's Tale*.' *Centennial Review* 28(1984), 204–22.
While tradition and her environment hinder Alisoun from realizing what she desires, her tale offers a chance for her to explore this issue (p 219). Chaucer exposes the conflict between standard morality and emotion when he alters the marital dilemma to focus on an issue of power as opposed to one of pride (p 220). See **381** and **823**.

1326 Peck, Russell A. 'Biblical Interpretation: St. Paul and the *Canterbury Tales*.' In *Chaucer and Scriptural Tradition*. Ed. David Lyle Jeffrey. Ottawa: University of Ottawa Press, 1984. Pp 143–70.
The hag's request to be respected for her wisdom is something rarely granted to a medieval woman (p 160). The hag's transformation is reflective of the Pauline advocacy of moving from the letter to the spirit

of the law (pp 165-6). See **824**.

1327 Quinn, Esther C. 'Chaucer's Arthurian Romance.' *ChauR* 18(1984), 211–20.

Because the *WBT* may have been initially written as an Arthurian romance without Alisoun or the loathly lady tales in mind, it should be examined in relation to other Arthurian romances. The *WBT* has extensive parallels to both *Sir Gawain and the Green Knight* and Marie de France's *Lanval*. Having Alisoun narrate the *WBT* underscores its fairy-tale elements.

1328 Robertson, D.W., Jr. 'The Wife of Bath and Midas.' *SAC* 6(1984), 1–20.

Since the word *wife* was associated exegetically with sensuality, Midas' betrayal by his wife can be interpreted as his betrayal by his senses (p 11). Alisoun reflects both Midas and her version of his wife. The knight, like Midas, cannot elevate his reason above his senses. The hag's promise to satisfy him prompts him to yield to her. See **827**.

1329 Ruggiers, Paul. *Editing Chaucer: The Great Tradition*. Norman, OK: Pilgrim Books, 1984.

Tyrwhitt believed *Flor* was a source for the *WBT* (p 136). He was also familiar with the more scholarly sources as well as *Mar*. See **828**.

1330 Sklute, Larry. *Virtue of Necessity: Inconclusiveness and Narrative Form in Chaucer's Poetry*. Columbus: Ohio State University Press, 1984.

Because her tale is autobiographical, Alisoun represents a fusion of fiction and reality (p 118). The *FrT* has no relation to the *WBT*. See **382**.

1331 Blake, N.F. *The Textual Tradition of the Canterbury Tales*. London: Edward Arnold, 1985.

See **830**.

1332 Blanch, Robert J. '"Al was this land fulfild of fayerye": The Thematic Employment of Force, Willfulness, and Legal Convention in Chaucer's *Wife of Bath's Tale*.' *SN* 57(1985), 41–51.

Willed force is illustrated in the incubus reference in the *WBT* as well as in the knight's rape of the maiden. Alisoun's reliance on fourteenth-century punishments in her tale is anachronistic (p 44). The queen's petition for Arthur's power violates the judicial process, inverts hierarchical order, and gives the knight no choice but to comply with her intent. The knight's offering property to avoid marrying the hag comments upon a common solution for rape in Arthurian times (p 46). The hag does not allow the knight to have a choice and uses the law to legitimize her desires.

1333 Item cancelled.

1334 Ferster, Judith. *Chaucer on Interpretation.* Cambridge: Cambridge University Press, 1985.
Much like Midas' wife, Alisoun cannot keep the secrets of her marriage. Speech acts as a purge for Alisoun (p 133). While the Midas digression casts a negative light on Alisoun, she tells it to assert that speech 'has no consequences' (p 136). The knight's use of speech to redeem himself counters this opinion. See **836**.

1335 Frese, Dolores Warwick. 'Chaucer's *Canterbury Tales* and the Arthurian Tradition: Thematic Transmissions/Aesthetic Transpositions.' In *Actes du 14ᵉ Congrès International Arthurien.* Ed. Charles Foulon et al. Rennes: Presses Universitaires, 1985. Pp 184–204.
Both Chaucer's *WBT* and Chrétien's *Perceval* contain psychological realism. The *WBT*'s ties to the Sovereignty of Ireland myths connect the tale to seasonal fertility themes that here have Christian overtones (pp 192–3).

1336 Kawasaki, Masatoshi. 'From Conflict to Harmony — in Case of the Wife of Bath.' In *Symposium on the Wife of Bath.* Medieval English Studies Symposia 2. Ed. Hisashi Shigeo, Hisao Tsuru, Isamu Saito, and Tadahiro Ikegami. Tokyo: Gaku Shobo, 1985. Pp 123–42. [In Japanese.] See **842**.

1337 Lindskoog, Verna de Jong. 'Chaucer's Wife of Bath: Critical Approaches in the Twentieth Century.' *DAI* 45(1985), 2520A.
See **384**.

1338 Pearsall, Derek. *The Canterbury Tales.* London: George Allen and Unwin, 1985.
The transformation tale has its roots in the human psyche (p 86). To Alisoun, the knight's committing rape is an attack against all women. The object of the pillow lecture is to strip the negative, patriarchal influence away from the knight and reform him into Alisoun's image (p 88). The true transformation that occurs is the knight's. Through his reform, Alisoun, represented by the hag, is allowed to bring forth her love and become transformed as well. See **845**.

1339 Reiss, Edmund. 'Romance.' In *The Popular Literature of Medieval England.* Tennessee Studies in Literature, 28. Ed. Thomas J. Heffernan.

Knoxville: The University of Tennessee Press, 1985. Pp 108–30.

The court of Richard II was probably familiar with the loathly lady tale before it was exposed to the *WBT* (p 111).

1340 Smallwood, T.M. 'Chaucer's Distinctive Digressions.' *SP* 82(1985), 437–49.

Chaucer shows unique narrative skill in his employment of digressions. Six of the *CT* contain significant digressions which do not further the narrative being told. These digressions primarily deal with general wisdom that relates to the specific issues of the individual tale (p 439). The *WBT* contains a 'two-fold digression.... The tale opens with five lines of narrative (III.857–61), then is briefly interrupted in lines 862–81 by the Wife's playful attack on friars; the narrative resumes for forty-nine lines (III.882–930) before a further digression of fifty-two lines ...' (p 438). These digressions maintain the readers' awareness of Alisoun as narrator. Chaucer attributes more enlightened qualities to the hag than other authors have given to her counterpart in the *WBT*'s analogues.

1341 Spearing, A.C. *Medieval to Renaissance in English Poetry.* Cambridge: Cambridge University Press, 1985.

That Chaucer was not an advocate of Arthurian romance is exemplified by its absence, except for the slight reference in the *WBT*. The fabulous elements of the *WBT* are incorporated by its teller for the sake of wish-fulfillment (p 36). The sermon on *gentillesse* is appropriate for Alisoun and Chaucer to tell, for both of them stem from self-made, middle class origins (p 98). Chaucer's penchant for summary is found in the *WBT*, which focuses on the central narrative after only 17 lines of introduction (p 169). The *WBP*, in relation to the *WBT*, shows two genres that depict relationships: fabliau and romance (p 216).

1342 Tsuru, Hisao. 'Alison's Sorrow — Her Old Age and Marriages.' In *Symposium on the Wife of Bath.* Medieval English Studies Symposia 2. Ed. Hisashi Shigeo, Hisao Tsuru, Isamu Saito, and Tadahiro Ikegami. Tokyo: Gaku Shobo, 1985. Pp 143–65. [In Japanese.]

See **851**.

1343 Williams, Michael E. 'Three Metaphors of Criticism and the *Wife of Bath's Tale.*' *ChauR* 20(1985), 144–57.

See **852**.

1344 Benson, C. David. 'The *Canterbury Tales*: Personal Drama or Experiments in Poetic Variety.' In *The Cambridge Chaucer*

Companion. Ed. Piero Boitani and Jill Mann. Cambridge: Cambridge University Press, 1986. Pp 93–108.

The hag's gentle discourse does not reflect the Alisoun of the *WBP* (p 102). See **856.**

1345   Burrow, J.A. 'The *Canterbury Tales* I: Romance.' In *The Cambridge Chaucer Companion.* Ed. Piero Boitani and Jill Mann. Cambridge: Cambridge University Press, 1986. Pp 109–24.

The five romances in the *CT* do not conform to the traditions of the genre. The *WBT* mentions Arthur as an opening reference, but it goes on to reveal comedy. Alisoun describes the Arthurian past as an age that was good for women, for in her tale females have power (p 111).

1346   ———. 'Chaucer's Canterbury Pilgrimage.' *EIC* 36(1986), 97–119.

While the Host and Friar are known for their direct insults, the Wife of Bath indulges in 'sly provocations' (p 106).

1347   Chmaitelli, Nancy Adelyne. 'The Theme of Synagogue, Ecclesia, and the Whore of Babylon in the Visual Arts and in the Poetry of Dante and Chaucer: A Background Study for Chaucer's Wife of Bath.' *DAI* 47(1986), 1722A–23A.

Certain imagery surrounding the Wife of Bath is indicative of the Synagogue and the Whore of Babylon, two themes with a detailed iconographic history. The *WBT* is a story of another character who recalls the Synagogue theme, the hag, who is transformed into a beautiful maid, an Ecclesia figure.

1348   Disbrow, Sarah. 'The Wife of Bath's Old Wives' Tale.' *SAC* 8(1986), 59–71.

Alisoun tells an Arthurian romance because its folktale elements underscore her image as an allegorical figure of carnality. Her old wives' tale further associates her with the Old Testament (p 61), for it is linked with Jewish oral tradition (p 64). Alisoun's presentation of pagan superstition is as ridiculous as her literal reading of the Old Testament in the *WBP* (p 71).

1349   Fleming, Martha. 'Repetition and Design in the *Wife of Bath's Tale.*' In *Chaucer in the Eighties.* Ed. Julian N. Wasserman and Robert J. Blanch. Syracuse: Syracuse University Press, 1986. Pp 151–61.

The *WBT* reveals little about Alisoun. Chaucer has assigned it to Alisoun for realistic purposes, but his main intent was to compare and contrast this tale with the other romances in the *CT* (p 153), specifically the *KnT.* The *WBP* and *WBT* illustrate the concepts of interpretation and misinterpretation (p 155). The meanings of *maistrye* and *sovereignty* have been misconstrued. Alisoun desires authority over her possessions, not dominance in marriage. The importance of the *WBT* lies in its presentation of shameful acts and the taking of vows.

1350   Fradenburg, Louise O. 'The Wife of Bath's Passing Fancy.' *SAC* 8(1986), 31–58.

The *WBP* and *WBT* exhibit a historical sense of the romance in which the nature of desire is viewed against the passing of feudalism (p 56). For Alisoun, the romance's only hope rests in reformation. Her performance highlights the process by which 'woman is constructed and bodies and texts feminized' (p 34). The post-feudal era marks a contrast between the romanticized past and the more practical future. Courtly love affirms masculine, aristocratic sexuality and makes the female an absent referent (p 39). The capitalistic era views fantasy as feminine and as a luxury. Alisoun's desire to tell a romance reflects her desire 'to renew the worn world' (p 43). The escapist element of the romance is indicative of 'the genre's potential as an instrument of change' (p 41). The *WBT* represents the 'enclosure of the woman in the interior of her desire' (p 44). That the hag's character challenges the social and sexual hierarchies is representative of the realistic threats women and the lower classes pose to tradition (p 52).

1351   Green, Donald C. 'The Semantics of Power: *Maistrie* and *Soveraynetee* in the *Canterbury Tales.' MP* 84(1986), 18–23.
See **861**.

1352   Grennen, Joseph E. 'The Wife of Bath and the Scholastic Concept of *Operatio.' JRMMRA* 7(1986), 41–8.

Alisoun's valuing of experience, which may be linked to the Aristotelian concept of *operatio*, is reflected in the hag's assertion that *gentillesse* stems from 'performance, practice, [and] works' (p 42). In light of this common bond, the pillow lecture does not seem as inconsistent with Alisoun's personality.

1353   Knight, Stephen. *Geoffrey Chaucer*. Oxford: Basil Blackwell, 1986.

The *WBT* emphasizes the threatening aspects of three traditional romance motifs: the hero's violence, the woman's power to aid the hero, and the hero's isolation and individuality (p 101). While the hag makes radical statements concerning *gentillesse* and poverty, she ultimately adheres to conservative cultural norms. She also does not maintain sovereignty as Alisoun does but yields it in turn to her husband. See **864**.

1354 Long, Walter C. 'The Wife of Bath as Moral Revolutionary.' *ChauR* 20(1986), 273–84.
See **866**.

1355 Mehl, Dieter. *Geoffrey Chaucer: An Introduction to His Narrative Poetry*. Cambridge: Cambridge University Press, 1986.
The *WBT* and *PardT* strongly reflect the personalities revealed in the prologues of their tellers (p 145). The *WBT* exemplifies an antifeminist dilemma addressed in the *WBP*. Alisoun's narrative presentation, however, is not entirely characteristic of her personality. While ostensibly a romance with some fabliau elements, the *WBT* addresses social and moral dilemmas (p 171). Its fairy-tale setting distances the reader. See **867**.

1356 Olson, Paul A. *The Canterbury Tales and the Good Society*. Princeton: Princeton University Press, 1986.
See **868**.

1357 Amsler, Mark. 'The Wife of Bath and Women's Power.' *Assays* 4(1987), 67–83.
See **874**.

1358 Bishop, Ian. *The Narrative Art of the Canterbury Tales: A Critical Study of the Major Poems*. London: Everyman's University Library; Dent, 1987.
The *WBT* is both the exemplum of the *WBP* and an example offered by Alisoun to young husbands (p 125). Alisoun's penchant for teasing makes it possible for readers to view the pillow lecture in a non-serious light. The hag wearies the knight with her long speech until he yields mastery to her (p 128). See **875**.

1359 Blamires, Alcuin, and Michael Scott, eds. *The Canterbury Tales*. Atlantic Highlands: Humanities Press International, 1987.
Alisoun's seemingly insignificant reference to Ovid during her Midas digression is a thematic link both to the concept of making choices in the *WBT* and to her own imperfection (pp 13-4). See **876**.

1360 Bowden, Betsy. *Chaucer Aloud: The Varieties of Textual Interpretation*. Philadelphia: University of Pennsylvania Press, 1987.
Alisoun has inspired a drama by Gay, a ballad collected by Pepys, and translations of the *WBT* by Dryden and the *WBP* by Pope (23). Blake has depicted her as the Whore of Babylon. Chaucer provides his readers with only a brief glimpse of the hag's ugliness through the knight's eyes.

1361 Crane, Susan. 'Alison's Incapacity and Poetic Instability in the *Wife of*

Bath's Tale.' PMLA 102(1987), 20–8.

Alisoun's concern that women possess power cannot be established through the romantic and antifeminist basis of the *WBT* for these traditions do not recognize female sovereignty.

1362 ———. 'Forum Reply to Esther C. Quinn.' *PMLA* 102(1987), 835–6.

Quinn (**1365a**) criticizes Crane's article on Alisoun's poetic instability (**1361**) for underemphasizing the distinction between the *WBP* and *WBT* and Alisoun's fictionality and for finding inconsistency in the *WBP* and *WBT*. Crane's response is to note that Quinn herself maintains a connection between the *WBP* and *WBT*, to define a character's fictional-vs-human quality, and to underscore the artistic merit of inconsistency.

1363 Delany, Sheila. 'Notes on Experience, Authority, and Desire in the Wife of Bath's Recital.' *HUSL* 15(1987), 27–35.

To ask what women most desire is to marginalize the female from humanity (p 33). Chaucer's rape of Cecily Champaigne and Philippa Chaucer's liaisons with John of Gaunt may have prompted Chaucer to add his own experiences and desires to the *WBT*. See **878**.

1364 Lindahl, Carl. *Earnest Games: Folkloric Patterns in the Canterbury Tales*. Bloomington: Indiana University Press, 1987.

WBT is one of the five tales that begins with an imaginary traveler. This image reflects the journeying of the pilgrimage (p 40).

1365 Mertens-Fonck, Paule. 'Art and Symmetry in the *General Prologue* to the *Canterbury Tales*.' In *Actes du Congrès d'Amiens, 1982*. Ed. Société des Anglicistes de l'Enseignement Supérieur. Paris: Didier, 1987. Pp 41–51.

See **395**.

1365a Quinn, Esther C. 'Forum: Alisoun's Incapacity.' *PMLA* 102(1987), 835.

While Crane (**1361**) accurately assesses the thematic importance of power and gender in Alisoun's performance, she neglects to note the Chaucerian alteration of literary genres that suit the *WBT* to its teller. The satire in the *WBT*, which Crane determines to be an indication of Alisoun's incapacity as narrator, actually reveals Alisoun's adeptness at challenging patriarchal institutions.

1366 Stone, Brian. *Chaucer*. Penguin Critical Studies. London: Penguin Books, 1987.

Despite its ostensible romance genre, *WBT* contains many Christian and classical allusions as well as Alisoun's personalized touches (p 90). See **252** and **890**.

1367 Taylor, Paul B. 'Wife of Bath, Pardoner, and *Sir Thopas*: Pre-Texts and Para-Texts.' In *The Structure of Texts*. Ed. Udo Fries. Tübingen: Gunter Narr Verlag, 1987. Pp 123–32.

See **892**.

1368 Williams, David. *The Canterbury Tales: A Literary Pilgrimage.* Twayne's Masterwork Studies. Boston: Twayne, 1987.

The *WBT* is a fantastical representation of Alisoun's life (p 68). Its fictional form allows Alisoun to create love that is not sin (p 72) and fulfill her desires. Ironically, it underscores the antifeminist tradition. Alisoun, like the knight of her tale, is both a rapist and a self-rapist (p 71). See **893**.

1369 Wurtele, Douglas J. 'Chaucer's Wife of Bath and Her Distorted Arthurian Motifs.' *Arthurian Interpretations* 2(1987), 47–61.

Chaucer's *WBT* deviates in plot from the more traditional Arthurian romances of *Mar*, *Wed*, and *Flor*. Among Chaucer's many alterations, the fact that the knight must yield to the hag before she transforms herself and that this transformation is independent of the knight's nature are crucial changes for the illustration of the lesson Alisoun intends to set forth.

1370 Bay, Marjorie Caddell. 'Chaucer's *Auctoritee*, *Maystrye*, and *Soveraynetee*: Rhetorical Control as Unifying Element in the *Canterbury Tales*.' *DAI* 49(1988), 1460A.

In order to unify the *CT*, Chaucer makes use of the romance genre, placing such tales at various points within the work. The terms *auctoritee*, *maystrye*, and *soveraynetee* appear frequently in the *CT* within frame structures that possess a prologue, body, and epilogue.

1371 Besserman, Lawrence. *Chaucer and the Bible: A Critical Review of Research, Indexes, and Bibliography.* New York: Garland Publishing, 1988.

The biblical quotations found in the *WBT* are annotated (pp 91–2). See **894**.

1372 Cooper, Helen. 'Chaucer and Ovid: A Question of Authority.' In *Ovid Renewed: Ovidian Influences on Literature and Art from the Middle Ages to the Twentieth Century*. Ed. Charles Martindale. Cambridge: Cambridge University Press, 1988. Pp 71–81.

Alisoun's Midas digression and the *ManT* examine the unreality of language. The Midas tale underscores the impossibility of 'private speech' (p 78).

1373 Davenport, W.A. *Chaucer: Complaint and Narrative.* Chaucer Studies 14. Cambridge: D.S. Brewer, 1988.

The *WBT* serves to underscore Alisoun's aggressive nature, yet it has enough of its own identity to withstand Alisoun's manipulations and digressions (p 55). That the *WBT* contradicts the realistic experience that is promoted in the *WBP* is in keeping with Alisoun's own dual nature, which is influenced by Venus and Mars.

1374 Fisher, Sheila. *Chaucer's Poetic Alchemy: A Study of Value and Its Transformation in the Canterbury Tales.* New York: Garland Publishing, 1988.

The pillow lecture represents Alisoun's concerns as a member of the developing middle class and as a woman in a patriarchal society (p 33). While the hag's views on *gentillesse* have classical origins, the context of these views, Alisoun's social context, is new. That value is found within the individual is important to Alisoun, who needs to discover her own worth (p 43). Her worth acts as a tool to re-evaluate antifeminist texts (p 48). Despite her triumph over antifeminism, Alisoun is unaware 'that she has not destroyed its methods' (p 92). She cannot perceive the transformation she has given to value or that she has misnamed her equal relationship with Jankyn.

1375 Goodman, Jennifer R. *The Legend of Arthur in British and American Literature.* Boston: Twayne, 1988.

The presence of Arthur in the *WBT* adds magic to the story. Chaucer's work is one of 'the most successful Arthurian pieces' (p 40).

1376 Hornsby, Joseph Allen. *Chaucer and the Law.* Norman, OK: Pilgrim Books, 1988.

The definition of *seuretee* (III.911) is ambiguous. The arrangement between the knight and the hag displays Chaucer's awareness of the legal procedure of bringing a contract to court (p 86). The knight's pledge of his word is legally binding, and the agreement is enforced by the court. Chaucer incorporates the legal definition of and punishment for rape into the *WBT* (p 118). The knight's pardon reflects the usual outcome of medieval rape cases.

1377 Kendrick, Laura. *Chaucerian Play: Comedy and Control in the Canterbury Tales.* Berkeley: University of California Press, 1988.

WBT goes beyond the temporary 'rebellions against repressive paternal authority' (p 124) in the fabliau. It advocates a replacement of the patriarchy. In using the romance genre and not the fabliau to establish this exchange of power, Alisoun's recreation is 'more seriously subversive' (p 125).

1378 Koff, Leonard Michael. *Chaucer and the Art of Storytelling*. Berkeley: University of California Press, 1988.

See **908**.

1379 Straus, Barrie Ruth. 'The Subversive Discourse of the Wife of Bath: Phallocentric Discourse and the Imprisonment of Criticism.' *ELH* 55(1988), 527–54.

See **915**.

1380 Canfield, J. Douglas. *Word as Bond in English Literature from the Middle Ages to the Restoration*. Philadelphia: University of Pennsylvania Press, 1989.

See **919**.

1381 Cooper, Helen. *Oxford Guides to Chaucer: The Canterbury Tales*. Oxford: Clarendon, 1989/rev 1996.

An analysis of the date, text, genre, structure, themes, style, and context of *WBT* within *CT* complements a thorough examination of the analogues of this work (pp 155–66). See **921**.

1382 Dinshaw, Carolyn. *Chaucer's Sexual Poetics*. Madison: University of Wisconsin Press, 1989.

The rape in the *WBT* signifies male society's economic treatment of women which, when done without her consent, is rape (p 115). The knight is an ignorant reader, violating the text in order to penetrate its truths (p 128). Alisoun undercuts the genre of romance, a genre appropriated to women, and incorporates her narrative digressions, techniques that go against 'masculine totalizing' (p 126). The *WBT* gives much attention to female desire. On the wedding night, the hag reveals the truth of her own text to the knight, for he has acknowledged her desire. See **922**.

1383 Elliott, Ralph. 'Chaucer's Garrulous Heroine: Alice of Bath.' *SMELL* 4(1989), 1–29.

The hag's sermon on *gentillesse* suggests either that Alisoun has designs beyond her own estate (p 18) or that she may be secretly yearning for Christian submissiveness (p 19). Her final prayer exhibits her true desire. See **399** and **923**.

1384 Fisher, John H. 'Assertion of the Self in the Works of Chaucer.' *MedPers* 4-5(1989–90), 1–24.

See **924**.

1385 Green, Eugene. 'Speech Acts and the Art of the Exemplum in the Poetry of Chaucer and Gower.' In *Literary Computing and Literary Criticism: Theoretical and Practical Essays on Theme and Rhetoric.* Ed. Rosanne G. Potter. Philadelphia: University of Pennsylvania Press, 1989. Pp 167–87.

The mutual valuing of sincere utterance in speech acts and *exempla* recommends the study of 'comparable *exempla*' (p 167) in *WBT* and *Flor*. Both works deal with female requests for justice and commitment (p 176).

1386 Knapp, Peggy A. 'Alisoun of Bathe and the Reappropriation of Tradition.' *ChauR* 24(1989), 45–52.

See **932**.

1387 McGerr, Rosemarie P. 'Medieval Concepts of Literary Closure: Theory and Practice.' *Exemplaria* 1(1989), 149–79.

Chaucer employs conventions of the *demande d'amour* in *BD*, *PF*, *KnT*, *WBT*, and *FranT* (p 168).

1388 Richman, Gerald. 'Rape and Desire in the *Wife of Bath's Tale*.' *SN* 61(1989), 161–5.

III.1039 should be translated to show that a woman desires both sovereignty *and* love from her husband. The knight's offer of his goods for his body (III.1061) echoes Alisoun's telling her husbands that they would master neither her body nor her goods and is in keeping with the theme of 'dominance and submission' (p 161). The knight's statement also recalls the *WBT*'s rape scene and the marriage debt of *WBP*. The role-reversal of rapist-turned-victim educates the knight about a woman's desire for true love and not for domination.

1389 Simmons-O'Neill, Elizabeth. '"Sires, by youre leve, that am nat I": Romance and Pilgrimage in Chaucer and the "Gawain/Morgne"-Poet.' *DAI* 50(1989), 135A.

Alisoun constructs both the history of antifeminism and that of her marriages into a frame for the *WBT*. This framework serves to show what society must move away from in order to gain the equality and grace of the *WBT*'s ending.

1390 Wetherbee, Winthrop. *Geoffrey Chaucer: The Canterbury Tales.* Landmarks of World Literature. Cambridge: Cambridge University Press, 1989.

The *WBT* emphasizes female generosity. The Midas digression signifies women's existence among men who are blind 'to their [male] natures and needs' (p 88). Female success in the *WBT* is still defined by the patriarchal institution of marriage. See **937**.

1391   Cooper, Helen. 'The Shape-Shiftings of the Wife of Bath, 1395–1670.' In *Chaucer Traditions: Studies in Honor of Derek Brewer*. Ed. Ruth Morse and Barry Windeatt. Cambridge: Cambridge University Press, 1990. Pp 168–84.

Alisoun is mentioned in literary works written between 1395 and 1670. She and the hag have served as models for literary characters in works such as *The Tale of Beryn*, Skelton's *Phyllyp Sparrow* and *Tunnynge of Elynour Rummynge*, Dunbar's *Tua Mariit Wemen and the Wedo*, Fletcher's *Woman Pleased*, Richard Johnson's *A New Sonet of a Knight and a Faire Virgin*, and Spenser's *Faerie Queene*, as well as several ballads.

1392   Cowgill, Jane. 'Patterns of Feminine and Masculine Persuasion in the *Melibee* and the *Parson's Tale*.' In *Chaucer's Religious Tales*. Chaucer Studies, volume 15. Ed. C. David Benson and Elizabeth Robertson. Cambridge: D.S. Brewer, 1990. Pp 171–83.

The hag is one of Chaucer's characters who exemplifies a successful, feminine persuasion of man. In the male-dominated society of the *WBT*, women do not agree with the policy of vengeance but advocate 'forgiveness and moral development' (p 177). The *WBT* also asserts female wisdom and ordered logic, as does *Mel*. The hag embodies the virtues she discusses and subverts the male hierarchy when she gains mastery over her husband. She does not, however, seek power over the knight but asks for his realization of her abilities.

1393   Delany, Sheila. 'Strategies of Silence in the Wife of Bath's Recital.' *Exemplaria* 2(1990), 49–69.

See **939**.

1394   Folks, Cathalin Buhrmann. 'Chaucer's *Wife of Bath's Tale, Sir Gawain and the Green Knight*, and the English Romance Tradition.' *DAI* 50(1990), 2062A.

Chaucer's *WBT* is an ironic treatment of the romance genre. In it, Chaucer creates unromantic characters and questions both the notion of chivalry and its values, yet captures some of the idealistic outlook found in the romance.

1395   Knapp, Peggy. *Chaucer and the Social Contest*. New York: Routledge, 1990.

See **945**.

1396 Laskaya, Catherine Anne. 'Representing Gender in the *Canterbury Tales.*' *DAI* 50 (1990), 2484A.
See **947**.

1397 Leicester, H. Marshall, Jr. *The Disenchanted Self: Representing the Subject in the Canterbury Tales.* Berkeley: University of California Press, 1990.
See **948**.

1398 Mann, Jill. 'Anger and "Glosynge" in the *Canterbury Tales.*' *PBA* 76(1990), 202–23.
Several tales in Fragment III and Fragement V focus on patience, the virtue that balances anger (p 211). The *WBT* illustrates masculine patience in acceptance of 'aventure,' while the Wife's shrewish behavior illustrates anger (p 214).

1399 Martin, Priscilla. *Chaucer's Women: Nuns, Wives, and Amazons.* Iowa City: University of Iowa Press, 1990.
The reversal of the knight's position from empowered to powerless equates him with Chaucer's 'reluctant bride' (p 58) heroine. Unlike this character type, the knight complains about his situation. The women in the *WBT* are polarized. The hag is Alisoun's 'mirror image' (p 61). Both Alisoun and the hag achieve marital reconciliation, but accomplish it through two different means. While the *ShT* seems to have been Alisoun's initial tale, the *WBT* allows Alisoun's 'idealism and wisdom' (p 91) to be seen. See **952**.

1400 O'Brien, Dennis. 'Academic Study in a Deconstructive Age, or What If the Wife of Bath Had Read Harold Bloom?' *CEA* 52(1990), 2–9.
An allegorization of *WBT* as literary history provides an alternative to the theories of Harold Bloom. See **955**.

1401 Spearing, A.C. 'Rewriting Romance: Chaucer's and Dryden's *Wife of Bath's Tale.*' In *Chaucer Traditions: Studies in Honour of Derek Brewer.* Ed. Ruth Morse and Barry Windeatt. Cambridge: Cambridge University Press, 1990. Pp 234–48.
Chaucer leaves the *WBT* open to multiple interpretations; however, Dryden's translation weakens the Chaucerian ambiguity. Having Alisoun as the *WBT*'s narrator moves the romance genre away from its traditional young, male aristocratic audience. Dryden's eighteenth-century mind-set broadens the concept of the individual woman to all womankind and restores the male perspective of the romance to the *WBT* (pp 241–2).

1402 Tigges, Wim. 'Romance and Parody.' In *Companion to Middle English Romance*. Ed. Henk Aertsen and Alasdair A. MacDonald. Amsterdam: VU University Press, 1990. Pp 129–51.

The *WBT* is a 'didactic romance' (p 138) that focuses on the knight's flaws and the harm he does to the maiden. Both *Sir Cleges* and the *WBT* examine the nature of *gentillesse*. Both *Wed* and *WBT* have their origins in folktales and have been tailored to suit the middle class (p 141).

1403 Windeatt, Barry. 'Chaucer and the Fifteenth-Century Romance: *Partonope of Blois*.' In *Chaucer Traditions: Studies in Honour of Derek Brewer*. Ed. Ruth Morse and Barry Windeatt. Cambridge: Cambridge University Press, 1990. Pp 62–80.

The translator of *Partonope of Blois* may have had the knight's reaction to his transformed bride in mind (III.1253) when he described the relations between Partonope and Melior (p 72).

✣ The Wife of Bath's Tale 1991–1995

1404 Beidler, Peter G. 'Transformations in Gower's *Tale of Florent* and Chaucer's *Wife of Bath's Tale.*' In *Chaucer and Gower: Difference, Mutuality, Exchange.* Ed. R.F. Yeager. Victoria, B.C.: University of Victoria, 1991. Pp 100–14.
See **195**.

1405 Bowman, Mary R. 'The Dialogue of Desire in the *Wife of Bath's Tale.*' *Hwæt!: A Graduate Journal of Medieval Studies* 2(1991), 9–15.
An observation of the interplay between male and female desire in the *WBT* may aid in our understanding of the story. The knight's challenge to find the answer to what it is that women most desire poses a challenge to Chaucer as well in that he was to represent female desire from his male perspective. Chaucer's perception of this dilemma may be seen in Alisoun's lion-painting speech. The *WBT* is a strong reply to the masculine misrepresentations of feminine desire in the preceding *KnT*, *MilT*, and *MLT*. In having her story begin with a rape, Alisoun shows how destructive male desire can be to women. Female intervention places the knight on a quest to learn what women desire and his next encounter with lovely women, the dancers, marks a change in what he wants from womankind. The hag's desire for marriage places the knight in a powerless role. He also grants the hag her desire for sovereignty. Alisoun does not reverse the genders in her story but focuses on modifying the male desire (p 12). According to Alisoun, when a woman achieves her desire, she does not enforce her will.

1406 Brown, Peter, and Andrew Butcher. *The Age of Saturn: Literature and History in the Canterbury Tales.* Oxford: Basil Blackwell, 1991.
See **966**.

1407 Eberle, Patricia J. 'Crime and Justice in the Middle Ages: Cases from the *Canterbury Tales* of Geoffrey Chaucer.' In *Rough Justice: Essays on Crime in Literature*. Ed. M.L. Friedland. Toronto: University of Toronto Press, 1991. Pp 19–51.

The *MLT*, *ClT*, and *WBT* reveal Chaucer's awareness and criticism of Papal Revolution law (pp 27–8). Because rape in the fourteenth century was rarely brought to court and death-sentences for the crime were rare, Chaucer's audience would view the events of the *WBT* as literary exaggeration (p 35). The *WBT* contains poetic justice; a rapist must surrender to female will. The submission parodies the standard submission of women. The *WBT*'s ending deconstructs its concept of justice (p 36).

1408   Fineman, Joel. *The Subjectivity Effect in Western Literary Tradition: Essays Toward the Release of Shakespeare's Will*. Cambridge: MIT Press, 1991.
See **968**.

1409   Frese, Dolores Warwick. *An Ars Legendi for Chaucer's Canterbury Tales: Re-Constructive Reading*. Gainesville: University of Florida Press, 1991.
See **405**.

1410   Hagen, Susan K. 'The Wife of Bath: Chaucer's Inchoate Experiment in Feminist Hermeneutics.' In *Rebels and Rivals: The Contestive Spirit in the Canterbury Tales*. Studies in Medieval Culture, 29. Ed. Susanna Greer Fein, David Raybin, and Peter C. Braeger. Kalamazoo: Medieval Institute Publications, 1991. Pp 105–24.
See **971**.

1411   Ireland, Colin A. '"A coverchief or a calle": The Ultimate End of the Wife of Bath's Search for Sovereignty.' *Neophil* 75(1991), 150–9.
Chaucer's particular choice of the word *calle* (III.1018) for a headdress serves to tie the *WBT* strongly to the Irish loathly lady tales. The Irish *caillech* refers to women of advanced years who have become nuns, yet it also is defined as 'hag, crone, witch' (p 157). In the Irish analogues, it is the *caillech* whom the hero must kiss. In the *WBT*, such women are the experienced ladies of Arthur's court.

1412   Johnson, Dawn. 'Some Views of Love in Chaucer.' *Pleiades* 12(1991), 59–63.
See **973**.

1413   Mann, Jill. *Geoffrey Chaucer*. Feminist Readings. Atlantic Highlands: Humanities Press International, 1991.

The *WBT* is an idealized vision of the male psyche rejecting its role of oppressor and undercuts the male fantasy of a woman's desire to be raped. The knight's transformation occurs after he becomes subject to female power. He must find out what women actually desire and is placed in the rape-victim's role when the hag claims him for a husband. The knight is given the responsibility of choice when faced with the antifeminist complaint in the marital dilemma of a beautiful wife not being faithful. Antifeminist thought fuels the tale's challenge to male domination (p 92). The ending of the *WBT* is a visionary glimpse of mutuality in relationships. See **197** and **976**.

1414 Mertens-Fonck, Paule. 'The Indebtedness of the *Canterbury Tales* to the Clerk-Knight Debates.' In *This Noble Craft: Proceedings of the Xth Research Symposium of the Dutch and Belgian University Teachers of Old and Middle English and Historical Linguistics, Utrecht, 19–20 January, 1989.* Ed. Erik Kooper. *Costerus*, n.s., 80. Amsterdam: Rodopi, 1991. Pp 189–99.
See **978**.

1415 ———. 'Life and Fiction in the *Canterbury Tales*: A New Perspective.' In *Poetics: Theory and Practice in Medieval English Literature.* Ed. Piero Boitani and Anna Torti. Suffolk: Brewer, 1991. Pp 105–15.
See **979**.

1416 Taylor, Paul Beekman. 'The Uncourteous Knights of the *Canterbury Tales.*' *ES* 72(1991), 209–18.
While noble knights exist in the *KnT* and *SNT*, six of the Canterbury stories contain knights who are far from ideal. The knights of the *MLT*, *WBT*, and *MerT* do not champion women but rather assault them. In the *WBT*, the hag saves the knight's life and forces her body upon him, turning the tables twice. The choice the hag offers the knight marks her conquest of him in a verbal battle in which she rapes him with words (p 214). Words subdue the knight's lust.

1417 Lindley, Arthur. '"Vanysshed was this daunce, he nyste where": Alisoun's Absence in the *Wife of Bath's Prologue* and *Tale.*' *ELH* 59(1992), 1–21.
See **1004**.

1418 Mandel, Jerome. *Geoffrey Chaucer: Building the Fragments of the Canterbury Tales.* Rutherford: Fairleigh Dickenson University Press, 1992.

See **1005**.

1419 Martin, Priscilla. 'Chaucer and Feminism: A Magpie View.' In *A Wyf Ther Was: Essays in Honour of Paule Mertens-Fonck*. Ed. Juliette Dor. Liège: Université de Liège, 1992. Pp 235–46.
See **410**.

1420 McKinley, Kathryn Lillian. 'Ovidian Narrative Technique in Jean de Meun and Chaucer.' *DAI* 53(1992), 1155A.
Chaucer's use of both Ovid's narrative techniques and his psychological explorations of character display themselves in both his selection of a fairy tale for the *WBT* that contains intimations of an inner world and in his alteration of the loathly lady tale tradition.

1421 Neuse, Richard. 'Alisoun Still Lives Here: Provocations, Politics, and Pedagogy in the *Wife of Bath's Tale*, *Hamlet*, and *Paradise Lost*.' *Exemplaria* 4(1992), 469–80.
While medieval women did not have a written text of their own (**1000**), they possessed oral textual abilities. The *WBT* is a glossing of Alisoun's experience that adds authority to her performance (p 470). The *WBT* manipulates the concept of textuality and exposes male authority as being 'based on a concealment of the phallus' (p 470). Alisoun finds pedagogy within matrimony in which the man is 'disabuse[d] ... of his sexual self-mystification' (p 474).

1422 O'Brien, Timothy. 'Troubling Waters: The Feminine and the Wife of Bath's Performance.' *MLQ* 53(1992), 377–91.
That the maiden is raped beside a river adds to the archetypal associations of women with water in the *WBP* (p 378). See **1008**.

1423 Patterson, Lee. 'Feminine Rhetoric and the Politics of Subjectivity: La Vieille and the Wife of Bath.' In *Rethinking the Romance of the Rose: Text, Image, Reception*. Ed. Kevin Brownlee and Sylvia Huot. Philadelphia: University of Pennsylvania Press, 1992. Pp 316–58.
See **1010**.

1424 Richmond, Velma Bourgeois. *Geoffrey Chaucer*. New York: Continuum, 1992.
While Alisoun's prefatory remarks about friars and concluding prayer for meek husbands give the impression that the *WBT* advocates female sovereignty, Chaucer's intent is to convey the importance of Christian living (pp 72–3). True mercy and concern for the reformation of a sinner are exhibited. The sermon on *gentillesse* emphasizes the teachings of Jesus Christ. The *WBT* ends with a happy marriage, a traditional romance

ending, that distracts the reader from the more serious issues of the story. Other discussion of what women want may be found in the *ShT* (p 90). See **1011**.

1425 Smith, Macklin. '*Sith* and *Syn* in Chaucer's *Troilus*.' *ChauR* 26 (1992), 266–82.
See **1013**.

1426 Tigges, Wim. '"Lat the womman telle hire tale": A Reading of the *Wife of Bath's Tale*.' *ES* 73(1992), 97–103.
The *WBT* teaches 'that what women do definitely *not* desire is rape' (p 97). This lesson accounts for the strong feminine roles and views within the *WBT*. Alisoun tells her tale in response to tales such as the *KnT* and *RvT* in which women must endure conditions enforced upon them by men (p 98). The reversals of power that occur between the knight and the raped maiden and between the knight and the hag suggest a 'psychological identity' (p 103) between these two women. This movement from woman as victim to woman as instructor and then to contented wife reflects Alisoun's own existence.

1427 Wood, Chauncey. 'Three Chaucerian Widows: Tales of Innocence and Experience.' In *A Wyf Ther Was: Essays in Honour of Paule Mertens-Fonck*. Ed. Juliette Dor. Liège: Université de Liège, 1992. Pp 282–90.
While the Wife of Bath, the Prioress, and the Second Nun do not form a significant group among Chaucer's pilgrims, and while their tales do not relate to one another, they share the common bond of widowhood, either through a domestic or a spiritual marriage. Although she has been a widow many times, Alisoun defines herself as a wife. Having been married at the age of twelve, the Wife has hardly lead a virginal existence. Subsequently, she defies the church's celebration of this state in the *WBP* and is rather unconcerned about the rape of the maiden in the beginning of the *WBT*. Alisoun has learned that gaining mastery in a marriage delivers one from the *wo that is in mariage* (III.3) (p 286). Thus the *WBT* ends with the rapist being dominated in his marriage by his wife (p 283). While Alisoun's personality is not merciful, mercy is thematic to the *WBT*. The knight has no mercy for his victim, the queen exhibits a questionable form of mercy towards the knight, and the hag wants to receive sovereignty, not to give mercy (p 287). The marital experiences in the *WBT* may be sharply contrasted with *PrT* and *SNT*, stories steeped in spiritual innocence. While the primary characters in

the *PrT* and *SNT* die, they find spiritual rewards in the afterlife. All that the Wife values will pass away. The *PrT* and *SNT* serve to provide examples of the value of virginity.

1428   Zauner, Erich. 'The Wife of Bath aus Chaucers *Canterbury Tales*: Ein Frauenbild aus der fruhen englischen Literatur.' *Moderne Sprachen* 36(1992), 7–14. [In German.]
The death of his wife influenced Chaucer's composition of the *WBP* and *WBT*, prompting him to search for the answer to what it is that women most desire.

1429   Bowman, Mary R. '"Half as she were mad": Dorigen in the Male World of the *Franklin's Tale*.' *ChauR* 27(1993), 239–51.
See **1019**.

1429a   Cuesta, Julia Fernández. 'A Pragmatic Approach to the Wife of Bath's Tale.' *SELIM* 3(1993), 103-16.
Through tricking Jankyn into submission, Alisoun gains control of her personal life despite the dictates of society. Pragmatically, then, Alisoun 'flouts the maxim of Quality of the Cooperative Principle' (p 110) with this accomplishment. Likewise, in having no choice but to submit to female sovereignty, the knight is manipulated and 'not saved' (p 115). Through his satire, Chaucer has created a text in which women implicate their own flaws.

1430   David, Alfred. 'Old, New, and Yong in Chaucer.' *SAC* 15(1993), 5–21.
The loathly lady offers a mere ten lines of defense concerning her age in the *gentillesse* sermon in comparison with her lengthy discussions of other topics. The *WBT* is itself rich because it is an old tale (p 16). See **412**.

1430a   Folks, Cathalin Buhrmann. 'Gentle Men, *Lufly* and *Loothly* Ladies, *Aghlich Maysters*: Characterization in *The Wife of Bath's Prologue* and *Sir Gawain and the Green Knight*.' *Noble and Joyous Histories: English Romances, 1375-1650*. Ed. Eiléan Ní Cuilleanáin and J.D. Pheifer. Dublin: Irish Academic Press, 1993. Pp 59-85.
Chaucer goes beyond conventional romance characterization in his creation of a flawed, nameless knight. He develops 'a scheming, opportunistic, but still appealing womanizer with all the worst features, as well as a touch of the charm, of the happy-go-lucky Gawain of the tale-rhyme romances' (p 60). While Chaucer's knight matures as he rises above his failings, the hero of *SGGK* improves by learning to accept his flaws. Alisoun's relation of the knight's story is indicative of

her 'rather capricious tastes, not only in men but also in literature' (p 61).

1431   Goodman, Jennifer R. 'Dorigen and the Falcon: The Element of Despair in Chaucer's *Squire's* and *Franklin's Tales.*' In *Representations of the Feminine in the Middle Ages.* Ed. Bonnie Wheeler. Dallas: Academia, 1993. Pp 69–89.
Just as Midas wants his wife to keep his secret in Alisoun's version of the Midas story, Arveragus requires Dorigen to 'conceal his cuckoldry' (p 87). Alisoun's outlining of a woman's need to speak is reflected in Dorigen's telling the truth to Aurelius and thereby saving herself.

1432   Hallissy, Margaret. *Clean Maids, True Wives, and Steadfast Widows: Chaucer's Women and Medieval Codes of Conduct.* Westport, CT: Greenwood, 1993.
While Alisoun is often aligned with the hag of the *WBT*, her tale does not tell us that beauty is what women most desire (p 177). The *WBT* shows that men should listen to women. While the fourteenth century allowed women to charge men with rape, the rapist was rarely prosecuted (p 179). In the *WBT*, then, women have the power to judge the rapist. See **413** and **1024**.

1433   Kamowski, William. 'The Sinner against the Scoundrels: The Ills of Doctrine and *Shrift* in the Wife of Bath's, Friar's, and Summoner's Narratives.' *R&L* 25(1993), 1–18.
See **1025**.

1434   Morsberger, Katharine M. 'Voices of Translation: Poet's Voice and Woman's Voice.' *PCP* 28(1993), 3–19.
Dryden's translation of the *WBT* exposed him to new potentials for his already well-crafted poetic style. He learned much about feminine voice and language. See **1027**.

1435   Odegard, Margaret. '"Alas, alas, that ever love was sin!": Marriages Moral and Immoral in Chaucer.' In *Censored Books: Critical Viewpoints.* Ed. Nicholas J. Karolides, Lee Burress, and John M. Kean. Metuchen: Scarecrow, 1993. Pp 144–58.
See **1028**.

1436   Petty, George R., Jr. 'Power, Deceit, and Misinterpretation: Uncooperative Speech in the *Canterbury Tales.*' *ChauR* 27(1993), 413–23.
The hag's misinterpretation of the knight's relinquishing his power to choose as an admission of her superior intelligence is Alisoun's

triumphant illustration of a woman being able to assert power through her language skills (p 419).

1437 Vance, Sidney. 'Contending with the Masculinist Traditions: *Sundiata*'s Sogolon and the Wife of Bath.' In *Global Perspectives on Teaching Literature: Shared Visions and Distinctive Visions*. Ed. Sandra Ward Lott, Maureen S.G. Hawkins, and Norman McMillan. Urbana: National Council of Teachers of English, 1993. Pp 101–8.

G.P. Picket's *Sundiata*, an English version of D.T. Niane's French version of *Soundjata*, is set historically in the thirteenth century and may be compared with epic literature of Western culture. Unlike Western epics, however, *Sundiata* contains a focus on the hero's mother and 'her struggle with the masculinist Muslim society of western Africa in her time' (p 102). This struggle, coupled with the presence of a shape-shifting hag, a rape, and a marriage between an ugly woman and a handsome man of the nobility, makes the *Sundiata* ripe for comparison with the *WBP* and *WBT*.

1438 Wheeler, Bonnie. '*Trouthe* without Consequences: Rhetoric and Gender in Chaucer's *Franklin's Tale*.' In *Representations of the Feminine in the Middle Ages*. Ed. Bonnie Wheeler. Dallas: Academia, 1993. Pp 91–116.

Both the loathly lady and Dorigen have 'a double commitment' (p 106). The old woman must be attractive and faithful to the knight, and Dorigen must deal with the roles 'both of traditional wifehood and of courtly mistress' (p 106).

1439 Wilson, Grace G. '"Amonges othere wordes wyse": The Medieval Seneca and the *Canterbury Tales*.' *ChauR* 28(1993), 135–45.

Chaucer has Alisoun refer to Seneca twice in the *WBT*'s pillow lecture. The references are used in a manner that is 'standard for the period' (p 139). Despite her downplay of authority, Alisoun, along with Chaucer, recognizes the value of Seneca.

1440 Blamires, Alcuin. 'Questions of Gender in Chaucer, from *Anelida* to *Troilus*.' *LeedsSE* 25(1994), 83–110.

See **1034**.

1441 Breeze, A.C. 'Chaucer's *Miller's Tale*, 3700: *Viritoot*.' *ChauR* 29(1994), 204–6.

The term *viritoot* may bear a relation to words meaning *old witch*, a phrase that could be applied to the loathly lady of the *WBT*.

1442 Daileader, Celia R. 'The *Thopas-Melibee* Sequence and the Defeat of Antifeminism.' *ChauR* 29(1994), 26-39.

See **1035**.

1443 Gallacher, Patrick J. 'Chaucer and the Rhetoric of the Body.' *ChauR* 28(1994), 216–36.

See **1037**.

1444 Weisl, Angela Jane. 'Gender and Genre in Chaucer's Romance.' *DAI* 55(1994), 1556A.

Chaucer manipulates the genre of romance in order to explore gender roles. Chaucer employs the Breton lay in the *WBT* to examine a world in which only feminized power exists.

1445 Yamamoto, Dorothy. '"Noon other incubus but he": Lines 878–81 in the *Wife of Bath's Tale.' ChauR* 28(1994), 275–8.

While Skeat (**4**), Winny (**48**), and Robinson (**38**) interpret III.878–81 to mean that elves impregnate women whereas seducing friars do not, the lines may be considered in another light. Medieval literature contains several references to incubi who beget children upon women, but incubi were more feared for their violent, even fatal, attacks upon people. Alisoun is thus emphasizing how trivial the annoying friars are in comparison to the deadly incubi (p 277).

445a Chance, Jane. *The Mythographic Chaucer: The Fabulation of Sexual Politics*. Minneapolis: University of Minnesota Press, 1995.

The *WBT* is a tale of a wicked husband. Alisoun incorporates the Midas digression, with its reflection on Midas' wife, to reflect her own role as wife and teller of truth and to compare her husbands with the deformed Midas (p 227). See **1048**

1446 Hallissy, Margaret. *A Companion to Chaucer's Canterbury Tales*. Westport, CT: Greenwood Press, 1995.

The rape scene connects the *WBT* to the *WBP* in that the rape negates the importance of a woman's will. The knight learns what it is like to be stripped of one's will. The loathly lady, as skilled in argument as is Alisoun, eliminates the knight's objections to her. The knight becomes educated through an experienced woman's teaching, not through learning the contents of old books. Alisoun's arguments in the *WBP* are thus exemplified in her tale. See **1052**.

1447 Hopenwasser, Nanda. 'The Wife of Bath as Storyteller: "Al is for to selle" or Is It?: Idealism and Spiritual Growth as Evidenced in the *Wife of Bath's Tale.' MedPers* 10(1995), 101–15.

The spirituality of the *WBT* lies in Alisoun's promotion of harmony and vitality in marriage and her denunciation of the church's established view of women as inferior beings (p 102). Reflecting the mystical visions of Margery Kempe and Bridget of Sweden, the knight's trial supports 'female understanding of reality' (p 104) over male idealism. Alisoun uses the Midas digression to show the realistic imperfections of marriage partners. The knight's willingness to receive female justice may be why his answer to the riddle goes unchallenged. On his wedding night, the knight learns 'to accept both contradiction and lack of certainty' (p 109).

1448 Lee, Brian S. 'Exploitation and Excommunication in the *Wife of Bath's Tale.' PQ* 74(1995), 17–35.

The rape in the *WBT* proves shocking to modern readers because of the casual way it is presented. While the raped maiden is a victim and an exploited commodity, she is also excommunicated from the tale through her abrupt disappearance from the story. A voice is found for her, though, in the voices of the hag and the women of Arthur's court (p 32). The knight's character undergoes a movement 'from being an agent of exploitation' to being 'the victim of the court's excommunication' (p 24). The *WBT* is concerned with rehabilitation.

1449 Taylor, Paul Beekman. 'Time in the *Canterbury Tales.' Exemplaria* 7(1995), 371–93.

While Alisoun is correct in having the loathly lady of the *WBT* teach the knight that the virtue of *gentillesse* transcends class boundaries, she errs when she has the old woman both assert 'that God selects recipients of gentilesse by entering time in order to manipulate his ordained providence' (p 381) and ignore the fact that all humans are born with this virtue. While the loathly lady emulates God in her promise of grace for the knight, she 'does not use time naturally to bear children' (p 391), and therefore, like Alisoun, does not reflect the creative process of God. See **1056**.

1450 Weisl, Angela Jane. *Conquering the Reign of Femeny: Gender and Genre in Chaucer's Romance.* Cambridge: Brewer, 1995.

Chaucer made use of traditional themes of Breton lays when composing the *WBT*, such as the interrelation between the worlds of reality and fairy. While the *WBT* contains the interplay of public and private worlds, it also incorporates Alisoun's immediate world. Alisoun contrasts the present, sterile world of friars with 'the fertile, generative qualities of the old world' (p 90), and she aligns herself with the old world by advocating oral tradition. The expandable quality of the lay genre allows Alisoun to incorporate her own ideologies into her tale. Her rejection of the friars is a rejection of masculine authority. The loathly lady, however, must use patriarchal authority in order to instruct the knight about *gentillesse*. The pillow lecture deviates from the lay genre in its length and in the morality of its subject matter. The *WBT* makes morality 'political, and therefore public' (p 96). Feminine law and justice triumph over masculine power and authority in the tale and feminine power becomes both public and private, yet Chaucer provides no femininst solution as he exposes a feminist problem (p 104).

1451 Beidler, Peter G. 'A Critical History of the *Wife of Bath's Prologue and Tale.*' In *The Wife of Bath*. Case Studies in Contemporary Criticism Series. Ed. Peter G. Beidler. Boston: Bedford Books of St. Martin's Press, 1996. Pp 89–114.
See **1058**.

1452 Finke, Laurie. '"All is for to selle": Breeding Capital in the *Wife of Bath's Prologue* and *Tale.*' In *The Wife of Bath*. Case Studies in Contemporary Criticism Series. Ed. Peter G. Beidler. Boston: Bedford Books of St. Martin's Press, 1996. Pp 171–88.
See **1059**.

1453 Fradenburg, Louise O. '"Fulfild of fairye": The Social Meaning of Fantasy in the *Wife of Bath's Prologue* and *Tale.*' In *The Wife of Bath*. Case Studies in Contemporary Criticism Series. Ed. Peter G. Beidler. Boston: Bedford Books of St. Martin's Press, 1996. Pp 205–20.
See **1060**.

1454 Hansen, Elaine Tuttle. '"Of his love daungerous to me": Liberation, Subversion, and Domestic Violence in the *Wife of Bath's Prologue* and *Tale.*' In *The Wife of Bath*. Case Studies in Contemporary Criticism Series. Ed. Peter G. Beidler. Boston: Bedford Books of St. Martin's Press, 1996. Pp 273–90.
See **1061**.

1455 Leicester, H. Marshall, Jr. '"My bed was ful of verray blood": Subject, Dream, and Rape in the *Wife of Bath's Prologue* and *Tale.*' In *The Wife of Bath*. Case Studies in Contemporary Criticism Series. Ed. Peter G. Beidler. Boston: Bedford Books of St. Martin's Press, 1996. Pp 234–54.
See **1062**.

1456 Morrison, Susan Signe. 'Don't Ask, Don't Tell: The Wife of Bath and Vernacular Translations.' *Exemplaria* 8(1996), 97-123.

See **1063**.

1457 Patterson, Lee. '"Experience woot wel it is noght so": Marriage and the Pursuit of Happiness in the *Wife of Bath's Prologue* and *Tale*.' In *The Wife of Bath*. Case Studies in Contemporary Criticism Series. Ed. Peter G. Beidler. Boston: Bedford Books of St. Martin's Press, 1996. Pp 133–54.

See **1065**.

1458 Slover, Judith. 'A good wive was ther of biside Bath.' In *Chaucer's Pilgrims: An Historical Guide to the Pilgrims in the Canterbury Tales*. Ed. Laura C. Lambdin and Robert T. Lambdin. Westport, CT: Greenwood, 1996. Pp 243–55.

While Alisoun 'is the exemplum of the feared autonomous woman' (p 250), her tale serves as an exemplum to her prologue. In the *WBT*, Alisoun attributes Eve's carnality to men when she creates a rapist-knight. *Sovereynetee* may mean equality to Alisoun (p 252). That both Alisoun and the loathly lady ultimately give up their mastery indicates that they possess both authority and the ability to regain it (p 253). See **416**.

ℰℴ Index

The numbers in this index all refer to individual numbered works in the bibliography, not to page numbers. Bold-face numbers after a scholar's name refer to items that the scholar in question has written himself or herself. We have not bolded the numbers for scholars who have edited a book that contains the work of other scholars.

heresy 555, 698
Hercules 675
Hermann, John P. 375, 376, 767, 771, 776, 1296
Hermaphroditus 1048
hermeneutics 737, 922, 971
Heseltine, Janet E. 466, 1096
Hieatt, A. Kent **46, 51, 238**
Hieatt, Constance **46, 51**
Higdon, David Leon **338, 641**
Hilary, Christine Ryan 72
Hilberry, Jane Elizabeth **931**
Hill, Archibald A. **905**
Hill, Frank Ernest **27, 31**
Hill, John M. **972**
Hinckley, Henry Barrett **213, 281**, 448, **1072**
Hippisley, John 362
Hira, Toshinori **329, 601**
Hirsch, E.D. 409
Hirsh, John C. **1038**
Historia Calamitatum 174, 638
historicism 409
history 287, 385, 391, 747, 954, 1350
history, literary 1400
Hobson, Robert 415
Hoccleve, Thomas 290, 485, 950, 1088
Hodge, James L. **226**
Hodges, Laura F. **414**
Hoffman, Arthur W. **302**
Hoffman, Richard L. **147, 148, 152, 153, 161, 319, 322, 344, 544, 574, 602**
Holbrook, David **560**
Holkham ms 1096
Holland, Norman N. **1172, 1180**
Holland, Thomas 415
Holloway, Julia Bolton 192, **368**, 403, **757**
Holmes, Sherlock 493

Holmes, Urban T., Jr. 125, 158, 494, 591
Holton, Sylvia Wallace **415**
Holy Orders 499
honde 656
honor 162, 639, 1234
Hooper, Vincent F. **32**
Hooper, W.H. 8
Hopenwasser, Nanda **1447**
Horace 468
Hornsby, Joseph Allen **1376**
Hornstein, Lillian Herlands **231**
horoscope 548a, 626, 952
horsemanship 286
horse 324, 631
hose 396
Host (see Bailly, Harry) 1237
House of Fame 539, 645, 1183
Howard, Donald R. **53, 224, 336, 575, 692, 758, 884, 1244**
Howard, Edwin Johnston **28, 553, 1153**
Hrabanus Maurus 139
Hrotsvit of Gandersheim 854
Hudson, Anne **906**
Hudson, Harriet **279**
Hugh of St. Victor 1016a
humanism 270, 564
humor 90, 206, 292, 623, 689, 815, 838, 868, 1041, 1057, 1073, 1099a, 1272
Hunt, Leigh 1088
Huntington Library 13
Huot, Sylvia 1010, 1423
Huppè, Bernard F. **146, 554, 1108**
husband, fourth 392, 462, 493, 511, 573, 594, 632, 649, 674, 683, 686, 696, 707, 724, 726, 792, 799, 805, 819, 834, 836, 897, 916, 925, 948, 965, 985, 1043
husband, sixth 213, 596, 673, 1224

696, 701, 706, 707, 717, 719, 724,
726, 727, 736, 741, 750, 754, 760,
769, 772, 773, 783, 799, 801, 805,
822, 831, 832, 834, 836, 838, 839,
861, 868, 874, 875, 879, 903, 916,
922, 925, 929, 945, 948, 951, 952,
958, 976, 977, 978, 985, 996,
1004, 1015, 1023, 1024, 1026,
1034, 1035, 1043, 1048, 1053,
1061, 1111, 1127, 1149, 1161,
1174, 1176, 1192, 1236, 1243,
1250, 1303, 1316, 1374, 1429a
Jankyn, the apprentice 594
Jankyn's book 88, 99, 123, 129,
140, 142, 151, 167, 169, 211, 289,
319, 392, 426, 513, 522, 539, 547,
560, 563, 590, 638, 651, 657, 659,
663, 676, 677, 702, 707, 708, 741,
745, 783, 787, 810, 822, 825, 836,
839, 862, 927, 929, 948, 984, 985,
993, 996, 1016a, 1023, 1045,
1048
January of *Merchant's Tale* 100,
234, 236, 264, 429, 494
Japhet 261
Jaques de Vitry 150, 475
jealousy 603, 712, 900, 965
Jean de Meun 75, 85, 86, 174, 180,
197, 233, 261, 273, 292, 340, 355,
424, 434, 457, 463, 520, 801, 862,
900, 1010, 1034, 1095, 1420
Jefferson, Bernard L. **259**
Jeffrey, David Lyle 809, 812, 815,
817, 824, 825, 829, 1326
Jehan le Fèvre 122, 177, 199, 801,
1010, 1106
Jelliffe, Robert Archibald **36**
Jerome, St. 48, 75, 83, 84, 88, 118,
123, 124, 142, 155, 160, 164, 167,
172, 174, 179, 192, 208, 209, 375,
420, 427, 455, 470, 509, 539, 540,
547, 607, 675, 693, 732, 738, 763,

787, 805, 807, 853, 899, 977, 992,
1016, 1031, 1064, 1095, 1252
Jerusalem 314
Job 1303
*Jobi Ludolfi alias Leutholf dicti
ad suam Historiam
Aethiopicam Commentarius*
280
Joce, St. 573, 704, 743
Johannes Balbus de Janua 139
John, St. 807
John of Gaunt 269, 1363
John of *Miller's Tale* 696, 995
John of Salisbury 83, 127, 142,
172
Johnson, Dawn **973**
Johnson, Richard 1088, 1391
Johnson, Samuel 418
Johnson, William C. 274
Johnston, Alexandra F. **907**
Johnston, Mark E. **245**
Jones, Richard F. **458**
Jordan, Robert M. **590, 737,** 739,
1225, 1232
journey 1132
Jove 539, 645
Jovinian 675, 805, 807
joy and bliss 640
Judaism 1348
judgment 1190
Judith and Holofernes 127
Jung, Carl G. 1242, 1266
Jusserand, J.J. **286**
justice 251, 1263, 1320, 1332, 1385
Justinus 234, 429, 1030
Justman, Stewart **693, 1039**
Juvenal 108, 137, 161, 179, 261,
1106, 1228

Kamowski, William **1025**
Kane, George **130, 821, 1110**
Karl, Otto **56**